Fablenoir

BOOK I

VIC SINCLAIR

Fablenoir

Book 1 of the Fablenoir series

Copyright © 2024 by Vic Sinclair

First published in 2024 by Urban Beanstalk Press

All rights reserved.

No part of this publication may be reproduced, distributed, or transmitted in any form or by any means, including photocopying, recording, or other electronic or mechanical methods, without the prior written permission of the publisher, except as permitted by U.S. copyright law. For permission requests, contact vicsinclair.author@gmail.com.

The story, all names, characters, and incidents portrayed in this production are fictitious. No identification with actual persons (living or deceased), places, buildings, and products is intended or should be inferred.

ISBN: 978-1-0687758-0-2

Cover illustration by Carlos Diaz

Cover design and logo by Miblart

Interior illustrations by ricerins

Edited by Brett Savory

Fablenoir

1
MAGICK & MURDER

'Give me another one. Hell of a night.'

I snatched the glass of whiskey off the bar and slumped into the nearest seat. The numb feeling I'd been seeking out the last couple of hours was starting to slip away, and my surroundings had become too real again. Too loud, too close.

I squeezed my eyes shut and breathed out viciously through my teeth. My tie was too tight around my throat. I yanked at it aimlessly until it was loose, and it slipped to the sticky floorboards. I let the whiskey wash through my body once again while I vaguely took in the blues tune wailing from the jukebox. I soon gave up, my ears greeted with the drunken murmuring and hollering of various other bar-dwellers instead.

It was a dull place. An overhead fan whirred loudly, practically dangling from the cracked ceiling, barely spinning as if it couldn't be bothered to do its job. Faded posters promoting bands that had broken up five years ago peeled away from the wooden walls; the big round tables were stained with old alcohol and probably vomit and piss.

Seeing double now, I looked out the window to my side, past the flickering neon sign out into the dimly lit streets. Nothing to see.

Everything seemed to be getting louder, and for a second I considered reaching for my gun and blowing my brains out there and then as a way of getting some rest, but thought better of it.

A rough laugh nearby took me out of that fantasy. I looked up from my drink to see the bartender above me. He was grinning, flashing his black teeth. I scowled and gulped the rest of my drink, my stomach burning.

'No offense,' growled the bartender, 'but the way I see it, you just ain't cut out for that line of work. Look at you. You care too much. I can tell.'

I scowled, confused. 'Excuse me?' I hadn't spoken since getting drunk tonight – I slurred even those couple of words.

'You've always been a real country boy, ain't ya, Jack? I don't get why you don't just take it back down south. Go with what you know.'

I'd had enough of this day. The stink of cigarettes and sweat was now shooting through my nose at a sickening pace. I pushed the empty glass away from me, snatched my tie off the filthy floorboards, and got to my feet. 'You barely even know me,' I said to the barman, not bothering to look him in the eye.

The barman shuffled aside when I shoved past him, but didn't shut up yet. 'You wanna know what I'd do in your position, what I'd do if I was your age?'

'Nope.' I dropped a twenty on the table and stumbled past the guy. He was still talking behind me, but thankfully my ears became selective about what they took in. The rest of my body wasn't so merciful. My stomach felt like it was devouring itself and my brain had pretty much been caved in with a mace.

It'd been another night of dead ends and failures. Ever since the new chief of the NYPD came in, that's what my career as a detective had come to. Dead ends. Failures. When I should have been investigating homicides, unlawful use of magick, and complex corruption scandals, I'd been assigned to cases of minor road traffic incidents and petty thievery, or maybe on a really exciting day, the odd complaint of shit being posted through a pensioner's door.

I should take some of the blame myself, sure. But when you spend most of your time drunk or going off the cliff on a magick bean comedown, you find it's easier to separate yourself from responsibility. I could clean myself up, yeah, but I'd discovered these last few years that whatever I do, I'm screwed. Because of that self-righteous asshole up there at the top of the food chain, wasted on power because he has royal giants' blood.

Allegedly.

I stepped out into the annoyingly bright haze of the purplish lights through the back exit, in the hopes I'd avoid the chaos of the city streets. Streetlights and air vents buzzed aggressively as I stood there. My fingers trembled, and a boiling rage danced with the heap of whiskey in the pit of my stomach.

I rolled up the sleeve of my coat, now soggy with alcohol, and checked my wristwatch: 1:48 a.m. It was around about shitstorm o'clock, and I needed to get home. Gunfights, illegal sorcery, trafficking right under the nose of every cop wandering the city, it would all be going down right now. Sure, I'd love to be able to put an end to it, and of course, I'd tried. But I'm just one guy, done with it all.

I slithered down the back alleys of just about the roughest area in town, and I'll admit, part of me felt right at home. Do I like that or not? Probably not, but it was the only sense of belonging I'd felt for some time.

Continuing my pleasant night stroll, I passed the back ends of clubs, warehouses, and convenience stores in the gloom and mist. When I reached an abandoned parking lot, I passed a substantial number of junkies and prostitutes who wouldn't have looked out of place in the morgue. I stopped walking and peered into the purple fog, making out the silhouettes of various figures slowly approaching me. It was straight out of a John Carpenter movie. After examining the scene like I was at some godless art gallery, I decided to continue my patrol. Experience has shown me waiting to find out what's lurking in these familiar shadows is far from a bright idea.

I wasn't far from my apartment now. Dance music boomed in time with purple neon lights bursting out into the alleyway. I made out a group of small figures gathered around a dumpster, yelling in harsh voices. I paused and scratched at my cheek, looking for an alternative way out – I wasn't about to get dragged into this shit.

'Oi! Detective?' called a hoarse voice. British, I think.

I sighed, sniffed, and shoved my fists into my coat pockets. I had a couple of magick beans on me if needed, and a Glock 19 in my holster. Like every other cop around here, if something went wrong and I felt like I had to discharge my weapon tonight, losing sleep over possible consequences wouldn't be necessary. Not in this department.

I tilted my head as the figures emerged from the purple fog and found myself reconsidering the whole consequence thing – I was being confronted by the Seven Dwarves, one of the most notorious gangs in the city, a gang with the top dogs of the NYPD firmly in their pocket.

I made a clicking sound with my tongue and wryly smirked at the ground. Today just wouldn't do me the favor of ending, would it?

'Gentlemen,' I called.

As I blinked away some of the haze, I realized there was another figure among the crowd of smaller men, a hulkingly brutish one, twice their size. He appeared to be carrying one of them by the collar, a brilliant way to get yourself stabbed to death. Blood loss from the legs while sprawled out on the odious ground of some back alley surely isn't anyone's idea of a good way to go.

'A nice evening for it,' I said, more to myself than them.

One of the dwarves came rushing over to me out of the fog. I stumbled back, my reactions slow and pathetic. Doc, the so-called mastermind of the gang scurried up to me, grim expression on his aged face.

'Easy,' I drawled, feeling the holster beneath my right hand. 'Who's that?' I motioned to the big guy in the haze.

A grin crept along Doc's face. 'Why not do your job and find out? Twat.' He spat on the ground and stepped aside.

'Fuck is this?' I murmured. I took out my gun and stepped toward the scene. The dwarves were yelling all kinds of insults and accusations, some of them aimed at me. Whatever they were, I blocked them out pretty effortlessly. I got a better look at the big guy – an ogre, unflinching, tough as hell, now with his giant hand wrapped snugly around the dwarf's throat.

'Alright, drop him,' I called, my gun now raised at the ogre's head. Quickly as my mind and body could muster, I surveyed the scene. Five of the dwarves here, two of them holding knives, Doc to my left, his beady eyes on me. A blueish shade of blood leaking from one of the ogre's calves, dripping swiftly onto the concrete, forming a puddle.

For a split second, I thought about calling it in, but that would've sooner ended up with me getting arrested, no doubt.

The ogre's black eyes met mine, and his voice boomed above the squawking raucousness of the dwarves. 'What are you gonna do about this, Detective?'

I breathed in sharply, again looking down to my left at Doc, who looked back and forth between us. This some sort of trap? Everything felt off, surreal. Like I was half sleepwalking.

The ogre fully turned his attention to me then, loosening his grip on the dwarf and letting him fall to the ground with a splat. I think he landed in the ogre's pool of blood.

He stood about seven feet tall, wearing a huge leather jacket and dark jeans, which the blood was still dribbling out of. It didn't seem to be bothering him at all. The air smelled like gasoline, booze, and iron. He started to walk toward me then, no limp, no grimace, nothing.

I was frozen where I stood, hardly noticing that the dwarves had stopped their yelling and were now backing away from the ogre. My face was level with his massive chest. I realized then that I'd lowered my gun.

'Look at you,' he growled. 'Just like the rest of 'em.'

Rain had started to patter against the dumpsters lining the wall of whatever club we were gathered outside. It trickled through my hair and down my face. As did my sweat. There was nothing for me to say.

The ogre gritted his teeth, maybe from the pain surely starting to come as the blood continued to pour. 'Slade, right?' he asked.

'Yeah,' I heard myself whisper.

He looked down, grimacing now, and a sort of laughing sound came out of his mouth. 'You people took everything from me. My wife, my children. I had to stand and watch them die because of you. What have you done? This city is hell. Everything's rotten, broken. And you haven't even noticed.'

My mouth was dry, ears were ringing. I needed a drink again, or a magick bean. I was crumbling. 'I . . . I don't know who you are,' I said to the ground. The rain was getting heavier. I shook my head slightly and looked back up at the guy, dwarves looking on. I noticed both knives they were holding were tipped with blue blood.

'What happened to you?' he asked, his voice reaching a lighter, weaker tone that made my hairs stand up. 'Where's the man that took down a goddamn *giant*?'

I felt myself shaking slightly then. Something was not right.

'I thought I heard them say you were one of the good ones,' he went on. 'Why won't you do something?'

'No, you don't— You don't know me.' *Did* he know me?

'My kids, they—'

There was a motion to my left. Blue blood sprayed across my face. I jumped back, blinded. I yelled something, then heard laughter. I wiped the blood from my eyes and saw Doc standing in front of me. He was in between me and the ogre, who was now on his knees, a stab wound in his stomach. I turned away, looked to the sky. Felt the rain on my face. It was all I could do.

When I looked back, I saw the ogre try to grab Doc by the face, and finally my body came to life as I brought up my gun again and called out, but I was too late. Doc slashed the ogre across the neck, finished him off.

'Miserable beast,' the leader growled.

I felt eyes upon me, but all I could do was stand and stare again, trying to process everything. Why was I so stunned? If they wanted to, the dwarves could've murdered me in cold blood there and then. There would be no punishment, no inquiry. Maybe in their eyes that wouldn't be to their advantage, do more harm than good. They wanted me to see this, to remember it. They knew I wouldn't – couldn't – stop them.

I was spiraling. I had to leave, but my body wouldn't let me. The ogre's body was completely still now, being battered with heavy raindrops. 'Who was he?' I asked the gang, my eyes fixed on the corpse. I patted my breast pocket, checking for my flask. It was there, so I drank.

Doc looked up at me with a mockingly solemn expression, then to the body. 'A loose end. Someone who needed to . . . not be around anymore, quite simply.' He raised his eyebrows, dead eyes meeting mine. 'He was attackin us! You saw.'

I chugged the last of my whiskey, shook my head at Doc.

'One of the good ones, are ya? That what you are? Oh, you showed it tonight alright!' he said, and snickered. The others burst into a chorus of laughter.

I gritted my teeth and holstered my gun.

'Call it in,' said one of the others. 'Dare ya.'

I didn't. I turned away, failed to light a cigarette, and started to slither through the alleyways in the general direction of my apartment. The dwarves jeered and laughed behind me. I blocked them out with a yelling voice inside my head. This night needed to end.

I passed through the near-empty blocks leading to my street, fleeting thoughts whirling around my aching head. I started to think about what they would do with the body, about the fact I was probably the only cop who knew about what had happened. Doing nothing. I'd turned blind eyes countless times before, but tonight was just screwing me up.

After typing in the passcode on the greasy keypad, I climbed the hollow creaky stairs leading to my apartment on the fifth floor.

Empty beer bottles lined the kitchenette sides, case files scattered on the floor. The smell of takeaway leftovers hit me as I staggered toward my dimly lit desk revealing the latest case file assigned to me. A speeding offense. Endless cases of missing women and children, and the NYPD assigns one of their best detectives a case involving some nineteen-year-old kid speeding through Queens.

A weird laugh forced its way out of me, then I started to bash my forehead repeatedly with my palms.

As if this would remedy all the drinking I'd done tonight, I went over to the kitchen sink and shoved my mouth under the faucet, letting the cold water rush through me. All it did was make me dry heave and splutter.

I stripped off my coat and my stinking shirt and collapsed into my desk chair, staring at the case file. I had a decision to make. Tomorrow morning, was I going to head over to Queens and issue some dumb kid a speeding ticket, or walk into Chief Cole's office and demand what I want?

As I tore the sheet of paper in half, the tip of my finger sliced open a little, the red of my blood staining the case file.

I made my choice there and then, in that drunken, fucked-up stupor. I could only hope I didn't feel quite as courageous when I woke up in the morning, hungover and alone.

The rest of my night was filled with vivid fever dreams and cold sweating, my mind racing even in my state of half-sleep.

When I woke up, courage wasn't exactly what I was feeling – more like unbearable sickness and disorientation. It took me a few minutes to even realize I'd woken up on the floor.

I decided I ought to go for the timeless remedy known as a glass of cold water. I brought it to my lips with the intent of delicate sipping, but my wrist jolted and washed the water down my throat in absolute desperation.

Straw-like hair dangled in front of my eyes as I caught a glimpse of my disheveled face in the mirror. Somehow I looked worse than I felt. I stumbled over to my desk chair and groped the pockets of my jacket. When I flung the thing upside down, cents and quarters clattered to the ground.

Then I found what I was looking for: the black metal container holding my supply of magick beans. A now limited supply, I shook the container around to find there were barely any left.

I dropped a pellet into my palm then held it underneath the sunlight leaking through my blinds. The multicolored shimmer of the bean never fails to mesmerize me, like I'm a baby quickly escaping some state of despair upon the sight of its crib mobile. I threw the bean down my throat along with the last of the water, clicking my neck, taking a deep breath and exhaling sharply as the burning sensation instantly started to grasp at my chest.

A minute passed and I felt like a new man, or at least as much as my system would allow. My temperature dropped and my vision cleared, the walls of my apartment beginning to shift and take on a more transparent form. Without trying, I heard various conversations and sounds throughout the building. I honed in on one or two for a few seconds – nothing to do with being some tattler; it's just a good way to adjust my senses.

I turned back to the mirror and brushed my hair out of my face. I looked my age again, not two decades above it. My blue eyes, although unnaturally glimmering a little because of the magick coursing through my veins, had life to them again, and my skin actually appeared to belong to that of a living person.

My use of this stuff is hardly a secret, especially to the others in the force, including my superiors. I usually try to take it in private to avoid the gawking of my peers, who find the whole situation fascinating, and are usually the ones trying to nudge me into telling them all about the day I got my nickname, 'Jack of the Beanstalk.' Moments like that more often than not end with me providing a dismissive expletive and moving to the next room.

As far as I can tell, officers like Chief Cole don't tend to care about my almost daily and illegal use of this substance, provided I don't use it to intervene in sensitive cases or, I don't know, harvest valuable and compromising information on people like him. Not that he would have any way of knowing. You don't need to channel sense-enhancing magick to dig up the dirt on the Chief Coles of the world, anyway. They can't bury every grim scandal or malfeasance-ridden story that comes out about them. The truth is, they don't need or want to because there aren't enough people in this city who care, so they don't need to invest the time and effort to lie.

I thought back to the ogre in the alley last night. He cared, he knew. But that wasn't enough.

With the effects of the magick bean now really kicking in, I put on a change of clothes, checked and holstered my Glock 19, and left the apartment, jogging down the wooden stairs to the ground floor so swiftly, I was almost floating.

When the magick beans take such a hold of you, staying grounded isn't the easiest thing. I'd need confidence and sharpness to confront Cole, but boiling over into blind arrogance and aggression was very much in the cards if I was careless.

I took my cruiser and made my way down Central Park West. It was pretty hot out, especially for fall, and barely a cloud in sight. Only the orange leaves of the trees either side of me and the glimmer of skyscrapers disrupted the vast blue of the sky. The streets, as usual, were swarming with taxis, people, creatures, angels, and demons. More demons than angels, most likely.

I tuned into my senses, looking out for a street that might be a little less chaotic and a little more traversable. There wasn't one.

A side effect of ingesting a mysterious and magickally engineered bean, which elevates your senses to the point where you can literally feel another person's heartbeat, is an excruciating and tormenting sense of restlessness.

After taking a few deep breaths and managing to subdue some of the hundreds of sounds and scents threatening to turn me insane, I switched on the red and white emergency lights hanging above the dashboard, blue ones at the rear window. The siren blared a few times and the traffic slowly but surely edged to the sides, just enough that I could sail through. It's illegal, but I was probably just about the only person on that street at risk of going deaf to New York chatter and traffic – although no doubt half the population of the city would claim otherwise.

When I made it through the worst of the obstruction, I let out a huge breath I didn't even realize I'd been holding in. My body relaxed and slumped into the car seat. Different voices and vibrations whirled past my ears, the same way traffic does on a highway with the windows down.

When I noticed how close I was to the station now, I realized there wasn't exactly a planned speech in my head, no specific case to make before the chief who'd been purposely steering me clear of the investigation I wanted.

I shrugged it off. Something was gonna come up.

I turned into the parking lot and parked the cruiser, the sky now gray, matching the dull appearance of the NYPD headquarters. The adrenaline shooting around my body needed to be tempered a little, so I took out my flask of bourbon from the glove compartment and swigged. Whatever ancient order or clan or mage that came up with these beans probably never intended for them to be mixed with liquor, but I'm innovative.

With the magick and its effects more muted, I headed for the sliding doors of HQ. And thank the gods I did get the magick under control because inside it was deafening. Officers and detectives shot around in all directions, waving around files and papers, yelling and cursing. Receptionists attempted to deal with angry and despairing phone calls in vain, lieutenants barking orders to various officers all around the lobby.

Everything in the place was painted white or gray, dented steel cabinets lined almost all the walls, and houseplants that had been dead for months sat in broken vases. It was humid and muggy, a smell of salt and fish haunting the air, and now I really was regretting taking the bean.

I plugged my ears with my fingers, which only slightly muffled the frantic yammering. For a split second, I had the naivety to think maybe the commotion was to do with the multitude of missing people, the story finally breaking through, the incompetent force unable to bury everything any longer. But after focusing on a few of the conversations around the room and building, I heard nothing but trivial arguments and officers being yelled at – not for failings that had anything to do with the people of the city, but their shortcomings when it came to protecting the reputation of some politician, or how an officer might have shot down an innocent person or creature a little *too* recklessly.

I had to scoff.

Shifting myself through the onslaught of bodies, I made my way to the end of the room, toward the double doors that led to the elevators. People were practically bouncing off me, thanks to the magick in my veins. Without it, I'd have been stampeded.

When I got to the corridor, I slammed the door behind me, the rambling and yelling now just muffled, not silenced. I looked down, realizing my fists were clenched. My eardrums were banging inside my skull. I used the elevator ride as another chance to try and compose myself, but all I heard was crashing machinery. I caught myself murmuring, then growling.

The ping of the elevator screamed into my ears and I stepped out onto floor seven. Up here it was a different world entirely. I still heard the chaos of the station, but it was far away, obscured. Up here, I only really heard the clicking of keyboards and the passing traffic. In amongst it, I also heard the deep rumble of Chief Cole's voice. It started to hush when I began walking forward. Like he already knew I was there.

The corridor was pretty impressive: wide and vast, its walls painted a blood orange. Plants and décor were placed symmetrically all the way down to the huge double doors at the end of the hallway, with blurred glass and ridiculously huge handles specially made for the grip of the descendant of a giant.

2
Dumpty

I found myself feeling for my handgun. Why? I had no reason to. As far as I knew I hadn't upset anybody – at least nobody important. I guess last night put me more on edge than I'd realized. I scoffed, concealing my holster with my jacket.

Muffled conversation emerged from the room ahead. One of the chief's doors was slightly ajar. Characteristically careless for him. I found myself wanting to listen. The little sack of magick beans in my breast pocket was practically vibrating with invitation. *Ah, hell*, I thought. I took it out, tipped one of the beans into my palm, eyed the people in the offices either side of me – not that they'd be able to stop me in any way – and threw it down my dried-out, aching throat. I gagged and spluttered a little, then tried to regain my composure. A woman on a telephone peered over her desktop at me, frowning slightly. I raised an eyebrow at her and headed toward the giant doors.

The bean's power started coursing through my veins almost instantly, that warm, tingling sensation. My body was light now, nearly weightless, yet grounded, heavy at the same time, powerful. I grinned, enjoying the moment a little too much, like I wasn't standing right outside the office of the police chief, listening for possibly sensitive info. I honed in on one of the voices: a nasally, rough one, unfamiliar.

'Oh yeah, sir, no, it'll definitely be taken care of. I just wouldn't let it happen, believe me, Chief,' it said. There was a grumble in reply – Cole.

Then another voice: a deep, polite, kiss-ass voice, complemented by awful, loud chewing sounds. It made me want to just walk away. That one I'd definitely heard before, somewhere.

Then it was suddenly very loud. I dropped my head to face the crimson carpet, instinctively shoved a pinky in my ear as if I was vacantly digging, absolutely not paying any attention to their conversation. I carried on walking toward the doors as if I'd only just arrived. One of the doors had now swung open, revealing the two owners of the voices. I'd been listening so hard I forgot to pay attention to their physical movements. Stupid.

The two forms in the doorway turned to me as they headed out. No clue who the first officer was – I'd never seen him before – so he must've been the owner of the nasally voice. The next part seemed to happen in slow motion. As he sauntered past me, he seemed to become possessed, his whole face morphing into a cartoonishly creepy grin, tongue squeezed between his teeth, deep wrinkles showing up all over his face. He had a neatly cut mustache and thinning brownish hair, slicked back to reveal his sizeable forehead. He was lean, medium height, pretty ugly. My eyes dropped to his name badge – 'Piper.' Nope, didn't know him, but he obviously wanted to make himself known to me for some reason. I'd managed to take in his wacky display, observe his features, and get his name, even though the moment had gone by quickly in reality. The magick beans aren't just about making me feel good.

I stared over my shoulder as this Officer Piper glided off, hands deep in his pockets. I think there was a snarl on my face.

'Jack,' said the other voice. One thing about the magick beans is you should never focus on one thing for too long, or the next thing just comes at you loud and fast, throws you for a loop. That's what happened then, and I had to loudly clear my throat in a pretty pathetic attempt to conceal the fact I'd nearly just jumped out my skin. 'You good?' said Special Agent Rick Hunter. They call him The Woodsman – I don't know why.

I sniffed, narrowed my eyes, nodded.

'I was just leaving,' he announced in a low tone, chewing gum smacking in his mouth. I wanted to smack it outta there. 'Need a ride?' He stood at about six-five, sandy blond hair parted neatly to the right above his square head, he had searching blue eyes and a triangular nose above that forever-chewing solid jaw. Always with the goddamn chewing. He was wearing his navy blue FBI jacket over what looked like a pretty damn expensive suit. His cologne was overpowering me, enhanced by the bean, but there was something underneath. I tried to focus on it – it was like flowers. Roses? And a sort of grassy smell. And rain. And . . . freshly discharged bullets.

'Naw,' I murmured, having to actually look up at him to meet his sharp eyes. 'I just got here.'

The Woodsman leaned back, peering into the office with raised eyebrows. Toward Chief Cole, I presumed. 'Okay,' he said, turning his attention back to me. And he just stood there for a few seconds.

I narrowed my eyes. Now what was this?

'You take care of yourself,' he said, edging past me at uncomfortable proximity. He joined up with the Piper guy and waited for the elevator.

I shook my head and stepped into Cole's office, unannounced. The beastly man was seated behind a huge oak desk cluttered with all kinds of paperwork – probably unsolved cases nobody had any intention of pursuing. Sunlight slipped through cracks between gray clouds, pouring into the room through three giant, arching windows behind him, casting shadows over the patterned carpet. The other three walls were lined with shelves filled with books he'd never read and awards he didn't deserve. It was a ridiculously large office. He's a massive guy, but it doesn't need to be this big. That's Chief Cole all over, though. Declarative, I guess.

'Detective Slade,' he grumbled, brow furrowed. 'You look . . . well.' His calculated pause in that observation was seeping with sarcasm. I knew I looked like shit, but hearing it from him was just something else.

'Sir.' I nodded. 'Not nearly as well as you.' That slipped out.

He leaned forward suddenly, custom-made office chair screeching in agony beneath his ass. He shuffled through some papers on his desk and opened a ledger, licking grotesquely at his sausage fingers before flicking through the pages. 'Scheduled a meeting, are we?' he asked, pretending to scan the contents. Performative.

'No. We need to talk about me, my career.' I really wasn't in the mood for this shit. I had to cut the crap, and I felt the magick bean's effect on my confidence surging.

The chief clasped those fingers together. I heard the dryness of his skin. 'Oh. Oh, *do* we? If that's the case, Detective Slade, I see no reason why you couldn't have put it in writing, or gone through the secretaries first. I don't much appreciate people just wandering in, I have to say.'

I knew why, too. I was lucky I hadn't walked in on some nightmarish scene involving the chief and some poor working girl, noon or not. Sweat trickled down his pink head already. He was getting worked up. On the inside, and maybe a little on the outside, I smirked.

Cole, as he tends to do, went on. 'Nevertheless, it's a conversation I am willing to have. Another day.' He began to rise to his feet, failed, and pretended he was only shuffling in his seat. He leaned back, clasped his hands on top of his mountainous belly, and said, 'You will find the door in the very location it was when you strolled in here, Jackson.' Good one.

I cleared my throat, then found myself taking a few steps forward. Now his face was like thunder. The mask was gone. 'I'm one of the best detectives in this force. My record *should* speak for itself, but it looks like I'll have to spell it out for you—'

'Slade, you will do no such thing.' He leaned over his belly. 'And I regret to inform you that you are far from the best detective in this force. Hell, boy, you're not even one of the best officers on this floor,' he spat.

I looked down at the case files spread over the desk, scanning them speedily, the magick coursing through my veins processing them instantly. 'None of these, Chief, have anything to do with what should be the biggest issue in the city right now. None of them are connected to the dozens of missing women and children. The numbers get bigger every day, or at least they might if someone was really following them.' There was fire in my voice now, my teeth clashing together. But I wasn't going to lose control.

'Boy, you'd better watch your damn tone.' A smirk crept across his fat face. 'And when did you become so, hmm, high and mighty, anyway? Yes, there was a time when, indeed, you shone as a police detective. Oh yes, very impressive – but those years are long behind us now, and since then I have seen nothing from you besides apathy and a . . . disdain for the work you supposedly do.'

It felt like my skin was tightening around my body. I felt hot, violent. I stopped my hands turning into fists.

'Not to mention your drug addiction there. You're lucky I haven't already taken your badge for that alone. And shall I delve into the tales of your greasy palms, misuse of citizens' private information, battering innocent bystanders, so on, so forth? The recently discovered . . . troubling accounts of events in your youth. Before you joined us.'

Man. He was pushing it now. I realized my hand had started creeping toward my holstered gun. Shit. Instead of taking it out and blasting his brains out there and then, I brushed the ends of my jacket with both hands in a fluid motion, like that's what my intentions were to start with. Now it was my turn to sweat.

Cole's tiny black eyes dropped to my hands, then he snarled.

Out of nowhere, I was on eggshells, serious eggshells, suddenly finding myself on the verge of making an insanely powerful enemy. And for what?

I cleared my throat again. It was drier than it'd been this morning. 'These cases I get assigned—'

'Nothing to do with me.' He waved a dismissive, thick arm, like a tree trunk with a shirt sleeve around it.

'I need something more.'

Cole reclined in his seat once again, that poor chair screaming more than ever. He sighed. 'So you step into my office, unannounced, and ask for it, something more?' It sounded like a question.

I nodded. 'Yeah.' The magick inside me was trying to alert me to something. Another presence.

'Well, that isn't how it's done, boy,' he growled. 'Work. Work for it.'

Someone was watching me.

Cole went on, raising his disproportionate arms to the sky now. 'It's the American way, isn't it? Get your head down . . .'

I switched his voice off in my mind, and slowly turned my head. That little freaky cop, Piper, was still there. He'd never left, never stepped into the elevator. He was trying to listen in, like I had with him. Fair's fair, I guess. He didn't know I was onto him – I could sense him through the wall, but I was out of his sight.

Cole had shut up. I almost started asking him about Piper and The Woodsman, but there wouldn't be any point. I'd already made this too dangerous, and gotten jack shit out of it. Just more eyes on me, probably. Well, that could make my life more interesting – there was always that.

I started to make for the doors.

'Ah,' grunted Cole, 'are we done?'

I turned to him. 'Don't ever bring up my past again.'

He jumped back a little, his face sinking into his chins. He paused for a few seconds, stunned into a rare silence. 'Was that a threat? You dare threaten me, boy!' he spat.

I quickly exited the room, leaving the door wide open. I'd made a mistake, but something was telling me I had no other choice. I heard my heartbeat in my ears. It was drowning out the booming voice of Chief Cole, insults and threats bouncing off the walls as I made my way down the corridor. I sensed the onlooking detectives in their cubicles behind the glass either side of me. They absolutely did not see this every day.

I reached into my right breast pocket, the one with the flask of whiskey in it, tipped my head back, and drank until the last drop. My ears burned, my fingers trembled. I saw my hair dangling in front of my eyes, drenched in sweat, vibrating. Someone was hissing 'fuck you' over and over. I realized it was me. This wasn't worth it.

None of this was worth it.

Too many magick beans in a short span of time. That was the worst of it. In an hour or two, it would be over, and I'd realize I was freaking out over a relatively small ordeal. . . .

I slouched in the seat of my cruiser, staring vacantly out the window, muffled chatter of officers walking by, flashing lights of vehicles leaving the parking lot, whirring of helicopter blades somewhere close by. It was all background noise. I just sat there, trapped in my head, turning over everything I'd taken in upstairs: The Woodsman, seemingly working with that deranged Piper guy; Cole's pathetic but wild fury; the sinking feeling in my chest and stomach that had stuck with me since last night.

And suddenly I was drunk again. 'Fuck this,' I murmured as I started the engine. I slammed down the lights at the top of my windshield and headed into traffic. I was taking today off, and there was nobody to stop me.

A few hours later and I was back to square one – drunk under the neon lights. This time, though, I attempted a stroll around the block. I'd decided wandering through a shithole at dusk was a step above waking with your face in a puddle of whiskey in a bar at one in the morning. Aiming high, as ever.

To be fair to myself, I wasn't as drunk as last night, but I guess it was still pretty early yet.

I trudged down the Manhattan streets with my hands plunged into my jacket pockets, staring at the ground, brain and skull thumping. I walked for two hours like that.

This was starting to feel like a new low. I started wondering how this could get any worse. I was literally walking in circles in the middle of New York, no sense of direction or control. There was just anger and frustration, but deep below, in a place I could barely access. Even my strongest emotions were tame and pitiable tonight.

I thought about calling it a day, heading back to the apartment, getting something to eat. But then what? Wake up the next morning, hungover and aching, drive down to the apartment and get assigned another dead-end case, if that? Surely Cole would have something in store as a form of punishment.

I could just hurl my badge at him, walk away.

My back was resting against the window of a bodega advertising trash magazines. I turned my attention to them, pulled out my lighter and lit a cigarette. Smoke drifted over the dirty window. When it'd cleared, I found myself staring at a magazine cover featuring a couple of gay centaurs in a compromising position, complete with oiled-up, shredded forms and a trippy, very obviously green-screened background. That was what my evening had come to.

How long had I been alone? The streets were empty. I didn't even know what time it was anymore. Icy fear crept up my back, stroked my neck. I took another drag of my smoke, a deep one. It was so quiet, the silence only broken by distant muffled music and light traffic a few blocks away from here.

Until I heard the screaming. Shrieking. Not the kind everybody's used to hearing around here – not some high lost soul, getting into fistfights with imaginary entities, not ghouls searching through garbage, or a wandering banshee.

Somebody was in trouble.

I waited for another yell. Had no idea where the first one came from. I threw the butt of my cigarette on the ground and stomped it out, one hand now resting on my holster.

'Please!' shrieked the voice, a woman.

It was coming from my left. I broke into a stride, then a jog. 'Police!' I called. 'Where are you?' I yanked my handgun out of its holster.

'Please, I think he's dying!' called the woman.

Almost on instinct, while running, I tipped one more magick bean into my palm and swallowed it. It started to work instantly. The magick shot through my veins, almost painfully this time.

Now I saw who the voice was coming from. Not clearly, but she was there: a pale, slim, blonde woman, dressed in black. I sensed her emotions a little now; fear wasn't one of them. But there was . . . excitement? I started toward her, holding up an arm. 'Ma'am,' I called, 'what's the problem? Hold it!'

Within a few seconds, she'd scurried away, vanishing into a cluster of corporate buildings. Not only gone from my vision, but well out of range of my power. I was almost definitely going to lose her. The overdose was working against me, not doubly enhancing my already heightened senses but destroying them.

'Shit,' I growled, slowing to a walk, panting, my chest tight and hot. My senses picked up on something else, though. Something dead.

Whoever or whatever it was, it was close to the old, shitty hotel around here – the Sultan. It's where a lot of people go to die, I'm sure, but this didn't feel like some poor sap locked in a room, drinking until he was unconscious, then plunged into the real thing. There was something more here.

As I got closer to the hotel, I spun in a circle, surveying the area for life, for that blonde woman who'd brought me over here. There was some activity, faint and fleeting, but none of it belonged to her.

A rotten stink penetrated my nostrils out of nowhere, and I leaned forward, expecting to send tonight's whiskey back up my system. It didn't come, I was just stuck there with that stench nestling itself in my nose. Now the beans really weren't doing me too many favors. I figured the stink was bad, anyway, but with my reinforced sense of smell, it was criminal.

So, unhelpfully, the overdose had decided to boost my smelling power alone, right when the stench of rotten eggs was flowing through the city air, and work against me when I needed to track the woman.

I coughed into my arm, peering into the distance. There was something there, a mass of white heaped on the sidewalk outside the Sultan.

'What the hell?' I whispered to myself. The thought of calling it in flashed across my mind – I immediately chuckled it away. Fuck that. This was mine.

Head on a swivel, I stepped up to the dead thing. A yellow liquid was trickling toward my boot, a line of it filling the thin cracks in the road.

Egg yolk.

I looked skyward, the Sultan soaring high above me. 'Huh,' I said.

Mr Dumpty'd had a great fall.

The smell was so strong now, so potent, I could taste it on my tongue, but the vomit still wouldn't do me the mercy of leaving my body. I felt it there. It was making me feel heavy and slow. The sound of my heartbeat was getting louder again, and so was the pounding of it, beating against my ribs.

I crouched to get a better look at the body. A tweed suit crumpled loosely around the smashed egg form, the facial features were distorted and disfigured, but Dumpty for sure. I got a feeling even my peers would've been able to figure that one out.

Business magnate, entrepreneur, millionaire philanthropist, oh, dear friend of the NYPD – the man-sized egg, Richard 'Dick' Dumpty, casting himself from a window of some three-star hotel in the dead of night? Cole would be all over this, and fast.

Giddiness was sitting in the pit of my stomach now, not lurking vomit. I got back to my feet and started pacing like some excited little kid waiting for Christmas morning. At this point, I hardly realized the side effects from my bean feast were getting genuinely bad. Tremors, blinking, blurred vision. I gave my face a slap and murmured some expletives to myself – words of encouragement.

I aimed to stay conscious enough to at least see how Cole and his buddies would react before things got messy. What a weird night. Couple minutes ago I was observing soft-core centaur porn through a shop window, then a few blood-curdling screams and horrendous whiffs of rotten egg later, I was at a crime scene any good detective in the city would sell their soul to stumble across.

A flaming feeling of rapture combined with genuine fear soared through my body. Things were happening.

I froze, gun still in my hand. A presence close to me.

People were suddenly near.

Maybe it was the woman's screams, or the sight of a man pacing in front of a giant, scrambled corpse egg on the ground that drew attention. Whatever it was, curiosity was brewing. I had to make this crime scene mine.

I stepped around Dumpty's corpse and peered into the lobby of the Sultan Hotel. No one inside, no one behind the desk, nothing. I looked over my shoulder, back at the corpse. It was one hell of a sight, this lump of shell and fleshy white, the sickly yellow of the yolk shining under the streetlight. I nearly felt for the guy, but only nearly and only for a second.

My eyes flicked to the right as a group of onlookers made their way toward Dumpty, creeping and shuddering.

'What the hell, man?' whined one of them, elven features, smartly dressed. A glamorous woman at his side gagged, and behind her a few others looked on, horrified.

'Yeah,' I said, heading toward them. 'Alright, stay back or clear off. Police business.' I chewed my lip, my senses alerting me to more people. I turned around. A crowd was starting to form.

A low murmur hummed around the street, cars slowed, some to

a stop, to get a look at the scene.

Someone said, 'Is that . . . Is that Dick Dumpty?' The murmurs grew into an excited chatter now, louder and louder. My head thumped. In most cases where a dead body is found on the ground for all to see, no one bats an eyelid, including the cop called in. Corpses aren't an especially notable sight to behold in these streets, but this was a person of note, a celebrity.

Someone clambered toward the corpse, some drunk kid. I thrust my boot into his stomach and he instantly crumbled into a heap. My grip tightened on the gun. The crowd got even louder, shouting at me, shouting amongst themselves. Fuck this. I fired my gun into the night sky five times. There was a chorus of screams as the crowd collectively ducked, some of them scrambling away completely.

I blinked tightly and groaned, my legs heavy and solid. 'Enough!' I yelled at the gawkers, hitting both my thighs in an attempt to get the blood moving. 'One of you must've seen something.'

I shifted my eyes across the silent audience, a few of them making eye contact, most of them still watching the body intently.

'Anyone,' I said. Nothing. 'Look, I can easily pin this on one of you unfortunate souls if I feel like it. Don't test me; it's been a long day.'

'Buddy,' said one of the onlookers, 'who the hell's gonna talk after you just assaulted an innocent man and fired your weapon for no fuckin reason?'

I looked down at the gun in my hand, felt myself smiling. 'What, uh, you implying I can trust any of you people to not to pull a knife on an officer of the law when given the chance?'

'What law?' yelled another voice.

I shrugged. 'Fair point, I guess. Now if no one has anything to contribute, get outta here; this is officially a crime scene.'

A few of them shuffled back. The rest just continued to stare.

I growled, cocked my gun and stepped forward, pointing it at their faces. 'Fuck off!'

And so they did.

As I watched them leave, I heard the sound of engines getting louder. Three NYPD cruisers came hurtling around the corner, each coming to sharp stops right outside the hotel. No sirens, lights off.

'What the hell is this?' I whispered to myself. I watched a few officers emerge from the vehicles. One more vehicle rolled up to the scene – a black van with its windows blacked out. 'Shit,' I whispered.

It was the King's Men.

Of course, there's no king here, it's a theatrical name given to an organization of darkly clad elite soldiers who serve Cole and others like him as a sort of task force intent on tackling, and usually covering up, shady shit. In short, this was bad news.

Four emerged from the van, every inch of them concealed by their pitch-black uniform, faces concealed by dark masks or helmets, each dressed in a black trench coat and black cowboy hat. The only color on them was the strip of red light across their eye line.

The normal officers just looked right through me and strolled over to Dumpty's corpse.

'Eh,' I called, trying to keep one eye on the King's Men, 'I want you to block off the street, call forensics, and start questioning residents of the Sultan. You listening?' One of the shadows to my right turned his attention to me. I looked away in case he saw me gulp.

'Thank you, Detective Slade,' boomed that familiar voice. My teeth started to grind. 'We shall take it from here. You may go home, get some rest.' Chief Cole squeezed out of the cruiser, followed by the Piper guy.

I headed toward him at a slightly threatening pace. I stopped short of striking his fat head. 'I'm not going anywhere. I found him; this is my crime scene.'

I don't even think he heard me – his tiny eyes were fixed on the body behind me. There was concern on his face. I'd never seen it like that before.

Piper stepped forward, arms folded, face wrinkled in a creepy smirk. 'This is ours,' he announced happily.

'Who the fuck even are you?' I said through gritted teeth.

He opened his mouth to speak but Cole's attention was back on me now. 'Have you forgotten yourself again, boy? Do not make me embarrass you in front of the general public. Oh, I think you'd highly regret that.'

I looked past his huge frame – the crowds were reappearing.

He turned to face them with open arms. 'Friends! Bear with us as we investigate this matter. We shall have answers for you very soon – that I can promise you. Please, make your way home; it is late.'

He turned back to me, face distorted with anger. 'That goes for you, too. Get out of here,' he spat in a whisper.

I stood my ground, trying to think.

'Hells, boy. Look at you. How can I rely on one of my detectives to be ready for a job at any given moment if he is wandering the streets in the middle of the night drunk and high?' He nearly knocked me off my feet as he brushed me with a tower of a shoulder, inspecting the body, huge hands behind his back.

'I'm on a case,' I said, voice shaky, legs nearly giving out at this point.

'No,' said Cole, not even looking at me anymore. 'You are not.'

There was a scraping sound behind me as Piper stepped up, breathing down my neck.

'You're gonna want to take a step back,' I warned.

'What's that, junkie?' said Piper into my ear.

That was it. I spun around and swung for him, putting all my weight behind the punch. All power, no accuracy. I missed completely as he jumped back. Next thing was soaring pain in my nose and head, and I was flat out on the concrete.

My ears rang and my eyes were wet to the point that all I saw was Piper's scrawny frame standing above me, highlighted by the pulsing orange glow of the streetlights. I realized there was laughter erupting now, muffled and loud, but not from that fucker Piper, and not from Cole – from the crowd. This was what they wanted to see. Who gave a damn about the body, about women and children vanishing from the streets every night? This, this right here – me knocked on my ass, lying in a stream of yolk in the dead of night, drunk and overdosing – this was the good shit.

I closed my eyes and shut down my mind.

But not for long.

Seemed my body's intention was to slip into a state of exhaustion and switch off the consciousness, but Officer Piper wasn't about to let that happen. He hurled an open palm across my face and I jolted back to life, scrambling to my feet, nearly slipping on the stream of yolk I'd been about to nap in.

I grabbed that asshole Piper by the throat with both hands. He instantly started spluttering, his stupid face going purple. I squeezed, squeezed hard until Cole stepped between us, wrenching one of my arms back with ease and shoving me across the curb.

Piper was trying to say something – I heard a few 'fuck's in there between the gagging and choking.

'Speak up, Officer,' I said, tasting blood on my lip.

I was engulfed by the shadow of Chief Cole, King's Men now standing beside him. Suddenly, I was a really small person. 'You are an embarrassment,' he said, smirking with resentment. 'What kind of way is that to behave at a *fucking* murder scene, boy? I have a mind to take your badge this very moment.'

Part of me felt like reaching into my pocket and handing it over right there – the part of me that wanted to end up unemployed and spending my last few days in this realm binge drinking in a bar until I was dead.

'You are suspended,' Cole proclaimed. 'Until further notice, I am freezing your pay, taking you off duty entirely, and you shall not be granted access to the station. Any open cases you are on will be assigned to other, more capable detectives.'

I shifted my eyes to Dumpty's body, now being thoroughly inspected by officials, evidence already being marked. 'You know,'

I said, clearing my throat, 'I haven't observed my colleagues getting on with the job this quickly in . . . well, years. Very interesting.'

Cole stiffened. 'Boy! Did you hear me? Suspended.'

'One hell of a time to suspend me.'

'I'm not entirely sure what the implication is there, but I'm going to have to ask you to leave this crime scene immediately.'

My legs twitched as all three of the identical King's Men raised their huge assault rifles at once and pointed them directly at my chest.

It was time to go. I raised my hands and slowly took a few steps back.

A smile crept across Cole's face. 'Attaboy,' he growled.

If not for the magick bean overdose hacking away at my system, I'm sure I'd have felt a sort of weight lifted off my shoulders.

But this was a good thing. Nobody was allowed to tell me it wasn't.

3
GIANTS

There was no shot I was leaving this thing alone. He didn't know it, but Cole had done me a favor with the suspension. He wouldn't be there to hold me back anymore – he wouldn't know where I was, and he couldn't give me shit cases to work.

He couldn't stop me, could he?

But I was still a cop, I still had power, and I was going to use it.

I had nothing to go on, but I needed to know what happened to Dick Dumpty. I just ended up in the middle of all that, and within minutes it was taken from me. I've never seen Cole show up at a crime scene like he did. Something was happening, and I wasn't about to let it slip by me, for better or worse.

Fuck Cole and whoever he might be working for – this was mine.

The next day, at about nine in the morning, my phone rang. Murky sun bled through my blinds, illuminating the stacks of papers cluttering my desk. My cell phone vibrated on top of them, nearly slipping off the desk. I answered it, greeted by a tired-sounding voice.

'Detective?' it said. 'Detective Slade?'

I hesitated a few seconds. 'Yeah, that's me,' I answered, rubbing my dry eyes. I noticed there was a tremor in my fingers.

No reply.

'Hello?' I said. Something was off.

'Sorry, I . . .' It was a woman's voice. She sounded close to tears.

'Ma'am, are you in danger?'

'No, no.' She cleared her throat. 'I wanted to ask you for something. I need your help. No one else is doing anything.'

'Can I take a name?'

'No. Not yet. I'm sorry.'

I breathed in, then out heavily. 'It would help the situation if I had your name, ma'am.'

'I don't know who to trust,' she said, voice quivering.

'I understand. What's this about?'

'You're a good man, aren't you, Detective Slade?'

'I don't know about that.' I walked over to the kitchen, poured myself a glass of water.

'Better than the rest, then, at least. It's my daughter. She's gone – been gone for two weeks now. Like the rest of them, just gone.'

I slowly took a sip of the water, then perched on the end of my bed.

'They won't do anything,' she said, 'the other cops. It's always the same shit, that they're looking into it, that she might just show up again in a few days. It's . . . It's fucked.'

'Yeah. Yes, it is.'

Then she was crying, trying to get her words out.

'Breathe, ma'am. Please, what's your name?'

'I can't do this.'

'Hold on. Talk to me. You don't have to tell me your name, but you can trust me.' I wasn't even sure if that was true, but something was happening.

'I hope they're right about you.'

I didn't know what that meant, and I didn't really want to find out. 'Just breathe, and speak to me.' I paused, rubbing my forehead, trying to think, prickles of anxiety all over my body. 'The timing of your phone call.'

She sniffed. 'What about it?'

'It seems . . . significant. Do you happen to be aware of an incident last night at the Sultan Hotel?'

She breathed down the phone, labored and shaky.

'Ma'am.' Still nothing. 'You need to talk to me, there could be—'

'Apartment seven, Drury Gardens.' The line went dead.

'Fuck,' I hissed, and almost on some kind of instinct, crept over to the window and peered through my blinds to the street below. I threw the window open, closed my eyes, and breathed. 'Get it together,' I whispered. Then I found myself looking down again. The ground and the people on it seemed so far away, and like they were shifting in awkward, broken motions. The sky seemed to be low and heavy. I chugged the rest of my water and backed away from the window.

Whoever she was, she knew something. My first instinct was that this was a trap, some kind of ambush, set up by Cole to snuff me out for looking in the wrong places. But I could almost feel some sort of pull – a pull I was finding harder and harder to resist. If I didn't go, I'd be wondering about this for months, while in the meantime, Cole swept more shit under the rug.

Midday and I was heading through the city on my way to Drury Gardens. I'd never heard of the place. Checked it out on my phone – a small hovel in Brooklyn, host of a number of crime scenes throughout recent years, nothing special.

So far I'd resisted the urge to take any more beans. At this point, they would do more harm than good. I took a swig of vodka and slammed the empty bottle into the glove compartment. Anything to ease the crashing and burning inside my skull.

Endless gray clouds hung over the street of skyscrapers. New Yorkers stared at the ground, scurrying in all directions. At a traffic stop, I made the mistake of looking into my wallet. Sure, I wasn't unemployed just yet, but things were hardly looking great for me.

I checked my gun, the gun that last night started seeming like an enticing option for me as I stood there in the dark, all fucked-up and lost. My mood had changed, though. If this was an ambush, I wouldn't turn this gun on myself; I'd take down as many of the other bastards as I could before it was all over.

When I reached Brooklyn, I flicked my GPS, which was blinking and threatening to shut off, as usual. Couple blocks from here. My heart was starting to boom again, ready for problems lurking in every shadow, every alley.

I growled and gave in. The bean shot down my throat and I took the next right, parking lazily by the sidewalk.

I heard and felt the crunch of the orange leaves beneath my boots as I stepped out of the car, my body once again coming to terms with the magick inside it when it shouldn't be. The sound of children laughing and yelling in the distance shot through my ears in waves, arms suddenly covered in goosebumps. I closed my eyes, leaned against the car for a minute, trying to take control of my breaths.

Hearing those children made everything feel worse.

I eventually opened my eyes and peered at the big, bronze gate to my right, next to it a rusty plaque – 'Drury Gardens.' It was one horseshoe-shaped building, red bricks, small windows, most of them covered with old newspaper, protecting the residents inside from whatever horrors might wait out here for them.

One of the gates was slightly open, so I went in, the thing screaming as it closed behind me. I winced. A slight wind breezed through the murky air, collecting piles of leaves and scattering them around the dead lawn. My hand rested on my holster.

I made my way to the block, scanning for number seven. The magick bean picked up on a few presences behind the walls. Sad, forgotten people. No immediate danger, far from it. Everything here was lifeless, invisible to everyone else. My hand relaxed and released the holster.

I approached the door of number seven, knocked three times. Someone was shuffling around and mumbling to himself in the flat next to this one. I heard the sounds of basic cable, some rerun.

A woman pulled the door of number seven ajar, tired gray eyes looking me up and down. She breathed in sharply, then swallowed. 'Detective,' she whispered.

Not quite. 'Are you alone?' I asked. No. She wasn't.

'Yes.'

My hand crept back to my holster. 'Are you sure about that, ma'am?' I saw her neck shift as she swallowed again. I placed my hand on the door and, through my heightened senses, felt her rapid heartbeat at my fingertips.

She pulled the door open more, motioned for me to step in.

I narrowed my eyes, took a quiet breath, and went into apartment number seven. My body stiffened. Whoever was with her was waiting on the other side of the wall, outside. I decided to pretend I had no idea, for now.

The woman closed the door and just stood there awkwardly, fingers intertwined firmly. Late twenties, frail, lean body, thin auburn hair, horizontal scars down each arm. She was wearing a loose-fitting black T-shirt and black skinny jeans. I could smell iron.

'Well,' I said, 'are you going to give me your name now?'

She sighed. 'Emily.'

'Thank you.'

The apartment was nearly empty. Just a few pieces of furniture placed in random corners, ugly, dark wallpaper peeling under the low, damp ceiling, a door leading to the kitchen hanging on by a hinge. And the window to my right, where the other person was: I walked over to it and felt Emily tense immediately. I paused and turned to face her.

'Can I sit?'

'Yeah, I— Sorry, yes, of course,' she said.

I sat in a leather armchair by the window. 'Are you going to sit down?' I asked.

She nodded. 'Uh-huh.'

'Good. Emily, let me just ask you right off the bat. Are you in danger?' Her hands were shaking.

'My daughter,' she whimpered, breaking into a sob.

'I know,' I said. The presence outside was filling my mind. I felt anger, brutality, resentment, fear, death. 'You said on the phone you haven't seen her for two weeks, your daughter. What's her name?'

Long fingers concealed her face as she sobbed. 'Ella.'

'Ella. Okay, thank you.'

'That fucking monster!' she cried.

I jumped slightly, eyes flicking from the window back to Emily. 'Scuse me?'

'It was him,' she hissed.

'Who? Emily, who?'

'How do you not know?' She clawed her fingers away from her face and stood up sharply. A dot of blood appeared on her cheek.

'Don't do that,' I said, also getting to my feet.

'Everything is so fucked-up, I can't do it.'

'Emily, what can't you do?' I said, hearing my voice getting louder now.

'I don't think you should be here.'

And neither did I. But I already knew there was no turning back. What else was I going to do – pass out in a bar at one in the afternoon? Go kiss Cole's ass so I could sit in a cubicle all day for no reason? My own heartbeat was getting violent now.

'But I am here,' I said. 'It's your chance to talk. I'm gonna ask you again now: Are you in danger? Is somebody threatening you?' I turned to the window.

'*Wait*!' she yelled.

I stopped.

'Fucking Dumpty. It's him, he's involved.' Tears were streaming now.

Fucking Dumpty. 'Involved?'

'That's why they killed him.'

'Who? Who killed him?'

She stumbled, almost falling to her knees. She held onto a side table, then punched it, again and again. 'Don't ask me!' she screamed. 'Please!'

'Okay, okay,' I said, backing up, hands in the air.

I thought about tumbling through the window, trying to tackle this bad dude behind the wall. But I couldn't. If this guy was blackmailing the mother, I'd more than likely get her killed. I've had enough blood on my hands in this job.

Emily had stopped attacking the table. She was completely still, leaning over it, face completely covered by her matted hair. 'Jolly Roger,' she said. 'Jolly Roger.' She said it like it was a question she was asking herself.

'Huh? Jolly Roger, like, the club?'

Her eyes shot up at me. I think there was a nod. Then, 'There was a man. Well, two men. Here.' Her eyes were red with tears. But there was some kind of defiance about her now.

I felt movement behind me. And an emotion. Apprehension.

'Two men?' I said under my breath.

'Tall. Blond like you, said he was from the bureau.'

My heart jumped. 'No, wait—'

A roar behind me. 'You fucking bitch!' screamed a voice.

I turned on my heel, aimed my gun at something at the window.

Emily screamed. A gun went off and it wasn't mine. Glass shattered.

'*Shit*!' I hissed.

I leaped toward the window and clumsily fired my gun at the attacker. He shifted across the lawn and fumbled into the passenger seat of a dark car. Emily was crying behind me. I focused on the license plate, but I couldn't get it. My vision was blurry, my body aching, failing me again. I realized my hands were gripping the windowpane lined with broken glass. My palms were bright red, stinging.

I flailed away from the window and dropped onto my knees beside Emily. Blood was streaming out of her stomach, the bullet deep inside.

'Fuck,' I growled. 'No, no, no.' There was no chance for her. I lifted her head up gently. She was choking, trying to speak. Blood trickled out of her nose and mouth.

She got one word out: 'Odette.' And then she was dead.

Sirens were already sounding. I had to get out now. I clambered to my feet, yanking open drawers, cupboards, looking for anything more than a name to go on. There was nothing else.

I fell into the hallway and sprinted out of Drury Gardens. People turned and looked, jumped out of the way as I ran through the Brooklyn street, a trail of my own blood behind me. My car seemed a hell of a lot farther away than it did when I got there. I climbed into it and took off. Peering into my rearview mirror, I just caught the flashing of red and blue against the townhouses, sirens blaring.

The crime scene was caked in my blood. I couldn't even escape back into the life of bar drinking and suicidal wandering now. I had to commit, or go down in flames.

A probably innocent woman lay dead, her child still missing, dozens more situations just like it in this city. And here I was, feeling alive again because of it.

After turning everything over in my mind for two or three hours that afternoon, I was headed to Long Island. I was weak, exhausted, hungover. The volume and intensity of magick in my system was really working against me – but for now, the only way I could overcome the crashing sensation was to eat another bean. Something was telling me there was no time for me to fall apart and let my guard down.

Jolly Roger is a freaky club by a beach on Long Island, run by a scumbag named Hansel. It attracts all the worst kinds of elites and bootlickers – Dumpty's crowd. 'Jolly Roger' was one of the last things Emily said. Why, I didn't know, but it was pretty much all I had to go on. That and 'Odette.'

I pulled up to the club and checked my phone. It was just gone six, so the place wouldn't be open yet. Good, this worked for me. I grabbed my newly purchased bottle of bourbon out of the glove box and took a swig. In theory, the alcohol would boost me a little, mitigate whatever damage my body had been sustaining the last twenty-four hours from magick. In reality, it probably wasn't quite working like that.

I slammed the car door shut, the shrieking of gulls breaking the quiet, and walked up to the front doors of the Jolly Roger. It was an old building – a strong plantation vibe with remnants of pirate-themed ornamentation that had clearly been gradually overlooked and dumped over the years.

The double doors looked about two centuries old, wooden cabin doors with purposely blacked out circular windows. I banged on them with an impatient fist. 'NYPD, open the door, now.'

'We're closed,' shouted a muffled voice on the other side.

'Yep. Open the door, anyway.'

Then one of the doors did open, only slightly, but enough for me to be greeted by the ever-punchable face of Hansel.

'I need to talk to you,' I said, showing my defunct badge.

'Oh, of course! When we're open,' he said with a grin.

I caught the door with my shoulder as he went to close it in my face, and swung it open with my arm, employing my added strength courtesy of the latest dosage of magick bean.

Hansel whimpered in shock and fear, flailing back as the wooden door crashed behind me. It was almost pitch dark in there, the only light sources being from the brightly illuminated bar and a bunch of neon signs over every wall. My boots stuck to the grimy floor with every step. I tried not to ponder what the hell it was and carried on approaching Hansel.

'Ahoy,' I said.

'Piece of shit!' he squawked, backing up. 'You can't just break into my establishment like that, Slade. Fuckin pig!'

I nodded. 'Hansel of the Forest, hm? Now we have the formalities outta the way, give me what I want.'

Hansel felt around behind him, refusing to turn away from me, and slipped into a seat against the black wall. I took my own opposite him, a large black table between us, a pool of bright purple reflecting into it from the giant, juicy neon lips on the wall. Hansel gawked at me stupidly, his mouth hanging open, revealing two rows of crooked yellow teeth, some missing. He had curly black hair, drenched in whatever product to the point it looked plastic, and wore circular black sunglasses, an ugly, oversized Hawaiian shirt, way-too-short denim shorts, and flip-flops. Flip-flops, in a place like this, with a floor as putrid as that.

'Goddammit, Slade, I don't got time for this!' he complained.

'That's simply too bad,' I said. 'I'm a cop.'

'No shit, pig. Now, what the fuck did you break my door down for?'

I scoffed. 'Don't be so dramatic. All you gotta do is answer a couple simple questions for me, then I'm gonna take a little look around.'

Hansel leaned back in his chair, made an over-the-top face of anguish.

'And then I'll make my merry way outta here, with you keeping your mouth shut, no matter who comes knocking next, alright?'

'Next?' he squawked.

I leaned forward, scowling. 'Yeah,' I whispered. 'I get the feeling I'm not the first unusual visitor you've had in here recently, and you damn well know I'm not gonna be the last.' I eyed him and his dumb outfit, his body language and facial tics telling me a story. I sat back again, taking in the place. 'Who owns this joint? Couldn't find shit online. Almost like it's been hidden on purpose.'

Hansel relaxed his body, pulled out something wrapped in plastic from his pocket. He shrugged. ''Sall public info, Detective. Go figure.' He unwrapped a red lollipop, letting the wrapper fall to the floor, and shoved it in his mouth, the stick pointing out of one of the voids in which a rotten tooth used to sit.

'Then you should have no problem telling me right now.'

'What do we pay you people for if you ain't even able to do a quick search on your phone?' He sneered. 'Embarrassing!'

'A young woman died today,' I said. 'She was murdered in cold blood. Her child has been missing for two weeks. She was living alone in a shitty apartment, terrified, paranoid. One of the last things she said to me before she died? Jolly Roger.'

Hansel made loud sucking sounds on the candy, then bit right into it with a loud crunch. He shuffled in his seat. 'What an interesting story. Junkie rambles about nothing, gets killed. I'll read all about it in tomorrow's paper. Seriously!'

The chair legs screamed against the floor as I shot up to my feet. I slammed my palms onto the table, leaning over this worm. He flailed his arms in the air, trying to shrink himself into nothing. 'Odette!' I yelled. 'What the fuck is Odette?'

'I don't know!' he yelled back, almost on instinct. 'I can't help if you ask bullshit questions like that!'

'This place is a pit of abuse, violations, dirty deals,' I spat. 'And you think I'm gonna think nothing of it being mentioned seconds before someone's murdered? *Think*. You know things.'

'I'm just the fucking manager!'

'Like hell.' I sighed, pulled out my wallet. I didn't have time for this bullshit. I threw a few bank notes at him.

'What's this?' he asked, sliding the notes toward himself and inspecting them.

'What does it look like? A bunch of flowers? Just talk.'

A grin crept across Hansel's face as he pocketed the cash. 'Oh, Jackson. You people are all the same. I love it!'

Violent thoughts danced around my mind. 'Emily Wyatt, who was she?'

Hansel paused for a moment, then sniffed hard. He crunched on the last of the candy and swallowed. 'I honestly have no clue. Not a name I recall hearing. But then, I hear a lot of em.'

I smiled. 'Fine. What about an FBI agent? How many of those do you get around here?'

'Ooooooh,' went Hansel, his voice high and shrill. 'Now *that* is a sensitive topic, ain't it?'

I feigned another polite grin, reached into my thin wallet, and slid a twenty over the table. Hansel tutted and rolled his eyes. I slid over a fifty. 'Specifically,' I said, 'one Rick Hunter, goes by The Woodsman. He been around recently?' I wasn't sure in this light, but I thought Hansel's face went a little pale then.

'Right,' he said, clearing his throat. He seemed to be sliding himself to the edge of the table.

I snorted. 'What, you think because it's dark I can't see you on the move? Make a run for it, I knock out your remaining fucking teeth.'

He raised his hands. 'Easy, easy. We're gettin along now, ain't we? Yeah, I know a guy goes by Woodsman. Tall guy, well-built, blond. Always got this pet guy with him – Piper, I think he's called.'

I nodded. 'Okay,' I said, my voice low. 'And who does he come here to meet? Other police officers, agents?'

'I . . . I guess. They ain't exactly flashing their badges around.'

'Describe them, the people he meets.'

'I don't know! Just guys, sometimes women—'

'Your women? Working girls?'

'Sometimes, yeah, sure.' He pulled another piece of candy out of nowhere, shoved it in his face hole. 'Listen, it ain't like I get involved, sit with them and shit. I don't know what to tell ya.'

'No, no. You're doing a wonderful job,' I said.

'Your good cop antics make me sick, Slade,' Hansel spat.

I chuckled, pleased with the review of my performance. 'Now, Dick Dumpty.' I was running out of money, but knew this one was gonna cost me. I threw seventy dollars across the table, some of the notes floating to the sticky floor. As Hansel scrambled for them, I readied myself in case he made a break for it.

Seemed he was too interested in checking the authenticity of the notes. He nestled back into his seat, checking out each paper. 'Dumpty,' he murmured.

'Yeah. He was found dead last night.' Hansel stared at me, suddenly wide-eyed. 'Made to look like a suicide.'

'Dead, did you say?'

'Big heap of scrambled egg outside the old Sultan. My crime scene. Or, it was.'

Hansel's mouth started twitching then, his eyes flicking around everywhere. His hands were suspended in the air, holding the note there idiotically. Suddenly he was nervous as hell.

I felt my eyes narrow.

'Dead,' he whispered to himself again.

'Talk,' I said. 'Did Dumpty happen to be one of the people The Woodsman and his friends hung out with around here?'

'Uhh . . .' Hansel's voice sounded dry and thin. Small and pathetic. 'Dumpty was a . . . regular.'

'Go on.'

'Dumpty was . . . Ah, shit! I can't!'

I shot up to my feet again. So did Hansel. I reached over the table and grabbed him by the collar. He shrieked, and two huge security guards came rushing over from some back room. I took out my gun and aimed it at the two guards, then at Hansel, who screamed piercingly at the top of his lungs.

'Tell them to fuck off,' I said.

Hansel had his eyes scrunched shut. He was gripping my fist helplessly. 'F-fuck off, you two!' he hissed. 'I don't wanna goddamn die!'

The two big men moved, slowly making their way backward, all the way to the bar. I turned my attention back to the pathetic man in my hand. Then I swapped my handgun for some knuckle dusters.

Hansel whimpered, recoiling into his Hawaiian shirt again. 'I'll be good, I'll be good!'

I shoved him back into his seat and positioned myself so I was standing about an inch away from him, staring down. 'Tell me everything. *Everything*!'

'Just— Just ease it with the brass knuckles, goddammit, please!'

I shoved my armed hand into the pocket of my jacket and stepped back a little.

Hansel pressed his hands against his chest, breathing deeply, harshly. 'I'm gonna be sick.'

'Oh, fuck me. No wonder, all you eat is that shit!' I said, pointing to the wrappers on the floor.

'Alright, listen, listen. Dumpty was in some business, bad business. Some kind of deal, okay, but I don't know the specifics, I swear.'

'Who does?'

'If I were you, I guess I'd – hoo boy – I'd start with the agent, The Woodsman. . . .' He paused, evidently trying to control his breaths. He looked up at me, eyebrows quivering above his blacked-out shades. 'But you realize now you've started with all this, you've practically signed your death warrant, right? I mean, you're fucked! And so is everyone you know!'

'Hansel,' I growled, 'I know *you*, don't I? Keep talking. What's with the egg?'

'Something about an arms deal, a gang upstate. Uhhh, girls.'

'Girls?'

'Working girls, I think. I told you, I don't know the specifics. But I— Ah, shit.'

'What?'

'Last night. He was here.'

'Who was here?'

'Fucking Dick *Dumpty*!' he screamed. 'Before he died, I guess. He was right here, in the club, with a girl.'

'Good. Sounds like we're getting somewhere, doesn't it? So, who was the girl?'

Hansel was almost trembling now, his voice quivering like someone was shaking him like a rag doll. 'God, I need a fucking drink. Okay, the girl I'd never seen before, I can promise you that. But you know, I mean, you must know, Dumpty likes em, uhh, younger.'

'I find that hard to believe.'

Hansel barked a nervous laugh. 'Really?'

'No,' I said. 'And you know that because he'd bring them here? We talking, what, seventeen?'

'I don't know. . . .' He took a deep, shaky breath. 'Young.'

I shook my head. My blood was burning now, on fire. Too bad he was already dead – spilled, splattered and shattered on the curb. I would've loved to have gotten the chance to smash his shell in with a hammer. Therapeutic.

'Sometimes boys, all kinds of beings, y'know,' murmured Hansel. 'Different creatures. But all around . . . a certain age. That was his type. But last night, it was totally different. Something was wrong, I think.'

'Go on.'

'Well, he was in here with a woman, some biker chick-type by the look of her. Mid- to late twenties, probably. But she never came to the bar, so I never got a good look.' He smiled and chuckled under his breath, staring off into the distance like he was reminiscing about some early romance. 'Which is a shame, because I wanted to.'

I sighed, shuffled closer to him. 'Oh, spare me that shit; I want facts, objectivity.'

He flinched. 'Blonde hair— No, like, gold hair. Kinda luminescent. Wearing all black, as far as I could tell. She had a kind of arrogance about her. For a woman, in a place like this, y'know?'

'Not really.'

'Well, she did,' he went on, going back to staring into the other wall. 'Obviously, it wasn't no date.'

'Obviously?'

'He looked stressed – scared, maybe.'

'You mean the woman was holding him hostage?' I asked.

'Sure, something like that.'

'What happened to them?'

'They left.'

'Yes, *when*?' I growled.

Hansel yelped. 'About midnight, goddammit!'

Suddenly I sensed some kind of movement behind me. When I turned to face the bar, the two huge security guards had gone. I took out my gun. 'Hansel?' I spat, aiming it at his face.

He flinched. 'What? What?'

I nodded over to the bar.

Hansel snatched off his shades and peered into the light.

'You playing some kind of fucking trick?'

'It wasn't me, I swear,' he said in a low, vacant tone.

I believed him. Nevertheless, I took out my cuffs and chained his wrist to the table leg, then took back my money. I wasn't spending the last of what I had on this dipshit.

'Ey, what the fuck are you doing? This is bullshit. I'm gonna call the cops. You can't do that, you piece of shit!' he screamed, tugging at the cuffs relentlessly.

I walked away from him slowly, gun raised and pointed toward the bar. 'Police,' I said. 'Show yourself.' There was a muffled groaning noise by the bar, sounded like a faulty car engine trying to start up. Then it went quiet, just the sound of Hansel whimpering and tugging on his cuffs.

I took in a sharp breath and whirled around the corner of the bar. There were the two huge guys, crumpled on the floor. One of them was motionless, cold and completely still like a pile of rusty scrap in a yard. The other guy kicked his legs out a couple of times, feebly, sluggishly, then stopped and died. In the darkness of the room, the pool of blood looked black like a void in the ground. Each of the men had a blade nestled snugly in his back.

'Oh, *fuck*!' screamed Hansel from behind me.

I turned on my heel, gun pointed at him and a black figure beside him. 'Hey,' I called, my throat suddenly closing up a little.

'Drop the damn gun,' said a voice quickly, a woman's voice, indifferent and cool. I saw a shimmer of metal beside Hansel's head. The barrel of a rifle.

'I'm police. Drop yours now!' I yelled.

'Ah, hell, I know that,' she said, her voice flourishing with a southern twang.

I heard the gun cock. My eyes were watery. The darkness seemed deeper than before, and I couldn't tell if she had the barrel aimed at me or the whimpering idiot to her left. 'I won't tell you again, lady,' I said, my finger resting on the trigger.

'Fine,' she said. And before I could register what the hell was happening, she seemed to bust Hansel's face with the butt of her rifle while somehow simultaneously conjuring a pistol out of nowhere, which she fired into my chest three times.

I flailed back with each bullet, arms flapping, head spinning. There was a deafening crash that sounded like a million empty glass bottles pouring into a landfill, and my body flipped over the bar and clattered to the ground.

I lay there in shards of glass, my chest tight and burning. Before everything went away, I saw the bodyguards' corpses in a heap at my feet above the bloody void. Now, I guess, I would join them.

Pain left me. My eyes closed.

4

Goldilocks

'Don't be so dramatic, Slade,' said a voice.

I woke up spluttering, the sour taste of vomit at the back of my throat. My eyes were clenched shut as dry coughs burst out of me. I couldn't breathe, and every cough felt like another bullet piercing my chest.

The bullets. I struggled to lift my eyelids. Something hellishly bright was shining in my face. I patted my chest, trying to feel for blood or entry wounds. There was nothing.

Eventually I forced my eyes open, the sun hovering above me, mocking and all-powerful. I ripped open my shirt, buttons popping, slicing through the warm air. Three black bruises sat there, the shape of a triangle.

That woman, she'd shot me with blanks. Never intended to kill me.

I yelled and looked up, one eye clenched shut. Her silhouette was suddenly there above me. Or maybe it'd been there the whole time. I scurried back, kicking my legs, trying to lift myself, hands planted into the rough ground.

My eyes started to adjust. A horizon of skyscrapers in the distance, enveloping blue sky, and the woman looking down on me. Her hair was as gold as the ball of fire behind her head, tied back into a blooming, high ponytail, a few strays hanging over one of her eyebrows, straight and narrow, whose shade was the antithesis of her hair. She wore a white vest and dark leather jacket, the barrel of the rifle protruding proudly from her back. She had kind of a pretty face, but feral. Piercing and arrogant. Her eyes were huge, like a cat's, wide-set, her irises a deep, deep brown. She had a smaller mouth, her thin, reddish lips a unique, uneven shape amplified by her deriding smirk.

She kicked at my boot. 'Get up.'

I growled through clenched teeth, trying desperately to summon energy, the will to get the hell up. 'Where am I? And who the fuck do you think you are?' I drawled.

The blonde woman sighed, looked into the distance, still with that smirk on her face, like she knew something I didn't. Which I guess she did, in fairness. 'I'm almost offended, Jack. You really don't know who I am?'

'Should I? I burst into a series of coughs again, finally rising to my feet. 'God, I need a drink.'

'Jess Robicheaux,' she announced. 'Some know me as Goldilocks. People like you, I'm talkin about.'

'Oh,' I said. 'Well, *Goldilocks*, I'm gonna have to arrest you now.' I started walking toward her. Until I veered off to the side. I cleared my throat and readjusted my course. 'You do not have to say anything—'

'You're damn crazy!' she said with a smile, then roundhouse kicked my head so hard I thought I was about to catch it in my hands. I flew to the ground again, landing hard in a puff of dirt. My vision blurred and flashed. Goldilocks was walking toward me again.

'Wait, wait!' I heard myself yell, muffled and far away.

She yanked my collar and stared deep into me with her near-black eyes. She was so close to my face, I could taste the mint on her breath as she spoke. 'Don't you ever point a gun at me again,' she said, her voice low.

I motioned at the triangle of black bruises on my chest, about to protest, but there was no point. I was too tired. I wanted to just sleep.

Goldilocks peered down at the bruises, briefly smiled, then sucked in her lips. 'Sorry 'bout that, but you left me no choice.' She rose to her feet, sun shining through her hair, and held out a pale hand, fingers long and dainty but somehow also strong.

After hesitating, I clasped it and she pulled me up effortlessly. I patted down my jacket and pants. They were covered in dirt. It was in my hair, too, deep and dry.

Goldilocks placed her hands on her hips. Like her hands, the rest of her was slim and lean, but still strong-looking. 'Gonna establish one thing right off the bat, Jack. You ain't arresting me – hell, you don't *wanna* arrest me, alright? You'll understand eventually.'

I couldn't help but let out a singular bark of laughter. 'You sure about that? I don't understand shit right now! One second you're firing blanks into my chest, the next almost detaching my head from my body, then helping me back up! To what, knock me down again? Screw it, go on, just send me packing.'

'Don't make me,' she said.

I sighed. 'Where are we?' I asked again, exasperated. The ground was a light yellow, brown in some places. Patches of dead grass sprung up in random spots. Behind me was some old shed, long abandoned. I could just about make out the city in the distance.

Goldilocks looked around, still cool but now with a hint of edginess about her.

I tilted my head.

'Someplace a little safer,' she murmured, to herself more than me.

'Than where? Can you tell me what's going on? Where's Hansel?'

Her head flicked to me then, her already big eyes wide and alert. 'He won't be talkin.'

'You kill him?'

'No. No, I didn't kill him, not yet. Don't worry about it.'

I scoffed. 'Very bold of you to try and dictate my emotions, tell me how I should react to things. What the hell do you want with me? I'm tired, I need a drink, and I want to go home.'

It was her turn to scoff. 'You ain't goin home! I'm not done with you.'

'*Done* with me?'

'If I was, you'd know about it. What can you tell me about Chief Cole?'

My head jerked up. 'What? Where did that come from?'

'Answer the question.' There was venom in her voice.

I shrugged. 'Not a whole lot more than what's already out there. We really gonna have this conversation out in the middle of nowhere? I can hardly talk. I. Need. A. Drink.'

Goldilocks kicked at the ground vacantly, a small wave of dirt floating toward me, like she was adding constant insult to injury.

I turned around in a circle. 'What time is it? Where the hell did I sleep last night?' Out of nowhere, there were cuffs on my wrist. 'Oh, screw this.'

'I ain't done with you,' she said again, then threw a sack over my head.

For the next half hour, I fought against the mass of vomit gurgling in the pit of my stomach as we raced to some unknown destination. I was on the back of a motorcycle, holding onto Goldilocks's waist for dear life, feeling a weird mix of awkward, confused, and angry. And I was still so goddamn thirsty.

I tried to distract myself from the nausea by wondering what the hell kind of woman parades around a detective with a sack on his head, going eighty through one of the liveliest cities in the world. Naturally I couldn't do much critical thinking, and the memories of what went on made the nausea worse, so I just counted the seconds and minutes until we were wherever this girl was taking me.

As soon as the motorcycle engine stopped roaring and I was heaved off the thing, the vomit started bubbling up my body. 'Gonna barf,' I wheezed.

A hand clasped my neck and there was a tearing sound.

Goldilocks had been considerate enough to slash an opening for the sack so I could vomit all over the sidewalk with dignity. I retched until I had nothing more to offer out of this hole.

'You done?' I heard Goldilocks say, and she grabbed my shoulder, steering me into a doorway, then guiding me up a very loud staircase. The floorboards shrieked with every one of our steps. When we reached the top, Goldilocks turned my body and nudged me from behind so I staggered forward, then ripped off the sack on my head. She slammed the door behind me, then rammed a key into it and twisted.

'This is my shithole for the time being,' she announced. 'Wait there; I'm gonna check nobody's been screwin with my stuff.'

It was some sort of loft – not an actual loft apartment, but a makeshift deal. Shady, illegal-looking, but not an entirely bad vibe. The wooden floor was well-polished, the brick walls decorated with various landscape paintings, the room lit by dim fairy lights and exposed bulbs. A leather sofa rested against the wall on my left, and there was a coffee table scattered with books and some empty beer bottles. The room was warm and smelled like frankincense.

I started creeping toward one of the blind-covered windows. Goldilocks appeared in front of me, mouth twisting slightly. I raised chained hands and collapsed into the sofa with an over-the-top sigh, cuffs jingling in my lap. Resignation had crept into my system and planted itself firmly into my recently emptied gut now. So much for stepping up.

'Got a drink?' My words tumbled out of my mouth and clattered into the silence.

Goldilocks said nothing, just peered at me while making her way to the fridge. She came back with two bottles of beer, snapped off the caps, and slid a beer over to me methodically.

I raised my eyebrows. 'Thanks, but . . . are you really gonna make me try to drink in handcuffs?'

She grabbed my wrist hard, her other hand resting on her gun holster, and stuck the key inside the cuffs. I almost heard my wrists breathe a sigh of relief as the cuffs slipped off them and crashed to the floorboards.

'Don't worry,' I said. 'I'm not even thinking about making a run for it or fighting you.' I chugged the beer.

She smiled sourly. 'I ain't worried.'

I kept drinking, like it was a precious flask of water I'd stumbled across in a desert. For a guy that'd just been shot in the chest and kidnapped, I was feeling better already. 'Hey, you got anything harder?' I asked, the head of the beer trickling into my stubble.

'Yeah, there's one thing.' She reached into a top cupboard and brought out a circular bottle. I saw my own reflection in its black glass, spoon-faced and as weary as I felt.

'Hell's that?' There was no label on it.

Goldilocks smirked, looking at the bottle proudly. 'Jabberwock's Brew,' she announced, pouring the stuff into two whiskey glasses. It looked like oil. She handed a glass to me. 'Cheers.'

I peered over the rim of the glass like I was expecting something to leap out of it and eat my face. 'What is . . .' I whispered.

'Drink it, asshole!'

I was too tired to argue. I figured I'd just sip the mysterious, gross-looking, probably poisonous alcoholic potion drink from the feral biker chick I'd known for about forty minutes. 'Yeah, fuck it,' I said, and gulped the gloop before bursting into another fit of spluttering and wheezing. 'What the *hell*—' I slammed the glass back on the table.

'Get ahold of yourself,' I heard Goldilocks say.

If it wasn't poison, it tasted exactly how I've always thought of poison as tasting. Like burnt rubber and licorice. It had the burning sensation of whiskey multiplied by a hundred, the texture bumpy and murky. 'Why would you willingly—' I wheezed before getting possessed by chesty coughs again. I noticed Goldilocks only had a sip of hers left. 'Goddamn. *Jabberwock*?'

Goldilocks shrugged. 'I don't care for spirits; this stuff was given to me by an old friend.' She took her last sip and winced. 'Least the bottle's nearly out now.'

I looked her up and down with narrowed eyes. The past few days felt like I was having the longest, weirdest dream I'd had in a long time. 'Are you gonna tell me what you want now?' I said, my voice dry, the almost-poison sitting in the back of my throat.

Goldilocks huffed, dropped into the armchair, strips of leather peeling off it. Looked like she'd found it in some dingy building and dragged it into her apartment – just like she'd done with me, I guess. 'You looking into this Dumpty deal, missin girls? Well, I think you're just about the only one who is.'

I twisted my mouth. 'Feels that way. What's it to you?'

The corner of her eye twitched a little as she gazed at nothing in particular. 'It's kinda a lot to me, Slade. But I don't trust you, don't know you yet. So I ain't tellin you everything you think you need to hear.'

'Well, can you at least tell me how you know my name?'

She looked at me, eyebrows slanting. 'Because I've been watchin you for a little while, and because you're Jack of the Beanstalk, giant killer. That's how.'

I shuffled in my seat. What did she know, really? 'That was a long time ago,' I said, now gazing into the distance myself.

'Sure. But it's your legacy now. We've all got our history, our breakthroughs, our accomplishments that get the wheels spinnin. Start the chain reaction.'

I scoffed. 'I wouldn't call what happened an accomplishment. I seem to be short on those these days.'

She watched me suspiciously.

'Why've you been watching me?' I asked. 'I mean, it's not like I've been up to a whole lot. Actually, that's a little embarrassing, not to mention creepy. Is that how you spend your time – staring at beat cops drinking themselves to death, pumping dangerous magick through their systems for a brief kick, waking up in empty bars with their bladders bursting, damn near pissing themselves under the table, only to go home, jerk off, pass out, do nothing at work, then do it all over again the next night?'

Goldilocks smirked that smirk again, resting her chin on her pale palm, caressing her cheek with slender fingers. 'I can't argue with you. That's a pretty damn faithful retelling of your life these days, ain't it? But no, that's not what I'm interested in. You've gotten complacent, yeah; depressed, probably; suicidal, maybe; a little more like your colleagues in the force, morality-wise—'

I stiffened in my seat and suddenly realized how tense my jaw was.

'Whoa there, buddy,' said Goldilocks, hand instantly on her holster. 'Don't you freak out on me now. Touchy subject? You don't like to be compared to your peers, hm? Because you're better than em?'

I sighed. 'Just tell me what this is.'

'What have you found out so far, about Dumpty's death, about missin girls?'

'Why would I tell some outlaw wannabe who just abducted me about such a sensitive case? You're goddamn entitled.'

'I'm goddamn determined,' she said before licking her lips and sitting back in her chair a little, as if she didn't mean to say it, like she'd just revealed a bit too much of herself.

'Okay,' I said. 'To find all the women and children?'

'To finish what I started. It's personal.'

'Your past, your legacy?'

'You really don't know who I am?'

'Aw, does that hurt your feelings, make you feel small?'

'Ha. Fuck you.'

'Get your hand off that holster,' I said.

'Hell are you gonna do about it, Slade? Arrest me? *That* would sure as hell make you just like the rest of em, oh yeah, goin after the people tryna do some right.' She raised her hand off the holster then, red fingernails tapping the arm of the chair. 'I need to know if you've got the nerve. I get the impression you started this job with the right ideas, had a fire in your stomach, thought you could bring down the right people, dismantle the oppressive systems, systems you would only go on to serve. But maybe that other you is still inside somewhere. I ain't askin you to like me, or trust me, no. I just need you to let me do what I gotta do, while you keep lookin in the right places. Because our paths, they're gonna cross, again and again.'

'What does that mean?'

'We can help each other. If you keep goin, you're bound to get some answers to the questions I think we're both askin now. I know who's behind all this, or at least I know some of em, these evil bastards.'

I chewed on my tongue, the inside of my mouth dry and heavy, still that bitter taste. I tried to weigh up factors in my head, possibilities, options, but I could barely think. Felt like my body was failing me, magick that shouldn't be inside me, eating away. My eyes nearly welled up, a sinking feeling deep in my stomach because I knew that, as always, I would only drop more magick beans down my throat the moment the pain got to be too much, or the danger swelled around me to the point I'd need something more. And where I was going, there was going to be nothing but danger.

I blinked, pinching at my nose and shaking my head. I saw Goldilocks's dark eyes peering at me, trying to read my face. 'I have to go,' I said.

Goldilocks sat back, almost flinching, her ponytail swishing as she shook her head. 'What?'

I breathed in deeply, burying the emotions, the fear that had just crept up on me. Or maybe it'd been there for a while now, waiting beneath the surface like magma.

'You can't just *go*,' she said, her voice hard, slightly raspy.

'You know what? Give me your number,' I said. 'I need to think. I'll call you.' I shrugged. 'Or I won't.'

Slowly, Goldilocks rose from the chair, keeping her eyes on me, and opened a drawer by the window. She took out two small phones. Burners. 'Here,' she said, lobbing it at me. 'Use this.'

I shoved it in my pocket. 'Yeah.' As I got to my feet and headed for the door, Goldilocks stepped into my path. She was only a little shorter than me, our eyes almost level. 'Walk out that door and don't come back, or I don't hear from you, I won't hesitate to put you down when we see each other again. You're either workin with me, or you're just another body in my way.'

I sniffed, searching for words that wouldn't show up.

She backed off, unlocked the door, then opened it. 'If you try anything, like telling your buddies to knock down my door, I'll know before you even think about it. You have no idea what you're messin with, and I ain't just talkin about myself, *Detective*,' she spat. 'You be careful now.'

'Thanks for the beer,' I said before trotting down the creaky steps, stepping out into the cold, dark air, my eyes scanning everything in the vicinity before the door had even closed behind me.

I got a cab to my apartment. It was almost midnight again. The entire ride home I'd been staring out the window, trying to think, peering down every street, every alley, watching shadows. My heart rate had been going crazy all night, beads of cold sweat trickling down my forehead, neck, wrists. My life seemed to be going from zero to a hundred, and it felt like there was nothing I could do about it. There was a stinging sensation in my eyes and nose as I went into the apartment.

I heard nothing except my own breathing as I flicked on the light, gun in hand, and slowly prowled the flat, expecting shadows. I checked the kitchen area first, making sure everything was where it should be, which is difficult when you leave shit all over the place. Then I checked the main living area, opening drawers, cupboards, even peeling my rug off the floor, looking for any sign of disturbance.

After checking the bedroom and bathroom and finding nothing out of the ordinary, I went back into the main room and stood in front of the big window. Across the street was another apartment block, bigger, fancier. I saw the usual silhouettes in the windows, outlines of rooms lit in all different colors – reds, purples, greens, golds. I thought I'd find some sort of comfort reminding myself that ordinary life was nearby. But comfort never came. I snapped the blinds shut and went to bed. It took me four hours to sink into sleep.

At about nine in the morning, I woke up to the sound of my phone loudly groaning against the floorboards. I jumped, wondering if Goldilocks was already utilizing the burner and trying to pull me into something first thing in the morning. I realized it was just my normal phone, and that was worse. Because the contact name was 'CHIEF COLE'.

I sat there in the bed, hair hanging over my eyes, room spinning. I stared at the phone sliding along the floor, wanting it to just stop. It showed no signs of doing so, so I hurled the covers off me, picked up the phone and accepted the call. I stayed silent, heard Cole's labored breaths down the line.

Finally he spoke. 'Slade.'

I swallowed.

'Slade, is that you?' Then there was a harsh cracking noise. I quickly realized that was the sound of his grinding teeth.

'Yeah,' I said, my voice croaky. 'Yeah, it is.'

'This morning I had a visit. I have to inform you . . . that you are no longer suspended,' he growled.

My mouth opened and closed. My stomach sank, but I wasn't sure why. 'What, why? On whose authority?'

'That doesn't matter!' he snapped. 'I expect you at the station within half an hour.'

I closed my eyes. Surely some kind of trick, a trap. My blood was all over the crime scene, back at Emily Wyatt's flat. Cole would've been the first to know once the King's Men arrived. Why wouldn't he just come storm the building?

'Who the hell made this decision?' I said, my voice shaking. 'Hello?'

The line was dead. I growled and threw my phone onto the bed. Unsuspended. Who would do that? Who does it serve? I still couldn't think. Even if my brain was actually working, I still wouldn't have known where to start.

My phone hummed again, but it wasn't the one I'd just thrown. I went to the foot of my bed, reached into my jacket pocket, and took out the burner:

Make your choice, time's running out. G.

No. I wasn't making any kind of decision the way I felt. I got dressed and went into the kitchen and fed myself a bunch of scraps from the fridge. At least it was something. A sack of magick beans was perched next to the half loaf of bread. Without looking, I snatched them and stuffed them in my breast pocket, then took them out again and dropped one in my mouth.

By the time I was in my car, I felt alive again. There was no feeling of guilt, no fear, nothing like that. I was good again, and I was going back to the Sultan Hotel.

I still had my badge, and technically, I was a detective again.

I started the siren and slammed the lights down in the windshield, racing into Manhattan, traffic parting in front of me, horns blaring, people and creatures scurrying across the streets.

I arrived at the Sultan with the rain gliding down, the kind of fine, lighter rain that looks more like a heavy mist. As I crossed the street in the shadows of clouds and skyscrapers, yellow cabs slowed and honked. I held out my police badge, staring up at the broken window high above, then looked down at where Dumpty had crashed into pieces.

No police tape now, no sign anything went wrong unless you happened to look all the way up to the smashed window.

There was an unfriendly looking gnome presiding over a newspaper stand a little down the street, arms folded stiffly, black pipe hanging out of his mouth, dropping bits of ash into his yellow-white beard. He glared at me from beneath huge, gray eyebrows, taking shelter from the rain with an umbrella. The newspapers, though, were left out to be soaked. I could still make out the headlines, including one that almost held my attention for over a second, announcing yet another scandal involving dark magick, orgies, and members of the Charming dynasty.

But there wasn't a whisper about one Dick Dumpty and his great fall. Nothing. I flicked through a few pages, finding nothing except trashy gossip and interviews with aging D-list celebrities and fake love potion recipes.

'Dumpty,' I said to the gnome vacantly, waving one of the newspapers at him. The glare remained.

Not a peep from the press, then. Dumpty *owned* half of them.

I shook my head and went back up the street toward the Sultan, approaching the double doors, taking cover from the rain under the portico, its wine-red paint job peeling off. I was getting a damn neck ache from the amount of head swivelling I was doing. Even with the magick in my system, the paranoia kept creeping back just when I thought it was gone. Momentarily gone, at least.

I pushed open the glass doors and stepped into the vestibule, a pathetic, ugly lobby with an apathetic teenager standing dumbly behind the reception desk. I noticed his pointed elf ears under shaggy brown hair. I walked toward him, holding up my badge.

'Police,' I said, and the elf kid straightened, scratching his head. 'Were you here night before last?'

'Wh— No, sir, I wasn't. Did— Did something happen?'

'Well, apparently not,' I muttered. 'Which is the room with the broken window?'

'Oh, I don't know; I didn't know there *was* a broken window, sir!' He put on a forced smile that looked more like a grimace.

'Okay,' I said, 'guest book. Now.'

His eyes widened. He looked at a huge leather-bound book on

the shelf behind him, back to me, then back to the book again.

'Come on. Hand it over, kid.'

'I don't know if—'

I slammed my hands on the reception desk and vaulted over it, the kid yelling and leaping to the side. I heaved the book onto the surface and ripped through the pages. And there was Dumpty's name – room 1215, one night.

'Room twelve-fifteen,' I announced.

The elf kid was staring at me, wide-eyed, cowering back. He swallowed. 'Sir, it's not—'

'Key?' Still he stared. 'It's alright, kid; like I said, I'm police. Key.'

He let out a loud sigh, swung open a cabinet of room keys, and handed me the one for room 1215.

'That's better,' I said. I made for the elevator at the center of the lobby. Everything was painted in the wine-red from outside, with blotches of black from dampness and leaks. The carpet was covered in a horrific floral pattern that made me feel like I was tripping. It smelled like ashtrays and wet dirt.

''Scuse me, Detective?' said the kid, timid. 'What exactly is going on?'

I raised my eyebrows and gave a vague shrug. 'Hell if I know.' I hit the elevator button and stepped inside, forced to face my petrifying reflection for the journey upward. If the magick beans were making me feel alive on the inside, they certainly weren't working externally.

Red blotches were plastered across my face, black eye bags drooped, stubble overgrown and uneven, straw-like hair now matted and greasy.

I stared at myself, mouth hanging open. *He* stared back, judging me mercilessly. My chest was tight, burning. I thought about how much worse I'd feel without the magick right now. I thought about how bad I'd be in a few weeks, days, when I take one bean too many. Then I shut down that thought, unholstered my gun, and stepped out of the elevator.

Room 1215 of the Sultan Hotel was waiting for me at the end of a long, wide corridor with dark brown doors on either side. Its door was larger than the others, and farther away from most of the other rooms. The only sounds were the honking of muffled vehicles and a newscaster's voice booming from one of the rooms behind me. The door of room 302 looked like any other hotel suite door. I knocked to no response. Before sticking in the key, I took out my gun, resting it against my thigh. I turned the key, but it jammed. I tried twice more, turning even harder. They'd already changed the lock. The urgent cover-up was well underway. I shook my head and laughed like an idiot.

Then there was a small creaking sound behind me. I stopped laughing and spun. Sunlight peered around the curtain to my left and shone into my eyes. It looked like no one was creeping up on me at all until I shimmied along the wall, holding up my left arm to shield my eyes from the light. Then I saw a little mouse poking its head around the tiniest door in the biggest hotel in New York. He was gripping a cane the size of a matchstick in his claws.

'Oh,' I said. 'Hey there.'

The mouse was wearing a pair of circular glasses, blacked out completely. He readjusted them and prodded at the floor with his cane, stepping out into the hallway. 'Ah,' he said. 'I don't suppose you, too, are here to stir up a racket, hm? Two hours sleep is simply abysmal.' He spoke in a quiet tone, as you'd expect, and had a mid-Atlantic accent.

I crouched down to his level, wondering if he'd find that patronizing, but then realized he couldn't see me, so it didn't matter. 'Racket, huh? I bet.' I put on my professional voice. 'I'm a police detective. I'm following up on the events of last night. Would you mind answering a few questions for me, sir?'

The mouse's nose twitched, then he stepped farther into the hallway, closing the miniscule door behind him. 'I was wondering when you would start asking questions, yes. I heard you all here fussing around in the early hours of the morning. See, I even dressed myself after being woken in case one of you came knocking on my door.'

'I see. Apologies for that, sir; it was a pretty damning situation that called for urgency.'

'What happened?'

'Well, that's what I'm here to find out. Let's start at the beginning. When did you first start to hear this racket, as you called it?'

The mouse tapped his claws on the side of his patterned red bathrobe. 'As I recall, the sound that initially woke me came quite a bit earlier than when the police arrived. It definitely seemed to be coming from the same room, though.'

'The same room the police were in? This one, the one across from here?'

'Yes, yes.'

'Okay, good. And what exactly did it sound like?' I asked.

'Well, first there was a very loud crashing sound. It sounded very much like someone was kicking at a door. I could be wrong, however – when I heard that, I was still in a dream. You know how the mind can play tricks on you,' he said, gesturing with a paw.

'I do, yes. Okay, this is helpful. What did you hear after that, when you'd woken up?'

'When I was fully awake and startled, I skittered to the door so I could perhaps listen in. I heard a man's voice, low and monotone, and also somewhat . . . patronizing, I would say.'

'Did you get to hear anything that was said? A threat maybe, or a question?'

'I'm afraid not. It was all rather muffled, and it happened so fast.'

'That's fine. How many voices were there?'

'Just the one, as far as I could tell. There were quite a few footsteps to be heard, though. They were coming from the other rooms – probably people panicking,' he deduced.

'Probably. How many different footsteps did you hear in the room opposite?'

His ears flicked. He scratched at them rapidly. 'Well, it was, of course, hard to pinpoint, but it sounded like just the one person. See, it was at this moment that I heard the sound of someone running, maybe six or seven footsteps in quick succession, and then the sound of smashing glass.' He let out a regretful sigh. 'It was as if someone leapt out of the window, Detective. Is that what has happened?'

I grunted and looked to the side. 'We don't know. Listen, uh, what's your name again?'

'Ridley, sir.'

'Mr Ridley, if anyone comes asking around about any of this, don't tell them you've spoken to the police. In fact, I think you should move out of here as soon as you can. It's too dangerous. Here, thanks for your help today.' I passed him a twenty, which was only a few inches shorter than him.

'Oh, how kind. I will promptly pack my things this afternoon, I've had quite enough of this city, anyway.' He rolled up the bill into a tube and tucked it under his arm.

I rose to my feet. 'That makes two of us,' I said. Yet I'm still here. 'Thanks again,' I said. The mouse bowed his head and I turned back down the hallway. Then I stopped. I couldn't leave the place without at least getting a look at Dumpty's room. It's not like I had restrictions anymore. It's not like I needed a warrant. I'd just turned a gun on my own chief. Nothing really mattered anymore.

I walked back to the door of room 1215. The mouse's door opposite was now closed. 'Mr Ridley, don't be alarmed. Police business. Just stay in your room,' I called. I took a step back, then thrust a boot into the door. It only sent a pain shooting through my leg. I tried again, this time barging into it with my shoulder. The door burst open, and I was in room 1215.

'What the fuck,' I whispered. I closed my eyes, then opened them again. The room was empty. Empty as in entirely bare. I was just standing in a concrete cube. No furniture, no carpet, and not even a window someone could fly out of. 'What the hell is this?' I said out loud. I felt the concrete wall; it just felt like a concrete wall.

I knocked on it, looking for some sort of hollow area. Nothing. I closed the door, opened it again. Nothing changed.

I stormed out of the room and shut the door. I headed back down toward the lobby. 'Hey,' I said to the receptionist, 'come here. I need to show you something.'

'What? What is it?' he said, dumbfounded.

'Just come with me, now.'

He wandered over hesitantly, and we took the elevator to floor twelve.

I quickly walked along the hallway back to room 1215 with the kid trailing, dragging his shoes across the carpet.

'Sir, could I just ask—'

'Shh,' I said. 'Come here, look at this. Do you have any idea what's going on here? Is this normal?'

He walked over, scratching his head. 'It's, uh, it's a broken door, sir. Did you do that?'

'What? No, not that, the goddamn room, look!' I pushed the door open wider.

He held his arms out by his side, mouth hanging open. 'It's just a normal room. What am I looking at?' he said, almost whining.

'I . . . Alright. What do you see?'

It was against protocol to use magick at the scene of a crime, but it seemed like that was exactly what'd happened here.

'Sir, are you okay? Should I get someone?'

'What? No, shut up. Listen. What do you see?'

'I just see a hotel room. I don't know!'

'Nothing weird about it?' I asked. 'Nothing broken, except the door? Everything seems normal?'

'Well, yeah. The room seems normal. You, sir, on the other hand . . .'

'Alright, never mind. Y'know what? Forget it, it doesn't matter. Look,' I sifted through my wallet, took out twenty-four dollars and eighty cents, 'here, take this. If any other police come snooping around, don't say I was here? Got it?'

He reached for the money. 'Uh, yeah.'

'Got it?' I said, louder this time.

'Right. I got it. I won't say anything. I don't want to be involved in this anyway, whatever it is. Thanks. You have a good day.' He took the money and trudged back down the corridor, counting the cash, then shoving it into his pocket.

I stood there, resting my hands on my hips, staring into the concrete abyss and wondering if I truly had the energy for this. Deciding I probably shouldn't be staying in any one place for too long – especially a concealed crime scene – I headed back outside and got into my car.

Now I was really feeling out of my depth. Dejected. I sat there with the engine off, the rain getting harder now, tapping, then crashing, against the windshield, like it was alive and angry, desperate to break in and reach me.

I gave a shudder and found myself reaching for the burner phone.

I called Goldilocks.

She picked up within two seconds. 'Detective,' she said, her voice cold down the line.

'Shit's getting weird.'

'Oh yeah, I'll bet.'

'Don't know what the fuck to do,' I said. 'What am I doing?'

Now, why would I ask her that? *This* is what it was coming to?

There was a quiet sigh on the other end, barely audible under the rain pellets shooting into the windows. 'Sounds like you're gettin closer to makin the right choice, that's what.'

My turn to sigh. I looked out the window. People rushed around like aimless ants, cars swerved around corners, a couple of my colleagues flew by in cruisers, pursuing anything but what was real, what was eating this city alive. I shook my head, biting down hard on my lip.

'You're runnin out of time,' said Goldilocks.

'Meaning?'

'How much longer can you live with yourself like this?'

I gripped the phone hard. 'What the hell do you know? I don't have to hear this shit from you. Who the hell even are you?' I breathed in, tried to gather myself. Everything was so damn loud, suffocating.

'What I'm meanin is, you could be doin a hell of a lot more. And we might be able to help each other. You *need* my help; no one else is gonna fix this.'

'Fix what?'

She stayed silent. Then, 'Get to Domino Park for five. If you ain't there, next time you see me will be the last because I'll be puttin a bullet through your tiny brain.' She hung up.

5

ODETTE

I didn't need another target on my back, especially not from a crazed outlaw. I didn't need any more enemies, and I was too damn tired for more showdowns. I decided I'd hear Goldilocks out. Because what else exactly *could* I do?

I perched on a bench overlooking the East River with my chin in my hands, waiting. My watch said it was 4:56. The sun was going down, its distorted reflection shifting in the water.

This part of the waterfront was completely submerged by the shadow of the Williamsburg Bridge towering above me. Drunks stumbled by, murmuring unintelligible things at me that didn't even warrant eye contact. I waited, ignoring them completely, and they just went away. Small mercies.

A young woman with a sweeping afro was practicing magick by the metal fence next to the water, trying to cast some kind of elemental spell on the river. I watched, half-interested, as the water twisted and speared up like a fountain. She kept sighing and clicking her teeth, not getting whatever result she was after. She appeared to have been here a lot longer than me.

It wouldn't be long before some cop with nothing better to do would come along and yell at her, or maybe even tackle her into the water.

'Hey,' I called. 'You know you can't be doing that out here, right?'

She looked over her shoulder at me, gave a sour look. 'Why don't you mind your business?'

'Trust me, lady, I work with guys who are nothing short of scum, and they'd take great pleasure in disciplining you for what you're doing. Harmless as it is.' I pulled out my badge and showed it to her. Her face went a little grave. 'I'm sorry,' I said.

She looked into the sunset, chewing at her lip, then waved a hand toward the river, and the dancing water collapsed back into its natural state.

'Try it out where no one can see.'

She nodded vacantly, then coasted away. I watched her as she went, then my eyes caught someone in the distance looking right at me. My heart jumped and I got to my feet. At this point, in my mind, anyone looking at me for too long was pretty much out to get me.

The figure got nearer, and the magick in my system identified it. It was Goldilocks. She cut a striking figure as she stepped into the subdued light of sundown, lean and sharp-looking, like she could slip into the shadows at any given second, which I didn't doubt she could.

The half-smirk was there again. She sauntered toward me, slowing the nearer she got. She wore a dark jacket over a black T-shirt, with dark crop cargo pants and trainers. Her hair was down now, flowing emphatically, kept out of her face with a black plastic headband, shining in the setting sun.

I rested on the fence, looking from the shifting water to Goldilocks as she stepped up to me. She stopped about a meter away, resting an elbow on the fence herself. She looked into the water, rubbing at a dark red fingernail vacantly. 'Made the right choice,' she said, still staring into the river.

I scoffed. 'It's a little early to say, I think. Why did you want to meet?'

She started eyeing the surroundings and random passersby with her big dark eyes, ready, I guessed, to attack some secret accomplice I didn't actually have who might've been hiding in the bushes. She looked down again, and I think I spotted a hint of . . . trepidation behind the eyes. I blinked and – if it was ever there – it was replaced with the familiar arrogance. 'Dick Dumpty—'

My ears pricked and I felt my head tilt.

'—is dead for good reason,' she continued. 'That guy was a monster, and every story you might've heard about him is true, and so are the ones you haven't heard, and probably never will. Pray you don't, anyway.' Her lip twitched. 'But he was just one creature, and there are thousands more like him in this damn city.'

She trailed off as a man walked by, uncomfortably close to us.

She cleared her throat and went on. 'If you or anybody else managed to get a lead on Dumpty while he was still alive, you'd have vanished just like that. Hell, it's probably gonna happen, anyway, while he's dead. These guys, they work from the grave. Now, the thing is, it was always gonna be you, wasn't it, Slade? There *ain't* nobody else, not in the New York Police Department.'

I shuffled a little, tapping on the rail. 'Well, who's kidding who,' I said. 'What I've started doing isn't out of some sense of integrity, or bravery, or – I don't know – passion. I think, more than anything, it's simply because I hate my boss. And right now, my only other options are drinking myself to death or just . . . ending.' For some reason I found myself smiling, then shaking my head at what I'd just said. Not that it wasn't a fact.

'Alright. Fine. I don't know you well enough to comment on that, but it ain't particularly important, anyway. What matters is that you've started it now. You see that, and I'm sure you know what it means. It means there ain't no turnin back. Never. You're gonna spend the rest of your life lookin over your shoulder, and fearin for the life of everyone you give a damn about.'

I chuckled. 'Lucky for me, I don't care about anyone. There's no one left. If I have to live my life just worrying about myself, well, that suits me just fine. Perfect.'

'What, really? No family? Friends? A girl?'

I straightened my back and wagged a finger. 'Hey, I see what you're doing. Don't try getting to know me. It's enough you've been watching me for however long; I don't need you to be my therapist.'

'If you don't want to die, you're gonna have to let me know you on some level, sooner or later. Trust me, I ain't here to make friends. I haven't been watchin you so I could track you down and invite you to a . . . barbeque, or whatever normal people do.'

I rolled my eyes and breathed in hard, patting the rails.

'But I'll go first,' Goldilocks said, brushing a wave of hair back behind her ear. 'I'll let you know something nobody on this earth or otherwise knows about me.'

'And what's that?' The sun was descending fast now, its reflection disappearing from the river, orange rays vanishing into gray on the ground. The streetlamps flicked on.

Goldilocks chewed her lip, eyes peering over my shoulder, then looking right into mine. She twisted her mouth and said, 'I don't think you'd be stupid enough to try and arrest me if I told you that I happily murdered Dumpty in cold blood, would you? Not only stupid, counterproductive.'

I frowned, thinking back to that night, Dick Dumpty's body smashed into pieces on the ground, the audience watching on, the woman screaming, alerting me to the scene. I thought about Hansel's description of a pretty blonde woman with Dumpty in the club.

Goldilocks leaned over the rail, folding her arms, staring cooly at the setting sun, clearly satisfied I wasn't going to arrest her. 'Motherfucker had it coming,' she murmured as my brain worked. 'Somebody should have done that a long time ago – before he got to ruin more and more lives.' She shot a hard glance at me. 'Your fuckin department shoulda got him.'

'So . . . So, why now? Why kill him that night? And why didn't you just come and find me?'

'I did come and find you, didn't I.'

'I mean without leading me to the scene on my own, and shooting me in the chest. Both of those were pretty avoidable.'

'Ah, you still ain't over that,' she said with a smirk, though a little smaller than usual. 'But listen, you really expect me to just approach an officer like some normal person? You may not know who I am, but I'm sure some of your peers do, incompetent as they are. And I don't trust you, not yet. I came to you because I got a feelin, but I don't *know* you.'

I felt my mouth twisting, my head shaking slightly.

'I'm bein hunted,' said Goldilocks, slowly turning to face me. 'If you ain't gonna try and arrest me for Dumpty, then I guess I can tell you the rest. Or some of it. Bad, bad people are after me, not just the law. I was in a gang, back in the south. Some people might call what happened to me groomin, but I won't. I knew what I was doin, almost all the time.'

'How old were you?' I asked.

Goldilocks turned her attention back to the golden ripples in the river. 'Fifteen.'

I narrowed my eyes.

'Papa Bear, they call him. Now, him, I'm sure you've heard of.'

'Him, yeah. Arminus something. Giant grizzly with connections to all kinds of gangs and politicians across the country. Gunrunner, right?'

She nodded. 'And you're about to become a lot more familiar with old Arminus. Because he's come to New York. Him and his gang.'

I breathed in sharply through my nose. 'Terrific,' I mumbled.

'I betrayed the bear, stole a whole lot of valuable assets from him, took off.'

'Why?'

She shot me a look as if the answer was obvious. 'Because I was done with him.'

I sighed. 'Well, if that's how you treat your accomplices, you're not exactly doing a great job of convincing me to join up with you.'

Goldilocks slid a pale hand across the rail and turned toward me.

There was a cold look in her eyes. Obviously, she had no time for my sarcasm right now. Her voice went dark, deeper. 'I said I don't know you, and I don't. But you ain't even on the same plane of existence as that thing. I don't know many who are, but I still know enough, and that keeps me up at night, makes me do what I do.'

I thought for a minute, feeling a little intimidated but undeniably intrigued. I pulled out a smoke, lit it, and took a few drags. I offered one to Goldilocks, who shook her head then stared.

'I'm convinced Papa Bear has a role in this,' she said. 'A big one.'

'In what?'

'Missin women and girls.'

'Huh,' I said, head pounding. 'Can't say I know a lot about the guy, but he's never come up in that context before. Not that I can remember, anyway.'

Goldilocks glared, her lips parting.

I held up my hands. 'But, before you say it, yes, why would he? He's a criminal mastermind who knows how to cover his tracks, etcetera.'

She relaxed, eyes slowly scanning the water. 'Before I left, things were startin to get real bad in the gang. Intense. Like, a whole other level of operations I didn't sign up for. Shit that went too far. The more I was recognized as a leader in the group, the closer I got to the bear. And the closer I got, the more I realized his ambitions. He had deals with the worst kinds of people, *big* kinds of people in big cities, mainly here.

'One night in his mansion, I snuck through hallways and doors I wasn't supposed to because I had to know what shit he was pullin.' She swallowed, a hint of vulnerability flashing in her eyes. 'His right-hand man, insane son of a bitch called Bluebeard, was in one of the rooms below the mansion, yellin and screamin. I heard other screams. Kids.

'I made a fuckin mistake. One I have to fix now. My revolver was loaded and ready, it was in my hand, and I was fixin to kick the door down and shoot Bluebeard in the brains, rescue the girls. But doubt pulled me back. I started thinkin about how it was a death wish, even for me, because I wouldn't have made it outta the mansion without bein caught, then killed. The bear practically has an army.'

I shook my head. 'Sounds like there was nothing you could have done right then.'

'I thought that at the time, not so much now.'

There was a nauseous sensation sitting in the pit of my stomach. 'Dare I ask what they were doing with the kids?'

She shook her head. 'I can't say for sure.'

I sniffed, stared at the ground vacantly.

'But what I can say is this: Dick Dumpty was there that night.'

I looked up. 'Dumpty?'

'Yeah. *Pretty* sure I didn't mistake someone else for him. How many eggs do you know? When I was raiding all the shit to take before I fled, I heard voices. Arminus and someone else. They came into the room I was in, and I was just about able to get myself in the shadows. It was him, Dumpty. They seemed panicked. Dumpty was freakin out, talkin about the walls closin in, things not bein how they should be. Papa Bear asked about a girl, and a king.'

'A *king*?'

Goldilocks shrugged. 'That's what I heard. It's what he said. But I'd already outstayed my welcome, and eventually Dumpty alerted the bear to me. I pulled out a knife as Arminus crushed his huge arm against me, his paw over my mouth. I stabbed him as many times as I could. I don't know what he's made of, but all it did was make him loosen his grasp. Only just. I slipped under his arm and got out. The door wasn't far. If it had been, I'd be dead.'

I said nothing for a while, thinking things through. Goldilocks's jaw had gone stiff, and I could almost hear the anger steaming inside her.

'I kicked Dumpty out the fuckin window.'

'You *kicked*—'

'Yeah. I didn't go there to kill him. I went to get answers. Work on helpin those women and girls. But I completely lost control.

Somethin took over. Seconds before I did it, I thought it'd feel good. It'd feel *right*, like I'd shifted the entire world in favor of the innocent. Or at least in favor of the good. But . . . there was nothin inside me after. I thought that meant I wouldn't want to do it again.' She looked at me. 'But I do. And I will. I'm gonna kill Papa Bear.'

After the sun had gone down, with the streets' roaming characters becoming shadier by the minute, Goldilocks led me to some dingy bar where she told me more of what I thought I wanted to know. She told me about the heists and gang wars back south; getting caught up in all kinds of predicaments involving dark magick and rare and brutal creatures I'd never heard of; and how she became one of the most feared and accurate shots at such a young age.

It was impressive stuff, sure, but it hardly made me feel any more relaxed around her, or like she could be trusted. In a way, the more I heard, the more I felt like walking away and burying my head in the mud.

But the pull is too strong. It's no longer an option. I can't explain it, but it's like some kind of force has me by the arm and is dragging me toward the danger, and I can't shake it off.

When Goldilocks went to piss, I found myself taking another magick bean. The booze wasn't hitting me at all, and I had to conceal my shaking hands between my legs as she told me more about her past.

I slept for about three hours that night, back at my apartment. Swallowing a bean so late was on me, but I knew I wouldn't sleep, anyway. Every time I closed my eyes, I saw the empty room in the Sultan, like some cursed concrete void that would never host any sort of life again. Every time I saw it in my mind, chills ran up my limbs. I remember imagining that's probably what it's like to be caressed by the abominable snowman.

I woke up in the morning with my eyes wet and mouth paper-dry. I thought of Cole's phone call. Unsuspended. I don't know whose decision it was, but it damn well wasn't the chief's. And I'm pretty certain whoever did make the decision wasn't looking out for me. No one's looking out for me.

Along with the empty room, the word 'Odette' circled around my mind all night. If I was no longer suspended, well, that meant I had access to police records. So after one more bean, a splash of water on my face, and more scraps of bad food in my stomach, I headed to the station, part of me anticipating some kind of ambush as soon as I stepped through the doors.

There was no ambush, but there were cold, hard stares from every direction. I saw the receptionist pick up her phone. She glared at me until I was out of sight. I stopped, and honed into the sound of her voice, courtesy of the magick bean.

Just as I thought – she was informing Chief Cole of my presence.

I cracked my knuckles and moved. When I got to my desk and switched on the desktop, I picked up on some distant rumbling. Unmistakable. It was Cole's footsteps, high above me, getting louder each second. A pencil on my desk sprung and hopped with every step. There was a long silence, then the sliding of elevator doors.

I peered out the opaque window screen and saw a huge dark shadow cover the carpet, and again with the footsteps, much louder now, uncomfortably loud.

Chief Cole gripped the doorknob and emerged in the doorway he could barely fit through.

'Chief,' I said vacantly.

'Jackson, my boy,' he snarled. Then he smiled, which made invisible snakes slither up my back and hug my neck.

'It's good to be back,' I said, squinting.

'Oh yes, yes, of course,' he said, almost in a whisper. 'Though you've not been assigned a case, as far as I'm aware, so what could it be that you're working on over there? Didn't you think it would be polite – *becoming* of you, perhaps – to pay a visit to me upon your return?'

I cleared my throat and frowned. The air closed in around me, forcing its way into my chest. Cole's body odor shot into my nostrils, amplified by the magick bean. 'Sir, I guess I just wanted to just get on with things. Y'know? I learned my lesson; now I'm here to work.'

Cole barked a laugh that attacked my eardrums. 'That right? Give it a rest, boy. Just because you are no longer suspended doesn't mean you can do as you please. You report to *me*, you take orders from *me*, as I'm sure you are more than aware.'

'And who do you take orders from?' I asked.

Cole's face shrank into a dull glare, then his mouth crept up at the corners.

'Only right I should know who made the call, isn't it?'

He breathed in through gritted teeth, making a horrible hissing noise. He paused for a moment, stuck in this creepy freeze-frame, then narrowed his eyes. 'It was the governor.'

I swallowed. I wasn't expecting an actual answer; the adrenaline from the bean was just making me dangerously cocky. 'Governor Charming?'

'The very same,' he boomed. 'Make of that what you will, boy. It doesn't matter, though. All of this, it all leads to one place. Remember that.' And then he left.

I sat there in my desk chair, leaning forward, mouth slightly open, wondering if he was offering yet another threatening but meaningless platitude, or actually telling me something in his usual asshole way.

Governor Charming. Him I knew very little about. As far as I could tell, just a member of yet another political dynasty playing with our lives in the shadows. The hell would he want from me? Like I said, whatever he wants, it wouldn't be for my own good.

I closed my eyes and tried to get control of my breathing, slow my racing heart. Suddenly I felt like a pawn in some nightmarish scheme. I had the urge to disappear, hopefully forever.

Goldilocks was right. I shouldn't be here.

I looked over my shoulder, glancing around the room. No one else was in here, but eyes were everywhere at the same time. That said, Cole hadn't even stuck around to see what I was up to here, hadn't tried to stop me. Had he been told to keep his distance by the same forces that brought me back into the force? I clawed at my cheeks, turned back round and logged into my account. I went into the database and typed in the word 'Odette.'

A list of results came up, all cases involving someone described as simply Odette, some kind of nightclub manager. I glanced through the charges – bribery and corruption, unlawful use of magick, money laundering, prostitution, human and creature trafficking. I pulled out my phone, snapping photos of each page as quickly as I could.

I got everything on my phone, then ripped open the computer and broke the hard drive. Can't say I was hopeful the powers that be hadn't already been alerted to my search, but I had to try something. I was becoming all too aware just how deep in this shit I was.

I scurried out of the office with my head down and left the block. I refused to make eye contact with anyone around me, bursting into the lobby and past the reception area. Voices and sounds all around were drowning me, pressing against my senses. Maybe within this commotion someone was calling my name, chasing after me. I never looked over my shoulder to find out.

The glass doors leading outside were a few yards away. I shoved past some gawking cop, almost tripping over, and spilled through the doors into the parking lot.

Only when I was on my own did I realize I hadn't taken a breath since getting out of the office.

I was shaking again, violently. Even the magick beans couldn't suppress it, or maybe at this point, they alone were causing it. Either way, I wasn't good.

I tried to take comfort in the fact I was never going inside that station again, but all I felt was dread. 'Shut up, shut up, shut the fuck up,' I hissed to no one, not even myself. It was just some sort of release, but a release of absolutely nothing. Something was eating away at me mercilessly. '*Goddamn.*'

I thought about taking a cab but couldn't even bring myself to use my phone. Instead, I just walked into the streets, doing my best to blend into the crowds.

About an hour later, I ended up in some coffee shop in Lower Manhattan. I needed to be somewhere unfamiliar, somewhere that made me feel a little more free. I took a glass of ice water to the corner of the place, where I sat in a brown leather sofa. Ivy leaves hung across the brick walls. Electronic jazz was playing out of the speaker above me.

I sunk into myself and looked at the photos I'd taken back at the station, glancing up every ten seconds to make sure no one was near me.

Nothing had come of these charges – they were all from the last five years, and all dropped. There were a lot of them, but they all came to nothing. Like a couple of cops had accidentally stumbled on a situation they'd have done better to avoid, upset the wrong people in the wrong places. I recognized some of the places this Odette owned, places that attract all the Dumptys of the city. But there was one establishment that really stuck out.

The Jolly Roger.

I shook my head and chuckled under my breath. Hansel, the slimy little bastard, knows exactly who Odette is, because it's his damn boss.

Odette's office was listed as being located in one 'The Seven Ravens', not far from here. The sun would be going down soon, and the city's night routine would begin. Ravens was where I was headed next. The pull that seemed to be determining my every move now was in full flux.

I overpowered the man on the door with ease.

This was a place for exclusivity, elites. There was no point in me even trying to talk my way in. With the magick bean's power pulsing through my body, I twisted the huge man's huge arm behind his back and flattened him on the concrete, then dragged his unconscious body into the alley beside the club. Even the alleyway looked high-end. No garbage, rats, or ghouls in sight.

I stepped inside the lobby and parted the strips of purple that separated the entrance from the club, instantly hit by a smoky, electric aroma. Lights flashed, people and creatures danced and mingled, some weirdly hypnotic electronic music filled the room. It was a huge space, mostly dark but dimly lit with neon colors in certain areas. Holograms and living things alike danced on elevated platforms.

A red-haired nymph ran her fingers through her hair, twirling and sliding around in time with the music. She stared across the room, right at me, beckoning me over. I frowned and started to walk in a different direction, pushing past suits and flesh.

I was going right for the bar. This was just about the worst environment possible to be in while high on magick that doesn't even belong in your system. I felt blinded, deafened, and submerged in a brooding sexual chaos. It was all unnatural and wrong.

The barmaid smiled, poured me a double of some kind of spirit. I'd pointed to a random bottle on the glass display behind her. I prayed it wasn't 'Jabberwock's Brew' or whatever the hell that poison was called.

I downed the drink and ordered another double before my brain could even register the flavor. Fighting fire with fire.

When I turned around to get another look at the place, a woman appeared right in front of me, smiling strangely.

'Hello?' I said.

She wore a long, black leather trench coat that reflected all the colors of the flashing strobes. She had a sharp jawline, nearly concealed by a fur lapel that splayed out to the sides. Her hair appeared to be dark brown, flowing from underneath a weird pillbox-type hat that matched her coat. On it was a silver brooch in the shape of a swan spreading its huge wings.

'Detective Slade?' she said politely, barely audible under the thumping music, her smile still plastered on. She held out a gloved hand, again with the shiny material covered in flashing lights, as if her whole outfit was part of the illumination setup. 'I'm—'

'Odette,' I said, shaking her hand tentatively.

She was short, with a small frame, but had one hell of a grip. She yanked me closer, shaking my hand almost violently. 'Why don't we go upstairs?' Still with the smile.

'Pleasure.'

She maintained her intense eye contact a few seconds longer, then let go of my hand. 'This way, Detective.'

Everything seemed to automatically part for her as she glided through the crowds, even the amenities. I followed her to a door framed by pink neon lights. She pushed it open, held it open for me, and drifted up some steel steps.

I tried to grab my senses by the throat, beat the shit out of them until I had control again. I wanted to focus all my attention on this small space, this strange woman, anything up here that might have been a threat.

The walls were painted black, exposed light bulbs illuminating the metal stairs. I watched Odette carefully as she climbed them in tall, black heels. I can usually get a pretty reliable idea of a person within seconds of meeting them, especially if they're involved in a case, but I was drawing a blank here. She was odd, absolutely, but that was all I could define about her character.

'If you wanted an appointment with me, Detective Slade, you

need only have contacted us.' She paused at the top of the stairs, turned around, and tilted her head. 'Paralyzing the doorman was a little unnecessary!' she said, almost giggling.

I frowned as she went through another door. 'Huh.'

I followed her into the room, a well-decorated space with a desk in front of a one-way window overlooking the club. The dark walls were all covered in tiny white lights that faded and shone again irregularly, like failing stars. A huge rug covered most of the carpet – more swan imagery, though this time its vibe was a little more occult-like.

'What's with the swans?' I asked as Odette took a seat behind the desk.

She smiled, but this time it wasn't unnerving. It was almost sad. 'Take a seat,' she said. Now that we weren't being drowned out by the music on the dance floor, her voice took on a soft tone, with an accent I couldn't place.

I did as she said, slowly, staring cautiously. She stared right back at me, one eyebrow slightly raised, lips turned up in the corners. She was early thirties, maybe – same as me – and had a fine nose, hazel-green eyes peering out from intense dark eye shadow, and winged eyeliner covered in silver glitter. Not same as me. Her skin was tan, a few freckles dotted about her narrow cheeks.

It was an unorthodox getup, more like that of some avant-garde model than a club manager. But interesting to look at.

'So, what have you come here to speak to me about, Detective? I'm simply presuming, of course, that it *is* me you wish to speak to.'

'I have a few questions,' I said.

'Oh. More questions about swans, perhaps? Or any other aspect of the furniture that might be troubling you? Or maybe a number of questions concerning my makeup, or my outfit, as you've been gawking at those since laying those baby blues upon me.' She smiled shyly, and placed a polished fingernail to her temple. Then she dropped the smile and just stared again.

I swallowed and repositioned myself in the chair. 'Uhh, no. No.

Be serious. I've come to you over a sensitive subject. Concerning the steep rise in abductions recently, or *presumed* abductions, I guess.'

She said nothing.

I took out my phone and opened the folder of photos I'd taken back at the station, keeping them out of her sight.

'If that's a phone you've got down there, I'm afraid I'm going to have to ask you to hand it over. Things like that aren't permitted in here. Strictly.' She held out her gloved hand.

'Yeah, that's not gonna happen,' I said.

Her glove squeaked as she balled her hand into a fist and withdrew it. A flash of that smile appeared on her face. 'Fine,' she almost whispered. 'I guess I'll allow it, this once. Since I quite like you.'

I frowned. 'You don't... You don't know me.'

Again the smile.

'Procurement of a person for the purpose of prostitution. Intent to receive money and/or benefits from a sex worker as a result of their services,' I recited. 'Uh, money laundering, all kinds of financial fraud, crimes concerning the unlawful use of magick, specifically dark and blood magick, and intent to traffic both humans and creatures.'

Odette shook her head, closed her eyes, and calmly said, 'No, no, Jack, *all* of these charges were dropped, as I'm sure you know as a serving detective. Don't waste your time with me. I can assure you, the answers lie elsewhere.'

I scoffed. 'That's not for you to say. A woman died the other day, shot dead in cold blood after speaking *your name*. Now, why might that be? Why did she want me to hear that, and who *didn't*, to the extent they would kill her for it?'

Odette licked at her lower lip, frowning slightly, staring at her own hands clasped together on the desk. 'Who— Who was this woman?' she finally said.

'Emily Wyatt.'

'Emily Wyatt?' She scanned the air, then opened a drawer by her knees. I stiffened and peered over the desk. Odette gave me a look.

'It's just a ledger.' She pulled out a large, leather-bound book and placed it on the desk.

'What're you doing?'

'Checking the records,' she murmured, slowly turning each page. 'Staff.'

'Don't know the names of your own girls, huh?'

Her eyes shot from the page to me, then back to the page. The floor was shaking from the blaring bass downstairs. Odette tapped at a line in the book. 'One of ours,' she said. 'Yes, I know her. Knew her.'

I scoffed. 'Doesn't entirely sound like you *knew* her, does it?'

'Enough. Miss Wyatt used to work with us, yes. I terminated her contract about two months ago now. She had gotten involved with bad elements. People and ideas that only brought her harm and, in turn, this establishment.'

'Like what?'

'Drugs.'

I laughed out loud. 'Give me a break. These places, they hand out drugs on a damn buffet table to their girls.'

Odette's face was cold. She saw no funny side, apparently. 'I'm not sure what you mean by "these places," Jack, but no, I'm talking about a certain kind of drug. Okay, not a drug, perhaps, slip of the tongue; I am speaking of a more organic produce not created or grown for the consumption of normal humans.' She paused, looked down, then up again. And I knew what was coming. 'Correct me if I'm wrong, Detective, but as rumor has it, it seems you might know a little something about that?'

'Don't go there, lady.' My voice was louder than I'd meant it to be.

'It wasn't an insult,' said Odette, in that weirdly soothing tone. 'I find it engrossing. Isn't it a relatively new phenomenon? For such commodities to have a real, meaningful, and powerful effect on a bog-standard human?' She widened her eyes, almost choking on her words. 'No, no!' she chirped, 'I didn't mean ... Forgive me. By no means do I consider you bog-standard—'

'Listen, it doesn't entirely matter to me what you consider—'

'After all,' she went on, '*slaying a giant*, no less, and at such a young age, too.'

I started shifting in my seat again. I didn't know what kind of game she was playing here, but I didn't like it. 'Can we move on?'

'Like most others, I don't know the ins and outs of what happened, obviously, and I won't ask, curious as I am. But that must have had quite an effect on you. So I don't blame you at all for your perceived addiction—'

'Shut it!' I hissed. 'Quiet, please.'

Odette frowned, started stroking her sharp chin. She looked genuinely offended or confused, as if she didn't recognize she was out of line. Some people don't believe they're ever out of line – they don't know it's possible for them. Because they've been told nothing but 'yes' all their life. Maybe she's one of them. 'We all have our pasts,' she whispered thoughtfully.

'Yeah, people seem to keep telling me that recently.' She cocked her head, but I changed the course of the conversation back to where it needed to be. 'You don't seem all that interested in Wyatt's death.'

'It's not that. It's simply that I saw it coming.'

'Oh, you did? Is that why *your name* was in her dying breath? Whatever groups she was mixed up in happened to show up and kill her right at that specific moment in time, while a detective was in the room. What would you have to say about that, Odette?'

'These things happen more than any of us seem to realize,' she said, her smile faint and distant.

'Her kid was – is – missing.'

Odette shrugged, fluttered her eyelashes lazily. 'I'm sorry. I just don't know. I wish I did.'

Pain shot through my head. I realized I was grinding my teeth. 'To move on, then – I take it you're aware of the death of Dick Dumpty. Now, I've seen no coverage at all in the press, but he was a client of yours, wasn't he?'

'A rich man in New York City. Of course he attended our venues,' she said. Her tone was different, like she was far away, somewhere else in her head and physically, barely in the room with me. 'He died, yes. At some hotel. Suicide, I heard.'

'Okay,' I said. 'And what was your relationship to Mr Dumpty?'

'I never said I had one.'

'No, but this is a pretty exclusive deal. With all your establishments, seems like the people who visit are in close-knit circles. You're telling me you never spoke to him.'

'Probably, yes. But I can't remember any particular interaction or conversation with him.'

'You don't remember any particular interaction or conversation with a seven-foot egg? I mean, c'mon, there are some weird characters around, but I've never seen anyone that looks quite like that.'

'Then maybe you don't get out much. I see all kinds of people, creatures, spirits, whatever, every night. What difference does it make, anyway, if I knew him or not? Dozens of people knew him.'

'Yeah, but so far, only your name has come up. There seems to be a connection. The missing girls, your establishments, Dumpty's death.'

I imagined Goldilocks in the hotel room, face-to-face with Dick Dumpty. I imagined his terror as she launched a kick right into him. I saw his flailing body falling from the sky and splattering all over the street below.

Odette narrowed her eyes, and I picked up on a slight tremble in her jaw. Was she seething? Scared? Either way, I knew she was hiding something.

We sat in silence a few seconds longer, the only sounds being the club ambience trying to burst through the walls and floor.

'Right,' I said, choosing my words carefully. One more thing lingered on my mind. 'Can you tell me if you know someone called Jessica Robicheaux? Goes by Goldilocks.'

A hint of recognition seemed to flicker in her eyes. But then again, it might not have been that at all. This woman was damn near impossible to read. 'No. I don't know who that is. Should I?'

I placed my phone in my breast pocket and sniffed. 'Forget it,' I said. 'I think I'm going to give up on you, for now. We both know there's nothing I can do, even if you are involved in this. In a way, I got some of the answers I need.'

Odette chuckled, her mouth twisting up in one corner. 'You don't sound like a man who has any answers. You aren't even asking the right questions,' she purred.

'What does that mean, not asking the right questions?' I said as I got up from the chair.

Again, Odette's smile faded, leaving a cold, unemotional air. 'Well, that *certainly* isn't the right question. I have one for you, though.'

'Shoot.'

'Do you really believe, in your heart of hearts, that you're ready for this? Meaning, do you truly think you can change anything on your own? Part of me would find it . . . inspiring if you do. The rest of me knows it's suicide.'

'Why are you so interested in what I believe? To me, you sound a little scared. Scared I'm about to open a cage of pixies that are gonna run riot and ruin everything you value.'

As the smile crept back, she shrugged, closing her eyes again. 'You're right, I'm scared. Of course I am. But that is *not* why.'

'Go on.'

'A word of advice, Detective. Just stop shining your light into these dark corners. You won't like what you find, and you're only going to get yourself killed.' She chewed her lip, staring down at the floor. Then she met my eyes again, sparkling glitter encircling her own like an army of fireflies. 'Or worse, you might just end up in a situation so stark, so wretched, you'll never be able to turn around again. Never escape. Trapped like a spirit that never quite made it to the next realm. And you'll hurt, and keep on hurting until you become so numb that you seek out real pain again, and you'll salvage all of it, just so you can trick yourself into believing you're really alive. Tell me you don't want that. Do you? Do you think you do?'

I snorted. 'Honestly, the more you people tell me I'm making the wrong choices, looking in the wrong places, the stronger my resolve gets. We'll see where that gets me, I guess.' I went through the open door and jogged down the steel steps. 'Night, ma'am.'

On my way out of the club, I went through the conversation in my head, recalling details and Odette's expressions, inflections in her voice, what she did or didn't say, even objects placed around the room. I was so far inside my own head, I barely realized where I was.

It was a stupid, stupid mistake.

How did I allow myself to not see it coming? Asshole.

A strong, hard arm had me in its grasp, my feet kicking aimlessly at the cold ground, splashing a puddle and spraying water across the street.

It pulled me back into an alley, the alley where I'd taken out the big guy on the door. While I flailed and fought, I saw a flash of the man's body on the ground. He was still there.

I bit into the arm as hard as I could, and whoever had hold of me shrieked and swore. I spun, but was greeted by a fist to the nose before I could do anything more.

I crashed to the ground. I was stronger with the magick bean in my system, but my pain tolerance was dramatically decreased. My eyes were suddenly wet and bleary.

'You fucking bit me?' said the man, towering above me while I tried to scramble back, skin of my palms shredding off as they scraped on the concrete.

'Hold it, hold on, hold on,' said another voice.

I tried to blink away the tears, blood pouring from my nose and into my mouth. The taste of iron filled my head.

'We oughta keep him at least a *little* presentable for the boss!'

I recognized the voice. From where?

I tried to get to my feet. 'Who the f—'

'Shut it! Shut the fuck up,' said the second voice, nasally and grating. I realized who it was. It was one of the officers from Cole's office the other night. Piper.

'You?' I breathed.

The other figure threw me against the wall, and I stretched for my holster.

Piper got there first, slowly removing my gun. 'Nope, nope,' he said almost playfully. 'Let's not do that. No need to take things *so* far, is there?'

I gave up replying. My mouth was filled with blood, anyway. I couldn't speak, and I was about to start choking. If I did, I never knew about it, because my lights were about to go out.

I slid down the wall and hit the floor, and Piper stood right above me, clicking his tongue. 'That's right, shut it all down, boy. It's a shame you'll miss the ride. I'm gonna be taking the scenic route tonight.'

'Odette,' I heard myself wheeze.

'What was that?' Piper said before snorting inwardly. Then his wet and warm spit splatted on my forehead. 'That bitch ain't gonna help ya! It's just us now, pal!'

I heard the scraping of boots on dirty concrete, then a fist hit me like a rock.

I was out.

6

JUST RIGHT

It seemed to take me hours to force myself back into consciousness. I was dreaming about corpses by the trees, and children being plucked from their beds by a faceless monster as if they were fruit. I dreamed about swans covered in blood and guts, and a woman with the apocalypse inside her. I dreamed about a king rising from the dead ground beneath our feet. And I dreamed about giants tumbling from the sky.

There was a bag on my head, tightened with something around the throat so I could barely breathe. All I smelled was blood, the dried parts stuck to my nose and above my lips.

I was moving along at a steady pace, felt the engine vibrating under my boots. I wanted to boot the back of the seat in front of me, but I felt like death.

It was the coughing that alerted Piper to my newly awakened state.

'With us again, are you, Mr Slade? I hope you had a good nap, my friend; you'll be needing all the energy you can get.'

I didn't bother speaking. He obviously wanted me to take his bait so he could verbally prod me even more.

'No, you're right,' he said. 'Don't waste your breath on me. We're almost there, anyway. Almost where, you ask? That's a secret, my friend, a big secret. I'll tell you this, though: You'll be catching up with some old friends.'

The car came to a halt. After a few seconds, I heard the sound of a gate opening. I let my head fall back and I closed my eyes. The magick bean had completely worn off again, as if Piper and the other guy had beat it out of my system. Now all that was left in me was a quiet rage and broken ribs.

When the car moved again, I felt we were going uphill. One of the car windows was open, but there was no sound of traffic or any kind of life. All I could make out was the sound of tires on gravel. My wrists were completely numb, bound by rough rope. My heart was beating hard, and getting faster.

'Here we are,' whispered Piper as we made a slow turn. The car stopped, the engine shut off, a door slammed, then there was silence.

About five minutes of it.

All I heard was my breathing, heavy and thick. And every breath hurt like hell. I cursed Goldilocks for making this more painful than it needed to be: Not only were my ribs probably digging into my organs, my chest was working extra hard after being dealt an emphatic blow by her blanks.

But, man, could I have done with her swooping in round about now.

The door beside me suddenly swung open and I was hauled out of the car by what seemed to be two men.

'Careful, gentlemen.' The wretched voice of Piper.

I immediately lost my footing and fell on my knees, but the strong, silent arms dragged me along and forced me to get back on my feet. The air was colder than it'd been all year. A choir of nocturnal birds screeched high above me. The brushing and creaking of trees joined it. My gut churned and shifted.

Something heavy scraped against the ground, the night air filled with a horrific screech, and I was shoved into an area even colder than outside. The concrete ground was so numbing, it sent a shiver through my boots, into my feet, and up through my entire my body.

'Oh yeah, chilly, ain't it?' whispered that prick Piper behind me.

We descended a spiral staircase. By the time we reached the bottom, I almost threw up.

Another metal door opened, and I was shoved into a different room, this one twice as cold.

The door crashed shut behind me and the sound of footsteps gradually quieted as I stood in the room, helpless.

I felt pretty certain I was alone. There was a low buzz humming around me, as well as the sound of liquid dripping into a puddle. Slowly, I moved around the room, bag still on my head, hands restrained. I extended them upward to feel around. Seemed a small room – floor, wall, a block I guess I was supposed to sit on, all concrete. It wasn't long before I really began to shudder, and my teeth chattered relentlessly. 'Fuck this,' I said into the straw bag pressed against my face. 'Ah, fuck *this*.'

This was the first time I'd gotten myself into a hostage situation in my twenty-nine years of ill-fated life. I had been trained for it but, of course, poorly, and I was absolutely clueless. I curled into myself in the corner of the room.

Eventually the door opened again while I was on the verge of what was either sleep or just straight-up passing out, so I scrambled onto my feet and slammed myself against the wall, grunting and practically hissing. Something was burning inside me, a fury, some sort of mania, things I'd been pushing down through years of agony. I felt things I hadn't felt since . . .

Hold it together, you bastard, I thought before trying to relax my body and gain more control over my breath, or at least as much as I could with a sack on my head.

I was greeted by a familiar sound; Piper's chuckle bounced off the walls that surrounded me, creeping into my ears. One hell of a torture method. He began to walk toward me, and I vividly pictured his repulsive saunter just by listening to the rhythm of his dumb footsteps. 'Right, Slade,' he said, merrily, 'time for your interview.'

Interview meaning brutal interrogation, I imagined. 'Yeah,

whatever, just tell me where I am, at least, will you?' I said, still leaning on the wall with my sack-head like some abandoned, crooked scarecrow.

'You are about to find out exactly that. Come with me up these steps, then I'll take that bag off your head before you go into the office. Sound good?'

'Yeah, that sounds good, Piper, sounds incredible. Whose office?'

'Hah!' he yelled. 'I'm quite surprised you haven't figured out where you are yet. You sure you're a detective? You are on the estate belonging to none other than Papa Bear, my friend.'

For a minute that was actually a second, my body froze and my mind went numb, before that rage, that horrible feeling, came burning up through my body again, and this time it took me. I charged forward wildly with my shoulder and pinned the officer against the wall, then I threw my head toward his face, then again, this time with a crack and a shriek, and I felt his warm blood meet my cold blood through the rough material on my head, and I struck him again, he screamed again, then monstrous heavy footsteps rumbled above me and got louder as I threw my head forward once more, this time only meeting the concrete wall.

I stumbled back, seeing nothing but weird patterns squirming around before me.

Piper roared, struck me with something, and thankfully, I was out cold again.

I woke up on a huge bed in a dark room. A warm room, though – one with actual furnishings and wallpaper and carpet. Flames flickered on the wall opposite where I lay, dancing in the dark.

A hint of the pain I'd been feeling was still there, but it was suppressed, dampened. If I wasn't alone in some bedroom I'd never seen before, I might have even gone so far as saying I felt content. But *because* I'd just woken up in a room I'd never seen before, and been beaten half to death by that piece of shit Piper, I was not content. I was seething, and determined to get out of there.

I slipped off the bed and tried to plant my feet into the carpet, but just completely crumbled and crashed to the floor. 'Fuck,' I hissed, gripping my knee. My joints were sticking, barely moving. Shapes and images flickered before me.

This wasn't the same as magick bean withdrawal – something else got in my system, was *put* there. I scrunched my eyes shut and held onto the bed frame, lifting myself up slowly. Suddenly, I weighed four hundred pounds. 'Those bastards,' I slurred under my breath.

When I finally got to my feet, I went stumbling back and smacked against the wall, causing some framed painting to crash to the floor. I peered down at it, hearing myself chuckle for no apparent reason, in a weird, shrill pitch that didn't sound like me. It was a spell, whatever was making me feel like this. I felt the magick working inside me, swelling and shooting around, taking control of my nerves and chemicals, harassing and marauding them.

Piper, or whoever set it on me, obviously didn't want me moving around too much, or remembering a whole lot.

I looked around the room, realizing I had my arms wrapped around my body as if I was still cold. I wasn't cold, but I was uneasy. Scared. There was a dresser, bed, some kind of writing desk in the room, and paintings, lots of paintings, all over the walls. My vision was so blurry, I couldn't see what half the stuff was, but the ones I made out looked pretty fucked-up. Sexually charged, with ambiguous undertones of all kinds of wrongness.

I quickly looked away, the uneasy sensation inside me nowhere near clearing off. I felt for my phone, trying to dig my hand into my pants pocket. But that was a problem because there were no pants there. I'd been completely stripped.

I marched over to the door at the end of the room, junk swinging, and grabbed the bronze door handle. It was locked, of course. I bashed my fist against it. 'Open this fucking door!' I yelled, or tried to. It felt like there was a tube of cardboard down my throat. Beyond the door, I thought I heard footsteps, then murmuring. Then there was definitely the sound of footsteps.

Keys jangled, the door unlocked, then swung open. I lurched forward, and swiftly smashed against the ground.

'Alright, get up, buddy. In,' said a new voice. A low southern drawl. He gripped me by the forearm and dragged me back inside my bedroom cell.

I punched the bed frame and pulled at my hair, then breathed in and out as deeply as I could.

'Yep,' said the guy. 'Sucks, doesn't it? Man, would I be embarrassed if I were in your position, Jack.' He chuckled, then stepped toward me. 'Naked and afraid, all alone in the dragon's lair.' He crouched down so his face was right in mine. 'Although, just between you and me, you're not quite dealing with a dragon – that was an overstatement.' He clicked his tongue and curled his face up into either a grin or a grimace. 'He's only a bear.'

I inhaled sharply between my teeth, my attention suddenly on my rapid heartbeat, undoing my breath work. Bear? *That* bear. I swallowed, but there was barely enough spit in my system, and I just choked.

'Aw, hell, Piper. Get this man a damn drink, will you? And some goddamn clothes. That's enough of this. I can't watch anymore! Go, you've had your fun, haven't you?'

Piper's silhouette was there in the doorway, lurking. I struggled where I sat, reached out at him, as if I could do any damage. 'I'll kill you!' I yelled. He slipped away, gone from my view, vanishing into the black.

'Shh, shhh, don't worry about him,' said this other guy. I realized then he was caressing me, stroking my bare arms and rubbing my neck with warm, damp thumbs. I swiped at him, and he closed his eyes in resignation, raised his hands. 'Fair enough,' he murmured.

He had bluish-black slicked hair, and dead, frosty eyes. Scars across his sandy complexion, a dark blue goatee. Something called to me inside my head. Goldilocks – she'd said something about someone called Bluebeard, an accomplice of Papa Bear. No doubt this was the guy. A raw depravity flamed behind his eyes, something I couldn't exactly place, but whatever it was made me feel more defenseless and violated than I already had been.

I was frozen. I tried to lift my arms, but it was like I'd forgotten how. There was no magick in this paralysis; it was just fear – fear that I told myself I shouldn't have been feeling. I told myself there was no time for it, that I needed to just power through it somehow. But it didn't happen.

'Where am I?' I said.

Piper appeared in the doorway again, holding a glass of water.

Bluebeard smiled. 'A haven. Safe from the darkness of the world outside. Officer Piper? Give the young man his drink.'

Again I tried to move, but everything was numb and static, completely dead, like I was a part of the floor.

'Open up, Detective,' said Piper. My tongue felt dry and hard against my teeth. He pressed the glass to my lips and pushed my head back. The cold water trickled down my throat and instantly I was choking. My throat was so parched, I couldn't swallow without nearly vomiting.

Bluebeard stood above me, arms folded, looking down at me with vicious, probing eyes. 'That's it, that's it,' he whispered as Piper emptied the glass down my throat. My eyes began to water, which meant luckily I didn't have to see that fucker's face so clearly. But I had a feeling I'd see it again vividly next time I closed my eyes to sleep.

'Why are you doing this?' I asked.

'Shhh, no, no. Save your energy, Jack,' said Bluebeard. 'Don't think about it. Just . . . be.'

I scowled.

Bluebeard headed for the doorway, one arm tucked behind his back, the other swinging at his side. 'There's a change of clothes in the dresser. You're gonna want to look presentable for the boss, right?'

'*Your* boss,' I spat.

Bluebeard chuckled and closed the door. This time he locked it.

I sat there for a minute, not even trying to move until I knew I could actually do it.

So, they'd brought me right into Papa Bear's manor, by the look of things. And I wasn't dead yet. I thought about what that meant as I tipped my head back against the frame of the bed. Did he want to use me, threaten me, eat me? My lips started trembling then, so I growled and snapped my head forward, shaking away the fear, the pain.

I felt totally doomed in that moment.

When I was ready, I got to my feet like a newborn griffin, scrambling and slipping and stumbling. I pulled open the drawer and, with a hell of a lot of aching pain, slipped into the soft white shirt and black pants. I noticed a pair of dress shoes by the door. I put those on and knocked on the door to be let out.

'Hopefully you've learned from your prior mistake, Detective!' Bluebeard's muffled voice said from the other side. I guess I had. I wasn't about to try anything this time. I wasn't going to prolong it. I just had to move forward, into the abyss of ambiguity.

Of course, there was nothing ambiguous about being dragged to a giant grizzly bear. It's what would happen *after*.

I was let out into the dark hallway. Slowly, I stepped into it, and Bluebeard led the way. Piper was nowhere to be seen now. A small mercy.

The journey through the labyrinth of candlelit hallways was much more a leisurely saunter than a case of being dragged. Bluebeard walked ahead of me, talking and holding his hands behind his back. I limped behind him, burying thoughts of escape that floated to the surface now and then.

Huge oil paintings covered the walls on either side of us, depicting various creatures and men and women in all kinds of poses and scenarios. They were all in the same style, probably the same artist. Some of the paintings were explicitly sexual, others with hints of eroticism about them. Some of the art was brutal and violent, then the next painting serene and peaceful but always with some unplaceable essence of despair and darkness underneath the paint. Eventually I just stopped looking at any of it; I didn't need to make myself feel any more uneasy.

We came to the end of one of the hallways. Bluebeard stopped, peered over his shoulder at me, then opened a door, leading to yet another hallway, pretty much identical to all the others – except at the end of this one, I saw two huge doors, their dark red paint illuminated by a sprawling chandelier.

'This way,' said Bluebeard, voice dry and raspy.

The whole building smelled like fire and whiskey. I thought about Goldilocks – here I was in her former boss' manor, barely on my feet, quite possibly closing in on my death. I wondered if she was actually the reason I'd got here.

'You look dashing,' said Bluebeard.

'Go fuck yourself.'

'Really. You'd fit right in.' He smoothed out his own blazer jacket and clicked his tongue. 'You can't even imagine the parties.'

We reached the doors.

I found myself staring directly up at the massive chandelier, almost hypnotized by its endless shapes and patterns, tiny details emerging with each second. I think part of me was hopelessly wishing if I stared at it long enough, it'd transport me the hell out of here. Naturally, that didn't happen. And Bluebeard pushed open the doors.

'Boss!' he hollered.

I froze and the screech of wood scraping against more wood rushed into my ears. Bluebeard sauntered into the room with the bear in it, the bear who was rising like a wave from where he'd been sitting behind a desk, and he stared down at me with small black eyes.

The bear, Papa Bear, Arminus.

Then it felt like everything else had frozen with me. No one was moving; there was no sign of life or time in that room. It was like I was standing inside a photograph.

What brought me back was the cloud of smoke that suddenly filled the room. The bear had a cigar hanging from his snout. Gold-rimmed glasses sat on the wide bridge of his nose. His fur looked aged but silky. He towered above me now, about twice my height.

I hadn't realized my throat could actually get any drier, but I can tell you it did just that.

'So, here he is, boss,' announced Bluebeard. He'd pulled up a chair to my left, sitting there with one lanky leg over the other. I only saw that in my peripheral vision because I couldn't look away from the bear.

He nodded once, slowly and thoughtfully, taking another puff of his cigar. I heard the moist, cracking sound of the bear's jaw as he opened it to speak. 'Yes, here he is,' he said in a rumbling voice that made my chest vibrate and quiver. 'Come here,' he said to me.

My feet, which felt like they'd turned into sandbags, dragged me farther inside the room.

The sound of the bear inhaling through his nose reminded me of a distant shore sweeping across a beach. 'Detective Jackson Slade' he said slowly, like he wasn't entirely sure that was my name. 'Jack of the Beanstalk. Jack the Giant Killer . . .'

Suddenly I was staring at the ground, at the expansive patterned rug that stretched sideways, wall to wall.

'Hey,' went Bluebeard, smiling with his eyes, but his mouth snarling, 'where are your damn manners? You look at the boss.'

But the bear held up a giant paw, turning his head to shoot Bluebeard a look of pity. 'That's quite enough, John. Do you not have your wives to attend to? Thank you for bringing Jackson to me. You will be called upon once more tonight, when your services are needed.'

Bluebeard shot to his feet, tugged harshly at the lapel of his jacket, and gave a sort of bow to the bear. 'Absolutely,' he drawled. He left the room, and the doors slowly swung shut behind him, leaving me alone with Papa Bear.

Razor-sharp white teeth emerged from the cloud of cigar smoke that almost filled the entire room. The bear was grinning, or grimacing, and just staring at me.

My heart was in my mouth. I swallowed it back down to where it should be and exhaled, shakily, slowly, quietly. I tried to stare back at him, knowing I was absolutely going to lose this contest. He wore a huge, patterned, dark green waistcoat. A black bowler hat sat on the desk in front of him, next to a reading lamp shining crimson red.

'I can feel your heartbeat from here, Mr Slade,' he growled. And at that point, I gave up trying to keep my panicked breathing quiet. He pushed back on the desk and rose from his chair, standing at his full height. That was when I looked away again. 'Here. This will take the edge off. I cannot have a conversation with a pathetic, shaking mouse.'

When I looked up, there was a tumbler of vodka with ice waiting for me on the enormous desk. The ice cubes rattled loudly as I took a couple shaky sips.

'I have to say, I expected one of the few people in this realm who can say that they slew a *giant* to be a little more . . . bold. No, not even bold,' he said with a rumbling chuckle. 'At least functional.'

'I'm functioning,' I just barely got out.

Again, he chuckled. 'Well, that's good, then, isn't it.'

Realizing I'd been sitting there with my nose buried in the glass – not even drinking – I looked up again and placed it on the desk. Who's kidding who – I was shitting myself so much, I'd been trying to hide in a tumbler. Embarrassing.

'I've never seen a giant,' said the bear. 'One of the last creatures

I must witness firsthand during my time in this world.'

'They don't exactly tend to hang out in the biggest cities in the world. Not any cities, for that matter. They don't like crowds,' I said.

'Quite. But the giant you killed—'

Here we go.

'—if only he could observe the crowds that gather round and gape and photograph his decaying corpse beside that towering beanstalk, their eyes wide, jaws hitting the floor. Once a force to be reckoned with, towering and full of pride, but now? A tourist attraction in the midst of nowhere, for the little people.'

I said nothing. I was used to people leaning in, irritating smiles on their punchable faces, waiting for me to explain what it was like, how I did it, how I'm still here. I never gave in, and today wasn't about to be any different. I lifted the glass of booze back up to my face, and this time I drank.

'What's your point?' I finally said, my voice coming out a lot quieter than I thought it was going to.

'That any of us can *fall*, I suppose.'

I shrugged, took another sip and puffed out my cheeks. 'Why was I brought here? I'm exhausted, scared, and quite busy.'

The bear chuckled. 'Busy, indeed. From the little I know of you and the situation you've found yourself in the past couple of days, you appear to be taking on quite the feat. A foolish endeavor, but undoubtedly admirable.'

'I think you know more than I do about what the hell it is I'm apparently taking on. Care to give me a clue or two?'

'Unfortunately, no. I didn't have you brought here to disclose any incriminating details you might be seeking. This isn't really about you at all. It's the evasive one, that slippery little wretch who always finds a way to vanish into the cracks. She has been a source of great *bother* to me, to say the least. She is a convicted outlaw, she can be arrested, detained. You are a serving police officer, and her apparent accomplice. Do you see where I am going with this?'

I swallowed thin air, tried to keep my newfound composure. Then before I knew it, it was gone again. Arminus had to have sensed my increasing heart rate again because a horrible smile crept along his snout as he eyed me up and down.

'I am not asking much of you, Detective. The girl is not to be trusted. I don't know what she has told you, or done to you, done *with* you, or even what she's up to, entirely. But she is a savage, a dangerous and clinically insane fugitive. And she is in possession of a number of things that belong to myself and this estate.'

I shuffled in my seat. 'Don't take this personally, but your other guy out there just stripped me and nearly fondled me, after using some illegal paralysis spell. The other one, a serving cop, stood there and watched with a smile on his face. He also almost broke my nose. Granted, I think I did *actually* break his, but he shouldn't have abducted me. What I'm getting at is, maybe the problem really lies with your recruitment staff?'

The bear wasn't impressed with my lame, long-winded joke. 'I won't speak for them. I wasn't there. But Goldilocks? Well, I can tell you I know her very well. Like she's my own daughter. In a way, she was just that, a daughter, but she let greed get to her head, and it seems only derangement followed. She betrayed the only family she's ever had, *killing* my associates in cold blood in an attempt to further anger me.'

'Dumpty?'

'Yes, Dumpty. That woman is a monster, and must be stopped, whatever the cost.'

I chewed my lip. 'At whatever cost to me, you mean. You're asking me to try and arrest her, bring her to you.' I shook my head. 'Your associate, then, Dumpty. Heard some bad shit about him.'

'Whatever do you mean?' the bear said in an almost mocking tone.

'I don't think I need to spell it out to a man of your stature. The woman you call a monster . . . she caught you one night, didn't she?

She heard things.'

'Ah, I would love to discuss what Jess thought she heard with the girl herself. If she were to come to me, I could do just that.' He chuckled. 'And a man of *your* stature, well, surely doesn't believe the ramblings of a killer outlaw just like that, does he?'

I decided to ignore him. The truth was, I didn't know what to think about Goldilocks. I wasn't about to blindly defend her honor to her former crime boss's furry face. 'What was Dick Dumpty doing here that night? Why so spooked?'

'I don't disclose my business to prying fools who don't know what they're getting themselves into. It would only do you undeniable harm to know anything of my business transactions. You have no right to ask me such things. And what would you do with the answers, anyway?' He scoffed. 'You are powerless.'

The bear was right; I knew that. I wasn't here to ask questions – my focus should've been getting out alive sooner than later.

'Now, they say that back when you wanted to be, you were one of the finest detectives in the force. You still have it in you, I am sure of that. Although your display today has been far from convincing.' The bear smiled. 'It's been a tough few days, hasn't it,' he growled. 'I must give you the benefit of the doubt. You clearly understand what it is I am asking of you. And have no doubt that *I* understand I am putting you in quite the position.'

Just as I was about to ask what was in it for me, Arminus pulled open a drawer below the giant desk and grabbed hold of something. 'There are more, much more, where these came from.' And he held up a small velvet sack, then threw it in front of me.

I swallowed. I didn't want to look inside. I wanted to pretend they weren't what I knew they were. But I couldn't – I was going to lose.

'Go on, take it,' rumbled the bear.

And I did, just like that. I tipped the sack and a dozen magick beans rolled out across the desk, rainbows glimmering. I held one between my finger and thumb and started turning it. It was legit, no doubt. 'Where did you get these?'

'The very same place I will acquire the rest of them, if you do as I say. This isn't the only payment I offer you, though, Detective,' grumbled the bear.

I battled with the urge to take a bean right now, and somehow won. I put them back into the sack. 'The other?'

'Mercy,' he said simply. 'I spare you from death. If you wanted, it may be that I even take you in, and you go on to live a life of luxury. You get everything you've ever desired, as well as things you didn't even know you could have.'

I scoffed. 'You hang death over my head, then employ me? Sounds kinda toxic. In fact, kinda explains why the people who work for you are . . . like that,' I said, picturing the grotesque duo of Bluebeard and Piper. I slipped the sack of magick beans into my breast pocket and started to get to my feet.

'Sit down,' boomed the bear, and I instantly did just that. 'We aren't done here. Your chief of police, Cole, tell me: Has he been acting strangely recently? On edge, perhaps?'

'How's that?'

'The man is compromised. Things have clearly started heating up. It is at this stage we separate the men from the boys, as it were.'

'Cole's always been corrupt,' I said. 'Literally his entire career. Can't say he's acting any more of a dick than usual, no. You two got a deal?'

'You don't ask the questions anymore, Detective. You're on my payroll now, after all.'

'I didn't say yes.'

'I don't need you to.'

My jaw tensed, my hands balled into fists. I thought about making some vague threat about storming his mansion with a squad of King's Men if he thought about messing with me. Then I immediately shut down that idea. Stupid. I didn't have that authority, and they were way more likely to side with the terrifying career criminal, anyway.

If I was in the shit when I was brought into all this by Goldilocks, I was absolutely up to my eyes in it by the time I woke up in this goddamn building.

I'd been staring down at the desk, stuck in my thoughts for a minute. When I looked up, the bear was surrounded by another thick cloud of cigar smoke. He was pondering something. 'It is something remarkable . . . to nearly deplete every known witch around New York of those precious beans.'

My face instantly went hot. Anger boiled inside.

'Quite the addiction. One has to wonder how it is you're still standing. The magick that creates those things takes an abundance of energy from the witches themselves, such is the power inside them. They must think you a leech. How many years now have they been supplying you? Of course, they would only do such a thing if they were getting – or going to get – something in return.'

'What are you talking about?' I heard myself say in the distance.

The bear rose to his full height and the rage inside melted into a heavy, churning misery. 'It started as soon as you came across that gold, didn't it? Money that could have saved your mother's life, that instead you invested into fueling your addiction. Failing upward all your life. I wonder what people would suppose if they heard that Detective Jackson Slade, climber of beanstalks, slayer of giants, left his poor mother to starve and die while he traveled the country, spending thousands and thousands of dollars on magick beans, living in ecstasy while his mother's corpse rotted away in that farmhouse, not to be found until years later.'

My fists slammed into the desk as I lurched forward. 'Shut up! Shut the *fuck* up! That is not what happened. You don't know anything, you don't know anything—'

'I know that you and the girl are not so unalike. But it does not matter. As long as the people never know, it does not matter.' Suddenly the bear crashed a paw against the table and charged around it, stopping just inches away from me. 'That was the last time you ever try to intimidate me, boy. Of that you can be assured.'

I was at his mercy. The part of me that wanted him to thrust his claws into my heart and get it all over with melted away. Instead, the adrenaline of resilience surged through me. It felt good because I had something to live for. I was in the middle of it all, and doing damage to these people was my only choice. It gave me a reason to keep going.

'Bluebeard,' ordered the bear as I turned away.

Said piece of shit emerged, swinging open the double doors. I stepped into the hallway, then turned back to the enraged bear. 'I know you didn't ask – you want to pretend you don't really care. But I know you do – of course you do. So I'll tell you how I did it – I let the giant underestimate me. That's it.'

7

THE DOCTOR

My stuff was returned to me in a garbage bag. I snatched it from Bluebeard and checked the contents – just my bloodied clothes.

'Phone,' I said.

Bluebeard reached into his pocket and held up my phone, then whistled for no apparent reason. 'You get this back when we're done with you, my good man,' he declared.

'And what about the other one?'

He chuckled. 'Cop with a burner phone? Big red flag. Imagine one of your colleagues caught you messing with that? I took the liberty of destroying it, did you a favor,' he said with a wink.

We were standing by what seemed to be the front doors of the manor – us, Piper, and a group of dead-eyed goons. I checked out the massive oil painting of Arminus and his family, all the bears staring proudly at me. Even the kids had some aura of arrogance about them.

I thought about spitting on it as we went out the doors, but my mouth was still so dry, I'd never conjure enough ammunition, even if I wanted to.

I sniffed. 'Whaddaya mean, done with me? This is it, isn't it?'

'You're gonna need a ride back into town, my friend! Did you think we'd make you walk? Ha! Look, just because we abducted you . . . we do still treat our guests with manners.'

Then Officer Piper perked up, his eyes bloodshot, dried blood crusted over in his moustache, a piece of tape over his broken nose.

He got right up in my face and I tasted weeks of booze on his breath. 'See what you did, ya fuckin' asshole? Look at this, look at me!'

'Alright,' said Bluebeard, resigned. He placed a hand on Piper's shoulder.

Piper swiped it away, nearly taking my eye out, and pointed at him. 'Don't you touch me, freak.'

Bluebeard just chuckled, shaking his head and flicking through a set of keys.

Piper suddenly thrust his fist into my stomach, all his weight behind it. I dropped the bag of clothes and keeled over, clutching my stomach and groaning. Pain surged through my torso and my breath abandoned me.

When I opened my eyes, I saw two magick beans on the carpet. They'd tumbled out of the bag in my breast pocket. I reached for them desperately, but Piper's boot came cracking down on my fingers. I yelled as my fingers crunched and the beans under my palm crumbled into the carpet.

Piper was laughing now, cackling. He was enjoying the hell out of this. I didn't even feel humiliation, no loss of pride. Just fury.

With my free hand, I clenched my fist together and struck Piper's dick as hard as I could. He screamed and jumped back off my hand, revealing a small pool of vibrant multicolored substance from the bean, sinking into the carpet. One of the goons grabbed me by the collar and crashed me against the wall. My arm smacked into one of the framed paintings and it fell to the ground.

Piper shrieked, one hand over his crotch, the other over his mouth, eyes wide. 'You fuckin idiot! Bastard! You're dead!' he yelled.

But he wasn't talking to me. The goon's grip released and I slipped down the wall. Piper whipped out a handgun from his holster and shot the guy once in the leg. He collapsed to the floor with only a grunt. 'Somebody tidy this up.' He pointed to me. 'Someone sack him and let's get outta here.'

'Alright, alright, enough of that,' said Bluebeard, still completely resigned. 'Give him back his deposit.'

'Fuck!' screamed Piper, still gripping his nutsack as one of the goons shoved the other type of sack back into my pocket. 'Why didn't you bind his fuckin hands!'

Bluebeard just chuckled in reply, then I felt a disgustingly warm touch as he held my arms behind my back, took some cuffs off Piper, and locked them around my wrists. Then it all went dark as something was placed over my head again, and I was guided outside.

A car door was opened and I was pushed into the vehicle. I recognized Bluebeard's touch again and fought the urge to throw up inside this bag, consequently drowning myself in my own vomit. 'That's it,' he whispered as I ducked into the car.

The two men slipped into the front seats and slammed the doors closed. Piper was still going on. 'Why d'you always gotta pull this shit?'

Bluebeard sighed. 'What?'

'Fuck you, man.'

'Yeah, fuck me. I'm not the one getting my ass kicked by the half-conscious guy, but sure, fuck me.'

'Shut the hell up.'

I tried to block out the insufferable whines and protestations of Officer Piper. Hell, I even started wishing Bluebeard would start talking more if it meant less of that guy.

Daylight crept in through the seams of the bag on my head. I was completely disoriented, I had no idea what time it was anymore. All I knew was that the sun was shining.

'Alright back there, fuckface?' called Piper. 'Shame you're missing the scenery!'

'You're an idiot, Piper,' said Bluebeard as the engine hummed on.

'*What?*'

'I don't know why you insist on throwing that bag over his head. If Jack here is foolish enough to descend upon Papa Bear's manor, he'll know exactly how to do it.'

'Yeah? Why's that?

'Because . . . his accomplice used to *work* for us! You dope!' Bluebeard yelled. It was the first time I'd heard him raise his voice. 'Of course, would be suicide for them to try it.'

'Yeah,' murmured Piper, and his voice got slightly louder, which I guess was from him turning to face me. 'It would.'

We drove on, only the sound of the engine and air outside an open window filling the silence. It was the most peaceful I'd felt in hours, and I was still a hostage.

'Officer Piper,' I finally said.

'Ahh, he speaks.'

'Cole put you up to this?'

He sighed, paused for a minute, then chuckled quietly. 'I ain't talking, Jack. Don't bother.'

'Whatever's happened here, well, you're, what, the cleaner?' Then there was a rough clicking noise, like the sound of marbles crashing together. I realized Piper was grinding his teeth.

'Don't go there, brother.'

'What's going on?' I was saying, getting loud now, uncontrollably. 'Is this what the fuck you signed up for? It was you who shot Emily Wyatt, wasn't it? Or someone you're working with. You're *all* involved with Dumpty, with the missing women and children. But it's me with my life on the line. You think you can blackmail me into staying silent, into letting you carry on?' Now I was yelling, no longer in control of what was coming out of my mouth.

'Quiet now,' said Bluebeard. 'You've got it all wrong.'

'Piper, you piece of shit, talk to me! What the fuck is going on!?'

'*Enough!*' yelled Piper. 'I ain't gonna listen to your bullshit. If you're not with us, then I will not hesitate to stop this goddamn vehicle right now and blow your brains out. I'll find the girl myself, then I'll splatter her brains all over the wall and play with her body for a while before hanging it from the top of Papa's mansion.' He was really screaming now. 'No longer will you be remembered as the man who took down a giant; everybody will know the truth, about how the coward Jackson Slade killed his own mother, became a junkie, and started having his way with a psycho outlaw and leaving his mess all over her headless body!'

My body suddenly jolted to the left, my head smacking into the window. There was a collective scream as the vehicle flipped. I tried to force my body against the seat, attempting to defeat gravity somehow. The car flipped again and again before we dropped hard into what felt like a ditch. It was over before I could tell if I was even still alive.

I heard Piper's breathing. He was wheezing and spluttering. 'What, what, what, WHAT?'

A warm wetness trickled down my forehead into my eyes. Here I was again, in another more than perilous situation with a bloodied sack on my head.

There was a metallic scraping sound as Bluebeard began to yell. 'No, no NO. Not you . . .' Then the unmistakable sound of the butt of a gun making swift contact with a skull.

'No, wait!' yelled Piper. Another crack against the skull.

The metallic scraping again. It sounded like a crowbar lodging into the door. I heard the door swing open, then two arms hooked under my shoulders. I was lifted out of the wreckage, then I fell to my knees.

The ground was soft and wet. I began tipping forward before someone placed a hand on my chest, gently pushing me back so I was resting against the upturned car. Someone slipped a key into my handcuffs. There was tugging around my neck. The sack on my head loosened, then was pulled off.

I let out a huge breath and instantly started to laugh for all kinds of reasons.

With my one open eye, I made out the face of Goldilocks, striking and radiant.

'Quite a suit,' she said, the familiar smirk returning. 'Shame you've wrecked it already.' She reached into a back pocket and took out a white cloth, dabbing at the blood over my eye. I winced and inhaled through my teeth. 'Sorry, sorry, hold still.'

The rising sun turned her dark eyes a glimmering bronze. They watched intently as she wiped at the wound.

'What the hell happened?' I said, sounding almost disinterested.

Goldilocks made a sound through her nose. 'You first.' She stopped tending the wound and stared into my eyes. 'Jack, what the hell were you doin over here?'

'I got a lead,' I said, the taste of blood thick in my mouth. Everything smelled like iron. My head was heavy and slow. 'I went to Odette's place, tried to piece things together, about missing girls, y'know. She's involved. Anyway, I left, went outside, ambushed. Woke up . . . in there.'

Goldilocks looked over her shoulder, then back to me, a severe look on her face, lips pressed together tightly. 'And he let you live,' she said, to herself more than me.

'He . . . Yeah, he let me live.'

Her eyes stayed fixed on mine for a few seconds, some kind of doubt working behind them. She put the cloth back to the wound, which was persistent in its bleeding.

I was getting woozy.

'Looks like this is gonna need stitches,' said Goldilocks, changing the subject. 'Or something. But you ain't goin to a hospital,' she added sternly.

'Hold up. Who are you to tell me where I'm going or not?'

'Oh, give me a break. I just saved your ass,' she hissed.

I sighed and checked the area out. We were in a ditch by the side of a road. There was nothing in sight besides clusters of trees and a sea of mist. Everything was gray now, the sun submerged in thick clouds. It looked like I'd spawned into a half-loaded video game map. 'Where is this?' I said, rubbing my eyes with my free hand, trying anything to fix my vision.

'Long way from the city,' said Goldilocks. 'And somewhere we shouldn't be hangin out much longer.'

I remembered the magick beans in my breast pocket then, their magick calling to me, right to my heart. I reached into the pocket, took out the little sack, and tipped the beans into my palm. I swallowed two of them.

Goldilocks shot me a look, arms by her sides, eyes wide. 'That gonna heal your wound? I'm tryna stop the bleedin here; quit jerkin around.' Then she grabbed me by a scruff of hair and reapplied the bloodied cloth once again.

I laughed, the magick shooting through my body. 'Good job these things have already kicked in.'

She shot to her feet, a revolver suddenly in her grip. She walked over to Piper, who was either unconscious or dead. The revolver hovered above his head.

'Whoa, whoa!' I called out. 'Is he alive?'

'Hell if I know,' said Goldilocks, then crouched next to him and took his pulse. 'Yep, afraid so.'

'Well don't kill him. I can question him, use him.'

'If I was gonna kill him, I woulda done it before.'

'Like you almost just did to me, too, huh.'

'Oh, knock it off, Jack. It was a perfectly calculated shot. If anyone else took that shot, you'd be sufferin a lot more than a head wound. You should be thankin me.'

I chewed my lip, laughing quietly to myself. 'Maybe I should be,' I muttered. 'Thanks.'

Goldilocks snorted. 'Naw, I don't want your thanks.'

Of course.

As power circulated through my system, I rose to my feet and dusted myself down. I was starting to feel something close to great, but this time, a nagging thought appeared at the front of my mind: that it wouldn't last, that the comedowns were only going to get worse. Then I would need more magick beans.

I thought about the bear. This was the power he had over me now. Had I really exhausted the witches' supply? Was it now a case of gaining magick beans through Arminus or not gaining them at all? If I didn't get them in my system consistently enough, I would practically rot to death. I couldn't help but entertain the idea that rotting away was looking like the best bet.

Bluebeard's mangled body protruded from a dead row of bushes behind the overturned car. I walked over, the magick telling me – despite the state of his body – he was still breathing. I patted him down, searching for anything I could use for evidence in the case, if you could even call it that.

'Nope,' said Goldilocks, suddenly standing by my side, slender hand on her hip. She held a key in her other hand. 'This is all he had on him. For the cuffs.' She reached into her pocket and pulled out my phone. Half the screen was smashed. 'And this.'

I took it, shoved it into my pocket though the thing was damn near useless now.

'Other than those, he wasn't carryin a thing. Probably knew there was a chance I'd screw him up, so didn't wanna carry anything incriminating. Bastard always did think ahead.'

'Damn,' I murmured. Then the bloody cloth fell from my head as I grabbed Goldilocks by the wrist. As soon as she made the slightest move, my senses realized what she was about to do.

'Hey!' she yelled, her face screwed up. 'No, this one *has* to die.'

'No, no, no,' I said, shaking my head. 'What makes him so special? He's as fucked-up as the rest of them. We can't kill him; I need him, too.'

'You don't understand,' she said as I loosened my grip. Suddenly she looked like a sulking teenager. 'You really don't... understand.' She stared at Bluebeard, his body a crumpled heap.

'I think he'll be feeling more than enough pain by the time he wakes up,' I replied. 'Look at his leg, definitely broken. He'll have scars everywhere, trauma, all of that—'

'Yeah, and knowin him, he'll enjoy it.'

This time, even the magick beans weren't enough for me to react when I needed to.

Goldilocks raised the revolver in a flash and fired.

My arm reached out, my hand burned with a brief sting as it wrapped around the firing gun. The bullet flew into a tree above Bluebeard's body and Goldilocks stumbled back. The revolver fell to the dirt.

Then Goldilocks let out a scream, a scream like a banshee, and clawed at the side of her face.

'Stop!' I heard myself yelling.

And just as soon as she'd yelled, she did stop. Her hands covered her heart, her face hidden in the mass of gold hair. Her shoulders rose and fell as she took slow, deep breaths.

It was near silent for a while. There was only the sound of a light wind streaming through the trees, and Goldilocks's shaky, boiling intakes of misty air.

Finally, she looked up at me. Her face was scarily blank. 'My bad,' she said. 'You're right.'

I realized I was still holding my hands out toward her in apprehension. I dropped them.

Slowly, Goldilocks stepped toward the revolver, leaves crunching beneath her boots. She picked it up, held it by her side for a moment, then holstered it, watching the motionless Bluebeard the whole time.

'Uh, what— What shall we do with them?'

Goldilocks sniffed sharply. 'Got this car parked up the road. The one I tailed y'all in.'

'Yeah, so how—'

'I'll get into that. Help me move him first.' She gestured toward Officer Piper, who was sprawled across the ground, close to the roadside.

'I'll do it,' I said. With the strength given to me by the magick beans, it was next to no effort lifting his limp body. I planted my feet into the ground and dragged him by his ankles up to the roadside. Goldilocks stood watching, hands on her hips, mouth slightly open. She'd tucked her hair behind her ears since the outburst. She looked less feral, but still agitated.

'Here,' she said, throwing me some car keys. 'Shove him in the trunk.'

I nodded, heaved Piper over my shoulder, checked the road for any activity, then walked over to the car, which was parked in the shade of a group of towering maple trees. It was a shitty gray sedan, a perfectly unremarkable car you wouldn't look at twice.

I pulled open the trunk, which squealed as it rose, and threw Piper inside.

Then I spun where I stood, listened, and ran back to where Goldilocks was.

Because something had moved nearby, and it wasn't her.

'Shit!' I hissed, letting myself slide down into the ditch.

'What?' said Goldilocks, whipping out her gun. I did the same.

I brushed past her, walking over to the wreckage. I peered around it, expecting to see Bluebeard's unconscious body. There was nothing there.

'You kiddin me,' whispered Goldilocks. 'How the hell . . .'

I honed in on my senses, all of them. I fell back a little, my grip on the handgun too tight. It was all noise – endless, vicious noise. Goldilocks was trying to say something but she was just another sound in the symphony of chaos. I focused on my vision instead. All I could pick up was the mass of leaves and dirt and moss. There was life, that's for sure, life absolutely everywhere. But each creature was indistinguishable from the other. What might have been an ant might have just as easily been a goblin, or a wolf, or a man. The forms I saw were just like the noise – endless, infinitely complex, catastrophically overwhelming.

'Jack!'

Then there was a deafening bang, and I collapsed where I stood.

It was all over. I was on the ground, streams of sweat mixing with the blood on my face. When I looked up, I saw the back of Goldilocks, staring out into the distance. I blinked and her face was inches from mine, then back in the distance, then back again.

I shook my head, wiped at my eyes, at the blood. 'What is happening?' I breathed.

I stared at Goldilocks – through her – and tried to get to my feet.

'No,' she murmured before looking over her shoulders. She pressed a hand to my chest. 'Forget him. You need help.'

I puffed out my cheeks. 'Yup.'

'I know a guy.'

'Hospital?'

She shook her head adamantly. 'Course not. Blood seems to be stoppin, at least.'

Pain came in waves. Where magick had been coursing through my veins, a soaring burning sensation now spread. It felt like the worst hangover you could ever have while still being alive combined with the motion of flying through a window, shards of glass sticking into every part of you as you descended for what seemed like an eternity.

For a split second, I felt a little smirk creep onto my face, realizing I was witnessing something close to what Dick Dumpty felt before he crashed into pieces on the Manhattan concrete.

I faded in and out of consciousness. This time when I opened my eyes, I was back inside a car.

We seemed to be coming out of the misty landscape and back toward civilization.

We passed a few gas stations, abandoned motels, and lonely houses. The city's skyline hovered on the horizon.

'He got away, but I'll find him again,' said Goldilocks, one hand on the steering wheel, the other near her face as she chewed her nails thoughtfully. 'Our paths are gonna cross a couple more times before this is all over, we can be sure of that. I *will* kill him.'

'Sure,' I grumbled, lifting my head from where I'd laid it on the car door during my slumber.

'How you feelin?'

'Just about the worst I've ever felt in my life. Yeah, it's up there. Damn.' I pressed my fingers to my eyelids. The magick beans were still doing their thing, whatever the hell their thing now was. It was like I had to manually switch off my senses to escape the pain, the noise.

What I'd just had wasn't sleep – it was my body giving up.

We took a right turn and cruised under the shade of the trees.

'Need to keep to the back roads,' said Goldilocks. 'You well enough to talk?'

I laughed, not entirely sure why. 'To talk?' I repeated helpfully.

'Yeah.'

'Maybe. Probably not.'

'I'd like you to,' she said, watching the side of my head. I avoided eye contact. I felt like turning my head would cause it to snap off. 'Talk to me. What did he want? Why are you still alive?'

'Right now I kinda wish I wasn't.'

'You'll get over it.'

Usually I would agree. It's hardly like I'm unfamiliar with comedowns from having magick inside me that probably shouldn't be. I'm a mess. But this was something else. As if the magick was malfunctioning in some way.

'The beans I took. He gave them to me. Arminus.'

'And you just couldn't help yourself, huh?'

'No, they seem . . . different. I don't know. I'm not sure he had anything to do with it. Why would he let me go in one piece and then fuck me up with some shady beans?'

Goldilocks tapped her fingers on the wheel to no apparent rhythm. Like she was on edge. 'Well, let's start with the first question – why did he let you go in one piece?'

I knew the question had to be answered, somehow. But I still wasn't ready to try and answer it. I thought about the supply of magick beans, and the bear's demand. Then I started to think about the effects of the beans I'd just taken, how they seemed to put me at death's door. Why would Arminus give me a sample that would mess me up like that? Hardly like it would tempt me back in.

Either he doesn't know something's wrong with them, or nothing's wrong with them at all, and I'm the problem.

'Well?' said Goldilocks, her voice suddenly loud and insistent. 'He wants somethin, doesn't he?'

'I don't know,' I stammered. 'Maybe he wants to use me, thinks I can play a part in his plans.'

'His plans? And what are they?'

'I don't know! You tell me, you're the one who worked for him.'

Goldilocks shook her head and pounded a fist on the wheel. We were traversing a blurred sea of trees, hypnotic green and blue. 'Slade, if you're compromised, you have to tell me. Now. Much as it pains me to admit, if you're workin with him, in whatever capacity, you're a danger to me – one of the only people alive who is.'

There was nothing I could say – certainly not the truth.

'Look,' said Goldilocks, 'I ain't anywhere near trustin you, and I wish I wasn't even in the position where I needed to trust another person, not to mention a cop. But as I told you, if we're gonna work together and actually pull somethin off, you gotta answer my questions.'

I scoffed. 'Somehow I don't see that working both ways.'

'It works how I say it works.'

Again, I went silent. I couldn't even think straight, let alone come to any important decision or conclusion. About anything.

'Whatever,' she said. 'Guess we'll have to come back to that.'

After a few minutes of unbearably tense silence, I mumbled, 'Where are we going?'

'Hatter,' she said.

I didn't know what that meant. I didn't ask. We just drove along the empty back roads in silence until we reached the outskirts of the city.

Goldilocks brought the car to a stop. We were in some suburban area. Everything was flat and gray, dark clouds rolling in low and fast. I watched her eyes as she thought, flicking across the horizon. She chewed her lip and sighed before eyeing the rearview mirror.

'We get tailed?' I asked dumbly.

'No,' she said. 'Who is he?'

'Huh?'

'In the trunk.'

Part of me had forgotten he'd been stuffed inside the trunk, unconscious and helpless. It brought me a little joy, the idea of him waking up in there, petrified and baffled. Though he was probably still in better shape than I was right now.

'He's Officer Piper,' I said. 'Nasty piece of work. Working for both the chief and the bear. Get the feeling he knows a hell of a lot.'

'Well,' said Goldilocks as she opened the car door, 'here's to hopin he talks more than you have.'

My head tipped back against the car seat. I let out a huge sigh, feeling all kinds of pain and frustration and confusion. I swung open the car door and joined Goldilocks by the trunk. She pulled it open and Piper's eyes stared back at us, wide and wild.

'You're up!' said Goldilocks with fake merriment.

Piper sucked in a breath, held up his hands, and yelled, 'You have to listen! Wait, no, please—'

Goldilocks grabbed a wheel of duct tape from the trunk, tore a piece off, and slammed it against his loud mouth. She turned to me, half smirking, half glaring. 'See, he can't wait to spill his guts.' She turned back to Piper, pulling back her jacket to reveal the glaring knife underneath it. 'And neither can I.'

'Stop,' I said, barely able to stay on my feet.

'What? You cut a deal?' She looked at Piper again. 'Slade cut a deal, huh?' she said, motioning to me wildly with the knife.

Piper only screamed underneath the tape in reply.

'You're crazy,' I murmured, leaning an arm against the car for balance. 'Can you tell me what's going on? Why are we here? Who's

Hatter?' And suddenly a repressed rage rocketed up through my body. 'Look, we *can't* just keep each other in the dark; it's too fucking dangerous to play these shit games. It's not funny. People are after us. We could be dead in a fucking second if we aren't careful.'

Piper whimpered.

'Yeah, Jack,' said Goldilocks. 'You just described my entire existence. You don't have to tell me. So be goddamn straight with me, or we're done for. Probably both of us, but definitely you. Why did you come back if you ain't gonna talk?'

'Come *back*? You abducted me, nearly killing me in the process! I didn't ask for this; don't pretend I did.'

Suddenly she gripped me by the forearm and there was fire in her eyes. 'Are we doin this?' she hissed. '*Are we*?'

I guess we were. She was right. I wasn't walking away from anything; I was putting myself in these positions, over and over, and I was going to keep doing it. The future was a raging black storm, volatile, bleak, repellant – but I knew I was walking into it now, no matter the toll. That much was pretty clear.

Goldilocks must have seen the answer in my eyes – I didn't need to say a thing. The flames dimmed. She released her grip and nodded faintly.

She glanced around the street. It looked stark and bare, like it was fading away. 'Alright, help me move him.'

'What is this place?' I asked.

'Somewhere we won't have to worry about peepin toms.' She shoved Piper onto his front, and he started kicking wildly. As I grabbed his flailing ankles, she tore off another piece of duct tape with her teeth and bound his wrists. We both stopped and stared at each other as a rumbling sound vibrated through the air.

I peered around the elevated door and saw two choppers flying across the sky. Rain began to pour. They were some distance away and didn't seem to be coming toward us, but I didn't feel like taking any chances.

'Eh, don't worry about it,' said Goldilocks before heaving half of Piper's body out of the trunk by his shoulders.

I waved her away, staring at the choppers until they were small black dots under the gray clouds. They flew back toward the New York skyline, barely visible now in the growing mist. The rain pelted down, soaking us through in seconds. The cold sent shivers up my spine. Goldilocks watched me impatiently as I grabbed Piper by the ankles. We heaved him onto his feet and Goldilocks slammed the trunk shut.

While I checked the street, I jumped at the sound of a blade unsheathing.

'Try anything, it's all over.' Goldilocks had her knife pressed to Piper's belly, hatred all over her face. The fear in Piper's eyes seemed to leave then, and he returned her a look of resentment. It made me uneasy, a little twitchy. 'Come on,' said Goldilocks, and we headed toward one of the houses, grabbing an arm each.

Piper's physical resistance was gone. He just walked along, glaring ahead with glassy eyes.

'This one,' said Goldilocks.

We came up to one of the houses, which was nearly identical to the others, besides being surrounded by a low metal fence. Goldilocks pushed open the gate silently, and we stepped onto the porch. The house was small and ordinary, its paint chipping off to the point it was more of a brown shade than the intended white. The glass in the windows looked frail, paper-thin, like a single tap of the finger would explode it into fragments.

The weird thing was the glass was like a mirror, not a window. You couldn't see inside at all; we just stared back at ourselves, standing in a void of dark purple mist.

I looked at Goldilocks. 'You seeing this?'

She smirked and pushed open the front door. It was already ajar.

I didn't bother asking any more questions – they weren't exactly getting me anywhere, and I was starting to think I was better off just observing.

We walked inside a dark front room, clearly disused and abandoned. The smell of wet grass flew up my nose, and I was suddenly cold, colder inside than out there. A black sofa bursting with stuffing sat across the room diagonally, surrounded by towers of taped-up boxes. Dark stains had been splattered across the white walls. I worried about what they were.

So did Piper as he tensed up again in our grip. He mumbled under the duct tape. Then he growled, and tried to plant himself where we stood.

Slowly, Goldilocks turned her attention to him, swiveling on her heel. She launched a fist into his stomach, just as Piper had done to me, and he hollered and bent over. Goldilocks tugged at him and brought him toward an archway that led into what was supposed to be a kitchen.

I wasn't even holding onto Piper now. She was in control, for better or worse.

In the kitchen, the window had been boarded up, letting no light in at all. Broken tiles were scattered all over the floor, and only a fridge occupied this part of the shithole.

Thinking I heard a sound nearby, I attempted to tune into my enhanced hearing. All the noise, the violent clutter, was gone. At least most of it. So some of the magick remained, and I realized there was a man downstairs, right below us.

Metal scraped against metal. A low voice hummed and murmured. Utensils clattered against wood. I also heard a weird wet, popping sound, like bubbles boiling.

I shifted my attention away from the stink of damp and focused on the smells down in the basement as we walked toward the descending wooden stairs. The aroma was nothing like anything I'd ever smelt before. It was completely unfamiliar, like it wasn't of our world.

Goldilocks clocked the look of bemusement that'd taken over my face and laughed, then she went down the steps. Piper following cautiously, evidently doing his best to not trip and crush his face even more.

At this point, the smell from downstairs was unrelenting, and I don't know if that's what finished me off or not, but my body'd had enough. Backing away from the first step, I hit the wall behind me and began to close my eyes. As I was fading, I felt an ice-cold substance cover my back, and the smell – the smell of another world, deadly and unearthly – seemed to turn into a physical being, and suffocate me with its unfathomable frame.

When I came back into consciousness, I was somewhere else entirely, as if I'd transported there. I seemed to be lying on a cold metal surface, my body held down by a force that wasn't actually there. Seemed to be somehow the same cold surface I'd felt while passing out before.

My head still hurt and I still felt like shit. Seemed as though I'd eternally feel like shit at this point.

I heaved my eyelids open, but they immediately snapped shut after being attacked by a blinding white light. I wheezed a horribly long cough that nearly suffocated me, and grasped at my throat.

A low, almost whispering voice, said, 'No, no, stay still. For God's sake, what a time to wake up.' Then it chuckled. Sounded like a British accent.

'I'm gonna piss myself!' I said, eyes still clenched shut.

The voice got a little louder. 'Don't you dare piss on my equipment, you blond bastard.'

Gloved hands grabbed at my shoulders, almost shoving me off the surface.

'G'wan, get off! Go piss in the corner if you must.'

Suddenly there was no more surface beneath me. I opened my eyes but could only see giant yellow blotches. My arms flailed out desperately, hoping for anything to hold onto. There was nothing, and I crashed to the floor, a bunch of metal tools clattering on top of and around me.

'*Bloody idiot!*' roared the Englishman among the symphony of clashing knives and scalpels. I could partly see now, saw it on the floor, bloodied surgical equipment. There was also an array of test tubes, spilling out weirdly colored chemicals onto the ground. I scrambled to my feet and turned to face the supposed surgeon.

Before I could even process my sight, a voice from behind said, 'Hell was that noise?'

I turned to face Goldilocks. 'What is this?' I asked in a pitch that took me by surprise.

The surgeon spoke. 'Well, Miss Robicheaux, your delightful companion here decided he ought to disrupt my surgical quest by wriggling around on the table and complaining about the state of his bladder. He then proceeded to attempt to fly almost, and evidently dealt some swift damage to some of my tools there, you see?' The man pointed to the collection of damaged equipment with a long, gray finger.

He was a strange-looking guy, to say the least. He was tall and slender, with gray, slicked-back hair and a stern, bony face. A white lab coat stained with giant patches of red and brown hung over his frame. He wore circular goggles with thick black lenses that took up half his face.

I glanced around the room I was in. Some sort of basement – broken furniture absolutely everywhere, stacks of boxes filled with books, and more surgical equipment.

'Jack Slade, this is Dr Hatter,' said Goldilocks, motioning at him flippantly.

Dr Hatter began to saunter toward me, outstretching a long arm, offering a gloved hand. 'I am, indeed, Dr Hatter. Jack, I presume?'

'Well, yeah,' I said, reaching out with my own arm, but then deciding thoroughly against it, shoving both hands deep into my pockets. I glanced toward Goldilocks, then back to the "doctor".

'Fair enough, then,' he said, throwing his arm into the air and turning away. 'Have it your way, you impolite little wretch.'

'What . . . What is this?' I asked Goldilocks again.

She smirked and folded her arms. She looked like a plotting cat.

'Dr Hatter,' she said to the man, 'afraid we need your help, your expertise, right now.'

I cleared my throat. 'I gotta say, these don't look like the premises of an expert of anything. We're in a rotting basement.'

Hatter chuckled, and it sounded like gravel dropping onto metal. 'Wrong, lad, wrong! Judge me only when my work is done – until then, keep your trap decidedly closed. To do my work, I require silence, and if not silence, then at the very least only the most minuscule of whimpers emanating from yourself, if the pain becomes too much.'

I looked toward Goldilocks again, like a helpless kid in a doctor's clinic, which I guess I kinda was, in a fucked-up way. Goldilocks's mouth was tightly closed. She shrugged. I could've sworn she was on the verge of erupting into laughter.

I wasn't.

'Now,' rustled Hatter, 'what is it *you* require? Might there be a faerie's poison gushing through your bloodstream, a wound that refuses to close, perhaps from the claws of a grizzly bear, or maybe a disintegrated limb that you might need replacing, inflicted by the darkest and most chaotic of blood spells?'

I sighed, the man's ramblings adding to my headache. 'Do I look like I'm missing a leg or an arm? And did you say "bear"? That's weirdly specific.'

If his eyes weren't concealed by the huge goggles, I might've seen them light up viciously as he grinned.

'Dr Hatter's an old friend, Jack,' said Goldilocks.

'Yes, indeed, it is so,' announced Hatter, stretching his back and placing his hands behind his head. 'We have a mutual former employer, don't we, dear? I have become privy to the young lady's resentment of the great bear, and I know her to be foolish enough to go to war with him.' Suddenly there was an air of severity around Hatter. His eyebrows furrowed behind the goggles and his voice fell into a harsh whisper. 'Jack, artless Jack, are you to tell me you have joined dear Jessica on these evident excursions?'

My mouth hung open for a second. I looked between Hatter and Goldilocks, baffled. 'You could put it like that, sure,' was all I could come up with.

Then Hatter pinched his goggles with long fingers and thumbs and lifted them from his eyes, pushing them onto his head, revealing hard, wild eyes that struck anxiety right into my soul. They seemed to tell me a brief history of his world, and maybe a world that was yet to come. I found myself looking away and swallowing hard.

Visions staggered through my mind. A jagged castle, twisting black towers reaching up to a crimson sky littered with winged monsters. A young, smartly dressed man in the cell of an asylum, hunched over a table, frantically murmuring to himself – or maybe to the hare that sat on the end of his bed. I felt the man's terror and his joy at the same time. It made me feel sick. Hordes of soulless beings gathered before their queen – she was frantic and beautiful. She demanded the company of her daughters, and that someone be beheaded. I tried to break out of this illusion, but I wasn't in control.

A young girl sat in the shadows of a cold, damp room, playing with her knives and waiting for a chance at violence. Then I saw that same woman, the queen, dark red hearts etched into her dress, blood dripping from her hair, and I felt like she was near me. Goldilocks was there, too, with death in the form of a great black cloud grasping at her. She looked at me with red eyes, and then I was dead.

That's when I broke out of the nightmare, my body jumping, then freezing in fear. The sound of my teeth chattering disrupted the silence.

'That seemed . . . lucid,' murmured Hatter.

I looked back into his eyes, but this time nothing seemed to happen. 'Fuck was that!?' I yelled.

Hatter began striding around the cellar, hands pressed together beneath his chin. He was murmuring, spitting words under his breath. I didn't catch any of it, but it was somehow instantly familiar.

'That guy,' I said, dizzy where I stood. 'That was you, in the vision.'

I noticed Goldilocks suddenly beside me, her eyes fixed on me, dark and intense. She said nothing, just observed me, her face pale.

'Hatter!' I shouted.

He stopped, slamming a fist on the work table. 'Where did you find this man again, Jess?'

Goldilocks stammered. 'He's a cop.'

'I *know* that,' he spat. 'But *where* did you find him?'

Goldilocks just arched an eyebrow, shaking her head a little.

He waved her off, then leaned toward me. 'Have you ever been to Wonderland?'

'What?' I said.

'Wonderland!' he yelled, long arms flying through the air.

I ducked instinctively. 'What— No! Where's that?'

'Good,' he said. 'Good, very good, marvelous. That's alright, then. I believe.'

'Doc,' said Goldilocks. 'What's the deal?'

Hatter took a deep breath, pinched the goggles, and placed them back over his eyes. 'The boy Jack, he saw things.'

'And what does that mean?' she said.

I cleared my throat. 'Like a vision,' I said.

'No, no, not a vision, my man. A glimpse into another realm. Fragmented memories, realities, futures that could happen, pasts that didn't, yet did. *Vision* implies something more certain, something yet to be that *will* be, perhaps. What you saw was through the eyes of a great many. Those were their memories, broken memories, but very real nonetheless. Not all of them were ordinary memories, and that would make the others extraordinary. Extraordinary *future* memories, of the sisters, of the guardian angel, of the knave, the dragon, and the others . . . I will not speak of them all, should not. There were countless realities rushing through you in seconds.

But you are not a worthy vessel.'

Now it was the doctor who seemed possessed, staring into nothing, rambling to himself more than to either of us.

He looked up.

'Forget all of this,' he said.

And I realized I already had. Everything I'd just seen had slipped out of my mind and spilled into the dingy air. I'd forgotten the visions that just seconds ago had given me a fleeting existential crisis. It was just like a dream.

'None of that,' Hatter went on, 'was meant for you.' He wiped at a piece of drool hanging from his lip. 'Was it?'

Goldilocks eyed me again. Hints of regret lingered on her face. Slowly, she stepped toward Hatter.

He jumped. 'Ah, yes, of course. Where were we? Let us put this episode behind us. I doubt it is a great cause for concern,' he said, forcing an almost nervous giggle. 'What is it you need from me, as you undertake this less-than-humble quest of striking down the great bear?'

Goldilocks smiled. 'It ain't that simple, Hatter.'

'No?'

'If Jack's with me, he ain't even really in it for Arminus. He's got his own reasons. Although I'll endeavor to suggest he's got a lot of good in him. More than me and more than you. There's a connection between the force he works for, Arminus and the missin kids.'

'Ahh,' breathed Hatter, then tilted his head. 'So you're going to war with the bear *and* the city's policing department, and those it seeks to . . . serve?'

Goldilocks shrugged, almost pouting.

'Well, that's much more humble!' shrieked Hatter, and then burst into a short fit of laughter.

Goldilocks walked over and pushed me back onto the metal table.

'Ey!' I called, feeling pretty delicate.

She pointed to the wound on my head. 'Case your doctor's eyes ain't noticed, *this* is what we need fixin.'

'Oh, certainly,' said Hatter, collecting himself. 'Easy. Too easy. Tedious, almost. Very well, you shall gain my aid here. Then I will name my price.'

I looked at Goldilocks. She was smirking. I frowned. 'Oh, I got just the payment,' she drawled.

'I believe you are aware that, these days, I have very little use for the American dollar.'

Goldilocks was nodding excitedly.

'My preference, when dealing with the subject of remittance, might be deemed unorthodox yet entirely *practical*. Yes, if you were to supply me with something that could aid me in my research and experiments, I would be stupendously grateful.' The doctor clasped his hands together and raised his shoulders, looking between us like a hopeful child. I was unnerved.

'I know your taste, doc,' said Goldilocks.

Next thing, I was stretched across the metal table, staring up into the blinding light. I squeezed my eyes shut then opened them to get a look at what Hatter was doing.

He was hunched over the worktable, murmuring again, looking for things, pouring weird liquids into vials and ceramic bottles. That sight brought one of the forgotten memories back to me – it was nearly identical to the guy poring over his desk in the asylum, the hare with wild eyes perching next to him on a bed. My heart started to race, and the memory slipped away again.

I turned my head to Goldilocks now. She stared back at me with a stony expression, her eyes slanting downward, chin slightly raised. It conveyed something between judgement and fear for me.

'Ahh,' went Hatter.

I jumped and swung my head to look at him. He was prowling toward me. A giant syringe protruded from his gloved grasp. The whole thing glowed neon pink, some kind of steam rising from it.

'What the hell,' I said, 'is that?'

Hatter's face was stern. 'I would absolutely, positively love to tell you, but I wonder if my efforts would be in vain. In fact, I can assure you they would be. The particulars of my medical procedures expand far beyond the modest, cozy amplitude of your brain, which is, may I remind you, in and of itself, dwindling as we speak.'

I gulped. It was comically audible. But no one was laughing, and I was pretty close to shitting myself now.

Hatter was right beside me, observing the syringe in his hand. The fluid inside looked alive somehow, like it had thoughts and objectives. Bubbles grew and popped. The stuff was nearly as bright as the lights glaring down above me. 'Have no fear,' he ordered, 'you are in the hands of arguably the most capable medical and or magickal practitioner in the neighborhood!'

The neighborhood. The empty neighborhood. I just hoped he was trying to be amusing.

'But don't take my word for it! Just consult the seven-hundred-and-eighty-second edition of *The Annual Enchantment Review*, in which I was voted Magickal Person Least Likely to Cause a Disaster! Or a certain volume, the number of which has slipped my crowded brain, of *Wonderland Weekly*, in which I was proclaimed Physicist of the Decade!'

'You just made that up,' mumbled Goldilocks.

The syringe was hovering above my head. The heat from the steam made my head sweat. My wound screeched in fear, and so did I, as Hatter plunged the syringe into my chest, the needle surely meeting my heart.

I gripped the sides of the table so hard, my hands went numb. I screamed and yelled, but the pain never came.

I was fine, I think.

The syringe flew upward, out of my chest and into the air. Hatter held it there, his mouth gaping, arms spread out. 'Behold,' he said.

I immediately looked down at where he'd stabbed me. It was glowing underneath my shirt, a swirling pattern, purple and pink. I ripped open my shirt to get a look, panting and heaving. It looked like a minuscule galaxy sitting there, working its mysterious magick I'd blindly just agreed to.

'Behold,' said Hatter again, in a low whisper. He lowered himself into a swivel chair.

Goldilocks peered over, then looked into my eyes, then my forehead. 'Hmm.' She nodded in approval.

'Tis all but done,' said Hatter as he swiveled away to one of the cluttered worktops.

For the first time in months, and especially the last few days, I felt strong, healthy. Genuinely well. And it was instant. It wasn't the kind of strength I gained from magick beans; it didn't feel artificial, temporary. It was real and good.

'What did you do?' I asked, watching the magick pattern on my chest spiral away.

'My work,' said Hatter proudly. 'I learned a great deal of such magick during my time as the Red Queen's personal physician, in her loyal court. Before . . .' He flew toward me in his chair with a rumble. 'Enough of that,' he said, patting my hand. 'Your payment?'

I heard Goldilocks's boots scrape the ground. She stepped closer. 'You're gonna love this,' she said to Hatter with a grin, and vanished up the stairs. There was a loud thump followed by the sound of shuffling footsteps.

I sat up on the table, then instantly lowered myself, realization hitting me in the head and heart. 'Oh no,' I murmured, watching the steps in anticipation.

Goldilocks returned, and she wasn't alone.

She ushered the subdued Officer Piper into the room. His eyes were red and wild with terror. He squirmed and shook, yelling underneath the tape plastered to his mouth.

Hatter shot to his feet. 'Yes! Perfection! A human body!' he shouted. 'And it's *living*!' He trotted over to a wooden chair and dragged it along the ground loudly. 'Put him there, that's it, that's it, yes.'

'Robicheaux,' I said, my voice flat. Suddenly the newfound strength was gone. I was deflated.

She looked at me, nothing behind the eyes. 'C'mon, Jack. What do we have to lose? He'll just become one less problem.'

'He'll become an even bigger one,' I said.

'What does that mean?'

Hatter fawned over his subject, muttering ideas and declarations to himself.

'We can't do this.'

'Why? You two *are* friends, then, huh?'

'No, you— No. It's not that. It's . . . fucked.'

'Well, we're playin a fucked game, ain't we? I thought you understood. Thought you got it, that this is how it's gonna have to be now. We take what we can get. And sometimes we gotta do things we don't necessarily like.'

'You seem to be enjoying it just fine,' I said.

'Man, step back. He's workin for your chief *and* Papa Bear. He chose this. The world's gonna be a better place without him, and you know it,' she hissed.

Hatter emerged, towering in the space between us. 'Now, now, you two. Is there really enough time for you to squabble like this? Bad things are coming, things much worse than what happens here.' He nodded toward Piper. 'If you are serious about your quest, you ought to get on with things. I can show you the door, if you like.'

'No, thank you, Doctor,' said Goldilocks, still watching me.

'Is the exchange done, then? He's mine?' There was violence in his voice now.

I buried my head in my hands. '*Fuck*.'

Goldilocks nodded.

'Excellent!'

Piper, he looked so small and frail then.

Goldilocks hauled him up, gripping him firmly by the arm, and pushed the offering in Hatter's direction. There he was under the bright light, in his glory – Hatter's payment.

I left the room.

As I passed Officer Piper, we made brief eye contact. In his eyes was the ultimate fear. I knew that look would stick with me forever.

Somehow, out of all the terrified faces I'd seen throughout my career – from kids suddenly left orphaned, or someone wrongfully sentenced to life in prison – I knew Piper's face was going to haunt me the most. Probably because the terror had been put there partly by my hand.

A shiver passed through me as I heard the sound of the duct tape being torn from Piper's face. He moaned and growled then screamed and pleaded as Hatter ushered him up toward the table and told him to stay calm.

As I started to go up the stairs and leave this place, I caught a glimpse of Goldilocks facing my way as she came to follow. There was something like a smile there.

'I thank you greatly for this lavish transaction, my dear Jack, my dear Goldilocks!' proclaimed Hatter. 'All the best to you – I do hope your accomplishments will be many. You know where to find me.' Then he opened up some kind of refrigerated door, pulling a long furry material out of it. It flopped limply in his arms, like some dead thing. I looked away.

'Wait, no! Fuckin wait!' screamed Piper. I wasn't waiting. I was leaving. 'You're making a mistake, goddammit! Don't do this! I'm a police officer! Jack, *I'm a fuckin police officer!*'

I walked through the house, out the door, into the front yard. Goldilocks followed. I slammed the door shut behind us, silencing the screams of Officer Piper.

8

THE PIED PIPER

Back in the car, I was numb, confused, and angry. Even though I should have felt physically okay now, I was completely conflicted, mentally exhausted. There was no point in me having this newfound strength if my mind felt like a swamp.

The streets became more familiar as we passed through them. We were headed through Queens, back toward Goldilocks's place. When I looked at my phone, it notified me of five missed calls from work. I swiped them away and put the phone back in my pocket. Goldilocks drove in silence until we came to a traffic stop not far from her apartment.

She was eyeing the rearview mirror as she spoke. 'How you feelin? Your head?' she said distantly.

'I uh... Externally? Much better. But the inside of my head...' I puffed out my cheeks. More silence. 'I'd be talking out my ass if I said I'm not a little concerned about possible side effects. Probably should have asked him about that,' I said, half-trying to introduce a little levity to the atmosphere.

'You'll be fine,' she said dryly, employing her benevolent bedside manner. Finally she budged, addressing the dragon that filled this interior. 'Look, you really mad about what just happened? Don't come back. You'll just be a hindrance. I ain't sayin any more on it.'

'After what we've done, what makes us any better than the guys we're going after?' I asked in a voice that came out so timid, I felt embarrassed.

Goldilocks was silent again for a moment. 'I can't believe you're even askin me that,' she said.

'Listen to me,' I said, trying to inject more authority into my voice. 'You might have murdered your way through life up to now, but there comes a point where that's not an option if you want to live. We have to choose our battles now.'

'And that's exactly what I'm doin, Jack. Don't you see that? We might've just saved your life by givin up that scumbag. He had to go, for *your* sake. And now, what happens to him happens.'

We pulled into Goldilocks's block. Her eyes seemed to spend more time on the mirror than on the road. The streets were dark and dead in the shadows of skyscrapers and enormous construction cranes. Like last time, the sidewalks were nearly empty, the shops closed or desolate. She parked behind the block of apartments, or storage rooms, and turned off the engine.

She turned to look at me.

I frowned back.

'He told you to kill me, didn't he?' she asked.

I hesitated. 'No, I . . .' My eyes flicked down, and I was staring into the barrel of a revolver.

'Don't lie to me,' she said. 'I smell it on you. The deceit.'

The words "you're crazy!" kept floating around in my head, trying to latch onto my tongue. I didn't let them. And who the hell would I have been to say the words, anyway? She was crazy on some level, but not here, not now. She was right not to trust me.

I started to think about the magick beans again, and I audibly sighed. Even though they'd done more bad than good recently, I still needed them. *Needed* them. They were going to kill me, but they were also the only reason I was still alive. I'd cheated death with them, battled through things that would have otherwise killed me with them. They'd become a part of me, for better or worse. The comedowns were just the price I'd paid for all the times they'd saved my life. If they're going to kill me, they're also going to get me where I need to go first.

Sweat dripped into my eyes. 'He wants me to deliver you to him,' I croaked. 'Alive.'

Goldilocks's lips curled up on one side. 'How long you been workin for him?'

I made a noise that wasn't quite a laugh. She reminded me of the existence of the gun, nudging it into my thigh. 'I don't work for him. I don't *work* for him.'

'Hell would you call it?'

'Being compromised.'

Goldilocks breathed in through her nose softly. Her brown eyes had turned black, and so had the sky. 'I came after you because I thought you were better than that. Now, I knew you were far from perfect, you're a cop. But I thought maybe you'd last at least a week before turnin,' she said with a smile full of pity.

'I haven't. *Turned*.'

'Nuh-uh?'

'Do you think I'd do it? Turn you in?'

She turned her mouth even smaller, her eyes narrowed. 'Do you *think* you'd do it?'

'I don't know,' I said. And I was being honest. Then something flickered in the corner of my eye, some kind of swift movement.

'Look at me, Jack, not out there. And give me one reason I shouldn't wash the fuckin windows with your blood and guts, right now.'

I shuddered, my eyes fixing on Goldilocks for a second, then back to where I thought I saw the motion. There were shadows, and a faint light gleaming on the top floor of the block of rooms, where Goldilocks's place was.

'Because,' I said, peering up at the room, 'you might have a more immediate problem. You expecting visitors?'

Goldilocks narrowed her eyes again, but refused to turn her head. If I was plotting an escape, she was too smart to fall for that. But I wasn't plotting anything – two figures wandered past the window of her apartment, barely visible through the blinds.

'Seriously,' I muttered.

She pressed the barrel of the revolver against my leg even harder as she opened the car door with her free hand, glaring at me until she was out and I was locked in.

'No!' I called.

She strode away, watching the apartment window from the shadows, careful to avoid any lights, and vanished round the corner of the building.

'Shit, *shit*!' I hissed, looking for a way out. The only way would be to smash the window. I desperately looked around for something but there was nothing solid enough.

The old car was a heap of shit – it wouldn't take a lot. Hatter's magick would be enough. I took off my jacket, wrapped it around my arm and crashed my elbow into the window. It shattered on the second attempt.

I pushed myself out of the car, shards of glass clinging to me but doing no damage. My gun rested in my holster – I took it out and checked the chamber, still full. I considered charging through the door, up the steps toward Goldilocks's place, and bursting in.

Instead, I opted for a stealthier approach, creeping up the hollow wooden stairs, gun raised. There was talking, Goldilocks's voice followed by a loud distorted kind of sound, not quite a voice. Or if it was, not human. Goldilocks's voice got louder, then there was the sound of quick footsteps, yelling and thumping.

And then the crack of a gunshot. The hall flashed white and I flew up the steps.

I crashed through the door to Goldilocks's place shoulder-first and raised my gun.

The first thing I saw was the black void right below me, a shape in complete darkness. When I looked up, I saw more of the shapes. But these ones were standing upright, in their brimmed hats, black coats, armed with terrifying assault rifles. Their faceless chrome helmets reflected the lights around the room. There were blue and red LED lights on their chest and collar. Goldilocks stood with them. They towered over her. One of them had a gun to the back of her head.

'Shit, wait,' I said.

The form below me started convulsing, bright sparks flying from its chest. A dark liquid trickled from underneath it, and then it was still.

'You fuckin *slime*!' spat Goldilocks my way.

'This wasn't . . .' I didn't bother.

'Detective Jackson Slade!' barked one of the King's Men, stepping toward me briskly. He pointed a monstrous shotgun at my gut. 'Stay right where you are. Lower your weapon. By order of the King's Men, you are under arrest for malfeasance in office.'

Behind him, the King's Man with his gun against Goldilocks's head said, 'Jessica Robicheaux, do not move. You are under arrest for murder, breaking and entering, robbery, battery against police officers, and engaging in organized criminal activity.'

'Drop your weapon or we will not hesitate to shoot,' said my King's Man. And they wouldn't. I've seen it.

My gun clattered to the ground, and within a second, the shotgun guy launched forward and smacked me against the wall, my head bouncing off it. He twisted my arm behind my back and flattened me on the ground. It didn't hurt as much as it could've, but the faint scent of blood hung in the air.

I secretly hoped a broken nose might prove to Goldilocks I had nothing to do with this shit.

The King's Man crushed my back with his knee and pressed my face against the hard floor with his gloved hand. 'Don't move,' he ordered. As if I could. Whatever these guys were made of, it was dense.

I heard Goldilocks grunt on the other side of the room, like she was struggling in the grip of the King's Men. Or getting ready to fight. At this point, I sincerely hoped she wasn't.

Then there was another voice, an unfamiliar one.

'Congrats, folks!' it said.

The King's Man on top of me let go of my head, as if he wanted me to get a look.

I turned my head, spat blood, and saw Goldilocks hunched over with a King's Man gripping each of her arms. She flicked her hair out of her face and stared forward, where the door was. There was a change on her face, something like confusion.

'We got em,' said the owner of the voice. It was a distorted and robotic voice, like the King's Men's, but a lot smoother. He drawled in a southern accent. 'Well done.'

A smile crept along Goldilocks's face. I squirmed against the floor, which vibrated as the sound of slow, heavy footsteps filled the room.

The owner of the voice appeared in my peripheral vision. I strained my neck to get a look, expecting some insane new model of the King's Men. But this thing didn't strike me as one of them at all.

It wore a wine-red wool coat, trailing all the way down to its ankles, with an impressive Stetson to match. Dark brown cowboy boots stamped along the floor and spun. The figure was facing me now, peering down. The sound of mechanical whirring accompanied its slow movements. My heart jumped a little as I looked into its face – a black, patterned balaclava covered the lower half of it, but its eyes glared into mine, human eyes, or almost human. They glowed unnaturally, and squinted as the thing gave a little chuckle.

No, this was no King's Man.

I looked back at Goldilocks, who now had a manner of confidence and determination on her face. I braced myself for whatever the hell was coming next, counting on Hatter's work to prove its worth again.

'And, gentlemen, when I say "we got em,"' the figure said in a low, cool voice, hands by its hips.

I inhaled.

'I mean you,' it growled, glaring at all the King's Men.

'Sir?' one of them said. 'SIR—'

Within a half second, Goldilocks's face turned to an almost joyful grimace. The King's Men raised their guns, aiming them at the cowboy figure, who whipped out two revolvers from holsters. The King's Man on my back yelled and I spun on the ground, knocking the shotgun from his grip and trying to get him in a choke hold. I didn't have time to wonder about how effective choke holds are on machines.

Gunshots went off, and flashes of violent light filled the room. The King's Man broke out of my stupid hold with ease and went to deliver a hard fist to my head. I just about caught it and launched my own blow to his chrome head. My hand rang with a brief shooting pain that was extinguished by both the adrenaline and magick in my veins.

As the King's Man's head snapped back, he reached for the shotgun on the floor. At the same time, I leaped for my handgun. Just as the soldier raised his shotgun to blast my brains out, I fired a couple rounds into his head. He crashed to the ground.

Goldilocks screamed on the other side of the room, and King's Men roared and growled, people crashed and tumbled. I stumbled to my feet and was suddenly in the grip of another King's Man. He clasped his hand around my throat and propelled me into the wall, which I felt partly give way under my back. The soldier drew a huge knife from the inside of his black coat, but he hadn't realized there was a gun in my hand.

Gasping for breath and not even entirely sure where I was aiming, I fired my gun over and over until the barrel was empty. The King's Man fell back but he was still standing, covering his gut with his hands. Then he charged right back at me, arms outstretched. Just before he reached me, the cowboy fired both revolvers, discharging bullets straight into the King's Man's head. He jolted farther and farther across the room until he hit a blood-covered wall, slid down it and crashed to the floor in a heap beside a couple of his associates.

Goldilocks struggled with the last King's Man standing, who was leaking blood from about fifteen different stab wounds, slipping and sliding in it. Even then, he was still too strong and nearly overpowered her.

'Oh, scuse me,' said the cowboy as it walked up to the soldier and smacked his head with the butt of a revolver until he collapsed, then fired one last bullet into the helmet. 'That should do it.'

Goldilocks scrambled over to her gun that had ended up with all the smashed-up furniture, and swung around, aiming it at the unknown figure, who sighed and held up its hands casually.

'I know, I know,' it said calmly, with a hint of amusement. 'I don't entirely blame you, Goldilocks.'

Goldilocks looked between the cowboy and me. I stood there with my mouth open and eyes wide, clueless. She shuffled where she stood, like she was about to make a rash decision.

'Someone expl—' I started.

'Shut up!' snapped Goldilocks, her gun still aimed at the figure in the red coat.

It stepped forward, slowly, methodically toward Goldilocks and lowered its arms. It hummed a robotic chuckle.

She grimaced and pulled the trigger. A loud click followed.

'Goldilocks!' drawled the survivor. 'Last time we met, you almost cost me my handsome face. I thought maybe this time around you'd have at least loaded your weapon.' He snatched the gun from her hand.

'Hey!' I said, stepping forward.

The cowboy peered over his shoulder at me, then turned right back to Goldilocks. 'Don't worry, I ain't here to kill you – not this time,' he said to her, tipping the brim of his hat. 'And you're not gonna retire me just yet, no, missy.'

The absurdity continued. I was feeling more and more out of my depth with every passing hour.

Goldilocks sighed, looking up at the cowboy suspiciously. 'Slade,' she said, 'this is the Marionette.'

'What?' I said.

The Marionette spun on his heels to face me. He took off his hat, revealing smart, chestnut, wavy locks, and bowed. 'Pleasure,' he said. Then, 'Oh, where are my manners?' He pulled down the balaclava to reveal the rest of his face.

At first I thought his skin was covered in burns or scars, but quickly realized that wasn't the case at all. It wasn't even skin. It was wood.

'Hi,' I said while observing his features, trying to be subtle but obviously failing.

The Marionette scooped his hat from his chest and placed it back on his head. 'Salright, buddy, knock yourself out. Doubt you seen my kind before. Specially since I'm the last of us. That'll do it.'

I saw now that the eyes, while designed to be lifelike, were completely artificial, and his mouth moved in an unnatural, staggered kind of way. The pine shell in place of flesh varied in tone, turning from cream to light brown. It was smooth-looking, apart from the chunk missing in his lower left cheek, revealing the wires and circuits beneath. That, I put together, was Goldilocks's work.

'Yeah, sorry,' I said. 'I haven't.'

Goldilocks was glancing around her war zone of an apartment now, looking extra pissed off. She started opening drawers and chests, gathering various items and cash out of them, and stuffing it all into a rucksack. 'Why you here if you ain't here to kill me? she asked aggressively while packing. 'We gotta go,' she said in a low tone as she pulled open another cupboard behind me.

'Well,' said the Marionette, his tone remaining super relaxed and cool, 'there *is* one helluva price on your head. That's for damn sure.'

She shot him a quick glance then carried on stuffing things into her bag.

'But it ain't you we're after. Don't you worry your pretty little self.'

She scowled. '*We?*'

I shook my head. 'Leave it; we need to move. There'll be more coming if they're not already waiting outside for us.'

'Follow me,' ordered the Marionette, heading toward the door.

I shared a glance of apprehension with Goldilocks. She then gave a nod, heaved the backpack over her shoulder, and we followed the Marionette into the darkness.

He marched on, barely checking the streets to see if there was any backup waiting to ambush us. He thrust his hands into the pockets of his trailing coat and walked on.

We followed, side by side.

'Where are we going?' I murmured to Goldilocks.

She shrugged. 'Don't know. But as long as we get away from my place, we should be makin progress.'

I frowned. 'I don't like it.'

'I don't like it, or *him* particularly, but like I say, we gotta keep movin.'

We carried on roaming the streets, the Marionette casually leading us to some unknown destination. Light traffic cruised by. The android's mechanical whirring was the only sound, other than engines that filled the night air. A few minutes later, sirens joined them.

We walked on, slipping through alleyways and quiet streets, the smell of piss and cheap food in the light, cold breeze.

'You believe me, that I didn't set this shit up?'

Goldilocks was silent for a while, glancing around us. 'Yeah,' she said, almost in a whisper. 'I believe you.' Then, 'But settin me up in this instant and aimin to deliver me to Arminus are two different things, ain't they.'

To that I said nothing.

'Not too long now,' called the Marionette as we started traversing another stinking back alley.

'How do you know him? I asked.

'Old rivals,' she said. 'We worked for different people, there were conflicts of interest, and more often than not, that resulted in us comin up against each other. Obviously, neither of us triumphed in puttin down the other, but I came closest, takin off a chunk of his face last time we met. Now, how he found me . . . I have no idea, but it's botherin me.'

'Huh. Well, where did he come from? Y'know, why is he, uh, like that?'

Goldilocks shrugged and murmured, 'Was never my business to ask; that wasn't the job. But what I will say – it gives him one hell of an advantage.'

A low rumble echoed through the alley then, and we both jumped. The Marionette was chuckling. 'Mumble all you like, Robicheaux, but you seem to have forgotten I can hear every word you say. Ha! Hell, every breath you *breathe.*'

Goldilocks scowled and made a clicking sound with her tongue. 'Alright,' she said, 'I'll bite now. Where we goin?'

'To a friend you don't know you have,' he said, glancing over his shoulder, eyes glowing, creepy grin on his face.

'I don't like the sound of that,' said Goldilocks, tension thick in her voice.

The wail of passing sirens shot through the atmosphere. The ripple of choppers hung far above us. I hadn't seen the force so determined in years.

The night sky was a void – navy blue and empty of stars or clouds. Everything was beginning to feel airless and cold. Even with this supposed help, I felt bad things coming.

I thought about how it felt in Papa Bear's place, to be toyed around with like that, manipulated. The feeling of waking up in a place I didn't know, with an unfamiliar magick in my body that wasn't put there by me. I felt Bluebeard's greasy hands on my bare shoulders and my neck again. I remembered how it felt to be trapped in a room with a grizzly bear who felt he could just use me to his advantage.

I wasn't going to end up like that again.

I cocked my gun and pointed it at the Marionette's back.

He stopped walking, sighed, and chuckled. 'I wouldn't do that.'

Goldilocks shot me a look and put her hand over her own

weapon.

'It'll take more than bullets to put me down. Ain't that right, Goldilocks?' He turned to face me.

'Why were you with the King's Men? Who sent you?' I asked.

The Marionette sighed. 'You really can't wait, can you? Okay. Fine. I was with those dumbasses because I'm undercover. I've been hired by someone you'll be meetin very shortly – if you, in fact, let me. I can't say their name, not out here.' He scoffed, and I imagined if he was physically capable, he would've spat tobacco to the ground at that moment. 'Put your gun down, buddy. You an amateur? Cops are after us, hell knows who else, and you're wavin that thing around.' The Marionette chuckled and gave a shake of his head that made me feel pretty stupid.

Even Goldilocks, ever-distrustful Goldilocks, gave me eyes of pity, while I slowly slipped my handgun back into its holster, trying to do it in a cool, relaxed way that said I was still in the right. The burning sensation in my cheeks and ears told me I had failed miserably.

My brain wandered away to reflect on how much tension I'd be relieving if I could've just swallowed one little magick bean there and then. To get to a place where I wouldn't need them felt like a pathetic dream. Voices in my mind told me it was, and I was inclined to believe them whole-heartedly.

The farther we went down the alley, the filthier it became. Rats scattered in every direction, vanishing into crevices or shadows, whispering to each other and giggling bitterly. I hoped I would accidentally kick one of the things across the ground. Mice are one thing, but the rats around these parts are demonic.

The Marionette touched something near his eye, then a bright white light flicked on, illuminating the alleyway, revealing the grimness we would have, in a way, been better off not seeing.

'Ugh,' went Goldilocks, covering her mouth.

'Almost there,' replied the Marionette.

At this point, with every step I took into that abyss of garbage and half-alive beings, I was getting more and more desperate to know where "there" was.

Families of trolls with missing limbs and rotting flesh lingered by giant trash cans, watching us with obvious fear and unrest behind their eyes. Elves, witches, humans, foxes, dogs, all kinds of creatures, hiding in the shelter, waiting for death. All of them shielded themselves from the Marionette's light, ducking and turning away. I'd never strayed so far into territory like this. I felt sick and depressed. Beside me, Goldilocks kept her eyes dead ahead, not daring to let them fall on any of the doomed souls surrounding us.

I don't think it would be an overstatement to claim the outlaw was even more on edge than I was. She was a traumatized child, being led farther into darkness.

Then out of nowhere, a ghoulish figure leaped out at Goldilocks and grabbed her by the shoulders, foam bursting out of its mouth. She went for her knife, but the attacker overpowered her. They crashed into a puddle on the ground.

Heart suddenly pounding, I grabbed it by the back of the neck, reached for my gun, and smashed the ghoul over the head again and again until purple and black brains splatted onto the ground. With a dry, wheezy growl, the thing fell to the side in a heap, twitching and shaking for a while before going completely still.

The Marionette's light cast over Goldilocks, who lay there in the puddle, stunned. It was the first time I'd seen her so helpless and vulnerable, and right there and then, I hoped it would be the last.

As she sat up, staring blankly at the corpse to her side, her eyes seemed to glisten with a veil of tears, and I felt my heart sink. I don't know if it was some heightened sense of empathy for her or what. My own eyes could've been stinging in that moment for a more selfish reason – that right there, in that burst of terror, Goldilocks was overpowered and shaken by a weaker creature, and it was me who had to step up and protect her.

I blinked away a feeling of shame and the self-loathing that was starting to surface. But I was right to feel that way.

'Are you alright?' I asked, holding out my hand. There was low murmuring all around us. The creatures shuffled and whispered, their silhouettes barely visible.

They were all unsettled. We were in their territory. This is all they had.

Goldilocks ran one hand through her wet hair then slapped the ground. She reached out to me with the other. 'Thank you,' she said quietly. She gripped my hand and I pulled her up to her feet.

The murmuring continued. All eyes were on us. I kept the gun in my hand, ready for another outburst.

Goldilocks tucked some loose hair behind her ears and walked over to the corpse.

It was one of the grossest sights I'd ever seen in all my years of police work in this city. The most striking thing about it was that it was the result of the city itself – its negligence, its crimes, its corruption. This is what's in store for you, this is your fate if you slip through the cracks. No second chances, no bailouts, not for the majority.

The corpse of Dick Dumpty flashed across my mind as I looked away from the dead hag.

And it gave me some joy.

The Marionette stood beside Goldilocks. 'It... *she* was probably going for your bag. Maybe let me carry that.'

She instantly backed off, shaking her head slowly. Now she took out her rifle and balanced it over her other shoulder. Everything was escalating, and she seemed to see this as a necessary precaution. I wasn't about to argue with her.

'Fair enough,' the Marionette purred with a smile.

'And could you turn off that light?' I said. 'You're gonna blind us.'

'Affirmative,' he said politely, and switched it off.

'Marionette,' called a woman's voice from the darkness. I swiveled round as another flashlight beamed our way, this one considerably less intense. 'Okay, it's you,' she said. 'These our friends?'

'Oh, indeed, Lieutenant, though I'm figuring they won't be so quick to call *us* friends.'

The owner of the voice stepped farther forward, hardly visible as she was enveloped from behind in white light, just a silhouette.

'Did you say "lieutenant"?' I asked, tensing up.

'They're a little on the jumpy side,' the Marionette said in a stage whisper.

The sound of a blade slashing out of its sheath echoed down the alley. 'Oh, you android piece of shit,' hissed Goldilocks, voice shaking. 'This time I *will* finish you.'

The Marionette just laughed. 'See what I mean, Lieutenant?'

The lieutenant flicked off her flashlight as the sound of sirens wailed through the night beyond this alley. She crossed her arms firmly. 'Well, they have a point, Marionette. You can be a complete shithead sometimes.' She looked at me then.

I felt unnerved that she could somehow see me, but I couldn't see a glimpse of her.

'Hi, I am Lieutenant Ilsa Corral, NYPD.' A police badge glistened in the weak orange light from one of the windows either side of us. Her voice was made up of complete authority and rigor. Her accent seemed to spontaneously switch from Bronx to thick Spanish.

I cleared my throat and took a couple steps forward. 'Nice to meet you. But I'd be lying if I said I was overjoyed to see a police badge. Obviously, you know who we are?' I uttered it like a question. I hadn't exactly stamped down any authority. Then again, I was in no position to.

'Yes. I know who you are, and I am not here to arrest you, Detective Slade. Or even you, necessarily, Jessica Robicheaux.'

Goldilocks shuffled where she stood. She was damn near sneering at the cop.

'We're here to help,' declared the lieutenant, before turning away and fading into the light.

The Marionette motioned for us to follow her. After a few

seconds hesitation and what was essentially attempted telepathy between Goldilocks and me, we did.

Somehow the darkness of the night seemed to shift a little then, like it'd backed off us, allocated us some breathing room. We left the vagrants behind us in the damned alleyway. Tonight they would fight to the death over the corpse I made, those that beat out their competition and consumed the spoils cursed to make it through another night, still breathing.

Ilsa Corral led us to a sprawling industrial park. Everything was gray, soulless under the massive white lights beaming down from above. The black sky swept into the horizon and met the sea.

Immense sheds, rigid square warehouses, and towering cranes stretched along as far as I could see. The sounds of mechanical construction and engines roaring filled the huge space.

The lieutenant stood before us, eyeing the scene, hands on her hips. She looked over her shoulder at us. She had thick black hair tied into a bun, and small, probing eyes that looked like they never closed for sleep. Although she only stood at about five feet, she was assertive in her body language and severe expressions. She wore a long, black raincoat over her uniform as if she was prepared for a storm only she knew was coming.

If she was truly an ally, I was going to feel a hell of a lot better with the lieutenant on our side. But I wasn't prepared to celebrate yet – not by a long shot.

'This way,' she ordered, and took off to the right, heading toward a smaller warehouse. Keys jangled in her hand. She found the one she was looking for, shoved it into the door firmly and swung open the entryway. She stepped to the side and beckoned for us to go in.

The Marionette obliged first, removing his hat and saying, 'Why, thank you, ma'am.'

I tried to peer past him as he sauntered inside, but could only see more grayness and harsh light.

I walked up the small set of steel steps, nodded at the lieutenant, and walked in. I heard a brief back-and-forth about carrying rifles out in the open, turning around to see Goldilocks still carrying it, still on edge. Lieutenant Corral smirked behind her and slammed the door shut. The snap of the lock turning echoed down the hall in which we now stood.

There wasn't much to look at. It was bland and lifeless. White tiles had been dislodged from the walls and floor. Another steel door hung loosely from its hinges, looked seconds away from crashing to the ground. An irritating buzz hovered above our heads.

The Marionette was leaning against the wall, arms folded, one leg up, observing us both. The fact that he was impossible to read probably wasn't helping Goldilocks's irritability.

'Okay,' said Lieutenant Corral, who was now standing by another door, 'now that we're in a secure location, I can explain to you both exactly what's going on here.'

'Please, go right ahead,' said Goldilocks with bold impatience.

The Marionette's eyes flicked toward her.

Lieutenant Corral pushed open the door and stepped inside. I followed, my ears pricking up at the sound of murmuring voices nearby. As soon as we entered the room, the two men stopped talking.

They were perched on a steel desk, chatting, arms folded and leaning toward each other. They were both dressed in shirts and vests, their sleeves rolled up. One of them was a tall, elven man with blue-white skin, intelligent emerald eyes, and long limbs.

The other was a human. He had dark skin and black hair, gelled back with a smart quiff at the front that refused to lie down. His eyes were round and discerning, and already made me slightly uneasy. He whispered something to the elf and hopped off the desk in a fluid motion. Then he drifted over to a hat stand, put on a black wool coat and matching fedora, and made his way out another one of the doors.

'See you, Bhatt,' said the elf.

'Later, friends,' said the man to the elf, then us.

I frowned and gave a small wave.

Corral nodded.

Goldilocks glared.

'He didn't seem to want to stick around for us,' I said to the lieutenant.

Corral half-smiled. 'The days here are long and taxing, Detective Slade. It's late. He'll be needing all the sleep he can get before he does it all again tomorrow. And that goes for you, too, Detective Vesryn,' she called to the elf.

Vesryn slipped off the desk and walked over to us, reaching a long hand out to me. I shook it. 'Pleasure,' he said in a silky voice. 'I agree, Lieutenant, but first allow me to greet the new subjects.'

Goldilocks shuffled again, probably at the use of "subjects." She declined to shake his hand.

I checked out the area, which appeared to be a makeshift office. It was in slightly better condition than the hallway outside the door, but still grimy. Which meant it gave the actual NYPD offices a run for their money. Desks and computers were scattered around the room, a few filing cabinets lined the walls, and there was even a private office in the corner, which I assumed belonged to the lieutenant. Whatever they had going on here, they certainly didn't want people to know about it.

Corral scraped a metal chair across the floor and sat on it backward, hands clasped together, rubbing her thumbs against her knuckles methodically. She left us to stand. 'Alright, so, all this . . . where does it start? Dick Dumpty, Arminus, missing women and children. Well, we have some ideas. We're making progress in our investigation. Slowly, yes, but this will take time. Goldilocks, as I understand it, you were once in the gang, correct?'

Goldilocks said nothing. She stared Corral's dark eyes down with her even darker ones.

'Perhaps you have some inside information you feel would be helpful to share,' Corral went on. 'And perhaps if you've told your partner here, well, you can both get us up to speed with things on your end.'

I chewed my tongue while glancing around the room, thinking. But I didn't know what to think yet.

'How do we know we can trust you?' I asked. 'The sensitivity of this situation, this *case*, if we can call it that . . . well, it's unprecedented. You could easily be working for Cole—'

'No, Jack. No,' said Corral, her voice hard. She was shaking her head side to side, eyes closed. 'I do not work for Chief Cole. Of course, *yes*, I do still technically work for him, but I have been undermining that man for close to a year now.' She seemed to be collecting herself then. Her face screwed up as she spoke. 'I have lost men and women through undermining the chief, pursuing this operation. At times I have questioned whether it's all been worth it. The death. Depriving my officers a life with their family. I have to live with that. Meanwhile the chief and everybody connected to him do . . . unimaginable things behind closed doors, then direct us, good people, away from uncovering their crimes. To the point where we must form a secret unit within the force to do good. You can trust us because we've been doing this longer than you, Jack, and we've lost so much along the way already.'

I stared at the ground, the silence filled by the loud electronic hum that droned on and on. When I looked up, I noticed the lieutenant's eyes were red.

She stood up swiftly and turned her back on us, putting her hands to her face. 'Vesryn,' she said, then sniffed.

Vesryn collected a folder of files from one of the desks and strolled over to us. 'In our investigations regarding the supposed abduction of women and children from New York City and surrounding areas, as well as the apparent murder of one Dick Dumpty, it appears that high-level police corruption has been a substantial contributing factor in these and other cases.'

I shrugged. 'Yeah.'

The elf cleared his throat and shot me a slightly annoyed look, then regained his composure. 'More than likely this corruption has been enabled by the chief of police himself—'

'Yeah, no doubt. He's as crooked as they come.'

'You've worked pretty closely with Chief Cole over the years, haven't you?' said Corral.

'No, I wouldn't say closely at all. I've been shut out of most of the important cases year after year.'

'He doesn't trust you?'

I shrugged. 'Trust me, like me, whatever; I've never been part of his inner circle.'

'Did you want to be?'

'Fuck no. Why would you ask me that?'

The lieutenant got to her feet. 'Because we can't risk you putting any of us in danger,' she said harshly.

I nodded.

Goldilocks continued to stand there in silence.

'Well,' continued Vesryn, 'we have gathered evidence that tells us the chief of police has, for a considerable length of time now, been making deals with criminal enterprises.'

'Robicheaux,' said Corral suddenly, but continuing to glare at me.

Goldilocks folded her arms and tilted her head.

The lieutenant shot her eyes to Goldilocks, then stepped closer to her. I felt my eyes narrow, and I verged on praying neither of them was about to do something reckless. 'I am well aware of your record, and I am well aware of your history with the Marionette here. I trust the Marionette, but can I trust you?'

Goldilocks screwed up her face, made her mouth small and hard. 'Kinda question is that?'

'I am assuming you're aware that your former boss is one of the people Chief Cole has been working with.'

'I know.'

'Well . . . Conflict of interest,' she said, her pitch going upward at the end.

Goldilocks blinked.

Corral stared.

'I'm sorry,' said Goldilocks, 'was that a fuckin question?'

'Hey, hey,' I said, completely uselessly.

Corral waved me away. 'You're an outlaw. You're dangerous. You were a member of Arminus's gang. Of course I need to ask you these things.'

'I don't have to be here,' said Goldilocks, smirking. 'Don't know who the hell y'all are and I don't need to. . . . Jack.'

'Huh?'

'We're leavin.'

'No. You're not leaving,' said Corral. I inhaled. Vesryn straightened his posture and slid his tongue along his teeth. And the Marionette just stayed where he was, arms folded, back against the wall.

'It's okay,' I said, either to Goldilocks, Corral or myself – I wasn't sure.

'We your prisoners now?' asked Goldilocks, almost in a whisper. Her slender fingers traced the patterns on her rifle.

'Stand down,' ordered Corral. 'Escalating will get you nowhere, I can assure you. We all need each other.'

Goldilocks scoffed.

'No. You have no idea,' continued the lieutenant. 'We *do*.' She cursed under her breath in Spanish and grimaced at the ground, then looked back toward us. 'The children. The women. They're being taken to a wood, not far from here.'

'What do you mean?' I said.

She motioned for me to stay silent, as if I could. 'Wait. They're being taken to the wood, and something is happening to them. We've got no evidence to suggest they've been killed but . . .' Her voice was trembling a little now. 'According to my source,

Cole's cops have been taking vulnerable women and children of any species from disadvantaged households and delivering them to *your* former boss's people, Robicheaux.'

Goldilocks's expression told no story. But her fingers remained in their creeping motion along the rifle.

Inside me, a nauseating sensation was brewing. It was made up of fury and hopelessness.

'We don't know how much the cops know about what happens to the vics after they're delivered, but that's not important right now. We do know the NYPD is also supplying weapons, and a lot of them, to Arminus's gang. I can't tell you the ins and outs of that aspect because we haven't got all the information yet, but this is bigger than I could've imagined.'

'Fuck,' I hissed, finding myself pacing around the spot.

'So, what have you got?' asked Corral.

'I uhh . . . There's a club owner, think we can get something from her. Running girls. A guy who works for her, too, has a place on Long Island. Have my suspicions he's deeper in this than I thought.'

'Good. Fine. We start with them.'

My mind was falling to pieces. None of this was particularly shocking to me – it wasn't unexpected – but the reality hit me there and then like a bullet.

It was about to get a hell of a lot worse.

Corral went on. 'We've completely lost our contact; we don't even know if he's alive anymore. Could quite easily have been found out, dropped in a ditch.' She walked over to a filing cabinet as she talked, bringing out another document. 'Hell, he could've turned, gone rogue. I cannot believe a part of me could think he *would*, but we just can't say for sure.'

'What do you mean?' I asked.

'He's supposed to stay in contact with me, keep me updated. I was getting intel every other night. About a month ago, it all stopped, and we've had to figure out everything else on our own.'

She sighed, pressed her fingers to her forehead. 'Officer Richard Hamelin was embedded in the bear's gang a year ago to gather everything he could and report back to us. Know him?'

Corral flipped open the file and handed it to me.

I felt Goldilocks step up beside me.

I flipped the file over. The page had a glossy photo of the cop attached to the top. That familiar face looked back at me. Though it was unfamiliar at the same time.

I was looking at the real cop, the man who'd gone into the bear's lair to do his job, not the scumbag who had reveled in my misery.

My heart sank. Every drop of blood in me must have stopped circulating.

I passed back the file.

'He goes by Piper,' I heard Corral say.

9

THE HATTER & THE JACK

'This should go without saying, but our operation is extremely dangerous and there is absolutely no room for error. Can I trust you to work with us?' asked Corral.

I suddenly realized she'd been talking for a while, but I hadn't heard any of it. I'd lost all focus. Corral looked at me as though she'd just asked me a question. I tried my best to get it together. Goldilocks was looking at me, tense, perhaps a little scared.

'You hear me?' said Corral. 'What's up with you? Can I?'

'Can you . . . uh, sorry, can you what?'

'Detective, are you even listening to me? I asked if I can trust you to work with us.'

'Hold on. Goldilocks and I are gonna need to talk about this. Uh, alone. As you said, this operation could be quite susceptible to oversights,' I said, fumbling through my words.

Corral looked to the side for a moment, visibly confused. 'No, I never said that. Did you hit your head?'

I turned away and guided Goldilocks back toward the door. 'Yeah, actually, pretty badly. Excuse me, one second.'

We shuffled into the hallway and pulled the steel door shut. Goldilocks took off farther down the corridor, about twenty meters away. I followed, grimacing and thinking haywire thoughts. She stopped and twisted on the spot, facing me. She put her arms out by her side. I did the same back at her.

'I knew this was a fuckin bad idea,' she whisper-shouted.

'The bad idea was leaving Piper with *your* guy.'

Goldilocks glared but, to my surprise, said nothing else.

'We can . . . work around this,' I said. 'We need them as allies. This is too big for just the two of us.'

'Man, we probably just killed one of those allies. We don't get out of this one. And how do we know they aren't actually workin for your chief, like all the others?'

'They're not, they're not,' I said, shaking my head. 'I don't think they are. Look, our main thing now is getting Piper back. We have to.'

She looked at me blankly, closed her eyes, then opened them again. 'Fuck that guy. He had chances to tell us but he didn't take em. He's probably compromised by the bear for real, we gotta forget him and move on. Leave these guys behind, too.'

I wandered from side to side, kicking at bits of rubble on the floor. The truth is, I'd never felt a sense of unity or camaraderie with my fellow police officers. There wasn't a single one I'd ever considered a friend. I never trusted any of them. Maybe that makes me the asshole, but everyone I'd ever worked with was just as bad as the people and creatures they were sworn to take down. I don't consider them my colleagues, just a mob of thugs always getting in my way. If Piper really was playing a part, it needed to be my mission to save him from the mess we put him in.

'Could you please stop kickin the damn floor?' said Goldilocks.

I looked up. 'We can't leave him. We need to go back to Hatter, now.'

'Goddammit, Jack, why?'

'Do you really feel nothing right now? It was your idea to use him as payment. This is mainly on you. Come on.'

'Who the hell else were we gonna use? Get it together.'

I stepped closer to her. 'I know you're not heartless. Do the right thing.'

This time it was Goldilocks who kicked at the ground. 'You

high and mighty motherfucker,' she said, then pursed her lips. 'Remember what you were up to when I found you in that strip club? Beatin the manager guy half to death for some answers. Don't lecture me about "the right thing."'

I laughed to myself and shook my head. 'Alright,' was all I could think to say.

'Besides, even if we did go get him back, you think that lieutenant is just gonna look the other way? I'm tellin you, this is trouble.'

'Look, I have no idea what she'd do, but one thing we can rule out is her arresting our asses. She'd be betraying her own operation.' I caught myself talking a little too loudly and checked over my shoulder. There was no sign of an audience, just the continuous buzz of the lights.

Goldilocks sighed. She was looking at the ground and thinking. 'I just wanna stop them. And I wanna kill them. They don't deserve life. You ever thought about *why* Papa Bear is collecting all these weapons, hm? What's the bastard up to? The sooner I put a few bullets in his brain, the sooner this is over. We need to act, Jack. Who knows how many lives are at stake, how many more victims these monsters have in their sights?'

'You're right. You are. But we need to go further than that. The problems won't stop when we take down the bear and the chief because they're baked into this city. We have to learn the truth, get it out there. If we don't, we'll just do this over and over again until we get killed. It looks like our best option is working with Corral. Yeah, you don't trust her, but who *do* you trust? She seems to know what she's doing. If we tell her what we know, we could take a massive step toward the end of this.'

'If we did that, we'd have to tell her about Dumpty.'

'That's right.'

She didn't say anything to that. She looked through me, then into my eyes.

'What do you say?' I asked.

'We ought to get some rest. I haven't slept in so long and I'm gonna start forgettin what's real. Tell the others we'll get back to em. We can sleep on it,' she said, starting to head back down the hallway.

I reached into my breast pocket and brought out two magick beans. 'What about Piper?'

Goldilocks stopped and turned around lazily, rifle hanging loosely in her hand. 'If you're in such a rush to go get him, I ain't stoppin you.'

'Take this,' I said, holding out one of the beans. 'You won't even need sleep. Come with me.'

'Fuck those things,' she said. 'I want good old-fashioned sleep. I'll find some motel.' Then she said in a low tone, 'Don't say a word about anything yet – not without me.'

I nodded, then swallowed both magick beans, kind of instinctively, vacantly.

She scowled.

'You know,' I said, 'I'd offer you my apartment for the night, but I figure it's probably one of the least safe places in the city for either of us.'

She carried on down the hall, raised an arm. 'Goodnight, Jack. Try not to die on me while I'm gone. I don't know how many more times I can save your ass.' She opened the entrance door at the bottom and vanished into the purple haze. The door slammed shut, then the other one instantly opened.

Corral appeared, looking at the entrance, then across to me.

I waved, blinked, then widened my eyes as the effects took their grip. I gripped my hips and turned away from the lieutenant, who was walking quickly down the hall toward me. Sweat sizzled on my forehead. I wiped it off, but it only came back within seconds. I planted my feet into the ground, tried to take control of my breath. In a few seconds, my focus would be perfect.

'Slade,' she said. Her voice had fingers. They stroked my ears.

'Yeah, hold on,' I said, still facing away.

She gripped my elbow and I screamed. My arm was polystyrene. I tugged myself out of her grip and slammed myself against the wall.

'Fuck are you doing? Where's Goldilocks?'

'Yeah one— one sec, I—' I slid down the wall.

Corral sighed, crouched, checked my temperature, undid my top button, ripped off my jacket. 'What is—'

'I'm okay,' I gasped.

A look of recognition washed over Corral's face. 'Oh, it's *those* things, isn't it?' Corral said. 'Magick beans, right? You know these things aren't for swallowing, you imbecile. No one knows what the hell is in those things. "Magick" is a little too vague, isn't it?'

My chest was getting tight, everything was spinning and shifting. And no, technically they're not for eating. I was having some regrets.

Corral tried to lift me to my feet. 'Come on, you need water.'

I stumbled out of her grip and crashed against the wall. 'I'm getting there, I'm getting there,' I said, panting. The usual effects seemed to be kicking in. I caught my breath once again.

'Of course, one of the few decent cops in this whole wretched city has to have a drug problem. Wonderful,' Corral muttered.

I managed to lift my head and straighten my legs. 'They're not drugs, Lieutenant.'

'Witchcraft, narcotics – what's the difference?'

I laughed, stumbling back slightly. 'That's a good one! Maybe you'll see someday.'

'Oh, you think I've not come up against witchcraft before?' she said, folding her arms and raising her eyebrows.

I waved her off. 'Put your eyebrows down. Not real witchcraft if you're talking like that.' I sputtered a laugh.

She turned away, muttering aggressively in Spanish.

'Okay,' I said. 'I'm good now, let's go.'

"Good" was a complete overstatement, but it was time to move. There wasn't really any other option anymore.

We went down the hall and headed back into the station-like

room. The Marionette and the elf cop had gone. Some of the lights had been turned off.

'Where did those two g— Wait . . .' I said.

There was a shift in my mind, a seamless adjustment. Everyone was back in the room except Goldilocks. Corral and Vesryn were huddled in a corner, talking quietly. I walked over. She was saying something to him about staying vigilant, something about trust, betrayal. She said goodnight and showed him out of a back door. The Marionette strolled over, tipped his hat and followed.

'I see,' I said to myself.

'What?' said Corral, peering into my eyes with her hawkish expression.

Seemed that doubling the dosage could unlock a whole new aspect of the beans. Whether it would be worth it in the long run – that I would have to discover the hard way. I didn't need things to be any more trippy, but hopefully I would be stronger now. 'Nothing. I guess the others took off for the night?'

'Yeah. I'm leaving soon, as well. First, I want to know what you know.'

'Honestly, Lieutenant, we essentially know as much as you do.'

'I know that's not true.' Her tone was low and somewhat menacing. She was an intimidating woman.

'Look, it's late. We're both tired and I'm drowning in my own sweat here. Perhaps we should leave it there for tonight and group up tomorrow. The thing is, I have something personal I desperately need to attend to tonight. I really need to get going. Here,' I took out my phone, 'take my number, call me in the morning. We can get right back to it.'

With the same cold look on her face, she brought out her own phone and took my number. 'Alright, Jack. But if you or your friend try anything, it's all over. That's mainly aimed at Goldilocks; she shouldn't be trusted.'

I just nodded.

She pointed over my shoulder. 'Shower's in there. There should be some fresh clothes around, too. If you need something to eat, grab anything from the refrigerator. We meet back here tomorrow morning. Oh, and if you touch anything you shouldn't, I'll know about it.' She unclipped a key from her belt and threw it over to me. 'That's for the main door. Lock it when you leave.'

'You got it. Thanks,' I said.

With one last lingering look, she walked over to a chair, grabbed her coat and backpack, and headed out the door, locking it behind her.

The effects of the magick beans still hadn't peaked, the sensation still rising inside me. I waited for a few seconds, then approached a filing cabinet. It was locked. I tried a drawer underneath one of the officer's desks. Also locked. Whatever was inside them should have been visible to me, even slightly, but I saw nothing. Probably some sort of cloak spell from the elf, Vesryn.

I thought about Piper, about what we'd done. Took a brisk, cold shower before changing into something that didn't smell of a week-old corpse. I froze as I did so, catching my reflection in the mirror: the clothes Papa Bear had given me. I was back in the room with him. His threat came storming back toward me. He spoke to me all over again: the story about my mother, how he would destroy my life if I didn't bring Goldilocks to him. He was a monster, a real monster. But not in the same way the chief was, or every other bastard criminal I'd come across in this city. There was something about him, something that put him on another level. From my first impressions, he struck me as a guy that very rarely makes mistakes, always miles ahead of the people in his way. People like me, and Goldilocks. Then again, he still hadn't gotten his paws on her, and that appeared to be driving him a little crazy, not that he'd admit that.

I broke out of that thought, mentally traveling back into the station. My brain was almost tingling now, like it was working extra hard to deal with the increasing flow of magick.

I put on a plain white shirt and black pants. A long, gray wool coat caught my eye. It was folded up among a bunch of jackets and bulletproof vests. I pulled it on, wondering if it belonged to one of Corral's deceased officers, or maybe Vesryn or the other guy that slinked off. It looked pretty good, so it was mine now.

The refrigerator hummed at me from across the room. I didn't need to eat, I needed to move.

I went into the hallway and wandered back out into the night, being sure to lock the door behind me. I followed the purple light and came out into the street. Behind me was pure darkness, where those dregs of society were lurking. I could see into the shadows, but I didn't want to. I called a cab for Hatter's place, or the nearest place to it I could think of. A bar called The Fisherman's Wife.

After five minutes of standing on the corner of the street, pacing and observing with searching eyes practically at the back of my head, the cab showed up. The driver engaged me in small talk, and I ended up in verbal autopilot the whole journey. I didn't really know what I was saying – something about how filthy the streets are around here, how weird the moon looks tonight. With that going on, I was allowed to drift off in my thoughts, watching the streets through the window, paranoid. It was only when I handed over the cash and stepped out of the cab that I realized how much I'd been talking. I'd never done that before.

I walked by The Fisherman's Wife, glimpsing in as I did so. Through the walls and windows, I heard meaningless, drunken conversations and confrontations. I saw that a fight was about to start. Someone was about to pull out a knife – minor injuries most likely, practically forgotten by the morning.

That took me back to where this all began; that night with the Seven Dwarves and the ogre. Shooting pain darted through my body, remembering the things he'd said, and how I've been complicit in those things for so long now. Not anymore. I couldn't live like that.

Turning the corner, I was met with the smell of beer and spirits floating through the warm air. The aromas were amplified, and I could taste each individual drink. It made me feel queasy more than anything. I quickened my pace.

The closer I got to where I thought Hatter's place was, the more familiar everything became. In that moment, the buildings around me looked as recognizable as the ones across from my apartment.

But in reality, they weren't. It was just the helpful illusion of the magick coursing through my veins. In the distance, a small building stood out to me, a blue glow cast out in the middle of all the other structures. It was the right place. I saw the yard, dimly lit but deserted. I saw those weird windows too, reflecting some ghostly version of me, small and submerged in a void. If anyone else was around tonight, would they be able to see this stuff, too?

I followed the blue glow, which was reaching out and appearing before me as a long, winding strip. The thought that this unfamiliar, stronger sorcery should probably concern me slightly dwindled at the back of my mind. What if I were to lose myself in its pull, if it took control of me?

Maybe involuntarily, I waved off the doubt and arrived at the front door. Another thought nibbled away at my confidence – there was only one of me. If this was a trap, then what? I thought about how I should approach the situation. Dr Hatter would surely be none too pleased that I'd come to take back my payment. The guy was unpredictable, a loose cannon. If it came to it, maybe I would need to restrain him, or worse. Then Piper. He wouldn't come quietly; he wouldn't forgive me, surely.

I looked around. There was life lurking, but it felt far away. I knocked on the door three times. Waited a few seconds and knocked again. There was no response, just the echoing bark of a dog in the distance. I supposed my only option was to kick the door down. I took a few steps back, then thrust my boot into the door. The bottom hinge flew off, and the door jammed into the frame diagonally. I realized I probably could've been a little more methodical about it, enhanced physical strength and all. A shoulder barge would've sufficed.

I grabbed the door and threw it to one side. I listened, expecting some sort of racket from below, but heard nothing. There was a faint yellow light at the bottom of the staircase leading to the basement. No moving shadows, no sound at all. I took out my gun and walked slowly down the stairs.

I'd forgotten the smell of the place – like a number of medicines, flowers, and small animals had been blended together and turned into some sort of potion. Then again, they probably had. That's probably exactly what I was smelling.

I came to the last step and peered into the basement: no one. Just a giant clutter of all the equipment that'd been there before. I tried to focus on any sounds, but everything I heard was coming from outside. I walked over to the counters, making sure I didn't touch a thing. They were covered with rusty utensils, bloodied gloves, and aprons. I felt uneasy again that this guy had "operated" on me.

'Hatter?' I said into the other end of the room. 'Piper?' No. 'Hamelin?'

Silence.

I went over to the area with the bathroom, no longer treading carefully. There was a ripped mattress on the floor covered with dark green stains. Above it was a tiny window covered by cardboard. Holding back a dry heave, I holstered my gun and lifted the filthy mattress. A desperate check for a secret hatch or something. There was nothing there except a family of spiders, which quickly dispersed into the corner. I could hear them whispering, panicked.

Then there was a loud noise: the sound of an engine. It was quickly getting louder. I focused on it and vaguely saw Hatter inside an old rattling car, turning into the open space up above me. He looked agitated.

I dropped the mattress and quickly moved into the bathroom, closing the door as far as it would go. The engine stopped and the car door slammed. He was muttering to himself as he noticed the lack of a door at the top of the staircase. He stomped down the stairs quickly and roared, swiping the mass of equipment off the counters, laughing as it crashed to the floor.

'Well, well,' he said, madness in his voice. 'I'm not alone right now, am I? Of course, I am never truly alone. You lot are always there, aren't you? But there is someone special among us tonight. An uninvited guest lurks in the shadows. Ha!'

Once again, I took hold of my gun. I was about to step out of the bathroom when I noticed he'd taken hold of something. It was a blade.

I pressed a hand to the wall and looked. He opened a cupboard and took out a tiny jar filled with a pure black liquid. He poured it onto the dagger, which began to make a sizzling sound, turning black itself.

'Ah yes,' said Hatter, 'quite beautiful.' He spun where he stood, pointing the dagger in my direction. 'You broke my door. I needed that.'

I almost replied, unsure if he was talking directly to me.

He began to walk. 'I would tell you it would bring me great displeasure to have to use this nasty weapon on anyone again, but that would simply be categorically untrue. Whoever you are, do yourself the favor of showing yourself before I make this thing eat away at your very flesh and bone, while you writhe and wriggle in a puddle of your own melting, steaming skin, and I stand there, watching, laughing.'

I decided then that I'd heard enough. 'Doctor, it's me. Jack,' I called. My voice was more authoritative than usual.

'Ah, "Jack," he says. A Jack. Could it be the hero of this story? Or a Jack of hearts, perhaps? He has come from the other land, quite possibly. It is quite fitting, indeed, that you would take my door from me, an object of security and safety. As you have taken so much from me already, in your great numbers, why would I be surprised that you are back once again, to end what you started?

Or perhaps it was I who started it, after all, and perhaps I am the real hero of this story. Let's give it a deserving conclusion, shall we? Now step out from the shadows, so that I might bury this blade deep into your neck, and begin the process that will see your undoing, and complete my redemption!'

'What? What are— Hatter, it's me, Jack Slade. You fixed my wound just a few hours ago. I'm a detective. Put the dagger down.' I put one hand on the door handle. 'I don't know what the hell you're talking about right now. It's just me. I'm gonna come out of the bathroom now. Please do not try and kill me. It won't go well.' I opened the door and stepped out.

Hatter was about four feet from me, holding the dagger out, his mouth hanging open slightly, eyes squinted. He smiled, and I didn't know what that meant. 'You again. Well, that was a waste of resources.' He threw the knife onto the floor and turned away, heading back toward the operating table. 'What do you want? Why'd you break my door?'

'I'm sorry, Doctor, I—'

'Put that gun away, you bloody child. Oh! Speaking of bloody children, that Piper fellow, he was an interesting one.'

'Was? Where is he, Hatter? I'm sorry, I have to take him back. He's a very important part of this investigation.' I paused, then swallowed. 'You kill him?'

Hatter was pacing. He looked even more agitated. 'Not quite, no. He's probably not dead. A lunatic, however? At this moment, I think so. I followed him as far as I could. See, young Jack, he made a dash for it. Wound me all around the goddamn city. I ended up on some country path. I believe he went into the woods. I don't think he's returning anytime soon.'

'How did you—'

'Before I began my work on him, I obliged in listening to what the man had to say.' He laughed. 'And he had *something* to say! He spoke of children running into the woods and never coming back. He told me about the grizzly bear, and a pirate, and you, and how this whole thing, whatever "this whole thing" precisely is, is infinitely bigger than what anyone is aware of.

Though, of course, he wasn't *really* talking to me, no. It certainly wasn't a conversation, rather the ramblings of a man who has seen far too much. In that moment, I related to him, in a way, yes. I did try and put in my two cents, as it were, but he was oh so focused on blabbing that, if I recall correctly, he failed to take a breath! In the end I was, unfortunately, completely unable to learn anything more. Pity.'

Even with the magick beans in my system, I couldn't figure out what to say. It was as if the effects had been subdued.

Hatter leaned against the operating table, his expression clearly indicating he was thinking hard about what was going on. He was trying to read me. 'You got the wrong man, didn't you, Detective? He was no crook; he was the one with the answers, and you brought him here to me in the trunk of your car as payment for a head wound. A human life, sir.' He laughed quietly. 'Oh dear, Detective, oh dear.'

'Shut up. Shut up. What did you do to him? Will it kill him?'

'*Something* will kill him. But nothing that I have done to him. I merely injected a serum into his veins. A little concoction I've been working on. Apparently, I didn't get the balance quite right, but that's what experiments are for, are they not? To put it simply, your friend Piper has gained the speed of a hare.' He slid on his goggles, crouched down, and pulled open a drawer, which hissed as it opened. An icy sort of gas erupted out of the compartment. 'Now, the last I saw of him, he was bounding down the lane, his body taking a quite hideous, monstrous form.'

'What?'

'As I said, the serum will not kill him. However, by now, I can only assume he has either been hunted down by whatever happens to be lurking in the woods tonight, or he has become half hare, half man, and is truly lost in the cold darkness, holding on ever so tightly to his sliver of sanity.' He brought out a small object from the refrigerated compartment.

I stepped closer to get a better look. It was a dead hare. I looked closer. It was riddled with tubes, a green liquid flowing through them.

'Old friend,' Hatter said quietly to the corpse.

I jumped back. 'What the fuck? What have you done?'

He just sighed and shook his head.

'You're insane, Hatter!'

'Clinically, I'm afraid,' he said, staring down at the hare. 'But I did save your life, Detective. I think you should remember that. You, on the other hand, have just ended that of a fellow police officer. Who is truly at fault here, I wonder?'

'Why? Why would you do something like that?' I buried my face in my hands. 'Fuck.' My legs were shaking, struggling to hold me. It was like there was no magick inside me at all.

Hatter turned to me, cradling the hare like a baby. Its dead black eyes gazed through me. 'Well, what exactly did you think I wanted a human body for? You quite clearly haven't thought this through very well.'

'I— It wasn't me. I—'

'What? Oh, it most certainly was!'

'I didn't know . . .'

'Oh, you boy, stop. You really ought to get out there and find him. He might just be the last person who can help you here.' He turned away again and placed the body of the hare back into the drawer. 'You must go to Snowdrop Wood, to the north of the city. I presume you are somewhat familiar. While I would not recommend entering alone, well, these are most desperate times for you, aren't they?'

'How am I supposed to find him? He could be anywhere in there by now.'

He darted at me, looking down on me with cold eyes. 'You're a detective, are you not?' Suddenly he gripped my jaw with cold, dry hands. '*Those things!*' he hissed, staring madly into my mouth, down my throat. 'Use them to your advantage and I don't doubt you will find him within moments, dead or alive.' I flailed and grunted, and he released his grip with a shove.

'It's not as simple as that,' I spat, rubbing my burning jaw. The man was so much stronger than he seemed.

'Do not lecture me. *I* am the doctor here! You would be wise to count yourself lucky the beans work the way they do with you.' He brushed himself down, lowering his voice. 'Now, I didn't notice a vehicle outside. Do you not have one? You can take mine if you must. I have other matters to attend to, therefore I shall not be joining you. Maybe I'll even get to work on the damn door you decided to destroy. . . . You will need to head north and enter the woods that way, through the marsh. That is where I lost sight of dear Piper.' He reached into his pocket and held out a car fob between his bony finger and thumb.

I took it and sighed.

He stood tall with his hands behind his back. 'If you bring him back to me, I can offer you a great reward. If you find him and decide not to bring him back to me, well, let us not forget I caught you trespassing and damaging my property. Perhaps you would like to entertain the idea that you *owe* me, sir.'

I opened my mouth then closed it. If I decided to retort the guy we would be there all night.

10

A Glimpse of Hell

If I were to find Piper, which I didn't have much hope for, there was no chance I would bring him back to Hatter. No, I didn't owe him. What I'd been a part of was sick. But we were desperate. I couldn't dwell on it.

As I drove through Upper East Side, my mind raced around, thinking back to each time I'd ever interacted with Piper, searching for any signs he wasn't who he seemed. I couldn't focus. My heart pounded. I gripped the steering wheel so hard my arms vibrated.

One more magick bean; maybe it would help. I reached into my pocket and took one, throwing it down my throat, then grabbing the wheel with both hands again, stopping myself from edging toward the sidewalk. It was busy out here. The paranoia that had been almost constant since finding Dumpty's shattered corpse whispered in my ears, hissing and taunting.

I unconsciously took out my phone with a shaking hand, went into my contacts, hovered a thumb over Goldilocks's number. Now my vision seemed to be failing me. Lights were everywhere, dancing and morphing, twisting into weird shapes and symbols. I wiped my eyes desperately with my sleeve. The streetlights hovered above me outside, floating alongside the car. Traffic lights transformed into horizontal illuminations, expanding and shrinking like elastic. I put the phone back into my pocket, rubbed my eyes again.

The sensation shooting around my body was indescribable, and there was no way of knowing if it meant I was getting better or I was about to pass out. It was when I brushed some hair out of my eyes that I realized how impossibly hot my skin had become. Thick sweat dripped into my eyes and onto my lips.

I was an absolute disaster, and about to head into one of the most mysterious and perilous places I knew, to rescue a fellow officer of the law who I betrayed, an officer who was either dead or suffering through an unimaginable experience.

My hands slipped along the wheel as I took a sudden left turn, onto a much quieter street. I knew roughly where I was, and I knew that the wide dirt road that led to Snowdrop Wood wasn't far from here. I was squinting now, which somehow allowed me to see clearly out of one eye, but not at all out the other.

Again I considered calling Goldilocks. I needed her. But I also knew I'd be putting her life at risk. If I went alone and never made it out, at least the one with the information would still be out there, even if she wouldn't work with Corral.

Corral, the name brought something like hope to the back of my mind. The fact that there was another cop in this fight, someone on the force I might just be able to trust, that was a big thing. I was far from optimistic, but there was something. Could she trust me, though? I was still hiding a dark truth from her. How could I tell her I'm responsible for the fate of the undercover cop?

My mind trailed off into wondering how she'd managed to pull it off, how such a high-ranking officer had been able to form a secret faction right under the nose of an authoritarian like him.

If she got this right, Cole would pay, and I would make sure I was the one who put a bullet in his fat head.

When I brought my attention back to the road, I realized the worst was over. I could see again, my temperature had lowered, and although I still felt like shit, the beans were working again. The amount of magick in my system was a joke, but desperate times, et cetera.

There were no sidewalks, not even a proper road, and no light except my headlights. Even the moon hid behind the giant trees that lurked either side of me. I was nervous as hell, and my eyes started to tingle as if they were about to leak tears. I blinked away the feeling and picked up the pace.

The engine rattled and groaned. Hatter said he lost Piper – Hamelin – at the entrance to the wood, whatever that meant. At the end of this road would be the vast abyss known as Snowdrop Wood, but last time I checked, there was no designated "entrance" for this place, just a long stretch of black trees vanishing into the distance either side of where you stood.

I wasn't even sure what good the beans would do me in this situation. Plenty of creatures that use sorcery or witchcraft can easily evade detection from whatever power is actually inside the magick beans. Consumption isn't how they should be used in the first place, but I'd been doing it for years without lasting harm.

The blackness ahead of me didn't seem to be going anywhere. It was as if I wasn't even moving. Everything looked exactly the same for miles. I rolled down the window a few inches, listening for any signs of life. At first I could only hear the weary engine and the sound of the tires crushing gravel and dirt beneath them. But then I began to reach across the area, as if my sense of hearing had wings and could glide above the mass of trees, listening, detecting.

The sound of running paws, leaves crumpling beneath them; hushed talking among birds; a blend of hooting and whispering. I heard a shrieking sound, which seemed only half human. It fluctuated between screaming and whining. Then there was a chorus of low murmuring, which sent ice trickling down my spine, a harmony of voices, chanting, singing. Warlocks, perhaps, cultists.

It was far away in the distance, but that didn't exactly make me feel any better about my situation. I didn't want to hear any more of what this place had to offer, so I rolled the window back up and sucked in a hiss that was supposed to cover up any other horrifying noises I might hear. It didn't work because the horrific combination of sounds had already made an imprint on my mind, and it followed me for the rest of the night.

I only realized how fast I was driving when the end of the lane came rushing toward me like a truck on the wrong side of the road. I slammed my foot down on the brake and yelled, my head thrown forward with the sudden stop. 'Dammit,' I whispered, hair dangling in my eyes again.

I swiped it out of the way and peered into what was ahead of me; it was the giant cluster of trees that welcome you to Snowdrop Wood. They were twice the size of the pines along the road, sweeping horizontally into the darkness that lurked to my left and right. That darkness seemed thicker and more alive than I'd ever known shadows to be. It seemed to be closing in on me, breathing on me. I pulled open the glovebox, almost as concerned about what I might find in it than what could greet me in the trees.

A scalpel, a collection of what looked to be old opera cassettes, and a flashlight. I grabbed the flashlight, doubtful of how useful the other items would be in this scenario.

I quickly noticed that I hadn't properly imagined the part where I step out of the car and walk into the wood yet. Suddenly I was regretting not calling Goldilocks. I thought about Hatter and the hare, and Piper, then forcefully knocked open the car door and took hold of my gun. I closed the door a lot quieter than I'd opened it, then stood there for a minute, keeping my hand on the car and leaning into it, ready to instantly slide back in and get the hell out of here.

I clamped my teeth together and growled something unintelligible at myself, then flicked on the flashlight. It illuminated the grass beneath me, which was touched by a light blue frost. I shone the light into the trees ahead. There were just leaves, thorns, and darkness. Then I pointed the flashlight higher into the sky, following the elevation until my arm was practically vertical. The trees rose into nothingness.

'Alright,' I whispered to myself, and took three paces – or meek shuffles – forward. I stopped, unholstered my gun, and aimed it ahead, gripping the flashlight just beneath it.

There was the sound of crunching leaves and frosty grass as I slowly made my way forward, branches and leaves that felt like blades trying to claw at my legs and ankles – which was better than some demonic creature trying to claw at my legs, but I wasn't feeling quite optimistic enough to rule that out as a lurking threat.

Continuing my shaky progression forward, I listened for sounds of movement or life, and focused my eyes to the sides of things far ahead of me that I thought might have been figures. The flashlight could only reach so far and the effect of the magick beans on my sight was only slightly helpful in the darkness. My hearing was my best friend in that moment.

'Piper!' I hissed into the darkness hopelessly. He could've been anywhere by now.

There was a shuffling sound, and I spun. I heard it again, distant then close. I frantically shone my light in all directions, the crunching of dry foliage apparently circling me, like a group of people were closing in. But there was no one. I stopped, took a deep breath, closed my eyes, and slowed my mind. I heard it again. It was on my left, moving farther away.

I kept my flashlight facing down, making sure I didn't fall into a ditch or step on some kind of animal or creature, following the sound with my ears. There was a combination of sounds stirring around the wood, but I would need to keep my focus on just the one or I could lose it. Neglecting the others was risky but necessary.

My strides became longer and my heart rate began to rise. I started muttering to myself in some useless attempt to feel less alone. Well, I *wasn't* alone, and that was scarier.

Then I saw something, and my heart sank into my stomach, which sank into my thighs, which tingled and trembled with fear. I involuntarily hid my face in the shoulder of my coat and repressed a gag. On top of a large, blood-stained rock a couple feet to my right, the flashlight had revealed a collection of bones, arranged in some kind of pattern. Or maybe it wasn't a pattern at all and my eyes and the beans were playing tricks on me, but they were absolutely bones, human bones. Some of them were splattered with blood, others pure white, and some partly crushed into dust. I mumbled to myself and snatched the flashlight away from the scene.

I was breathing heavily now, the cold air stroking my face and hands like an affectionate ghost. Then I found myself puffing my cheeks and peering over at the bones once more. What if this was Piper? If this was the fate I had brought him to, I would not be able to forgive myself. And how would Corral take this?

I gasped and choked on air as I spun to my left, flashing the light around aimlessly. The noise was close. I thought I heard the sound of claws digging into earth. 'Who's there?' I said weakly. I cleared my throat and breathed out sharply. 'Show yourself now. I'm police.' More sounds, a whole chorus of them coming from deep within the wood. I could've sworn I heard voices. 'Shit,' I whispered, edging closer to the shuffle, which was surely coming from about three meters away, at most.

Then I stopped moving.

Fur. Blood. Entrails. All caught up in the thorns.

I looked down to my right, in shock, in terror, in guilt. I found the source.

I saw what was making the sound, saw where the blood had come from. I saw him. Officer Piper, Rich Hamelin, dragging himself toward me, half the body of a man, the other half that of a hare.

'*Oh, fuck. Shit, fuck, holy* . . .' I said after looking again. Then I started to sob. I was crying relentlessly, my eyes stinging immediately, tears trickling down onto my trembling lips, onto my shoulder as I buried my face in it. I started to make noises I'd never made before. It became a meltdown.

I clawed at my own forehead and peered through my fingers like the coward I was, at the horror I was responsible for. The suffering I had caused, a sort of suffering I'd never even imagined possible.

It was the worst thing I had ever seen.

It was the look on his face, or what remained of it. I only recognized one of the eyes as his, the other wild and bulging, sticking out of his deformed skull. He was staring right into me through the flashlight, going through a transformation so horrible, the sight of it burned through my whole being and brought me crumbling to my knees.

I couldn't comprehend what I was seeing or feeling. Two thirds of his face had started to take on the characteristics of a hare. There was one long, gray, flappy ear hanging down to his chin, protruding from a lump of purple, rotten flesh. The entire lower half of his face was covered in matted fur, his mouth twisted and warped. It was open slightly, and he made a faint wheezing sound beneath my strangled cries.

I saw rips in his clothes, fur-covered muscles bursting through the tears, and as far as I could see, his lower half had become entirely replaced.

I stumbled back, hit a tree, and my body just gave up on holding me. I fell to the ground, dropping my gun, heels slipping along the gravel as I went.

Splayed out, I sat there and stared through wet eyes at a sight that would haunt me until my death and surely after. As I looked on, everything inside me weakened. I didn't want to look at him but there came a point where it was impossible to look away. I wiped the stinging tears out of my eyes, but they only returned a second later.

All I could think about in that moment was how this man, Rich Hamelin, was just another man in this hellhole who might have wanted what I want, who was prepared to go to great lengths to do his job, and I'd helped turn him into this. My heart was in my stomach. My limbs were shaking, frail and useless.

I saw that Hamelin was trying to open his mouth, making a breathless groaning sound, then reaching out a mangled arm. I crawled toward him, still shining my flashlight at him. I lowered it so he could get a proper look at the bastard who'd sentenced him to this condition.

'I'm sorry,' I got out between shaking breaths. 'I'm so sorry.'

I realized that the moonlight was now casting its glow upon both Hamelin and myself, breaking through the leafless giant trees.

Hamelin appeared to wave me away with his outreached arm, then rolled onto his back with another groan. He was looking up at it, the crescent moon, his one human eye with its eyelid heavy and flickering. I had to look away when I saw the great patch of blood on his stomach, a wound infested with bark and leaves and weird, unnatural colors.

'What do I . . .' I said, losing track of my words as I said them. 'I don't . . .'

Hamelin's eye flicked to me. 'Sh, shh.' He managed to hold a finger in front of his deformed mouth, then shook his head slightly. Then there was a subtle motion for me to lean closer, which I only noticed when I'd wiped the next clump of teardrops from my eyes. I sniffed, wiped my nose with my sleeve, and leaned in. He breathed in harshly through his mouth, wheezing and shivering.

I scrunched my eyes shut and listened, my body freezing out of horror and guilt.

'Cole,' he whispered. 'Cole knows. The wolves. Children . . . in the woods. A sacrifice.'

'What? I—'

'Shh. The bear. The bear . . . and Cole. Dumpty, Cole, Bear. Wolves. In here, the woods.'

'Wolves in the woods?' I said, my voice cracking.

'Yes . . . A cult. They all know. . . . They all know. Find them all. And Ilsa Corral.'

'What about Corral?'

'Work . . . with her. Find them all.'

'Find who?'

I swear then a hint of a smile flashed across that mouth. 'I t-told you . . . I was a cop.'

I let my head drop, and I gritted my teeth. 'I'm so sorry.'

'I think . . . Corral has a rat. Warn her. Find him. Please . . .'

I nodded, my words failing to form.

'There is . . . a place. Listen to me, Slade.'

'I am. I'm sorry. I am, I am—'

'There is a place . . . they take the children, the women. If you can make it . . . make it into Bloodstone, then find what I've left behind. . . . It will lead you there. To Koppelberg . . .'

'Hold—'

'Listen, dammit,' he growled. 'You never . . . listened. My residence, it's the room adjacent to Arminus. Find . . . the evidence. Concealed in the desk drawer. And kill that fucking bear, Jack. Somebody . . . kill that fucking bear And the chief. Just kill 'em.'

'What have they done? What have *I* done?' I breathed.

'I can't h—' Suddenly he hissed, placing his hand on the wound on his stomach.

'I'm calling an ambulance,' I said, fumbling for my phone.

'*No*,' he said, then spluttered a cough. 'You can't.' Then he said, 'You just have to kill me. Shoot me in the head. Shoot me in the fucking head.' And a tear trickled from his eye, which then closed gently. 'Do it. . . . And, Slade, you have to protect each other. Protect each other. There aren't . . . many of us.'

I covered my face with both hands, repressing a sob and shaking my head.

'Now, do it. Look at me. It's over.'

With one hand still over my face, I unholstered my gun and held it in my lap.

'Thank you,' whispered Hamelin. 'It's not your fault. You're doing . . . me a favor.' He groaned again and clutched his neck, sharply breathing in. 'Things are worse, worse than you think. Darkness everywhere. I don't wanna be here anymore. Shoot . . . shoot me, then run, run out of these woods. Or you'll just join me.'

I breathed out, got to my feet with a stumble. I wiped my eyes again, and aimed my gun between Rich Hamelin's eyes. 'I'm going to shoot you now, Officer Hamelin,' I said, my voice trembling. 'We won't forget you.'

He opened his eye and took one last look at the moon and

the stars that surrounded it. He closed it again, then whispered, 'Goodnight, comrade.'

I fired the bullet into Officer Rich Hamelin's skull, and ended the pain.

I pressed the side of the gun against my forehead and stood for a minute, desperately trying to gather myself, the stalking chill of the night's air creeping about my body. I felt for my phone, waiting for my mind to regain its composure, waiting for the right decision to come to me. There were sounds deep in the wood: life, movement, communication. I picked up the flashlight, shone it into nothingness. The light was flickering. I was shaking like crazy.

The stench – and God knows what else – emanating from the wounds in Hamelin's corpse hovered around me. I'd have to carry the body to the car, show Corral and the others what had happened. I'd have to come clean about my part in this, about Goldilocks's involvement. There was no more time for secrets.

I looked down at my phone, thought about calling the lieutenant, but there was the sound of branches and twigs snapping, and it was near. I flicked off the light, held my breath.

Hamelin did warn me; he told me to get the hell out. But I needed to know why. So I lifted one foot off the ground, starting to go deeper into the wood. I stopped instantly. Reason grabbed hold of me, and the effects of the magick beans still coursing through my veins started to make themselves known again. I closed my eyes, pressed my foot back onto the ground, and breathed out.

After opening my eyes, I looked through the trees, heard murmurs of life again, clearer than before, but still too distorted for it to make any sense to me. I figured there and then that it was supposed to be that way. I concentrated hard, trying to remain as focused as I could, despite my mental state.

Then there were patterns. Red flames soaring through the night sky, forming symmetrical shapes beneath the moonlight. Figures were sweeping past the blazes, a movement that resembled a dance or a fight. There was something off about the flames, though. It wasn't fire; it was something else, something uncanny.

Chanting and screaming rose above the trees, which made pimples spike up from my back and arms. And for a brief moment, I thought I might have heard the cries of children. And maybe that's what caused the last spark of energy to go out and my legs to bail on me, because a second later, I fell to the dirt again, lying, barely conscious, beside the warped corpse of Rich Hamelin.

It took almost everything for me to even heave myself up, but something told me that death was a very distinct possibility in that moment, and I promptly needed to get to safety, wherever that was.

When I placed my hands beneath Hamelin's corpse, I had to internally force down the river of tears, which was again trying to make its way out of me. Everything was so surreal. Whatever I'd gotten myself mixed up in, it was something way beyond what I'd ever imagined, and nothing I was prepared to face.

And still that irrational part of me that loves to take the driver's seat in my stupid brain was telling me to go and investigate what the magick beans had shown me. I told it to fuck off, then lifted the corpse off the ground with a drawn-out growl. The corpse was as heavy as I thought it'd be, and my legs almost buckled beneath me again. When I lugged the body over my shoulder, I stumbled back and pinned my boots into the mud, feeling the warmth of Hamelin's blood seeping into my shirt. I repressed a gag and headed toward the general direction I came from. The feeling of unwanted eyes burning into my back had become an all too familiar occurrence since coming across Dumpty's corpse – which, in itself, felt like months ago – and this moment was no different.

I trudged through the dirt and bushes, barely lifting my feet off the ground. I knew if anyone or thing was watching me and they wanted to come get me, they would do that with ease, and I'd be dead before even getting the chance to drop the corpse to the ground and reach for my gun. I doubted I'd even have the willpower or strength left in a single finger to pull the trigger.

I stumbled onward, and the sounds roaring into the night sky sent a wave of chills through my body. My hunger to investigate them here and now was surfacing again, trying to drag me back into the wood.

I cursed under my breath, foam blasting from my mouth, and finally came to the patch of dirt and gravel that led to Hatter's car. I followed it, desperately picking up speed as the old motor appeared in front of me. My legs crumbled again, and both Rich Hamelin's corpse and I met the concrete ground, but not without me taking a faceful of car hood first for good measure.

With what little strength I had left, I dragged myself to the trunk and heaved the corpse inside. And then that was it. I fell to the ground again, my body refusing to do anything more.

Staring up into the black sky, listening to the howling and screaming of some horrific darkness within the wood, I lay there and cried.

11

CROSSFIRE

My mother sits in her chair, looking through me because I may as well not be there.

I watch her for a while. The room is silent besides the ticking of the grandfather clock and the humming of the radiator. Their quiet, familiar commotion suffocates me. I look outside, through the dirty window, the glass about as thick as my mother's useless bones.

The beanstalk, it looms there proudly, only a little of the soaring thing visible from down here. A sort of rotten green, strangled by clumps of moss. It always looks as though it's staring into our house, intrusive, overbearing, dominant.

I look back at my mother, who's practically chewing on her chin, frowning. Disturbed angry eyes.

'Mom,' I say. For no real reason.

She spits on the floor in reply.

I shake my head and step toward her. She growls at me, grabbing her knife from out of nowhere. She aims it at my eye from across the room and throws it. It lands two feet in front of her and she begins to scream. Kicking the air, sinking into her chair.

All I can do is scratch my head and swallow.

Outside, I look up to the shining blue sky, which is penetrated by the enormous stalk. I still haven't made up my mind whether there's a beauty to it. I'm leaning toward no, although the armies of tourists say otherwise.

But it's the giant's corpse slumping beside the stalk that really brings in the sightseers. And no one would argue that it's one hell of a sight. A creature like that, not seen for hundreds of years, thought of as long gone, sprawled along the fields here in the middle of Arkansas. They were supposed to be long dead, and while this one looks different from the ones in the stories, it's sure as hell a giant. They aren't dead, just moved, changed. And it was me, local loser Jack Slade, that brought them back.

The corpse doesn't only bring tourists to this sad lonely town, but worshippers. Or cultists. People claiming to be descendants of the giants. Which is bullshit. They come in the night with their torches, chanting, hollering, and laughing. Sometimes they try to climb the beanstalk, always they fail. People have fallen to their deaths; I think it's at four now.

They all want to come see me, 'Jack of the Beanstalk,' to ask how I did what I did. One of the guys – a fat, long-haired kid a few years older than me – likes to call himself the leader of the cult. He asserts that he's a direct descendant of Old King Cole, and that one day he'll reclaim his throne, whatever that means. He's the most unhinged of all of them. The worst.

Days pass, and I drink through them all. My mother still says nothing, just looks through me at nothing, walks around the room, over and over and over. One day, she steps on the knife she'd thrown and just laughs. I offer to help and she slaps me in the face, hard. My mother is forty-two, but you'd be forgiven for mistaking her for eighty. She's a ghost of a woman, and I've always thought she'll haunt this house, this whole town, long after she dies. She'll haunt me, too.

One night, sleep evades me so ruthlessly that I go out for a walk, planning to wander anywhere. Before I leave, I grab my bottle of whiskey from the kitchen and look at the grandfather clock. Four thirty in the morning.

Up until recently, I could never look at the giant's corpse under the moonlight. It lies there, twisted and decrepit like some massive, deformed branch. At this point, it's almost just another part of the landscape to me. The glow of the moon makes the body a blueish gray, cold and dull. No cult tonight.

I walk into the woods, which is illuminated slightly by the hint of a rising sun. I can just about make out the path in front of me. But I abandon the path because I've walked it countless times already. It leads to a grim diner by the river where the fishermen like to hang out from the late afternoon until sundown.

The tingle of the whiskey kicks in, and I stumble through the leaves and branches, falling onto one knee a couple of times. Here the trees are taller, thicker, and the sapphire sky has gone almost completely out of view. I clear my throat after realizing I'd burst into a series of giggles, a twitching sensation in the pit of my stomach, a lump in my throat. My eyes begin to water.

Then the whiskey bottle in my hand is suddenly empty. I throw it to the side and exhale, standing still for a moment, careful not to stroll into some hole in the ground. Then when I look up, I see it: someone in the distance, or at least it looks like someone – it's too dark to tell for sure. I squint and look slightly to the side of the figure, a silhouette, symmetrical and still. When I raise my hand in greeting, I get nothing back. 'Hello,' I call. Nothing again.

When I conclude I'm talking to a rock, the shadow suddenly darts toward me, and just before I scream and fall on my ass, I see a smokey velvet form trailing behind it violently. When I hit the ground, I feel my palms burn as they scrape against a nest of thorns. My eyes force themselves shut and my body pushes itself firmly against the earth as I instantly realize what I've just run into. 'Not you,' I whisper, my eyes still scrunched shut, fists held over my head.

In a low, ragged voice that resembles the purr of a dying cat, the witch says, 'Up with you, boy. Jack the Giantslayer, frightened to death by an old hag. Wonder if they'd put that in the songs.' Then she makes a dismissive groaning sound, and I hear her shuffle away slightly.

I open my eyes and scramble to my feet. From the little I can see of the witch's face, I'm glad it's dark.

'Don't be lookin so repulsed now. Last time you stumbled upon an old woman of my kind, you caused that thing to flourish!' She was pointing through a gap in the cluster of trees behind me. The beanstalk twists and sprawls into the clouds.

I look for a second, then back to the shadow. 'Yeah, well,' I say, quiet and low, 'I wouldn't actually consider that a great moment in my life; it's done a hell of a lot more harm than good.' That wasn't a lie. Killing the giant was barely a triumph; it was a fluke. My mind begins to scramble, looking for a way to get out of this. To just go home.

'Look at you. Trapped. Stuck in that little old house with that evil woman. Is this what you envisaged for yourself, boy? It was one of my sisters who set you on this path. I'll take your hand now.'

I see the outline of her hand, more of a claw. I hope she only means metaphorically.

'I suppose you be needin guidance again. We been watchin, probably we will for a long time. Liberation's comin, Jack.'

A wave of chills starts to circulate around my body. A fox screams in the distance. The witch starts bustling toward me, and a breeze floats along the ground, becoming more aggressive with each second. Leaves start hurling themselves at me; the trees above moan and creak. I have to plant my feet into the soil to stop myself falling again.

There's a light with no apparent source cast around the witch's figure. I see her face, withered and ancient. Her eyes are silver, her skin is white. Her cracked lips tremble as she steps closer. And when I blink, I swear I see my mother before me, more dead-looking than usual, the rags and the dark, misty shape floating around her.

'What is this?' I say, my voice sounding a lot calmer than I feel.

The witch draws in a ragged breath and places a pale, rough hand on my cheek.

I find myself reversing slowly until I bump into a tree, staring into the ghostly eyes of my mother. It's impossible to look away.

'There is a path, Jack,' she says, with the voice of my mother. 'I see it, through the haze, the fog, the sorrow, the fear. The demons you have to face, they are far from here.'

I rub my eyes, look into the witch's. My mother's face is gone. So is her voice.

'Boy, there are things you must uncover, darkness that you will thrive within, beasts to conquer. Leave this cursed place. Your momma cannot keep you.'

I struggle for words. My mind feels weak. Eventually, I open my mouth. 'But how would you know this? What do I have to find? Help me.'

'Ohh,' groans the witch. 'They sprawl, Jack, they sprawl. There is loss, there is great pain, there is death, finality. But there is comfort in these things, yes. Fulfilment. I see them, the bright lights under which you will spend your years, where, if you fail to be vigilant, you will perish, boy. The spirits you will come across are dark, twisted, some purely evil. The adversity you faced here in your sleepy town was the first of many battles.' She pauses for a moment, her hand still pressed against my face. Her blank eyes seem to widen a little. 'Blood of the giants,' she says.

'Could you make it a little less vague?'

'No.'

'Oh.'

Suddenly her eyes return to a normal state and she pulls her hand away, long nails scratching my cheek. 'There's only so much you can understand for now, preserve your spirit, your fire. Somethin's comin, giantslayer.'

Don't call me that, I think. But my mouth fails me again. Understandably, I have questions this woman probably wouldn't answer, anyway. They all morph into one, and I just make a sound that goes, 'Eugh-uh?'

The witch buries a hand into her rags and reveals a small, bronze case. She opens it slowly, then I see my own face, dumb and confused, looking back at me. She begins to spit some sort of weird, violent language at me.

My face in the reflection fades away, and a second voice starts to chant back at the witch. A male voice, deep and imperious. It's coming from the mirror, smoke gliding deep within the glass. It looks like some sort of optical illusion. But I know it's no trick because then I see my mother in the mirror, and the voices stop. She looks dead. Again, deader than usual – like, conclusively dead. She's in a heap on the kitchen floor.

I swallow and end up choking a bit because my throat's gone so dry. 'What . . . What did you do? That real?' But I know it is.

'Now, go, Jack.' The witch snaps shut the mirror.

'What did you do?' I ask, louder.

'There's no sadness within you, is there?' she says. Then she laughs quietly. 'Go on, tell me you feel the sadness, boy. Try it.'

And there is no sadness. A lump in my throat again, but not from grief or loss or sorrow. Guilt. Guilt from feeling none of those things. I shake my head.

'The journey into light begins,' she drawls. 'The sisterhood'll be watchin, followin, guidin.'

I have to ask the obvious cliched question. 'Why me?'

The witch just closes her eyes and turns away from me.

'Why?' I say, the wind suddenly picking up again.

I walk toward her, my arm stretching out, and when I touch her cloak, she seems to evaporate into thin air with a howl of the wind. My hair flies across my face and I stumble back into the tree. There's a final weak whisper of wind, and I'm standing alone beneath the trees again.

I run home, a sudden shadowy terror wrapped around me all the way. I burst through my front door and see it: the corpse of my mother stretched out across the wooden floor. And it's the most at peace I've ever seen her.

And for me, still no sadness. Not even numbness. I stand there, doubting the sense of loss will ever come over me. I feel shaken, confused, angry.

And free. Fortunate.

My mother's magick bean supply, sacksful, sit on the counter. They glow slightly, as if to tempt me. There are beans by my mother's face on the floor, too. Her downfall. They killed her long before the witches.

Tomorrow, I leave this place.

I woke up to what felt like someone rubbing my face with the rough side of a sponge over and over. When I managed to force my eyes open, I scrambled back across the ground, seeing the blurry, ecstatic face of a small dog, panting then barking. I clenched my eyes shut again and rubbed them aggressively. I felt like a newly reanimated corpse. 'Hello, dog,' I said, then suddenly remembered the actual corpse I had in the trunk of Dr Hatter's car. 'Shit,' I growled, and shot to my feet, a burning ache bursting in my legs. I crouched over and groaned, feeling for the roof of the car to grab hold of it for balance. The dog continued to yap. The sun blasted into my eyes.

There was a woman's voice. 'Careful, young man! You don't look too well, not well at all. Don't trouble yourself too much; the ambulance is coming. And the police, I believe. Here, have some water.'

I blinked rapidly and my eyes finally focused on the figure standing beside me. There was a woman who heavily resembled the dog she was now pulling back from me with a leash. I looked down the road, listening for incoming sirens. 'Police,' I said vacantly. 'No.'

'Yes, son,' said the busybody. 'I was going for my morning walk, you see, and I happened to stumble across you in a heap. I was so worried, I thought there may have been some sort of brawl happening or – oh, the gods forbid – *a murder*. Oh, I was very disturbed by the scene. At first, I didn't know whether to call—'

'Alright,' I said. Her babbling was tempting me to just fall unconscious again. 'Thank you, ma'am, you shouldn't have,' I said, smiling. '*You shouldn't have!*' Now I was half grinning, half grimacing.

'Anything I can do to help,' she said sweetly. I wanted to run her over.

'When was it that you called?'

'Oh, must have been about ten minutes ago now. Just sit tight; I'm sure you'll feel much better soon.'

I chuckled. 'Sit tight, yeah.' Then I got into Hatter's car and started the engine.

At surprising velocity for an older woman, she shuffled to the car window and knocked on it with her cane. 'No, no, no!' I heard her say, muffled on the other side of the glass.

I closed my eyes, checked the rearview mirror, and rolled down the window.

'Young man, I don't think it's safe for you to drive. You're in a very bad way!' she pleaded.

I sighed. 'Ma'am, please, I'm a detective with the NYPD. I can check myself in to the hospital. If you don't mind, I'm very busy and I need to get out of here. Thank you for your help. Have a nice day.'

'Still, I really think you ought to at least wait for the police to arrive. Surely they'll want to investigate this little area, as well,' she said, waving her arms about, motioning to the giant trees above us. 'May I see your badge, young man?'

'For what?'

'You said you were a detective, no?'

I clenched my fists around the steering wheel and smiled. No way I was about to give her my identity. 'I don't *have* my badge on me right now. Now, please step away from the vehicle.'

The woman was unimpressed. She folded her arms and stared.

I sighed. 'My name, ma'am, is Piper. Officer Piper.' I started the engine and started to roll up the window.

'Thank you, Officer Piper. You have a nice day now.'

I nodded. 'Fuck you,' I whispered.

The engine rattled and wheezed as I turned, heading down the path back into the city. I caught a glimpse of the old woman's dissatisfied expression and clenched my jaw shut. If I was about to be brought down by an old hag, I'd just have to laugh.

My streak of feeling like absolute trash continued. I was going to smash my record. My mind was racing again, a carousel of images and thoughts flashing around my head, too rapid to even contemplate. I wasn't even sure where I was supposed to go next. All I could do for a while was imagine how I'd like to have the news broken to me that one of my best undercover colleagues, who was making a breakthrough in an extremely dangerous and sensitive case, had essentially been sacrificed by an ally, perhaps blowing up the whole operation in my face. I came to the conclusion there was no ideal approach. Half of me was preparing for Corral to just blow my brains out, the other half wanted to let that happen.

And Hatter. What was I to do with that psychopath? He was as guilty as me. Corral would surely want him arrested, hell, killed, if it came to it. The guy may have saved my life, but he'd quickly destroyed another. I hadn't even begun to ask what the hell he was aiming for with this fatal experiment. What reason could he possibly have had to do this? I realized I ought to do my research on this place, this "Wonderland".

Just when I'd decided where I was heading to next, I saw an ambulance speeding down the lane, followed by a cop car. I grimaced and made a low, guttural groaning sound, could only hope these cops in particular weren't familiar with me. And I wondered if such a cop existed around here anymore.

When the car was within a few yards, I put my hand to the side of my forehead, faking a scratching motion. It was a pointless attempt at evading them because my elderly friend back there was obviously about to start running her mouth. So once that cruiser was further down the road, all I could do was slam my foot against the pedal.

I caught myself exhaling slowly and deeply through my mouth when I was halted by traffic, caught on the edge of the city. My eyes flicked to and from the rearview mirror. I was sure my former colleagues would show up within seconds.

And then they did. I looked up at the traffic light, which was still red: about five vehicles in front of me, and an infinite number, including the cops, behind. Their lights were flashing. They blasted the siren once. Then I saw the passenger door open, and out stepped a uniformed officer. For some reason, I tidied my hair and cleared my throat, starting to put on another persona.

As the officer walked along the sidewalk, manic honking started to erupt from the traffic. I breathed out, rolled down my window, and cleared my throat again. The officer peered into the car.

'Hello, sir,' I said.

The officer's face was unreadable because it was mostly covered by a giant pair of shades. He was sucking in his cheeks and pursing his lips.

I raised my eyebrows, waiting for something bad to happen.

He pressed his tongue against the inside of his lower lip then smiled an ironic smile. 'You follow us,' he said. Then he wandered back over to his vehicle and overtook me as the traffic started to shift. I did as he said and tried to think of a plan. I had, indeed, met him before – in Cole's office when I was contemplating shooting my boss in the head. I pulled out my phone, cursed under my breath, and called Lieutenant Corral.

'Jack,' she said, answering immediately.

'Lieutenant, okay, hey. Uhh, I think they might have got me.'

'Who has?'

'Cole's guys, they're leading me someplace. They're in the cop car in front of me. I uhh . . .'

'Okay, where are you?'

I looked over my shoulder, then to the sidewalk. 'I'm on Laconia Ave, but I don't know where they're leading me.' We were heading into quieter areas of town, pedestrians and vehicles vanishing with each passing minute. 'Lieutenant, I think they might be about to kill me,' I said, then swallowed hard.

'Can you stall?'

'I can try.'

'Stop the car.'

'*Goddammit*,' I hissed. 'Are you sure?'

'Do it. Make a scene, you'll probably need to. I'm on my way.' She hung up.

I smacked the wheel with the palm of my hand. Then I slowed the car and pulled into a massive parking lot, sprawled out in front of an abandoned mall.

I heard the screech of tires as the cop car turned back and followed me. I stopped the car. In the rearview mirror, the mystery cop was walking toward me again, this time with a little more conviction, agitation. He was holding a shotgun. I checked my gun, slipped it back into the holster.

Once he reached the car, he tapped on my window with the weapon and foiled my plan of crashing the door into his face by stepping a meter back from it. He motioned with his head for me to step out of the car, chewing gum in his mouth aggressively. I got out, staring down the two barrels in front of me.

'Hands,' he murmured.

I slowly raised them, placing them on top of my head. My hair felt greasy and moist. He motioned for me to turn around, and I did. All I heard was the sound of distant traffic and popping gum.

'What happens now?' I said vacantly.

He cuffed me and stabbed his shotgun into my back. 'I await my orders. Then we await the chief.'

'Oh, good,' I said. 'Been a while.' I looked the guy up and down. 'Recognize you. Been by Cole's side for years, huh? What's the name again?' I asked, my voice monotone and scratchy.

Shades just chewed and glared behind the black lenses.

'Know who I am?' I asked politely.

Then a car door slammed shut in the distance. The driver of the car that'd pursued me slowly wandered over. He was an older guy, the kind of cop who probably talks about the day he gets to retire and very little else. As he got closer, I saw the grim look on his face. He looked me up and down, then spat on the ground, his thin gray hair flapping wildly in the wind.

The man with the shades approached him, muttered something, then came back to me. He was going for the trunk.

I turned to him, my brain scrambling for something to say. All I could do was draw in a breath before my chin was met with the butt of the shotgun. I yelled and fell back onto Hatter's car, then was gripped around the throat by the older guy. I spat out blood. 'Wait,' I breathed.

'Wait? Wait?' said Shades. 'Fuck is that smell?' He was talking almost in a whisper, barely opening his mouth. He nodded at the car. 'What's in this trunk?' he asked, but he didn't wait for a reply. He handed the old cop the shotgun and opened it up. He'd barely seen what was inside before suddenly spinning away from the discovery and retching and coughing. 'The fuck?' he said, his shades now balancing on the end of his nose, revealing beady, dead eyes.

I didn't bother explaining or lying; he knew full well that I was Jackson Slade, a dead man in his eyes, regardless. I just smiled instead.

'What is it?' growled the old guy to Shades, while seemingly subconsciously raising the shotgun to my face, his finger tickling the trigger.

I licked the blood from my chin.

The cop whipped his glasses off his nose and gave Hamelin's corpse another look. His face shriveled up. 'I have no fuckin idea, but it ain't right,' he said, then turned away and spoke into his radio.

The old man shot me a look, his expression an ugly blend of confusion and anger. 'What is it?' he growled.

I frowned back at him, my face aching. Everything suddenly felt supremely grim. I tried not to let my eyes wander anywhere near the corpse.

Shades wandered back over and stared into my eyes, hands on his hips and trademark aviators back on his face. 'This is it for you now. It's over,' he said in a whisper. The other cop tightened his grip on the shotgun and aimed it between my eyes. Shades lowered it vacantly and said, 'Not you, not like that.' He spat on the ground and slammed the trunk shut before reaching into his breast pocket and drinking from a flask.

'Can I get some of that?' I asked. I meant it.

He threw a solid fist right into my stomach. I fell onto my knees and wheezed. Then he grabbed a fistful of hair and stuffed me into the back of his cruiser. The punch really connected, because I started gagging and coughing, slumped there across the car seats.

'Don't you get sick,' he said. 'Don't want to embarrass yourself in front of the boss, now, do you?' He slammed the car door, and I yelled through gritted teeth, an outburst of pure frustration, fury and, I think, fear. Eventually, I closed my eyes and listened to the distant chorus of New York traffic.

Sirens blared, naturally, but when they started to get louder, I peered out the window. There was a calvary of about five police cars streaming into the vast stretch of dead parking lot, lights flashing, engines roaring. Behind them, a couple of shiny black vans, presumably filled with King's Men. The vehicles swarmed past me and came to a halt close to Hatter's car. I recognized some of the cops who emerged from the cruisers, some half-decent people, all dragged into this shitshow. But most of them were just outright corrupt scumbags. A few of them were heavily armed, proudly displaying assault rifles and the like. My vision was blurry, so I squeezed my eyes shut a few times, and when I opened them again, I saw that horrible, monstrous figure climbing out of his vehicle.

Chief Cole slammed his door shut and waddled over to the trunk containing the increasingly famed corpse of Officer Hamelin. Cole's gross form filled me with a sort of rage that only he could inspire in me. There were five armed men escorting him, most of them with their heads only reaching just above Cole's elbows. From this distance, I could properly witness the absurd height of the monster. I watched as one of the officers opened up the trunk. When Cole saw, there was no change on his face, as expected. In fact, I think I saw a smirk. He'd seen worse. He'd created worse.

There was brief exchange between the officers and Cole, some kind of gesture, and then Shades heaved me back out of the cruiser. 'Walk, boy,' he grunted.

I found my eyes were fixed on Chief Cole a few yards ahead of me, and I began to walk. Underneath the rumbling of the wind, I heard murmurings of all the officers around me. There were about twenty men and women, stationed in a scattered pattern across the stretch of parking lot, which had taken on the form of a concrete desert.

My staring contest with the back of Cole's head ended when I saw a group of silhouettes emerge from the black vans to my right. The King's Men stalked toward the scene with purpose. This time there was no Marionette commanding them. I was alone.

Corral needed to show up fast. What she'd be able to actually do once showing up, however, was a different story entirely.

Chief Cole slowly turned on his heel to greet me, a grimace on his face, which then turned into a soulless, mocking smile.

I slowed my walking and came to a stop about five meters from him. The King's Men stationed themselves around me. This was extremely high security for what was either going to be my arrest or execution. I guess more people hated me than I'd realized.

Cole took two steps toward me while looking thoughtfully at the ground with that smile stuck on his face, scratching the side of his nose with a finger that could've passed for a pork sausage. He then stretched his shoulders and puffed out his chest which, of course, also caused his belly to bulge at me. I let the revulsion creep over my face. He gripped his belt, sighed loudly, and shook his head.

'Look at this,' he said, motioning to the swarm of police that looked on. 'Take in this display. This little army of good, incorruptible police men and women, summoned here because of the misdoings of a certain little loose cannon, eh? Our resources, which would otherwise be applied to this great city and its people, have had to be lugged down here in the middle of an abandoned parking lot to apprehend you, the rogue ex-cop who just won't lie down. Oh, Jack, it's humiliating! Isn't it?'

I said nothing, just let things play out.

Cole looked at the ground and shook his head again, lowering his voice. 'I do regret we could not stop you sooner. Slimy rat that you are. A murderous scoundrel, too, I see.'

The sounds of wind and distant traffic hung over us all in between each phase of silence. I listened out for the sound of one more incoming vehicle.

The chief gripped his suspenders and began walking toward me. 'What ungodly thing have you created and placed into the trunk of your vehicle?' he asked quietly. He looked to the gray sky, frowned, and slowly paced about before me, raising his voice. 'You continue to outdo yourself, I must observe that. Reluctantly, of course, because as I'm sure everyone standing here today is aware, to witness the result of a homicide strikes me in the very center of my big old heart, no matter how many times I may have witnessed it. But from a former detective? It is unthinkable. Yet here we are.'

A smile crept onto my face because I was filled with disbelief, yet also found the whole act entirely predictable.

'Oh, he smiles,' growled Cole. 'There is no room for corruption in my police department, nor my city, *our* city. I'm afraid there is no future for you here. In fact, I am going to have to tell you there is no future for you, period.'

Some of the King's Men shifted a little, trigger-happy as usual.

'Jack, you have two rather obvious options here. After you tell us whose body this is within the trunk of your vehicle, I will shoot you in the head. If you refuse, well, I'll quickly be able to ascertain this corpse's identity, and you will only be sentencing yourself to a rather elongated and messy demise.'

I laughed and turned my attention to the onlookers. Here we were again, my boss and I providing a public dispute before a big crowd – he just loves that shit. 'I'm sure the chief's glaring hypocrisy isn't lost on any of you,' I said, my voice weak and tired. 'He threatens to murder me without trial—'

I was interrupted by a gunshot and a bullet nestling itself into my boot, half an inch away from making contact with my actual foot. I stumbled back, tripped over myself, saw Officer Shades pointing a revolver right at me. Cole stormed over and snatched the gun from his hand. 'Enough!' he roared. 'Hold your fire, ridiculous man.'

With a wince, I thrust myself to my feet, the sole of my left boot torn open. I turned away from Cole and his lapdog, looking out at the distant road. Two black sedans were making their way to the scene.

'What's this about?' demanded Cole. 'Who called for backup? Hell, did you even *search* the man?'

'We did, sir,' someone said.

'Jackson!' the chief barked. 'What is this?'

I just shrugged. The King's Men marched onward, shoving past me, guns aimed forward.

Then there was a distant roar, a loud, rumbling engine. To the east, there was some kind of large vehicle heading right at us, growing larger with every passing second.

This part wasn't in the arrangement.

Cole snarled, murmured something to one of the officers, who then took off in a cruiser, lights flashing, and went to meet the oncoming truck.

I looked at Cole. He was looking at me, and I thought he just might skip the theatrics and shoot me where I stood. But he didn't. He was going to see how this played out. The black sedans came to a halt as the King's Men approached them, guns still pointed, distorted voices ordering those inside to step out.

I squinted, hoping it would aid my failing vision. The first figure to emerge from the sedans was suited up in a long, reddish-brown coat and a cowboy hat. A feeling of relief rushed through me: the Marionette, surely the most talented gunman I'd ever met, and I imagined his skills were soon going to be very valuable once more.

To the left, the huge truck was still closing in, being approached slowly by the King's Men.

Ahead of me, Lieutenant Corral followed the Marionette out of the sedan, rising out from the passenger seat quickly and confidently, brushing aside one of the King's Men while showing it what I assume was her badge. There were five other people that followed, including the two that I'd met back at the station. I turned to look at Cole again. This time he was grinding his teeth. A chuckle slipped out of me.

Shades appeared at my side, glared into me through the aviators. Then Cole materialized at my other side, lowering himself right beside my face so I could smell everything on his wretched breath. His eyes were fixed on Corral. He muttered, 'You're digging yourself into a very bad situation here. I'm not sure how you expect this to end, but I can tell you that your snooping will bring much more harm to you and your friends than I would ever endeavor to inflict. Your life is essentially done now; it's everyone else's that are at stake. Make your next move very carefully. Now, what's in the truck?'

I looked over at the eighteen-wheeler parked in the distance, a few yards away from the entrance to the abandoned mall. It was a glamourous beast. I saw glimmering white light from the looming, subdued sun reflected off its burgundy finish. The officer who'd gone to investigate stepped out of the car and placed his hands on his hips, presumably ordering the driver to show some identification. My guess as to who was in the truck was as good as Cole's, though he would never believe that.

As I was looking on, the chief gripped my collars and yanked me toward him in a manner I was getting pretty accustomed to. 'What is this?' he snarled, then licked at his lips aggressively.

'Excuse me, Chief!' a female voice said behind us.

FABLENOIR

I looked over my shoulder at Lieutenant Corral. I must've looked like a helpless, battered animal, seized within the jaws of a vicious predator. She was trailed by the Marionette, the two rebel officers I'd briefly met before, and a small group of other officers who I assumed also belonged to our faction of subordinates. If anything was about to erupt, we were still massively outnumbered. A horrible feeling swirled around in my stomach for a moment as the thought that Rich Hamelin should've been here, too, made itself known in my mind.

'Lieutenant Corral,' said Cole, his voice a rumble of disdain poorly masked with an attempt at mild cheeriness. The guy was seething. He suddenly dropped his feral eyes to me, realizing he was still clutching me with a fat, chalky fist, then stepped back, pulled out a handkerchief from his jacket, and dabbed at his red, balding head. 'Lieutenant, we are dealing with this situation. This traitor and murderer is to be disciplined as I see fit; you have no part in this. I urge you, order you, to stand back.'

'Actually,' interjected Corral with force, 'this man is part of my investigation and I'm taking custody of him – with respect, sir.' She then gripped my wrist and pulled me toward her, away from the bemused chief, who I was still watching closely. 'Detective Jackson Slade, I am arresting you on suspicion of murder. You have the right to remain silent. If you give up that right, anything you say can and will be used against you in a court of law. You have the right to an attorney and to have an attorney present during—'

Chief Cole's vacant expression had been taken over by a gross grin, the elastic skin around his mouth forming deep, uneven creases.

'Don't move,' said a shaky voice from behind me, one I didn't recognize.

Corral sighed down my neck. 'You fuck,' she said after a pause, a tone of disappointment and resentment in her voice. Then there was a chorus of panicked whispering and the sound of firearms being whipped out of their holsters. 'Seriously? exclaimed Corral.

'Un-fucking-believable.'

I dared to turn around. The first thing my eyes took in was the sight of Corral with each hand beside her head, jaw clenched. Someone was pressing a gun to the back of her head.

It was one of her own, the other guy from the secret station whose name I never got. Surrounding him were the rest of rebel officers, including the elf, Vesryn, weapons drawn, aimed at both Corral's betrayer and the chief.

'Shit,' I whispered, feeling my eyes wide and darting.

Corral shrugged and rolled her eyes. 'Yeah,' she said passively, 'I know.'

It was almost comical, and I found I had to push down a laugh traveling up my throat. Or maybe it was actually an incoming eruption of hysterical tears. Either way, there was no time to wait and find out which. 'What is this?' I asked, either to Cole or the man with his gun to Corral.

King's Men marched toward the scene, raised their weapons to Corral and her people. Two of the soulless soldiers appeared either side of me, guns at my head. I looked into the blank metal helmet that cased whatever was inside it, if anything, and I didn't feel the fear I was supposed to, just resignation.

Cole cleared his throat loudly and spoke, a recovered self-satisfaction in his voice that made me want to cave his huge skull in. 'Ultimately, my dear boy, it looks like the lady lieutenant here got it a bit wrong – that is, her recruitment process for this little rebellious project she's put together! I admire your spirit, Ilsa.'

'Fuck off,' she spat.

'But,' Cole continued, as if he didn't hear her, 'in the end, honor, justice, integrity, and all those values my spectacular department holds dear and integrates with every aspect of its work, will always prevail, and overcome the harmful, childish antics of the few who choose to rail against them. Your friend, Detective Bhatt here, merely did the right thing, and informed me of your ridiculous efforts to overthrow and *undermine* our work.' He shook his head and put on an exaggerated, sad expression. 'Shameful. Sad.'

'Cole,' said Ilsa Corral. 'After you kill us – and I know you will because I'm more than familiar with your track record – you will go down, excruciatingly, horrifically. Things have already started, the skeletons are about to come tumbling out of a very large closet, and lots of people want you dead, *will have* you dead. You will be eaten alive for your violations. You're too fucking arrogant and blind to even take these words entirely seriously, I know it, but I believe I can plant a couple seeds of fear in your psyche for now.'

As the chief abruptly burst into a belly laugh followed by a fit of disgusting, wet coughing, I heard sudden movement behind me and a grunt from Corral. I spun to see Bhatt grappling with her, gripping her shoulder and digging his boot into the back of her leg so she dropped to her knees. Two of the King's Men went to help as Detective Bhatt pushed the barrel of the gun to the side of Corral's head, and another two gave me the same treatment.

I collapsed to my knees before the giant frame of Cole, who was now hacking into a large cloth. When he was finished transferring a lung into it, he flung it down in front of me and wiped his mouth. 'Oh, Lieutenant,' he said, his voice croaking, 'I thank you for those words. We shall see if they have the desired effect upon me, but I must admit, I am a *little* skeptical.' He chuckled again and spat out a slimy ball of green onto the ground, then adjusted his tie and folded his arms across his massive chest. Meanwhile, I battled internally with a brewing load of vomit.

Throwing his head to the side, Cole suddenly roared, '*WILL YOU GET THAT TRUCK AWAY FROM HERE, YOU IN-COMPETENT MAN!?*'

The officer in the distance, who was still arguing with the truck driver, replied with the waving of arms and an unintelligible shout.

'For God's sake, go and see what he's playing at,' said Cole to a squad of King's Men.

They took off immediately in a synchronized rapid walk.

'And so, this is the part we've been waiting for, ladies and gentlemen. It's time to dispatch the traitors. Detective Bhatt, if you will, I think it only fair for you to be the one to do the honor. You may now sentence Miss Corral to death, for she has brought great shame upon us all.'

Bhatt gave the chief a cold smirk, and took up a position before Corral. He pointed the gun between her eyes. I saw most of her face as the detective stood between us. Her dark eyes met mine, then she looked her executioner in the face. She was a picture of valor.

'I always hated you,' Bhatt said in a lofty half-whisper.

Corral scoffed. 'No you didn't. You're just a fucking sellout.'

I looked away quickly. I squeezed my eyes closed and clenched my fists so hard, they shook.

Then came a bang. But not from Detective Bhatt's gun.

Everyone instantly turned their heads to the side, and then chaos ensued. A small army of figures started to emerge from the back of the stationary eighteen-wheeler next to the mall. The officer who'd been wrangling with the truck driver was flat-out on the ground in a pool of blood, his head spread out in bits.

The King's Men who had gone to investigate were shot at with automatic weapons, firing their own guns into the growing crowd as bullets went through their own bodies. They all fell dead except one, who'd taken cover in front of the huge radiator grill. Just before I moved to dart away, I saw one of the gunmen shove a gleaming blade into the surviving King's Man's head.

I rolled to the side in a heap, not knowing what the hell was going on but hoping it worked out for the best. My ears rang, the sound of gunfire and screams amplified into pure carnage in my head. My senses were out of control.

Corral's officers scrambled for their guns, the Lieutenant herself launching an elbow into Bhatt's stunned face. She managed to grab hold of his revolver and blast a bullet through his neck.

Chief Cole stumbled my way, panting, reaching clumsily for his own gun. I darted for cover, falling behind one of the parked cruisers, desperately trying to find a way to break out of my cuffs.

Cole was now aiming his gun at Corral while shifting away from the action, tongue hanging out of his mouth.

'*Ilsa*!' I yelled, and she jumped away from the gurgling half-corpse of Detective Bhatt, a bullet from Cole's gun firing past her shoulder. '*Fuck*,' I hissed to myself, because I saw that about half the rebels had already been gunned down by the King's Men.

I gasped and fell back as someone slid into cover beside me. It was Vesryn, pistol in one hand, the other glowing with a dark green energy. 'Here!' he called to me, then blasted a beam of green enchantment straight into the handcuffs. They split off from my wrists and sizzled on the ground.

'Shit, thanks,' I said between breaths, and he slid a semi-automatic pistol my way. I gripped it and peered over the cruiser, teeth clenched together, scanning the scene for Corral. I found her backing off from where the main cluster of Cole's officers and King's Men were. She and her allies dispersed and got to cover themselves. I fired at Cole's officers, whose attention was now split between us and the gunmen quickly descending on them. 'Who are those guys?' I yelled to Vesryn.

He fired three rounds over the car and ducked for cover again. 'I don't know,' he called back as a bullet skimmed the roof of the cruiser. 'Keep yourself alive and you might find out.'

I leaned over the hood and aimed the pistol at Cole. He was a vulnerable target, and the King's Men knew that. They covered him as best they could, fully committed to sacrificing themselves for their supreme leader. Bodies went down as bullets ripped through the air in all directions, screams of agony and barks of orders beneath the roaring of the distant truck, which was now lighting up the scene with its great headlights, charging toward us all.

'Goddammit!' I yelled, as Cole was escorted into one of the large, bullet-proof trucks by a squad of King's Men, most of them collapsing to the ground after achieving their objective. It didn't matter how accurate the magick beans made my aim when the King's

Men were this well-drilled at guarding Cole, especially amidst chaos like this.

The black truck protecting Cole began to hurtle away, and then my eyes widened as I realized it was on a collision course for the eighteen-wheeler. It was about to get T-boned into oblivion.

'Oh, boy,' said Vesryn, gripping my arm and dragging me to my feet. 'We ought to move *right now*.' We stumbled to the next area of cover we could find, behind a row of large storage containers beside the desolate mall. The gunmen roared and hollered as the giant truck sped toward Cole's vehicle, and a booming metallic slamming sound was followed by the screeching of tires against concrete, as the armored vehicle containing the chief of police went spinning wildly across the parking lot and then tipped and crashed onto its side.

The eighteen-wheeler had stopped in the middle of the battleground, and there was a brief quiet before all hell broke loose again. The King's Men, intruding gunmen, and Corral's remaining rebel officers all opened fire. I caught a glimpse of the Marionette, cutting down his opponents brutally with a whole arsenal at his disposal. He threw a revolver to his side, aimed a closed wooden fist toward a police cruiser with about four officers behind it, all shooting incessantly at the bounty hunter, who never even flinched, and fired three small rockets from beneath his wrist.

I saw them swirl in a circular motion across the parking lot littered with bodies and vehicles, and blast the cruiser and officers in an eruption of fire and smoke. The flames whipped at the sky and flared up into a mountain of destruction. I had to throw myself back fully behind cover again as the heat roared against my face. Beneath the crackling and roaring of the fire, I heard screeches of anguish as bodies burned and the Marionette continued his slaughter, taking every bullet as if they were no different from the raindrops falling from the black sky.

'Lieutenant!' called Vesryn, and I saw Corral and a couple of rebel officers making their way from cover to cover, the Marionette standing his ground as a distraction.

I shot wildly into the crowd of King's Men to provide more cover as Corral and the others sprinted toward us.

'No!' yelled Vesryn, and I saw that one of the rebels had received a bullet straight through the skull. It'd come from Shades, who was standing right in front of the flames, aiming his revolver at Corral. The elf then appeared beside me, blasting a spell into the ground, ripping it right open from where we stood all the way to Shades, who flew back rapidly and was engulfed by the wall of fire before I even had a chance to raise my gun.

Corral and the officers took cover with us as the gunmen continued their rampage. 'Where's Marionette?' called the lieutenant while reloading her pistol.

I looked out into the chaos, saw the android walking in reverse toward us, firing bullets at the gunmen and King's Men with pinpoint accuracy. 'Oh, he's fine,' I said. 'What about you? You good?'

'Yes,' Corral replied stoically, 'I'm fine.' Her eyes scanned the chaos before us. 'My comrades not so much. Dammit! What the fuck is happening here?'

I said nothing, hearing the rate of fire decreasing suddenly. The Marionette appeared from behind the wall, dozens of bullets encased in his wooden shell, and about half of his coat reduced to gaping holes.

'Ruined my finest attire,' he said almost cheerfully, then brought out yet another weapon from his utility belt.

Corral gripped my shoulder and peered past me to see what had happened. 'Holy shit,' she murmured.

Scores of the gunmen were now standing in clusters across the parking lot, most of them aiming weapons at the few remaining King's Men and police officers, who'd dropped their guns. There was a loud thud, and everyone turned to look at the eighteen-wheeler. Ash and rain flew across the scene, and the giant frame of the one who looked to be behind this destruction emerged from the thick black smoke.

Papa Bear – tommy gun in his paws, cigar hanging from his snout – surveyed the scene, his long leather coat trailing across the blood-soaked ground.

'Oh my God,' whispered Corral as she looked on, pistol in hand.

I saw a figure scrambling across the ground, groaning and wheezing desperately. The bear stopped in his tracks and looked down at the man with apparent pity, letting the machine gun hang by his side. It was the cop, Shades, burned to hell yet grasping onto a sliver of life.

He struggled to his feet, yelled, and stumbled forward, blasting bullets into the ground then pointing his revolver toward the towering creature. The bear simply swiped at Shades's arm, which flew off cleanly as a high-pitched scream echoed across the parking lot, then Papa Bear shoved his claws into Shades's neck, effortlessly raising him to the sky for all to behold, and flung him back into the flames.

The display was met with raucous cheers, and the bear continued his pacing. 'Chief Cole!' he roared as he strode over to the toppled armored vehicle.

A weird feeling of dread and anticipation came over me. I immediately wondered how unfulfilled I would go for the rest of my life if Papa Bear was about to murder his business partner, my rightful kill.

He slammed his gun onto the metallic surface of the vehicle, sunk his claws into the hinges of the door, then ripped it off and hurled it across the parking lot like a frisbee. I jerked back and puffed my cheeks as the door crashed against the wall near us. Then I heard a sound that gave me more delight than it probably should have. Chief Cole whimpered and screamed as the bear peered into the truck, and I saw two wide arms protruding from where the door once was, flailing and thrashing pathetically.

I looked around at my allies with a smile on my face, but was only met with vacant glances as everyone looked on in shock. I dropped the smile.

Papa Bear reached into the truck and extracted a blood-covered Chief Cole, who just tipped over onto the ground, limbs loose, with a wet smack. It was an insane demonstration to take in, and I couldn't quite figure out how to process it.

Cole slid himself across the ground, backing away from the bear, grumbling and pleading.

Papa Bear picked him up off the ground and slammed him against the underside of the armored vehicle. I saw Cole clutching at his own throat, his chest heaving up and down, eyes scrunching shut. He threw his head to the side and projectile-vomited blood.

'Nobody start feeling sorry for this *pendejo*,' muttered Corral to the rest of us. 'He's gonna get what he deserves, one way or another.'

'Speaking for myself,' I said, 'I have absolutely no intention of doing so.'

Papa Bear's voice boomed across the parking lot like he was speaking into a megaphone. 'Now. I want to make this quick, Cole. Take this demonstration of violence and death as a warning. It did not have to be this way, as you well know. If you choose to continue denying me my resources, I will continue to deplete yours. Like this.' He turned to the crowd of surviving King's Men and officers, raised his machine gun to his waist, and fired at them until he was out of bullets. The bodies lay there in a heap.

I involuntarily smacked my hand against my mouth and drew back, resting my head against the storage unit and staring into the black clouds for a minute. The raindrops felt ice cold against my skin. There was a rumbling, and at first I thought it was the sound of thunder, but then the parking lot flashed with white light. I looked back around the corner. Four NYPD choppers formed a circle in the sky, casting a spotlight onto Papa Bear, whose leather coat flapped and lashed from the force of the propellers. He pressed a paw down on his trilby and gazed up at the copters.

'Ma'am,' purred the Marionette from behind us, 'don't you think it's best we skate while we can? There'll only be more reinforcements from here on out. True, I'm not paid for my advisory capability, but it seems to me that this is a good opportunity to regroup and plan our next move.'

The logical voice in my head agreed entirely, but I was also desperate to see how this played out.

'Hold on, Marionette, I know,' said Corral, eyes fixed on the scene ahead. The Marionette retreated a little, his body looking like a battleground in itself yet functioning with no apparent difficulty.

'I tend to agree, Lieutenant,' said Vesryn. 'We have lost many today; we cannot afford to lose any more. Jackson is in our possession again, and that beast over there has Cole on the ropes. This is essentially the best outcome we could have hoped for, all things considered.'

Corral shushed Vesryn with a wave of her arm and looked at me with the corner of her eye. 'What do you think?' she said irritably. 'We can hold out here a little longer, call in everyone I trust as backup and attempt to apprehend both the bear and the chief, or we retreat and start it all again. The enemy is weakened, and I think now is our chance, but I won't make the call if you don't think it's the right thing to do.'

Vesryn whispered, 'Only one of the enemies is weakened, Lieutenant. The other, perhaps the greater enemy, appears to have the world at his feet.' The elf paused, then swallowed. 'And Ilsa . . . There's no one left to call in.'

Corral's eyes were wide, almost glazed over, as if she'd only just realized her allies had been slaughtered.

Chief Cole was now signaling something to the choppers. It looked like he was telling them to stand down. Papa Bear remained unmoved, just glaring into the beams shooting down from above.

I thought about the fact that Corral didn't even know about Hamelin yet. I heard the growls and screams from the scene at the wood again, terrorizing my head. I thought about the fact that I hadn't heard from Goldilocks, wondered where she was. I realized she may have missed her chance to take out the bear, stupid idea as it might've been. I sighed and pressed my fingers to my temples, a heavy feeling in my chest. 'We should go, Lieutenant,' was all I said.

Corral looked at me, probing with those eyes. Then she turned away again as the sound of the choppers got louder, then quieter. All four rotated in the air and started heading back toward the city. For whatever reason, they were leaving their chief of police in a heap, bleeding in the rain. But it was by his own orders. Papa Bear stood over Cole, growled something to him and turned away.

A singular armored van was making its way toward Cole as the bear and his men disappeared round the back of the eighteen-wheeler and slammed the back doors shut. Four armored police officers rushed to Cole and heaved him to his feet, then dragged him along with great effort, pulling him into the van.

'Well,' said Corral. 'Looks like we're an afterthought for now. Let's go, while we still can. We have a lot to do.' She shot a look at me. 'And a lot to talk about.'

12
Sweet Tooth

Those of us that survived had fled the scene in a couple of the sedans that Corral and the others arrived in before the massacre. Thankfully they'd been parked pretty far away from the action, so there was no damage to any of the cars, and no reason for us to be stopped by anyone in the horde of police cars making their way through the city toward the littered parking lot. The military was out, too, followed by ambulances and fire trucks.

People stopped in their tracks, packing the streets to get a look at the cavalry. I noticed the skies were clear of choppers. It didn't look like anyone was being hunted down or pursued; it was more like a cleanup operation, with extra reinforcements to hold back crowds of curious, panicked civilians, and to subdue and threaten any prowling journalists who may actually feel like doing their job.

If there was anyone around who might recognize any of us, particularly the pretty damn distinctive Marionette, they didn't have a chance at catching a glance because the rain was now pelting down on the windshields, blurring us beyond recognition. It was only late afternoon, but the clouds that engulfed the tops of the skyscrapers ahead were so thick and dark, it seemed like the sun had set hours ago.

We stayed silent for the duration of the journey back to the station. There was a potent feeling of grief filling the car, and the use of words felt pointless and stupid.

Corral treated an injury to her wrist the whole time, never looking away from the blood-stained bandage on her hand until it was time to step out of the car.

We turned into one of the wider alleyways that led toward the makeshift station, sirens from the dozens of vehicles either at or near the shoot-out territory still wailing in the distance. The Marionette rolled down his window and said, 'Y'all wait a moment. I'm gonna check we're clear; Bhatt might not have been the only rat.' He turned to Corral. 'Keys, ma'am?'

'Yeah,' Corral replied, snapping them from her belt and passing them over.

The Marionette nodded, opened the car door, and stepped into the dark alley, turning on the flashlight built into his head. It flickered at first, so he thumped at his ears as if they were full of water, then it lit up the scene.

Corral sighed and looked at me. 'Seriously, I had no idea he was a rat. What does that make me? I almost got us all killed.'

Hamelin flashed in my mind again. 'It wasn't your fault,' I said.

'But it could've been prevented,' she replied quickly. 'How did you know, anyway?'

'Know?'

'When you texted me, before all of that, you said there was a traitor in my ranks. What made you think that? How did you know?'

'I uh . . . We should talk inside.'

'Jack,' she said, and I was reminded how unprepared I was to tell her the truth.

I fumbled with my words for a moment, weird sounds that were supposed to turn into sentences coming from my throat. 'Look, I just want you to know, before we go any further, I'm for real. I want things to change. I didn't know before if I cared enough to try and make things better, or if I was just playing games because I've got a death wish. But I think I've now realized that I've wanted to step in and fight all along; I was just too much of a drunken, fucked-up heap of a broken mess to know it. I'm committed, and I'm gonna help unravel everything, *everything*, and I—'

'I got it,' she interjected, 'I got it. Just be straight with me. You have to tell me everything now, and then we will begin to change things. So, I ask again, how did you know Bhatt was a rat?'

'Alright,' said the Marionette, peering into the car. 'Looks good to me. Let's all head inside and put our feet up, huh?'

I glanced across his damaged shell as he swung away from the car. Wood was splintered and broken, his fancy coat punctured with bullet holes. The Marionette now seemed to struggle as he headed toward the station. I'd never seen a robot limp before.

Corral kept her eyes on me while opening the car door. She turned away and got out, slamming the door behind her. I followed, climbing up the little steel staircase that led to the station entrance and heading inside. It was freezing and there was a weird metallic smell hanging in the air. I went after Corral, who was heading for one of the office rooms. 'Ilsa,' I said.

She turned on her heels, hands on hips. 'Come in here,' she said, cocking her head to the room. I followed her in, my hands gripping each other behind my back.

Like the rest of the station, the office was bare and bleak. Only the essentials were in place: computers, files, weapons. Corral noisily dragged a steel chair from the corner of the room and pressed down on my shoulder.

I flinched at the amplified screeching of metal, then sat.

She looked into my eyes for a moment, mouth clamped shut, eyebrows furrowed, then she pulled up her own chair opposite me. 'You're shaking,' she said. 'You've been shaking for about a half hour.'

I looked down at my hands. They didn't even look like my own, like they'd been ripped off and replaced with the hands of a week-old corpse. They were shaking alright, trembling, quivering. Drawing my attention to the abysmal condition of my body was just about the worst thing Corral could do, bearing in mind what I was about to tell her.

'You look absolutely terrible,' she continued, not looking so hot herself. 'If you don't wind up dead because of these dangerous enemies you've made, it'll be those drugs that take you. You realize that, right?'

Now it was really hitting me, the pain and the confusion. The adrenaline I'd had left in my body during the gunfight was gone. Magick remained, but it was lame, weakened somehow. 'I . . . I need water or something. I'm sorry, I might collapse.'

'Damn right you might.'

'Where can I get some water, or whiskey?' I said, stumbling to my feet. 'Please, I need a fucking drink.'

'Sit down! You'll get a drink when you tell me what I want to know. What I *need* to know.'

I looked at her with my mouth hanging open, my dry tongue resting on my bottom lip. My body crashed back into the metal seat.

Corral leaned forward. 'I don't want to see you like this, trust me. But I gotta push you here. Tell me what you know. I need to know now, right now. This is serious shit.'

'That . . . That it is. Alright.' I swallowed, my throat so dry, I almost choked on my own saliva.

'What made you say I had a rat?'

I thought back, half-picturing scattered memories. 'As you're aware, I was carrying out my own investigation before meeting you. When I found Dumpty's body a few nights ago, I took on the case myself, despite that fuck Cole's orders. We know what he's like, right? We know what he's all about. So when he started insisting he took care of it personally, well, naturally I suspected nothing less than a cover-up.'

'Yes. Cole has a long, long history of corruption and . . . immorality. If only you'd stepped up sooner. You've been a detective, what, ten years now?'

'Listen, it's not so straightforward—'

'But I'm glad you did decide to do what you did.'

I ignored the somewhat backhanded compliment and moved on.

'It got to the point where I was actually pointing my gun in Cole's face, and I was dismissed—' I paused a moment. '—and subsequently hunted down across the city, basically the entire police force wanting me dead. So, welcome to the club.'

Corral raised her eyebrows briefly and fiddled with a pen. 'Tell me about your girlfriend.'

'My what?'

'The blonde with the gunslinger act.'

'Goldilocks. She's not my girlfriend, and I'm not so sure it's an act. She's dangerous. And she's an ally.'

The lieutenant scoffed. 'So where was she tonight? I mean, I'm sure her gunmanship and ruthless style would've been useful in that shitshow we just went through. Weird that she just disappeared from your side once things really started heating up.'

'It's not like that. I don't know where she is right now, but I told her to get some rest last night. I'll give her a call once I acquire the luxury of a glass of water.'

'Is she the one who told you about a rat?'

'No.'

She just stared, pen between her teeth, eyes scanning mine.

I went on. 'To tell you the truth, I don't know a whole lot about Goldilocks. You won't like this part, but she used to be in the bear's gang.'

Her eyes narrowed into black slits.

'One day she overheard a conversation between the bear and the egg man himself – something to do with human trafficking and gunrunning. Obviously that's not what she signed up for, so she stole some very valuable things from Papa Bear and ran away. She betrayed them, Ilsa. She wants nothing to do with them, and she wants Papa Bear's head clean off. She wants to bring that about herself.'

Corral tipped her chair back a little and looked up at the ceiling.

My ears were hot.

'Did that girl kill Dumpty?' she asked.

'Yes,' I said. 'She did.'

She nodded. 'She doesn't seem like much of what you might call a team player.'

'Maybe not. But I owe her my life.'

'You trust her?'

'I feel like maybe I've abandoned the whole concept of outright trust, to be quite honest.' I licked my lips, covered in scabs. 'I believe her integrity. And I think in some ways, she wants what I want. What we all want here.'

'And what is it that we all mutually want here?'

'Revenge, I guess. Justice. A transformation. I don't know. I suppose I'm trying to say we're all wanted dead for a reason. Reason being . . . we're trying to do the right thing in a bad, deeply broken world.' The deformed face of a dying Rich Hamelin flashed in my mind.

Corral stuck out her bottom lip and nodded thoughtfully. 'You haven't always tried to do the right thing, have you?' she sternly.

I stayed quiet, not exactly knowing how to respond to that.

'How did they find you? Today, I mean, before the shoot-out.'

I puffed my cheeks and exhaled loudly, hoping to deflate into an empty sack of skin. It didn't work. 'Rich Hamelin is dead, Ilsa.'

She swallowed. Her eyes stayed on mine. Then after a few seconds, she nodded absently, like I'd just told her what I'd eaten for breakfast this morning. 'Okay,' she said. 'Okay.'

'I'm . . . I'm so sorry, it was—' I flinched as she suddenly pushed her chair back and rose to her feet. She floated past me, walked out the door, and returned a minute later with a glass of water and a bottle of unopened whiskey. She placed the water next to me, pulled out a drawer behind the desk, placed two glasses on it and poured the liquor into them. The glass came sliding along toward me.

All of a sudden, I really didn't want it.

She took a sip herself, staring at nothing. 'What happened?' she asked quietly.

I realized the glass of water in my hand was now a glass of air. I wiped at my mouth with the sleeve of my jacket. 'It was my fault. I cut a deal. I had no idea. I was a fucking idiot.'

'You cut a deal? What deal? What do you mean you cut a deal?'

This wasn't getting any easier. I thought maybe by now a way to explain things while sounding reasonable would materialize in my head, but it wasn't going to, exceedingly dehydrated or not. 'We traded Hamelin, who we thought was Officer Piper at the time, to a crazed physician or magus or someone, for his, uh, expertise.' I tapped at my head, even though that meant nothing to Corral as the wound was completely invisible. 'It just sort of happened. We were frantic, rushing. It was stupid. It shouldn't have happened.'

Corral sat there stunned, jaw clenched so hard, it was shaking. She suddenly let out a sharp breath and shook her head. I fidgeted nervously. 'What the fuck kind of physician is this?' she asked.

'I don't know. His name is Hatter. Goldilocks knows him.'

'Of course. Her again. So, what, Hamelin never revealed his true identity to you, even as you were trading him off for some goddamn medicine?' There were tears in her eyes now. She poured another glass of whiskey.

I thought back, hearing his screams as we left Hatter's place. My entire body felt numb. 'He didn't have a chance to; there was never a moment where we were alone together. And I sure as hell didn't suspect him as a good guy. He really nailed that Piper role,' I said dumbly, trying to lighten the mood.

'Yeah. That was his fucking job,' replied the lieutenant.

I looked down at the table.

'So, how did it happen? What did this nutjob do to him?'

'I . . . I'm sorry, Ilsa. I'm so sorry.'

She shrugged.

I tried not to choke on my words, everything I'd seen flooding into my mind at once. It was like I was being transported back there, watching him die all over again. 'Hatter was evidently using him as some kind of test subject. I don't know exactly. Like he was trying to transform him into something. He had half the body of a rabbit, or a hare.'

Corral stared at me, eyes narrowed, mouth making an O shape. 'What?' she finally said.

'Seriously, the man's insane.'

'And you willingly gave him one of our own. A human being.'

'I didn't know.'

'A *human being*!' she yelled. 'That's the point, Slade. Now what's the fucking difference between you and the bear?'

A minute filled with silence passed. Corral shook her head and poured me a glass this time.

I sipped, coughed with my mouth closed. 'I've made some mistakes, many mistakes. That's the worst one. It'll haunt me forever.'

'I certainly hope so.'

I thought for a moment, remembering all the little details of the night before, trying to retrace my steps. 'Hamelin was onto something. He knew he was dying but he wanted to follow through with whatever it was he was doing,' I said. 'Snowdrop Wood.'

'What about it?'

'That's where I found him. Dr Hatter said he'd managed to escape, so he chased him through the city in his truck, saw him heading into Snowdrop Wood. Hatter didn't go in himself, though, just went back to his lab, or whatever you'd call it. So I went there myself.'

'Hold up, hold up, what?' said Corral, waving a hand in the air. 'How did he not catch him if he was in a car?'

'I don't know exactly what Hatter was trying to achieve with that experiment, but he'd apparently managed to combine the genes of a hare with Hamelin. Until it all went wrong, I think he was able to run as fast as a hare.'

'Jesus Christ,' Corral said loudly, almost smiling with disbelief.

'What the hell is this?'

'Gets worse,' I said.

'Wait, why would the guy create something like that but then just abandon him once he got into the woods?'

'Obviously not worth the risk, the awful shit that's supposed to go on in there.'

'Yeah, well, he sounds like a pretty awful guy himself.'

'When I tracked Hamelin down, he was almost dead.' I stopped talking.

'Go on,' said Corral.

I breathed in sharply. 'I don't want to go into it. I won't. But he was suffering so much. And it was my fault. He told me about a cult, children being taken to the woods. Sacrifice. He said that they all know. Who is "they"? He told me I have to trust you, that I need to work with you to find out what the hell is going on. And then he told me you probably had a traitor in the squad.' I finished the whiskey, my eyes stinging viciously. 'He told me to end his suffering, so I did.'

As I turned my body to the side, staring down at the floor, Corral stood up and put her forehead against the wall.

I got up and slowly approached her, not knowing whether to stand beside her or keep my distance. 'His evidence is in Bloodstone,' I said. 'It's in his room at the bear's mansion. He said . . . Koppelberg. Know what that is?'

'Jack,' she said, still processing everything else. 'You fucked up, you really did. Richard Hamelin's death will be a costly setback in this operation. He was one of our most valuable assets and obviously he was bringing us the intel we need to one day bring down Cole and the others, and now we don't have him. That's your fault, and you should've told me sooner what'd happened. But we have to move on now. We have to get it together before more people are kidnapped or killed. I can't imagine what messed-up shit is going on, and clearly it goes all the way to the top, which puts us in massive danger. So we must tread carefully but with impact.'

I just nodded. I had more to say, although I didn't know exactly what, so silence seemed to be the best option for now.

'I'm keeping my eye on you. You did a terrible thing, so know that I think differently of you now. If I catch a hint of a fuck-up or another selfish action, you're gone.'

My heart sank and twisted a little. I nodded again.

She then opened the door to the main room and signaled for me to follow. 'We will seize Arminus and the evidence when the time is right. First, we can gather more information. We must go to your insane friend's home and question him on what the hell he was doing, then we will arrest him.'

I jogged up to her side. 'I don't think he's gonna go anywhere, honestly. We need to prioritize Odette first, stay hot on her trail. Dumpty was seen in one of her spots before he died. We can get more from the club manager.'

Corral stopped, breathed in through her nose, and placed both her hands on my shoulders.

'We need to get the victims back, right?' I went on. 'That's where we start.'

'Fine,' said Corral. 'But we *will* get the sick doctor.'

'And what about Goldilocks?' I asked.

Corral paused, her expression dark. 'Just . . . call her, get her back over here. Make no mistake about it, Jack: I do not trust her, but obviously we wouldn't have come this far without her. Can bet I'll be keeping an eye on her, too.' She looked across the room at the Marionette and Detective Vesryn, who seemed to be pretending not to pay attention. 'We all will.'

The red sun watched from the river as we pulled up to The Jolly Roger. This time, I wouldn't let myself get ambushed or shot in the chest with blanks (as valuable a sequence of events that turned out to be). This time, I would find out what else Hansel had going on in that place. It wasn't just some nightclub. It only made sense he was doing more for Odette than just balancing the books. The guy was weak. I was going to walk through his club and see what he was hiding.

A couple of young, willowy guys stood out front, raking leaves and hauling garbage bags. Probably also collecting needles and lost items of clothing from the night before.

Corral stopped the engine and eyed the club in silence.

Vesryn cleared his throat. 'I think we ought to move quickly, Lieutenant. Won't be long before people start forming lines,' he said. 'For some reason.'

The lieutenant shot him a look with her side-eye. 'Yes, Vesryn, I know,' she said, pushing open the car door.

We followed, and approached the front doors. One of the men looked up and peered at us from under his cap. A smoke hung from his lips, his face lined with wrinkles and blemishes that had formed too soon in his young life.

Corral showed her badge. 'Hansel in?'

The guy looked straight to the other one, who'd gone completely still, rake tucked under his arm. He shrugged.

'I'll ask again—'

The old kid's eyes widened slightly. 'Uh.'

'Go on, go fetch him,' I added. 'Tell him Slade just needs a quick word. Nothing to worry about.' I smiled, not overly warmly.

He threw his garbage bag into a steel container, flicked his cigarette onto the floor, and disappeared into the club.

The air smelt like fish and smoke. The fumes coasted up my nostrils while we waited. I started to taste it.

Eventually, the door reopened, and the old kid stepped out, eyebrows low. I peered round him and saw a visibly petrified Hansel. He jolted slightly and started to point.

'Whoa, whoa,' he said, his voice already shaking. 'Why the vests, huh? You here for a damn shoot-out on my property?' He looked around, maniacal. 'And where's that fuckin' chick at? I ain't dealing with this, nah, nah—'

There was a jangle of handcuffs behind me as Corral marched up to Hansel. Vesryn beckoned the other two guys over and motioned his hand horizontally. He'd either cast one of his spells or the kids had just waived any sort of resistance as they stepped eagerly to where he was signaling.

'Oh, hey, no, now what is this shit?' whined Hansel as the cuffs snapped around his wrists. 'Didn't we already go through this, Slade?' he spat.

'No,' I said. 'Not this. Show us the warehouse.'

Hansel sneered.

'The warehouse.'

'Warehouse? What fuckin' warehouse?'

I launched my fist into his stomach as hard as I could, then grabbed him by the curls on his dumb head. 'Show us the warehouse.'

He made a sound somewhere between a growl and a wretch. 'I'm gonna—'

'Do nothing,' snapped Corral. 'Except show us the *warehouse*, and then get in the back of my cruiser.'

'Fuck you.'

Corral simply shoved him through the doors of the club. We went in while Vesryn stood with the other two guys.

Inside, the lights flashed pink and green. Staff lingered around the bar. There was no music.

'Everybody out!' shouted Corral. A couple of too-young-looking bartenders scattered out the exit. A man in a loud suit and fedora looked between us all, eyes wide, then followed the girls.

'Where's security?' I said.

Hansel shrugged, bottom lip sticking out like some sulking preteen.

'In the warehouse?'

'There ain't any fuckin' security,' said Hansel.

'Ah, man, too bad,' I said. 'They given up on you, that what it is?'

Hansel said nothing. We kept moving toward the back of The Jolly Roger until we arrived at a black door.

'This it?' said Corral.

Hansel nodded. 'Sure.'

I pulled out my gun then swung the door open. Aside from a cardboard cutout of some pirate, which I almost discharged a bullet into, there was no one inside. Just boxes and crates and . . . sweets.

There was a crash behind me as Corral shoved Hansel onto one of the wooden crates. 'You sit there,' she said.

'Goddamn,' I muttered. 'This what your addiction's come to, Hansel? Say what you want about me, you asshole, but at least I haven't got an entire depot of beans in my name.'

'What exactly you expecting to find in here? Why me? Why always me?'

Corral gave him a look of pure disdain.

I flung open the lids of some of the crates. Pile upon pile of sweets. 'Why you?' I said. 'Well, why work for Odette? Papa Bear? Dumpty?'

'I never even *met* those guys!'

'Bullshit,' I said, flinging open another crate. I tore into one of the sweet packets. The packaging was completely unbranded, not even serial numbers. The sweets were wrapped in red foil. I threw one toward Hansel. He didn't move. The sweet addict didn't even try to catch the candy flying his way, cuffs or no cuffs.

Corral looked at me. 'What is it?'

'That's interesting, isn't it? Not gonna indulge, Hansel?'

'Fuck you, man.'

'Yeah,' I said, taking another sweet out the packet and unwrapping it. I held it up to my mouth and watched Hansel. He just scowled.

Then I stormed over to him, grabbed him by the throat, and shoved the thing into his mouth.

Corral jumped back. 'What are—'

'No!' screamed Hansel.

'*Why*?' I screamed back. 'Bite it!'

Hansel kicked and yelled, tried to bite down on my fingers. I took another candy, pushed it up to his mouth, and he bit that instead. He went out like a light. His body folded up and flopped onto the floor.

I looked down at him, chewing my cheeks hard, heart pounding. 'Well, there you go,' I said to Corral. I knelt and pulled at Hansel's jaw. A light emanated from down his throat. 'Look at this.'

Corral peered down tentatively. 'Magick?'

'Uh-huh. Of some sort. Whatever it is, obviously it's effective at shutting down the system. If it works like that on a fully grown man, well . . .' Corral nodded. I didn't need to go on.

Corral got to her feet and took in the sight of the warehouse. 'Right. I'll call this in; it's a crime scene now.'

'Ours.'

'Yeah, don't worry. 'Course I'm only gonna tell my guys.'

'You got any of your guys left?' I asked.'

The lieutenant looked down. 'A few. No one else can get near this. Including Robicheaux, got that?'

'I don't even know where she is.'

'Right, but eventually you're gonna,' said the lieutenant, her eyes piercing.

A flash of anticipation swirled through my stomach at that, even though part of me was starting to believe she was done with it all entirely. But I mostly expected to see her again. 'Right,' I said, smiling internally.

'And when he wakes up, whenever that is, he'll be inside a cell, and he'll tell me where we can find this Odette. You really think he'll know?'

I shrugged. 'She owns this place. He's gotta have some idea. And no matter how much he holds out, you push him. You *push* him.'

'Thank you, Slade. I've done this before.'

'Maybe call me when he wakes up.'

'Detective. I know what I'm doing.'

I nodded.

'Be in touch.' The lieutenant pulled out her phone and made some calls.

I slipped out the back door and into the evening. My teeth chattered with adrenaline. My fingernails buried themselves in my palms. I closed my eyes and fought for control of my mind and my body. The stink of fish and smoke closed in on me once more.

Later in the night, Lieutenant Corral called. Hansel was awake, and ready to blab.

On the way over to our station, I sent a couple of texts to Goldilocks and got nothing back. Resentment was starting to become cold, real anger. But that anger would shift into paranoia and fear. As if I needed any more of that crashing around my head.

I was thinking back on nearly every decision I'd made in the past couple of weeks, wondering which ones were about to come back in the form of a bullet or two in the brain. The more I thought, the fewer of them I ruled out.

I opened the steel door and stepped into what served as our interrogation room. The place itself almost seemed a little too bright to serve its purpose, but one look at Hansel and I could tell it wasn't going to make a difference. He was about to talk, if he hadn't already.

Corral turned to me, arms folded stiffly, jaw clenched. 'Word from Robicheaux?'

'No,' I said.

'Didn't think so,' she replied with a cold lingering look.

'Hansel,' I said, 'what you got?'

He was almost smiling, his face twisted up in all kinds of expressions; the one he settled on was terror. 'Well, I'm fuckin dead, ain't I? Whatever happens,' he whined.

I shrugged. 'You tell me. What *could* happen?'

Hansel's beady eyes flicked around the place. They were shot and red. 'Look at this. This ain't no real jail! You're not even real cops anymore, goddammit. You can do whatever the fuck you want to me now, huh? And that *robot* out there, what the fuck?'

Corral rested her hands on the steel table. 'Don't worry about him. And we're not gonna kill you. Don't be a moron. We want answers to our questions. Then we can help the people that you've hurt.'

'But not the ones that are already dead, Hansel,' I said.

'What?' he croaked. 'I already told this lady: I didn't hurt nobody, and no way did I *kill* . . . I just gave 'em the candy.'

I straightened my back and sighed. A numbness was on its way, ready to strip away any pity or humanity I might've had left.

'P-please. I didn't realize what I was getting into—'

'Oh *fuck off*,' I said. 'Where did you think any of this was gonna go? Magick-infused candy that knocks you unconscious after one bite. What did you think was happening?'

'I didn't— I guess I didn't think. I was a fuckin idiot,' he said through tears and snot.

'Tell him what you told me,' Corral ordered.

He looked up, then back down at the desk, shaking his head and clenching his jaw.

'Talk,' I murmured.

'It was all that fuckin *swan queen*. It was all Odette.'

My eyes narrowed. I took a few steps closer. 'What was, Hansel?'

'It was always for her. The candy. She would send her people, from the other clubs. The Roger's hers, too. But I didn't know I would be . . . so involved. Fuckin hell.'

'Who'd she send?'

'Like, vans, guys in vans, to take the candy.' He chewed on his tongue while slowly shrinking into himself. 'Sometimes there were cops, too.'

'What cops?' said Corral.

'I don't know, I— I never saw em, never got a good look. Never wanted to, neither. Didn't wanna know too much, y'know? Just . . . One was tall, pretty damn tall.'

Corral leaned closer. 'Alright, Hansel. That's all good. But you still haven't told us about the candy, the sweets. The magick, how does it get in there?'

Hansel glanced up, then down again. He sighed loudly and grabbed at his curls. 'That's witches.'

The lieutenant glanced my way, as if the inclusion of witches somehow made me involved.

'Where are they?' I asked him while watching Corral.

'Nuh-uh, sorry. I ain't fuckin with the witches. Even if I have got some shot of getting outta this alive . . . I tell you anything about them, it's all over. Besides, I can't think straight about em. They mess with your brain. Couldn't tell you shit if I wanted to.'

'Can you tell us what *type* of witch?'

'What? No . . . How many types are there?'

I shook my head. 'Forget it.'

Corral ushered me toward the back of the room with her head down. 'Well, I cannot lie, I'm mostly out of my depth with witchcraft. I wouldn't know where the hell to begin here. You? You must.'

My eyebrows shot up my forehead. 'I must? No. . . . No, not at all.'

'Why would witches be providing criminals with their *spells*?' She paused. 'Why do witches provide you with magick beans?'

My eyebrows crashed back down. 'I don't like where you're going with this, Lieutenant. Not in the least. You think there's a correlation? I am not the same as this asshole.' I stepped back toward said asshole. 'Not the time,' I said over my shoulder.

Corral glared back and approached to stand beside me.

'Alright,' I went on, 'so what did you get in return? Cash?'

'Yes,' said Hansel.

'And did she directly tell you why she wanted magick-infused candy from you?'

'No.'

'No,' I said. 'Otherwise you wouldn't have done it, right?'

Hansel glared through angry, teary eyes. 'She . . . She never told me. But eventually I started to figure things out. You hear things in this work. Women and th-their children, mostly.'

'That's right,' I said through gritted teeth.

'Taken.'

'Where?'

'The wood.'

'Yes. The wood. And do you know why they were taken to the wood, to Snowdrop Wood?'

'I heard things—'

'Yeah? You *heard* things?' My knuckles pressed hard against the steel table. 'And you were complicit in these *things*, weren't you, Hansel? Weren't you? *Answer* me.'

'I ain't gonna go that far—'

I slammed the desk, charged round it. Then I cracked Hansel in the jaw with my fist. 'I don't give a fuck what you think!' I hit him again, harder.

'Detective!' yelled Corral.

'You filthy scumbag.' I heaved him up and pushed him against the wall. Corral grabbed at my waist. 'Where's Odette now, huh? Tell me where she is, you filth.'

Hansel panted and flapped. 'I don't know!'

'Detective!' This time Corral pulled harder and I let Hansel go. He turned into a ball in the corner of the room.

I caught my breath, wiped the sweat from my eyes. 'I told you I wouldn't kill you. I meant that. Stop fucking crying and tell me where to find your boss.'

'Shit!' he yelled. 'Well, what do I get in return?'

At that point, I almost went back on my word. My gun was crying out. Instead, I started chewing on my knuckle so hard, I tasted blood. I kicked a chair. Even the lieutenant flinched.

'In return,' I said, 'we won't hold you here any longer.'

Corral's arms waved. 'Slade—'

'We'll take you in properly. Then someone, one of your buddies, will come along within the hour and you'll make bail, right?'

Hansel peered up at me. 'Yeah, I guess, but . . .'

'I won't say shit. Neither will Lieutenant Corral. In fact, we're more screwed than you are. Nobody's listening to us who could get you into trouble.' I wondered then how true that really was.

'Well . . . Then what? What if they come get me? And kill me?'

'Who?'

'That fuckin swan queen,' he hissed.

I shrugged. 'I don't know, steer clear of lakes. That's not my problem. I'm doing you a favor here, and you're asking for more?'

'Slade,' said Corral again, 'you're not in charge here.'

'What would you do with me, lady?' whined Hansel.

'Shut the fuck up,' she barked. She stepped closer to me, dark eyes narrowed. 'What is this?'

'Trust me,' I said.

She scoffed at that. '*That* is not happening anytime soon. But if you think this is the way to go about it, fine. Any more blood is on your hands.'

I nodded.

Hansel stared at us with hope in his eyes. It made me want to knock him out.

'Alright, Hansel. Let's hear it,' I said.

He gave me an address.

'Hm. Makes sense,' I said.

Corral cuffed him and made a phone call.

I got into my car and set off toward Swan Lake.

The rain hammered against the windshield furiously. I drove against it, heading north through a valley that supposedly enveloped Odette's estate.

Even now I couldn't escape the company of Lieutenant Corral. She called my phone, which sat in the dock. She was supposed to be an ally, I know, but I'd set my mind on this, and I didn't feel like inviting her to hold me back.

My finger hovered over "decline" for a few seconds, then I sighed and took the call. 'Lieutenant,' I said, not too shy about letting her know I didn't want to chat.

'Jack, you should rethink going alone. Just wait, think about this – you need backup.'

'Lieutenant, we're running out of time. There *is* no more waiting.'

I just hung up.

A few minutes passed and there was nothing but darkness, hills, and the sound of raging rain. Then my phone went again.

'Shit, what now,' I hissed.

It was a text alert from Goldilocks. It said, 'Alive. Call me soon.'

I smiled, then grinned, then heard myself chuckling under the bullets of water crashing against the windshield. I thought about calling her there and then, but looming over the fog and hills, something was reaching into the sky, black and twisting. It was a spire.

I took a right down a winding, muddied path, enclosed by bending trees and shrubs. Branches reached out and caressed the car as I drove. I was going downhill, more steeply than I was comfortable with.

The tires slipped and struggled against the deep mud. Something rattled angrily.

It went on like that for five minutes, then I was in a clearing, a huge valley that seemed like it shouldn't *be*. Down the middle of it was a wide flood of black water, dotted with small white specks. And in the distance, in the shadow of the colossal hills, a castle.

The whole sight made me feel sick, like I'd stumbled upon some world I had no right seeing.

I was getting used to stumbling upon things not meant for me, but fear was still nestling firmly in the pit of my stomach.

I continued driving along what there was of a path by the side of the massive lake. I looked across it as I went, watching the swans gliding across in their formations, sprawling, strong wings and intense eyes like pits. Some of them took an interest and swam closer to the car.

Then there were more, hovering right beside me. I jumped and shot a look to my left – they were there, too. Dozens of them sitting on the lake, watching while the others escorted me to my destination.

I smiled a little, then shuddered.

The castle drew nearer. From the distance, beneath the hills and beside the stretching lake, it'd taken on the look of a kind of cottage. But now, right in front of me, it was a real castle, soaring above me in all its glory.

In a way, it was ugly, asymmetrical, shabby. It had three huge towers, the tallest topped by a swan statue. The others were surrounded by gargoyles. The windows of stained glass looked dirty and dead. No lights glowed inside. It looked unlived in.

I stopped the engine and took a deep breath. The swan escorts seemed to split into two groups, some flying back to the lake, the rest sitting outside my car or surrounding the castle. I frowned and got out of the car.

The rain, which felt like it was becoming hail, pelted down on me hard, so I threw my raincoat over my head before I suffered a concussion, and ran into the small courtyard.

Another swan statue rested in the middle of it. This one was wearing a crown, perching atop an ancient, crumbling, flooding water fountain.

I banged on what could only be the entrance. The doors thundered and shook as I hit them.

'Open the door!' I yelled under the chorus of crashing rain. I splashed over to a side door as cold mud sprayed the back of my legs. I pounded on that one, too.

One of the doors of the main entrance thumped open.

My hand dropped to my holster and I jogged back over.

'Who do we have here?' said the man at the door. He was tall and lanky, with long, graying hair tucked behind his ears. He had matching stubble that covered a jutting chin, and two black blocks for eyebrows that his bluish eyes seemed to be struggling under.

'Detective Jackson Slade,' I said. 'NYPD.'

The man had a small glass of liquor in his hand. He tapped it with long fingers, letting his eyes drop to the ground.

'Can I come in? Is there an Odette inside? Who are you?'

The tall man smiled. 'So many questions!' he said between bright white teeth. 'Firstly, I'm sorry, but no, you can't come inside. You're already trespassing, in fact. Do you have a warrant, or even a badge?' He asked it like he was asking to borrow a pen.

I gritted my teeth. 'I don't need a warrant,' I mumbled, showing my badge.

The man squinted, then pulled out a small pair of glasses. 'Detective . . . Jackson Slade,' he said. He sounded thoughtful. Either I was about to be met with another tiring interview about that one event all those years ago, or he knew me for more . . . contemporaneous reasons. I felt myself tense up a little. Why could I feel a sense of familiarity now, hovering at the back of my mind?

'Yeah. Just stand aside, sir.'

The man finished his drink, and the glass slipped from his fingers. It smashed into pieces at my feet. His face was expressionless.

'Was that a threat?' I asked.

The man looked at the ground, then at me, almost sheepishly. He cleared his throat. 'Sorry,' he said softly. He began to crouch toward the shattered glass.

I felt for the cuffs on my belt. 'If you don't move outta the way, I'm going to have to cuff you. Is Odette home?'

On cue, a woman appeared on the wide spiral staircase behind the man. She froze, her hand clasping the wooden banister. The man slowly looked over his shoulder at her. It was Odette, but not like I saw her before. The bravado had been stripped away, leaving a small, scared woman who'd just emerged from, more than likely, a really comfortable bed. She grasped at her robe and touched her hair lightly, letting it fall over her face.

'I can still see you, Odette,' I said, unfastening the cuffs from my belt. 'Jig's up.'

The man turned to look at me again, one eyebrow raised. He took off the glasses and slipped them into his pocket. His jaw hung open a little.

'Oh, no, don't worry,' I said, holding up the cuffs. 'I got two pairs of these.'

Odette hovered where she was, the chestnut brown of her hair turning orange in the dim firelight.

The man swallowed hard, then looked down at the ground in sorrowful confusion, his chunky eyebrows slanting upward.

Odette took a few tentative, slippered steps down the staircase, trying to get a look at the man's face. With the light glowing more freely on her now, I saw how pale her skin was. And it wasn't from the lack of makeup. Through her hair, I saw two dark rings encircling her eyes.

My hand still hovered over the holster. It was shaking slightly. From the cold rain, I hoped.

Behind me, a cluster of swans sauntered and flapped in the rain. Most of them were looking right at me. Somehow that put me more on edge than this weird couple at the door.

I looked down a little, then up. 'I can see you're scared,' I said.

'Shall we just get this over with? I'll be taking you to the station.' I cleared my throat and said, 'Sort of,' under the rain.

Odette inched closer. She wouldn't take her eyes off the man.

'This your husband?' I asked her. 'You her husband?' I asked him.

'Siegfried?' she murmured.

'What have you . . .' croaked Siegfried in reply.

I clasped the cuffs in my hand and placed them around Odette's wrists. She was shaking. Too bad.

'Detective,' she said. 'Don't, don't.'

I just shrugged.

'What is this?' asked Siegfried, his eyes glistening.

'Sir, I'd appreciate it if you came down to the station, too.'

'I uh— I'm . . . I'm stunned,' he said.

I eyed him, then pulled out my phone and quickly typed out a message to Corral, glancing back up at the two as I did it. 'Some people, or some*one*, will be over to search the place,' I said. 'Come with me.'

Siegfried looked between me and Odette. 'Yeah but . . . Wait, you don't have a warrant. What is—'

'Calm down,' I said. 'Be more like her.'

Odette stared at the ground.

'In fact,' I said, and snapped the second pair of cuffs on Siegfried.

'That's just rude,' he proclaimed.

'Get in the car,' I said as I marched them over to it. I opened the doors and pushed them inside.

'Look,' said Siegfried, 'I don't know what's happening here, but you can't just drive away with the *castle unlocked*!'

'Where are your keys?'

'On the side.'

I jogged over to the doors, hopped over Siegfried's smashed glass, and grabbed a comically large iron key sitting on a table. The thing felt as heavy as my gun. I lodged it into the keyhole and clicked it shut. I got back in the car and started the engine. The swans started to close in again.

'Well, aren't you going to wait for this search team?' asked Siegfried.

'No. We have a mage, he'll be fine.'

Siegfried glared at me through the mirror and turned to the woman. 'What have you done, Odette?' he murmured.

'Stop talking,' she replied.

I smiled, placed sacks on their heads, and started driving.

13

REUNITED

It had gone midnight now. Lieutenant Corral waited for me outside our station. She glared.

I slammed the car door shut. 'How'd it go?' I asked.

She shrugged. 'Took him in. Did what you said we'd do.'

I nodded. 'How long you reckon before he's out again?'

'Few hours, probably.'

'Then what?'

She scowled. 'That was *your* idea. What do you think?'

'Fuck him,' I said. 'We can't hold on to all these people. He won't come after us, anyway. He's a coward.'

'And his connections? You think about that?'

'Well, I've got his boss right here, and her husband. Couple less to worry about. Heard back from Vesryn?'

'Not yet.' She motioned toward the car. 'Come on.'

I unlocked the car doors, scanned around the area. No sign of life, just drifting cranes and roaring machinery on the horizon. We escorted Odette and Siegfried into the building, and my attention quickly drifted elsewhere as Corral sat them at the table and removed the bags from their heads.

'Wh— What happened to him?' I asked, motioning to the Marionette.

'Yeah,' said Corral without looking at me. 'That's another thing I needed to tell you about.'

The Marionette tilted back, resting on a chair by the steel table in the main room. His eyes were out, his circuits were visible, and his arms hung by his sides. Even then, his large form was intimidating and he still seemed to be alive, aware somehow. I narrowed my eyes and watched Corral as Siegfried glanced around the room, wide-eyed and jittery.

'System must've finally given up after the damage he took at the parking lot. Well, "given up" may not be the term. He is resting. Believe it or not, I've been through this before,' said Corral, hands resting on her hips. 'He'll be fine, I think.'

I looked at the wires and circuitry protruding from his chest and neck. 'Fine?'

Corral shrugged. 'Well, maybe he's not been *this* bad, but there's nothing we can do right now.'

'We need him,' I said. 'He saved our asses out there.'

Corral pursed her lips, sighing. 'We got priorities. Come on, get in here.' She pressed her arm against the door and I stepped inside, taking one last glimpse at the Marionette's broken form.

Siegfried was sweating violently. His breathing shuddered and wavered. I took off his cuffs.

'Water,' croaked Odette.

'Put him in another room,' I said to Corral, keeping my eyes on Odette.

I could sense the lieutenant snarling at me. 'What other room?'

'Hm. Bathroom'll have to do.'

'Wh-wh—' went Siegfried as he was pushed through the door.

'Water,' whispered Odette again.

As usual, the buzz of faulty old bulbs filled the silence.

Her eyes were vacant. In the castle, I sensed some sort of emotion, but now there wasn't even that.

I stopped looking at her. It felt wrong. But *she* was wrong. A minute went by. I sighed and tried to look again. Eventually, she looked back, and this time there was something behind the eyes. In them, too – tears.

'What happened to you?' I asked, observing the pale skin, the sunken eyes, the matted hair.

'Detective, I was sleeping.'

'Right.'

Corral stepped back into the room. The door crashed shut behind her. Odette jolted, then tucked some hair behind her ear. Corral handed her a cup of water, and then it was gone.

'I need more,' said Odette.

I crossed my arms, staring down.

Again, Corral glared at the side of my face; again, she vanished.

'Children—' I started.

'I'm not going to talk, Detective.' Then tears trickled down her cheeks.

And she didn't.

In the main room, I looked at the message from Goldilocks again. Corral appeared, sporting a thick raincoat. I slipped my phone away.

'We have to let the guy go,' she said. 'Like you said, we can't keep hold of everyone. That is not what this place is for, Slade. It's dangerous enough holding the woman.'

I nodded. 'Fine.'

'They found nothing at Swan Lake. Nothing incriminating. And Vesryn is thorough.'

I nodded. 'Right. Yep.'

She just stood there, like she was waiting for something. Then she jangled some keys and went into another room. She returned with Siegfried, and placed a sack back over his head.

'What is—' he hissed. 'This really doesn't feel like normal police procedure.'

'It's for your own safety,' said Corral.

'And my wife? Does anyone plan on telling me what the hell's going on? Where am I going to *sleep* tonight.'

'Now look who's full of questions,' I said, then sighed. 'You're free to go back to your grand old castle. We'll let you know about any developments with Odette.'

'This is ridiculous,' he hissed as Corral marched him across the room. 'I'll be contacting your chief about all of this,' he announced.

'He'll be utterly horrified, I'm sure.'

I followed Corral as she marched Siegfried out into the rain. She stuffed him back in the car and slammed the door shut. 'Vesryn should be back soon,' she said. 'I'll wait here until he's back.

I nodded. 'I'm gonna take off.'

'To where?'

'I don't know. Probably some bar. Then somewhere with a bed.'

'Detective, you can sleep in there,' she called, pointing at our station.

'Yeah, I could do with a couple hours away from . . . all of this.'

'Yeah?'

I frowned. 'What, you don't trust your guys to watch over our prisoner? It's—'

'No. Not that.'

'Ah. Hey, I just got our suspect on my own, didn't I? You still don't entirely trust me to be out of your sight?'

Corral held her hands out by her sides. 'What do you think?'

'I—'

'That was rhetorical,' she said sternly.

I smiled.

'Make sure you're here early tomorrow. Like you said, we can't wait any longer.'

A few minutes later, there I was, in a bar, for what felt like the first time in ten years.

I'd called Goldilocks as soon as the lieutenant had pulled away, and after giving me no answers about where she'd been today, she told me to meet her at some underground bar in a disused subway station.

The place was dimly lit by some archaic oil lamps hanging from the stone walls, and the whiff of whiskey and incense immediately greeted me and started to calm my thumping pulse.

The ceiling was way above, almost entirely hidden in darkness, with just a few glimmers of light revealing it was covered with surreal abstract artwork. The place itself was pretty small, with about a dozen people inside, either sitting at the round oak tables or at the bar, which had massive stained glass windows behind it, portraits of all kinds of enigmatic figures and creatures, their faces staring intently and ominously from above.

As I stepped inside, I eyed each customer from behind the hair hanging over my face. I was trying as hard as I could to bury myself in my coat. Only a serpent-headed, yellow-eyed man sporting a fedora in the corner of the room paid me any attention, but overall he seemed pretty disinterested and quickly returned to tonguing his liquor.

The sound of instrumental synth-pop droned beneath the quiet chatter of the groups of drinkers behind me. I ordered a glass of brandy from the tall, blue-haired woman behind the bar. A temptation to relax pulled at me, but I just couldn't let it happen.

I stared down, sipped the brandy, feeling the warmth of it flow down into my chest. Before I knew it, I'd drifted off into a daydream where I found myself surrounded by people in the middle of Central Park in the year 1996, inebriated, carefree, gaping over at a band on a huge stage and singing along to corny alternative rock hits I'd forgotten the words to, or never really knew.

I snapped back into reality, a grim feeling in my heart, my blurred reflection shining back at me from the bar surface. In that reflection, I saw a slow movement – it was somebody taking a seat next to me.

I did an involuntary sharp intake of breath and looked. I narrowed my eyes.

'Huh,' I went.

Big, brown eyes glanced back at me, and small, red lips curled into a smirk for a second. Goldilocks wore a black Stetson, brown straight hair flowing from under it. Her black leather coat almost reached the floor.

'So. *Where* the hell have you been?' I asked, a little louder than I'd meant to. I toned it down. 'Most definitely had a moment or two out there where we could've done with your skill set, I'll put it that way . . . You dye it?'

'What? Oh, nah, part of the hat. Listen to me,' said Goldilocks, hunched over the bar, same as me. We didn't look suspicious at all. 'I think I got something—'

'Oh, *we've* got something, too – or some*one*.' I finished my drink.

'We? Oh, we. She turned you in yet?'

'Listen, Odette is in our custody – for now, anyway – and if she talks, we could be cracking this thing wide open.' I ordered a vodka. 'Today . . . we lost a lot of people—'

'Yeah, ain't surprised. Y'all don't know what it takes to deal with that damn bear—'

'*Well*, where were you?' I hissed.

'I was tellin you! I said I *got* something. I was at the estate, the bear's estate, and I was scoutin things out. When I saw he'd left the place, I figured it was a good time to check out his security detail.'

'His security? You worked for him,' I said, vodka burning through my chest. I peered at the glass. Strong stuff.

'He's changed things. I think he's— Not scared, but wary, maybe.'

'Expecting, what, you?'

'Expectin the worst. Which, yeah, would probably, in his mind, arrive in the shape of me.'

'I'm sure you feel all badass saying that, but remember, this isn't about you and him.'

Goldilocks shrugged. She looked offended. 'It's a big part of it. Something else you should also know. If he was keepin the victims someplace in the mansion, like when I came across them with Bluebeard, well, not anymore. Can't tell if that's a good or bad thing.'

'Shit,' I said, trying to think. What was it Hamelin had said? That they'd taken the women and children someplace ... The evidence in his room. If anyone could grab it ... 'So, what, you've decided, then? It's time for you to break into his mansion and kill him in his sleep?'

'Not in his sleep. I want him to know it was me turnin off the lights.'

I sighed. 'Again, this isn't about you being a badass. If you *have* to do this, be careful about it.'

She waved the bartender over, then started nursing a bottle of beer.

'How was it, anyway?' she asked.

'How was it?' I echoed. 'How was what?'

She widened her eyes. 'That damn shoot-out, outside the mall.'

I blinked. 'What do you want me to say? I supposed to review it for you? People got shot up and burned. . . . It sucked.'

We silently sipped our booze.

I glanced over my shoulders a few times, relieved to find nobody seemed to give a shit about us – they were just enjoying the drinks and atmosphere. I couldn't remember the last time I'd been around that.

'I should let you know,' I said finally, 'if you thought Ilsa didn't trust you to begin with, well, now it seems like she just hates you.'

Goldilocks nodded, wiping at beer foam with her sleeve. 'Ilsa? Wow, you must be close.'

My eyes narrowed.

'That's fine by me,' she said. 'Maybe she'll stay outta my way—'

'I don't know about that. She's very ambitious. Determined. Far as I can tell, she'll be looking at bringing you down, too, before this is all over.'

Goldilocks nearly choked. 'Hell! What a glowin reference! Wait, lemme get my shades; it's too damn bright.'

'Stop it.'

Suddenly a severe look crossed Goldilocks's face, and I was reminded who I was dealing with. 'Jack, to be perfectly honest, she probably ain't even gonna make it through this alive. And if she comes for me, she absolutely won't. Really need me to tell you that, though?'

I said nothing.

'And you may not like it, but the reason I'm gonna survive and she isn't is that she just ain't gonna go as far as me. I've just got that ... instinct. I'm used to it. I know how to ki—' Her eyes flicked up and across the room. 'I know how to do what needs to be done.'

I frowned and went for another swig of liquor. My teeth were met by tumbling ice cubes, nothing more.

'This one's on me,' said Goldilocks with a glare, and handed the bartender some cash.

'This better be my last,' I said. I was starting to get too comfortable already, too loose.

Goldilocks scowled. 'You've been here five minutes. Let go a little.'

The bartender snapped open another cold bottle of beer for Goldilocks, who swigged it while pushing away an empty.

I paused and watched her for a moment. Things about her seemed different now. I didn't know what they were, and I couldn't tell if it was for better or worse. She glanced at me, then away again, frowning slightly.

'I don't like that we've got more cops involved now,' she said after a while. 'But you know that. Whatever.' She swiveled on her seat and pointed at me with the bottle. Some beer splatted onto the floor. 'The way I'm goin about this ain't changin, no matter who you involve, so don't go expectin it to.'

I had to let out a little laugh.

'What's funny?'

'Like I'd expect that.' I swigged my drink.

Then gagged immediately.

Now she was laughing. '*That's* pretty funny!'

I spat the Jabberwock's Brew back into the glass and snatched Goldilocks's beer out of her grasp, fighting more gags.

'That's my fuckin beer!' she said through laughs as I swigged it.

'Ah, no, no, not this,' I gasped, the oily taste of Brew still clutching onto my suffering throat. It burned its way down my body and made a home in my stomach. I figured it wouldn't be there long.

Goldilocks was laughing silently into her knuckles while glancing around the room.

'Hell of a way to attract unwanted attention,' I wheezed. 'Is there ever a quiet moment with you?' I ordered water and washed away the horror.

'Well,' said Goldilocks, regaining her composure, 'you can't say you didn't deserve it.'

'*What?*' I hope you force some of that down you-know-who's snout before you do what you think you're gonna do.'

'Actually, he likes the stuff. Say what you will about the big guy, but he's sure got taste.'

'Seriously?'

'Nah,' she said through another smug chuckle. 'This is the only place in town I've seen servin that gloop. I couldn't resist. Sorry,' she said, and took another big gulp of beer.

While she did, I thought about the horror I'd been repressing at the back of my mind for the last couple of hours. I had to tell her about Hamelin. Goldilocks needed to know what we'd done.

I felt the muscles in my face relaxing, or going numb. I stammered. 'I found Officer Hamelin last night,' I said.

Goldilocks placed the beer bottle on the bar. 'Who now?'

'I uh . . . Piper. He was . . . working for the lieutenant. He was working for Corral.' My head started to thump.

Goldilocks watched me, her chin raised. She cleared her throat. 'Jack, what do you mean you found him? We left him with . . . Hatter.' She trailed off. 'What'd he do?'

'Did you know what he would do?' I asked, my voice louder. I took quick breaths, trying to force down the pain.

'And you're sayin . . . Piper was workin for Corral?' said Goldilocks. She sounded far away.

'Rich Hamelin was an informant. He was undercover, gaining intel on the bear and everything he was getting up to. Everything he *is* getting up to. He was like us, Jess. He wanted what we want. To save those innocent lives. He's dead now. Because of us. Because of Hatter.'

Goldilocks gazed around awkwardly and drank more beer. 'Well, shit, that's uh. Yeah.'

'We did this,' I said. 'We have to carry this on our shoulders forever now. We *both* do, forever.'

Goldilocks glared, then nodded. 'Things ain't ever gonna be the same. That was gonna be the case regardless of this. If you come out the other side, you're gonna be a different person. There's no goin back. I think you know that already. Maybe we made a mistake . . . Well, yeah, we *did* make a mistake with Piper, Hamelin. *I* made a mistake. But we'll keep makin em, Jack.'

I looked up, shaking my head slightly, my vision blurred.

'I hope we get stronger, and if we keep fightin we will. But you don't go into a war like this and make it through with clean hands. That just ain't happenin.'

Right now I could hardly hear. The scenes replayed in my head as Goldilocks spoke. The images that would be there forever.

But she was right, of course. What, did I really expect the insanity to cap here? Was it like I believed what happened to Hamelin was going to be the worst of it? Of course not. My memories of the detective in that wood would be joined, sooner or later, by equally terrifying ones. Worse ones. I knew, I always knew.

But you just can't prepare yourself for things like that.

'I'm sorry,' said Goldilocks. She said it vacantly, half-heartedly, but I knew she meant it, or she at least *meant* something. Underneath it all, she had a good heart, didn't she?

She didn't even know what had actually become of Hamelin yet.

I sniffed and straightened my back. I had to move past it, as best I could. Whatever it means to move past hell.

That doctor, though. What the hell did he want?

'Hatter,' I said, glancing toward Goldilocks. 'The things he did to Hamelin . . . I . . . Where the hell did he come from?'

Goldilocks breathed in slowly. 'Says he's from another realm,' she said, staring and raising her eyebrows slightly. 'I'm inclined to believe him, shit I've seen him do. Says he got here by accident. Opened up a portal, some hole in the ground, many years ago. Says he was escapin the clutches of some evil tyrant who was burnin his homeland to the ground.'

'Hatter wanted to escape tyrants and he wound up *here*? Now I almost feel bad for the guy,' I said, trying to bring in a little levity. For myself more than anything.

'Comes from a place called, kinda ironically, Wonderland,' said Goldilocks. 'Heard of it?'

'He's from there?'

'Yup.' She took another swig of beer. 'Whatever he's done to Hamelin, I'm guessin knowin Hatter comes from that place explains it slightly more?'

'Well.' I shrugged. 'Not like I know more than the next guy about the place. All I really know is down or up there, time works very differently and everyone's mentally fucked-up. Heard people call its residents *underlanders*, as, like, a slur of some kind.'

Goldilocks shook her head. 'He never really told me much. Well, nothin that made any sense to me. No idea if he was even tryin to make me understand. Guy just likes runnin his mouth. From what I gather, he served in his queen's council, was kicked out, and ended up wreakin havoc the kingdom before escapin here after some kinda trial by combat.'

I frowned, trying to take it all in. 'He served in a royal council and now he sits in some basement trying to turn people into rabbits?' I said. Then, 'Hares.'

Goldilocks glanced over at me with narrowed eyes.

I told her everything.

And before I knew it, there was more alcohol in my system than there'd been in *some* time. Weirdly, I didn't feel as drunk as I might have. It was like the booze was focusing all its energy on numbing the horrible sensation I'd felt in my mind while recounting what'd happened in the wood.

Time passed, and I realized there was hardly anyone in the bar left.

Goldilocks scratched at the side of her face and stared at the bar. 'With what happened today, and last night, I uh . . .There's surely gonna be a lot more of that. Well, it's guaranteed, ain't it? Lot more people are gonna get hurt before anything gets better out there – *if* it ever gets better out there, which I guess we damn well want to happen and . . .' Her voice was thick with booze as she drawled. She seemed to be analyzing the empty beer bottle in front of her while she spoke. 'So, I'm just checkin.'

'Checking?' I asked.

Goldilocks scratched at her face again, looking somewhere between confused and disturbed. 'Yeah, yeah, I'm just askin.'

'Asking? You didn't ask any—'

'*Yeah*, I'm like . . . askin if you're okay,' she said, then frowned at the floor.

I didn't know what to say or think for a few seconds. My mind tuned into the shapeless music in the background, then back again. 'I'm fine,' was what I said.

She sharply turned to me and leaned forward, which made the light catch her eyes so they became two piercing voids. 'I'm tryna ask— *trying* . . . to ask if you're alright.'

I laughed and shuffled in my seat. 'That's the same question!'

'No, no it's not, it's . . .' she struggled.

'How many of those deep are you?'

She looked between me and the empty bottle, silently said something, then closed her mouth. Her face softened into a small smile and she relaxed her hands on the counter, spreading her long fingers. 'I'm shit at this,' she said. 'Hell, that's only my fifth bottle, I think—'

'You're shit at drinking, or being nice?'

'Looks like both, doesn't it.' She shrugged and pulled a sarcastic face.

Then there was a little tugging sensation in my throat. I grimaced. It didn't seem to be the Brew up to its sickening tricks, or another bout of horrific withdrawals. As I looked over at Goldilocks, the feeling asserted itself, and wound up in my chest.

I cleared my throat. 'I, uh—'

'You don't have to say anything,' she said, waving me away.

'What about you?' I ended up asking.

'What about me?'

'Are, uh, you okay?'

'Yeah. Yeah, I'm fine. If you're okay and I'm okay and we look *out* for each other, then we're both alright, right?' She blinked heavily, almost sneering at her own words.

I clinked her empty bottle with my glass of water. 'Well, alright,' I said.

She gave a tense smile.

And then there was a stranger's hearty laugh behind her. A man leaned forward into view. He raised his tumbler and grinned. 'Aw!' he sang. 'Now kiss!' There were beads of sweat on his forehead, and scuffed black hair protruding from a purple, brimmed hat, set low in front of one of his eyes.

Goldilocks spun off the bar stool.

'Whoa, whoa!' went the guy.

I stood up.

The man's face turned dark with disturbance. 'Oh, yikes. You're not *siblings*, are you? Ahh, I've been a fool.'

'Get lost, friend. Thank you,' I said.

He stayed where he was. He wore a purple wool coat, dark waistcoat, and smart dress shoes. Probably some Wall Street asshole left behind by his banker buddies. But his patchy facial hair gave me second thoughts.

'Don't force me to escalate,' spat Goldilocks.

I tried to get a look at the guy's face as I stepped closer, but his features were hidden in shadows. I kept my hands close to my hips.

'Oh, I apologize, I do,' he said, his voice high and giddy with hysterical drunkenness.' He downed the last of his drink and slammed the empty glass onto the bar.

'Sir,' said the bartender, staring him down.

The man removed his hat, turned away, and swept at his hair, which was drenched in rain or more sweat or both. I thought I saw his hand trembling. He carefully placed the hat back on his head, then skittered toward the entrance rapidly.

Goldilocks turned to me, one eyebrow raised. I shook my head.

'It's not always in my control!' shouted the man as he stumbled away. 'Not always. Sometimes I just can't help it!' He marched through the door, his voice echoing down the tunnel outside. He babbled and sang until he was finally drowned out by the music and the returning chatter of the room.

The bartender watched us with an eyebrow raised. 'You know that character?'

'No,' I said, shaking my head dismissively and returning to my seat.

Goldilocks was still watching the door. 'We should get after him,' she said.

'Not a good idea,' I said. 'No, we don't need to get involved. Just some drunk.' I patted Goldilocks on the shoulder and she returned to the bar stool. People watched us, but seemed more empathetic than anything. No one knew who we were.

Now that my head was up, something caught my eye that made my stomach twist a little. Behind the bar, rising high up the wall, was a stained glass mural, a sea of faces looking back at me. One of them looked very familiar.

They were legends, supposedly, of the city and beyond. It was a masterfully crafted thing, no doubt, with shimmering multicolored accents and details framing fairy godmothers, old knights, werewolves, angels, witches, outlaws – and Old King Cole's fat face in the middle.

I felt my mouth twist. I looked at Goldilocks, who glanced at me then up at the mural in anticipation. Reds, greens, and purples flickered in her eyes. I signaled to the bartender. ''Scuse me, miss? What's with this?'

She knocked the door of a fridge shut and came over. 'What's that?' she asked.

'See this, this artwork. Old King Cole,' I said, obviously not making a lot of sense to her.

She blinked and took a look for herself, then shrugged. 'Ah, I think it's just for character, to be honest,' she said, smiling. 'I don't think it's supposed to be an . . . endorsement of some of the figures on there. Especially not, y'know, him.'

'Yeah,' I said, not taking my eyes off King Cole. He stood huge and tall above everyone else, big red beard and hair enclosing a face that was identical to his descendant, my former boss. He beamed back at me with death in his eyes as my blood ran cold.

'Funny,' said the bartender. 'No one's ever really mentioned it before, not that I recall, anyway.'

Goldilocks reappeared in my peripheral vision. 'What is it?'

'Know who that is?' I said, nodding toward the centerpiece. 'In the middle.'

She narrowed her eyes at it. 'Nah.'

'He's another Cole. The . . . biggest Cole, literally. A giant who lived hundreds of years ago.'

'Like the one you—'

'No, different. King Cole wasn't really a giant. He was a sort of mutant. He manipulated people and things to become like that. He was a tyrant, killed and tortured thousands himself, ordered women to be abducted from their homes and brought to his fortress for his entertainment, then disposed of them when he was done.'

Goldilocks seemed to flinch slightly. 'Some things just don't change. And you're sayin, what, that's the chief's great-great-great-great-grandfather or something?'

'I don't know how the bloodline works – I really don't *want* to know – but there must be hundreds of Coles out there.' I didn't say any more – a sense of hopelessness was starting to outweigh my drunken buzz. I shook my head.

She leaned forward and crossed her arms, peering at the stained glass. 'You really can't get a minute's rest in this town, huh.'

A stranger got up from his seat and stumbled slightly, brushing against Goldilocks's back. She jolted and spun her head to face him. The man, drunk and evidently threatened, apologized and made his way toward the exit. The hum of chatter was slowly fading. It was almost closing time.

Goldilocks stared past me. 'Before here – New York, I mean, and before the bear – I was in a gang, a different gang. Back in Texas. I did something that sort of . . . shifted my whole reality. Months after it happened, I would lie there at night, haunted, tellin myself that good *would* come of what I did, that it happened because in the end, I'd do some good. Whatever "good" means. I think in the end, I stopped tellin myself that entirely because nothin was gettin better, and nothin *is* gettin better.'

I cleared my throat. 'And, uh, what was it you did?'

'I murdered the man who took me under his wing.'

I stared down at my hands and nodded.

'Solomon Grundy was as close to a good man as I'd ever met at the time. Yeah, he was a criminal, but he was also so much more than that. He fought all his life, startin at five years old, back in the fifties when his parents were taken, *forced* to be servants in some fucked-up estate, and he walked half the goddamn south, gettin by on next to nothin.' She swallowed and shook her head. 'But he didn't just fight for himself, he fought for all of us, even when we didn't deserve it. Which was most of the time.'

'So why did you do that?'

Goldilocks looked at me for a second, then down again, the brim of her hat concealing her eyes. Her voice shook a little. 'Because I was scared. I'd started makin a name for myself, doin what I do, and after a couple years with Grundy, when I was eighteen, the bear's enforcer showed up.'

'Bluebeard?'

She nodded. 'He blackmails me, makes me take him to the boss. Wants me to poison him with some kinda skin-eatin potion provided by Hatter, who was commissioned, I guess, by the bear at the time. I don't do it like that, but regardless, I still do it. Two bullets.'

'Look,' I said, scrambling in my head for the right words, 'you were a kid—'

'The worst part is, Grundy's ready. He draws his gun before me, but he misses.'

'Wh— Why is that the worst part?'

'Cause he did it on purpose. I'm there on my knees, cryin next to his dyin body. I scream at him that he missed on purpose. You know what he says? He says that he was done, anyway, and that it was *inevitable*, that *I* am inevitable.' She shot me a look, her eyes glistening now. 'What does that mean, I'm inevitable? Why?' She was studying the mural again, glaring at the jolly face of Old King Cole.

I looked between the stained glass and her. My throat closed up again. She was almost pleading for an answer, one that wasn't mine to give. Again, the tightness in my chest. I was sure the booze was playing a part in my feelings, but there was also a raw empathy here that left me near-panicked.

Goldilocks wiped at one of her eyes, smearing black makeup

across her sharp cheekbone. She mumbled something under her breath, then reached out and lightly pushed at me. 'Sorry,' she murmured, getting to her feet.

'No. It's okay,' I said. 'Let's get out of here.'

'Sure,' she said, nodding.

I felt for my wallet, but Goldilocks stopped me and pulled out a small pouch of cash. She smirked and dropped it on the counter.

'Courtesy of Arminus,' she whispered to me, that familiar smirk creeping back onto her pale face.

The bartender looked at the pouch with quietly eager eyes, and nodded thanks.

I took one last look around the room, almost waiting for someone, or thing, to jump out. Nothing did. My eyes were pulled back over to the mural, to the king. My body tensed up. A half hour at best of something close to peace, cut short by paranoia, and the memory of genocidal legends. Their scions roam and play today, near limitless power at their fingertips, raping the helpless masses, just as their ancestors did before they became heroes etched into books and paintings and stories.

And here we were, stupid and angry enough to take them on, regardless of our relentlessly dwindling numbers.

We rose from the tunnel and onto the surface, stepping beneath the sheet of night and steel.

Returning to either of our apartments wasn't an option; we were well past that point. It had gone two in the morning and we were out in the icy rain, buzzed and hunted, making our way to an old motel.

Despite her recklessness, Goldilocks had moved her bike into storage a while back to avoid detection, and the old car she'd been using was sitting somewhere in the motel parking lot. So we walked through the Bronx with our heads down, staring at neon puddles until we were something resembling safe.

The motel she'd checked into was nothing more than what you'd expect. Its purpose was to keep us alive through tonight. And then maybe the next couple nights if we got that far.

I checked myself in with the surly receptionist. My ears had only her labored breathing, distance police sirens, and the obnoxious ticking of a clock that was about twenty minutes behind for company.

I glanced over at Goldilocks, who was standing at the other end of the room, waiting to go upstairs. The irritation I felt must have been pretty transparent on my face as the woman agonizingly entered my details one finger at a time in between hiccups, because Goldilocks's cheeks expanded in repressed laughter as she looked my way.

I hadn't seen her smile so much. Actually smiling, laughing, not just smirking. And there was something behind her eyes that wasn't anger or the urge to kill. Was it just the booze? Or was it something else – some kind of feeling of twisted glee as the stakes got higher and the bodies piled up around us? Maybe, in some horrible way, that's when she felt safest.

Seven minutes later, the receptionist handed over a key and gave me vague instructions about getting the most out of my stay. Then the woman grinned and coyly asked if I happened to be "from the TV."

I smiled, said no, and scurried off.

Everywhere we went now, we just had to keep our heads down.

My room was just down the hall from Goldilocks's, a space in not-horrendous condition with a view of the sprawling highway and rising towers. The sky took on a navy tint. Tiny red and white lights flashed high above the skyline. I pictured a chopper's floodlight pouring in through the window, me pissing the bed and scrambling around for safety.

Goldilocks gave me a tired smile from the hall and headed to her room.

'Hey,' I said. 'Don't go disappearing anytime soon.'

She nodded and closed the door.

Aside from the screech of the bed frame as I tried to get close to comfortable on the mattress, the motel was almost tranquil. Through the flimsy window, I heard the hum of distant air ducts at work and the muffled sound of light traffic on the highway.

With soothing booze in my bloodstream and fear subsiding for the night, I drifted off.

14

THE FISHERMAN'S WIFE

By morning it felt like a wad of cardboard had been wedged halfway down my throat. I woke to the commotion of my own dry coughing and heaving, flailing for a glass of water as if one would conveniently be sitting by my bedside, as if the drunk me from last night had the foresight to put one there.

I ran into the bathroom and found myself drinking from the shower hose and internally thanking Poseidon.

Golden haze streamed into the room. I checked my phone – just gone eight. I thought about calling Corral and letting her know when I'd be down at the station, but the idea of even talking made me feel nauseous. More water, this time from the faucet.

I got changed into my damp clothes and answered a knock at my door, gun behind my back.

Goldilocks stood there, looking the antithesis of my miserable state, with a pile of clothes in her arms. The brown wig was gone, her usual blonde hair tied up in a scraggly bun. 'G'mornin,' she said, strolling into my room and placing the clothes on my bed.

Now I had no choice but to talk. 'Mor . . . ning,' I managed. 'What's all—' I choked on my own words and went into another round of spluttering.

'Figured you could do with a change of attire,' she said. 'And here, guessin you need this.' She threw an ice-cold bottle of water my way.

'Oh, *yes*.'

She presented my new wardrobe – a plaid blue-and-white shirt, pair of brown pants, and a baseball cap.

'Ugly,' I said, 'but it'll beat the feeling of old, cold sweat being pressed up against every inch of me.'

Goldilocks walked over to the window and stared into the distance.

'You seem, well, fine,' I said, starting to swap out my rotten clothes for the new ones.

'What does that mean?'

'Well, you look . . . good and, y'know, not like you've spent the morning throwing up.'

'Wh— Oh, right. Well, damn, considerin your track record, I gotta say, I really didn't expect you to have the alcohol tolerance of a newborn fairy.'

I raised my eyebrows. 'Actually, the faerie can *drink*; you've obviously never hung out with any. Maybe not the newborn ones, but . . .' I adjusted my new outfit in the tiny mirror on the wall. 'How's this?'

Goldilocks spun around, nodding and smiling. 'That's it! Keep your head down and even the King's Men wouldn't be able to tell you apart from every other trucker in this town.'

'Good, great,' I said. There was a pause that seemed to go on longer than it really did as Goldilocks folded her arms and chewed her lip, watching the carpet intently and vacantly at the same time. I was almost scared to ask what she was thinking. 'You good?' I asked. 'You're thinking about your next move, aren't you? Against Arminus.' I stepped closer and she looked up. I sighed. 'Will you at least come down to the station? Not *the* station, our station, Corral's safehouse. We can't get too far ahead of ourselves. Let's see how this plays out.'

Goldilocks took a long, deep inhale, her lips pressing together, eyebrows furrowing. 'I'll go with you. Very least I wanna talk to the swan bitch, alone.'

'Alright, I don't see the lieutenant letting that happen, but let's just . . .'

She glared at me with black eyes.

'You're back,' said Corral without emotion as I entered the safehouse. She was transfixed on Goldilocks behind me – no acknowledgment of me. I saw Corral smile wryly, and Goldilocks did the same back, one corner of her mouth turning upward.

The lieutenant's smile sunk away.

I peered into the main room. People were there. 'Hell are they?' I asked. Three officers huddled by one of the desks, whispering and glancing over at us. They looked so young.

Corral sighed. 'They are the last of the officers I trust. Ambitious, talented, uncorrupted. Their hearts are firmly in the right place. This I know.'

One of the officers smiled at me, a woman. Or probably a girl.

'They're teenagers,' I said.

'They are my— our last hope,' said the lieutenant, watching them. 'The gods know I didn't want it to come to this, but everyone else is dead, Slade.'

'So you're gonna sacrifice these young lives next, because you've run out of options?'

My head flew back as Corral's open palm met my face. The *smack* echoed down the hall. The kids snickered.

Goldilocks grabbed hold of Corral's arm.

'Whoa, whoa,' I said, motioning to Goldilocks, cheek burning like hell.

'I wanna talk to the prisoner,' said Goldilocks.

'You cannot.'

'Why?'

'I transferred her. She's not here.'

I looked to the sky, then Corral.

Goldilocks actually loosened her grip.

'Transferred her? Why would you do that?' I murmured, almost to myself.

Corral turned to me sharply. 'Because it's too dangerous keeping her here. After Bhatt, we cannot be too careful about these kinds of things. I transferred her to the city—'

'But she'll be bailed out by this afternoon!'

Corral sighed. 'She already has been.' She stormed past me, farther into the station.

Goldilocks followed, snarling. 'Jack, I told you! This bitch—'

'Close your mouth, outlaw,' hissed Corral. She slammed the steel door shut behind us. 'You are the last person I wanna hear from, you got that? And *lose* the rifle!'

'Fuck you.'

Corral turned to me again. 'And Hansel is dead.'

I laughed. 'Hansel's dead? What do you mean, he's dead?'

'Well, obviously he outlived his *usefulness*,' said Corral, angry now. 'Someone figured he ratted, obviously, and—'

'Who knew we had him? Wait . . .'

Corral stared. Her eyes burned with intensity, hands dug into her hips.

'Did you do that on purpose?'

Goldilocks came closer. 'What, what did she do?'

'Did you transfer Odette, knowing she'd be let out within hours and have the rat, Hansel, murdered?'

Corral didn't say anything.

Goldilocks put a hand on the lieutenant's shoulder. 'Hell, if you did, you would almost have my respect!'

'Not now,' I said.

Corral jerked her shoulder away from Goldilocks's touch. 'I transferred Odette,' she said, articulating each word, 'for the integrity of this operation, and for *our safety*. If anyone found out she was here, it would all be over. We are hanging on by a thread as it is.' There was a hum from Corral's pocket. She took out her phone and went into one of the rooms, but not before giving Goldilocks another icy glare.

Why would Corral want Hansel dead? If she did do this on purpose, it was a side of her I was not expecting, and a side that made her significantly more dangerous. I thought about what she could possibly gain from it. Surely nothing, besides one less part of the puzzle to worry about. Unless there were things she hadn't told me.

Goldilocks gave me a knowing look, then went up the door Corral had gone through and pressed her ear against it.

The door swung open and Corral stormed through. Goldilocks leaned back and stepped to the side, smiling with her eyes. 'Fucking goddammit,' said Corral, typing something into her phone.

'What is it?' I asked.

'I just found out where Hansel's body was found.' Her voice was trembling with adrenaline. I held my hands out by my side, waiting. 'Your wood, Slade, where Hamelin went. Snowdrop Wood,' she said.

I looked to Goldilocks, who was chewing her lip, eyes wide, suddenly sincere.

'Let's go,' she said.

'You wait,' ordered Corral, and she burst into the main room, heading toward her squad. She gave her instructions and yelled at them to move, then turned to me. 'Vesryn has had eyes on some of the dirty cops; it's how he found out about Hansel. He is already there, hopefully still hidden, but we need to join up with him immediately and make our move.'

'*What* move?' I yelled as she marched off.

'Screw it,' she called back. 'We're going to arrest them all.'

'*Fuck*,' I hissed.

'*What* did she say?' hollered Goldilocks.

'This is it,' I said.

Goldilocks clenched her jaw, glaring at the back of Corral's head as the lieutenant ducked into the passenger seat of one of the cars.

We joined her. The driver hit the lights and we led this small, surely doomed, cavalry onto the highway.

The two cars raced along the gray world, sirens blaring, and visions of what I saw that night, what was put into my mind in Snowdrop Wood, presenting themselves again – faded, but *there*.

We arrived near the scene under an hour later, beneath a cluster of thick, gray clouds and a spattering of rain. Along the way, I'd managed to just about convince the lieutenant that hurtling into the wood with our sirens on would be impractical, and even detrimental to Vesryn's life.

We parked up in the mouth of the wood and stepped out into the frosty air. The dead grass beneath us crunched and snapped. The air smelled like soggy leaves and distant smoke. I caught my reflection in one of the puddles, which stared back in complete vacancy. My skin was nearly as gray as the sky, my eyes shot and heavy.

My hangover was hardly a problem anymore – my body was starting to fail me again because there was no magick inside it.

'Water,' I murmured to Goldilocks, holding out a hand. 'Please.'

She looked at me with concern in her eyes and passed over the bottle.

Water is not magick, but it was all there was.

Corral crashed the car door shut and cocked her gun with aggression. 'So, this is the place,' she said to no one in particular. The tween cops emerged from their sedan. 'We cannot get this wrong people, and you—' She shot a look at Goldilocks. 'You don't leave my sight.'

Goldilocks looked at the ground, and there was a pang in my stomach. I thought maybe it was a look of defeat, but of course, I was wrong. She stepped over to the lieutenant, every other officer visibly tensing, some shifting nearer to the outlaw.

'Robicheaux,' said one of Corral's kids. He had close-cropped hair and round, innocent eyes. And he was in no position to question Goldilocks. Whether he knew it or not, he was on the verge of asking for a lot of trouble.

I shook my head at him. He glared back.

The other two had their hands hovering over their holsters, staring intently.

Goldilocks looked Corral dead in the eyes, inches away from her face. '*Or*, we play to our strengths.' She bucked her custom rifle over her shoulder and nodded toward it. 'You think this is the time for worryin about me? Get your fuckin priorities right this time, Lieutenant,' she spat, then wandered over toward the dying undergrowth on the perimeter of the wood.

Corral's jaw seemed to vibrate, but she said nothing. The three young cops eyed the back of the lieutenant's head with visible concern.

Goldilocks turned to me, placing one boot on a small hill and cocking her head.

I followed.

'Slade,' said Corral from behind me.

'You want us to march directly into whatever the hell's goin on in there?' asked Goldilocks. 'No. We'll flank 'em. I can take out some of their men—'

'We're *not* here to—'

'—*if* it comes to it,' finished Goldilocks. She dropped her head down as a brief silence hovered. Then, 'You think it won't come to it, Corral? You think they'll come quiet?'

Corral's face was hard. 'It doesn't matter what either of us think, kid. What matters is that we are prepared for everything.' She signaled to the rest of her team, and they began their descent into the darkness of the wood.

'Good luck, Lieutenant,' I said.

Corral turned, two quick looks between me and Goldilocks. 'Yeah,' she said.

Goldilocks was already trudging her way through tall, brown grass and the bed of moist mud beneath. I sighed and followed. Every step was a small battle, and I kept gripping onto twigs covered in thorns, branches that gave way as soon as I touched them. *She*, though, eventually seemed to glide through the field, occasionally turning back to glance at me as she went, the same almost pitying look on her face each time.

I grunted and mumbled and struggled until we reached a much more walkable area, a clearing with a stronger, more forgiving foundation.

I looked up at the sky, feeling small and alone as the rain tumbled down. Goldilocks did the same, rifle hanging by her side. She squinted as she stared up, looking the clouds over as if there was some vantage point up there she had to reach. Her mouth hung slightly open, raindrops trickling off the brim of her hat, onto her forehead, down her face, and settling in the crevices of her hollow cheeks. She closed her eyes for a moment, her sharp, pale nose twitching as she breathed in the air. I wondered what she was feeling right there and then, but only wondered. It wasn't the time to talk.

I scanned what I could see of Snowdrop Wood, the mass of black trees swallowed up by hostile mist. There was no knowing what was beyond, not from here. What I did know was that the place didn't look any more forgiving in the daylight.

Goldilocks slowly lowered her head and pursed her lips, then glanced over at me. We kept moving.

As we walked on, the weight of where we were, what was happening, how far we'd come, seemed to be setting in for both of us – we didn't need to speak a word, it was just there, hanging invisibly but heavily in the misty air between and around us.

There was something in Goldilocks's movements now that I'd not seen before, a sort of solidness. No swagger, no arrogance. There was only resolve, and a real tension in every step. This made me feel worse, my own limbs cramping up at the idea of fucking it all up as we moved across the field.

Twigs crunched as Goldilocks came to a sharp stop. She held up a slender hand without turning to me. I stopped and swallowed. Her gaze seemed to be on the wood – the trees round here were easier to see through, most of them dead and bare. There was movement, people walking, patrolling.

'Get down,' Goldilocks hissed, swinging her rifle into both hands. I did, wide-eyed and clumsily, hand fumbling to my holster. She peered down her sights and curled a finger around the trigger, aiming at something I couldn't see.

Mouth gaping, I stared at the side of her face uselessly and tried to mentally prepare for chaos. It didn't come yet, though. Slowly, Goldilocks lifted her chin and opened both her eyes, glaring into the distance intently. 'Well, hell,' she said, 'there's the big man himself.'

I crawled over, hands splashing and sinking in mud, and peered over the long, dead grass. Yeah, now I could see. That unmistakable frame, that labored, dragging walk. From here he was just a gray silhouette, but Chief Cole had come to pay the guys at the crime scene a visit. Make sure the cleanup was in order.

'This one's yours,' Goldilocks whispered beside me.

My eyes were fixed on the chief. He was limping, all patched up with bandages from his heroics at the shoot-out, seemingly grunting orders to his officers. The mural at the bar last night flashed in my mind, the joyous, gleefully evil face of Old King Cole taunting me.

'Hey,' said Goldilocks with a nudge. She was holding her rifle out to me.

I grabbed it with both hands without noticing, without taking my eyes off the chief. Everything Corral had said this morning was burning away into a cloud of ashes. Her plan, these goals, all of a sudden they meant nothing to me. I thought about the people – suffering, dead people – whose blood covered this man's hands, how all his life he'd gotten away with absolutely everything he wanted. About how he'd even gotten into this untouchable position in the first place – by being a descendant of a literal giant of history, a king whose story had been rewritten again and again so the very idea of him could be blindly worshipped for eternity by people who never cared, never *would* care, about the disgusting truth. Because it was easier like this.

The rifle in my hand. I could kill Chief Cole, end his reign. It was too late for the people who were gone or living through hell because of him. But by killing him now, I'd prevent it from happening again by his hand.

'Jack,' hissed Goldilocks.

But then what about the replacement? The other Cole, literal or otherwise? I wasn't up against a man; I was up against a structure, a cult of depravity whose desires I still didn't understand. If I killed the man now, my life, Goldilocks's life, Corral's and the others' lives, they would all hang in the balance more than ever. And it would be for my own selfish pleasure.

'I can't aim for shit with this thing,' I said. I wasn't even looking at Cole anymore; I'd fallen inside my head.

Goldilocks snatched the rifle and pulled it out of my weak grasp. She aimed, remorseless purpose in her dark eyes.

'No, wait—'

'Wait?' she said, finger tightening against the trigger. 'Goddamn, Jack, the longer we wait, the—'

Her body jerked back and blood splattered across my face and into my mouth as I breathed in. Everything went crimson and then her body fell onto mine, struggling and kicking.

I wiped the blood from my eyes. I scrambled beneath her. '*Shit, shit, shit!*'

Goldilocks rolled off me and onto her back, hissing and cursing, alive. I saw the blood leaking from her left shoulder, joining the rain and mud on the ground.

'Fuck,' I breathed, tearing at my shirt and trying to make something that could serve as a bandage.

Goldilocks yelled, pummeled at the ground with her good arm, then drew her revolver from out of nowhere. She spun as she did and blasted shots in the general direction of Cole and the others. I heard a distant robotic yell under the rain and the splat of a body hitting the drenched deck. Goldilocks fell back to the ground, grasping at her wound again, teeth clenched together.

I pulled out my gun and aimed over the grass, fired a few times at an approaching black figure and got down again. I crawled over to Goldilocks.

She swiped at me like a defensive cat. 'Forget it!' she yelled. 'It's nothin. Hold 'em the fuck back. *Shoot*, dammit!'

I threw myself to one side, then rose above the grass again. The King's Man trudged through the mud, some kind of submachine gun in his grasp. I saw Cole and the others retreating. The King's Man turned to me, raised his weapon instantly, but not before I fired three rounds into his body. He fell to the ground. I looked to Goldilocks.

'Go!' she yelled. 'Go find the others. I'm behind you. You'll be alright?' she asked.

'*Me?*' I yelled back. 'What about you, the one with the gaping wound?'

She thrust herself to her feet, wincing. 'Go!'

I shook my head and did the best I could to run through the deep mud. The main bulk of Snowdrop Wood was clearly visible now, as if it'd come to us. There was gunfire coming from it.

'Come on!' called Goldilocks.

I blinked, then she was ahead of me.

'How the hell?' I said out loud, stumbling after her. What was she made of?

She inhaled through her teeth with every other step, storming through the pain. It gave me a sort of drive to wholeheartedly fight whatever we were heading toward. It was like nothing could bring her down. For all the will I was gaining, my mind was still foggy as hell, and an evil sensation clutched at my shoulders as I moved.

We came to a clump of dead bushes. Goldilocks took out her knife and sliced away at the bone-like branches with her functioning arm. I tried to take control of my breathing as I aimed my gun in front of me, but it simply wasn't happening.

I was staring at the blood seeping from Goldilocks's wound when I almost dropped to the ground at the sound of gunfire. More of it, lots of it, crashing and echoing throughout the wood we were heading into.

'*Fuck*,' I hissed as, somehow, Goldilocks sped up ahead of me.

She panted and growled as she went, seemingly repressing the effects of her injury with sheer adrenaline. 'That way,' she called. She shifted to the left and stumbled down a rise into a clearing. She managed to land on her feet. I didn't. 'Up, come on!'

I jumped up as she gripped and yanked my sleeve. I was aiming my gun in every direction, wary of an ambush. Now the gunshots were close.

We burst through another load of naked bushes and came out to another clearing, this one darkened by the enormous trees above us. The ground was soaked in blood and rain. Corral and Vesryn took cover behind some stumps. There were bodies splayed across the area.

And two King's Men, on their feet. They looked disoriented as Goldilocks and I emerged. One of them spun to shoot us. Goldilocks took her shot, rocketed a bullet through his skull. I took out the other one – two bullets to the chest. They both dropped dead.

Goldilocks fell onto her knees, breathing heavily. I placed a hand on the shoulder that didn't have a tear through it.

'What the *fuck* happened?' yelled Corral. There was blood all over her face, a wound on her forehead. She shoved me with more force than I was expecting.

'Back off,' said Goldilocks, rising to her feet, hand over her wound.

'I've lost...' Corral closed her eyes, bit down on her lip too hard. 'I've lost so many. Look at this.' She motioned to the ground. Rain was pouring down on about ten corpses, three of them in police uniform. '*Fuck!*' she yelled.

I felt blood pumping in my head, my breaths still labored. It was a massacre, *another* massacre. The trail of bodies was getting longer every day. Those kids, they looked younger than before. Like children now. The girl lay in a heap below me, blonde hair reddened, wound in the neck.

Next to her, a body with countless wounds, gunned down until it no longer resembled a person. Against a tree, bullet wounds all over his chest, the big-eyed boy slumped. Those eyes were wide open. His dead stare shot toward his leader. His lieutenant had marched him and the others to meaningless deaths.

'Cole,' said Goldilocks. 'Jack, go!'

Corral was fighting back tears of fury.

'Lieutenant,' I said. 'Ilsa. We have to get the chief.'

She shot me a look, eyes red and narrowed.

'They'll send more King's Men. There's four of us left.'

'I can count, Slade. I did watch them die,' she whispered.

'He might not have made it out yet,' I said, backing away. 'Come with me. We have to take him out.'

I noticed Vesryn slowly heading deeper into the trees. He paused, turned around, and came back to us.

'Do you hear that?' he asked, his pointed ears twitching. 'They're already here.'

Goldilocks cocked her revolver.

'You three,' said Vesryn, 'that way. If you stay, we all die.'

Corral looked at him, frowning.

'I will conjure a barrier. I can hold them off for a little while, but you have to run. There will be vehicles near the entrance you can steal. Chase down Chief Cole. Do what you have to do. Complete the mission.'

'I'll stay,' said Goldilocks. 'I'll pick 'em off from behind your shield. You'll live and we'll lose the trail.'

'Vesryn, just come with us, quick,' I said.

He thoughtfully shook his head, turning away from me. 'They will obliterate us. And Robicheaux. You remaining here would be suicide. Even you wouldn't stand a chance.'

She shook her head. 'I can—'

'Go,' said Vesryn. A purple glow began emanating from his hands as he held them by his sides.

Corral covered her mouth and turned away. She grabbed my arm and began to lead me out.

Goldilocks held the elf's shoulder, saying something I couldn't hear, then joined us.

There was a low *boom* sound as he began to cast his spell, waving his arms slowly in a fluid, delicate motion. A large purple wall of rippling magick grew from his hands, covering the clearing from one side to the other. Then the King's Men emerged at the top of the rise, aiming their guns immediately.

I stopped, my heart pounding. 'You're a good man, Vesryn,' I said.

Bullets began to blast onto the wall rapidly, their impact muffled. Vesryn turned his head to face us. 'Give it everything you've got, Detective. For the victims, for us, for yourself. And Ilsa,' he called, his eyes glancing at Goldilocks, then at me, 'it's time to start playing it their way.'

Corral took a deep breath, closed her eyes.

'Now, run,' called Vesryn.

And we ran for our lives, into the trees and back southward to the entrance, where Cole, as desperate as us, would be fleeing in panic and terror. Vesryn's sacrifice had bought us invaluable time – time that could finally give us the upper hand. I felt my heart sink when I heard the bullets cease.

We had a good hundred yards on the King's Men who'd ambushed us from the back. There was time to escape if we played it right.

We slid across the drenched mud and made it to the road. There were a few abandoned cruisers with their lights flashing, but no sign of Cole's high-security van.

Goldilocks rushed toward one of the cruisers, smacked the roof of it with her palm. 'Still runnin'!' she said. 'Must've belonged to the fucker who ran over there to rip a hole in my damn arm.' Then she skirted round the vehicle and opened the driver's door.

I stayed where I was, my mind foggy and dazed.

Corral stepped forward. 'No,' she said.

Distant gunfire.

Goldilocks shot the lieutenant a look. 'What's that? No. What do you mean, no?'

'You are not driving, move.'

'Trust me,' said Goldilocks, her voice louder now, 'I can drive a whole lot better than you, even with one of my arms outta the picture. We're gonna need the very best behind the wheel if we're to get away from these guys and catch the chief.' She turned her attention back to the car.

Corral lurched forward.

'Hey!' I yelled pointlessly. And then I noticed she had drawn a gun.

So had Goldilocks, whose leg extended behind her in a flash and cracked into the lieutenant's knee. The gun went off, a bullet flying into one of the nearby trees. Corral growled as Goldilocks followed up with an elbow to the side of the head before tackling her to the ground. The outlaw drew her own gun, pointing it right between Corral's eyes. 'I only need one arm to finish you off,' she murmured quickly.

'Stop now. STOP!,' I shouted, imagining the King's Men storming past Vesryn's corpse and bursting through the trees behind us any second. I moved forward, about to intervene, but Goldilocks quickly holstered her gun and brought Corral to her feet. She confiscated the handgun she'd pulled on her with no protests from the lieutenant. She was in complete control – of the situation and her own disposition.

Corral now had a completely vacant look on her face. The look of defeat. Rain poured all over her face, blending with the blood from the fresh wound on the side of her face, provided courtesy of Goldilocks's elbow.

Goldilocks loosened her grip and Corral got into the back seat of the cruiser, slamming the door.

I rushed into the front passenger seat as Goldilocks took the wheel. I sighed through my teeth, and so did she. The difference was, I did it out of frustration and sorrow, while she did it because she was clearly in a huge amount of pain.

We accelerated down the muddy road, wipers fighting hopelessly against the now nearly horizontal downpour. I looked over my shoulder, past the slumped figure of Corral – who sat with her head against the window – and into the trees, where I could vaguely make out a pattern of red and blue lights from the King's Men's masks.

Goldilocks looked into the rearview mirror. 'Yeah, I know,' she said sharply, apparently sensing my fear, and sped even farther until we reached a turn. We slid precariously around the bend and out of their line of sight.

There was a long silence as we drove back toward the city.

Eventually, Goldilocks broke it after peering into the mirror again, this time at the crestfallen lieutenant. 'Can't we all just... get along?' she said in an almost cheerful tone, but her voice quivered from the pain of the gaping wound.

Another silence.

Then Corral, in a subdued, hoarse tone, said, 'Well I guess now we got two reasons to find the mad doctor. Get you some treatment, and then interrogate him.'

Goldilocks smiled. 'That's more like it.'

15

SOMETHING WICKED

We abandoned the cruiser a few blocks from Dr Hatter's quiet street. The sun was gone, and the warm rain spat on us as we walked toward his house.

Ilsa Corral trudged slightly behind us, head low. She looked pale, sick. Goldilocks hadn't returned her service weapon. The lieutenant hadn't even asked for it.

It seemed as though the doctor would have nothing to fear from Corral, not now. She was broken.

Vesryn had died for us. Those *kids* died because she put them in the line of fire. She knew they weren't ready for this. But they were dead now. From here on out, there could be no more failure, and no moping. Could she not see that? And still, some irrational part of me felt bad for her. Probably because, despite it all, we're all in this shitstorm together.

'Alright,' said Goldilocks, sighing as we reached the doctor's house.

Corral started as Goldilocks thrust her boot at the front door, swinging it wide open and crashing it against the wall.

Dr Hatter went about his work, hunched over vials and potions lined up on bloodied worktops. This was the first time I'd seen him since he sent me to track down Hamelin, and I had some opinions to share with him. Right now, he seemed entirely unbothered. He'd been expecting this.

Goldilocks had her rifle pointed at Dr Hatter's head from across the dingy room. She cocked it and motioned for him to move away from the desk he was leaning over.

He turned and grinned.

'Alright,' I said, 'why are you smiling?'

Hatter slowly – very slowly – reached into a breast pocket and brought out a cloth, then dabbed at his forehead. 'I'm smiling because – well, look at you all. Lost souls, well into the fateful night of victory or despair. Admirable, I suppose, how you've taken such a weight upon your own shoulders, but arguably foolish.' He frowned, some kind of expression of deep thought combined with lunacy on his face. '*Arguably*, I reiterate, because . . . maybe not.'

Corral looked at me out the corner of her eye. I looked back at her and shrugged, trying to telepathically tell her, *This is just how he is*.

He went on. 'There is something about you. And you, you're new.' He gestured toward Corral flamboyantly. 'Certainly a valuable asset, I'm sure. I must admit, I feel an inkling of hope for your cause, an inkling.'

I stepped forward, looked Hatter dead in the eyes. 'What were you thinking?'

That pondering expression again, this time exaggerated. 'You'll have to be a tad more precise. I think I've thought many thoughts on many different occasions, like most. Oh! Are you talking about the policeman?' He laughed, and I held back the urge to throw a fist his way. 'Shan't have you getting too passionate about how that played out when you traded him TO ME!'

He yelled so loud that his voice seemed to multiply, surrounding us all in this dungeon of horror. His face had suddenly contorted into an expression of passionate rage. Goldilocks edged forward, finger on the trigger. I jumped a little.

'Ain't no excuse,' said Goldilocks.

Hatter chuckled, his face back to normal. It unsettled me. 'Goldilocks, my dear, you of all people should be the last to open their mouth on a question of ethics, morality. No. I won't have it from you. I respect you, that much you know, but you are quite out of line on this one. Now, stop pointing that blasted weapon at my face and let us have a civilized conversation. Would you all like some tea? I shall get the kettle on. How does that sound?'

He attempted to saunter to the room behind us. Goldilocks stepped forward again, gripping the rifle harder. 'Fuck your tea!' Then she lowered her weapon involuntarily, grimacing and hissing while clutching onto her wound.

'Yes,' said Hatter vacantly, 'that is a nasty little wound. I see how you expect this to pan out, my friends. You break into my abode and threaten me with a gun, for some inexplicable reason, and then you suggest I heal this rather substantial bullet wound. Sounds entirely fair when you put it like that!'

'And then we arrest you,' mumbled Corral, finally glancing up to properly meet his eyes.

Hatter feigned surprise.

'Hatter,' I said, 'you know why we came here, or at least why *I* came here. I want an explanation. An explanation of *why* you did that. Is there not a single part of you that wants to question your insane decisions? What is . . . wrong with you?'

Goldilocks cleared her throat. 'Yeah, but first, let's see to the gapin wound in my arm?' She put away the rifle.

Hatter relaxed.

Instead of the rifle, she brought out a revolver, hopped onto the table, and aimed the gun at his head.

Hatter assumed his former rigid state.

'If I get the slightest suspicion you're tryna play one of your games, you're dead, Doctor.'

'Fine, fine,' said Hatter. 'That's fine. Very well, let's begin.'

There was a sincere look on Goldilocks's face as she removed her coat. She glanced my way and nodded.

I felt somewhere between sleep and death. Everything that had gone on the past few days was catching up with my body. And that's without even factoring in the bean withdrawals. The fact

Cole had slipped away again seemed to generally bring my morale lower again. Not that it had been sky-high at any point so far.

I thought about Vesryn, about the others who I barely got to meet, how they were caught up in this terrifying shitstorm, and now it's only Corral left out of her group – Corral, who was barely herself anymore. I thought about Hamelin's corpse, now in the hands of the NYPD.

'Hatter,' I mumbled. 'Hatter.'

'I'm . . . working.'

I ignored him. 'Is there any way anybody could trace the corpse back to you?'

'What corpse? Oh, *the* corpse.' He peered intently into the wound, going at it with nasty-looking utensils. 'What, you mean you *lost* it? What a waste.' He sighed loudly. Goldilocks grimaced, revolver nonchalantly pointed toward the doctor. 'I suppose it was all a bit of a failure, all things considered, so not too much of a loss.'

The flippant way he spoke about this made my jaw quiver and fists clench.

'Well, unless those who now possess it have within their ranks some sort of physician or alchemist or wizard – and one who is anywhere near as capable as myself – then there is a very slim chance. Very slim, indeed.' He looked up and pulled a face. 'Otherwise, it's damn near impossible. Oh, I do hope you haven't got me into trouble,' he said in a low tone.

'You *are* in trouble,' said Corral. 'With us.'

'I see,' he said, returning to the wound.

Corral lightly slapped my arm with the back of her hand. 'Can we talk?' We shuffled into the back end of the room, careful to avoid stepping on the abandoned syringes decorating the floor. 'You look awful. Again.'

'Ups and downs,' was all I said. It was all I could think of, if you could call what was going on in my head thinking.

'I'm not blaming you for what happened. Maybe I overestimated us. Maybe this whole thing is unwinnable and my guys died for nothing.' She was tearing up. 'There is blood on my hands. There is.' She looked up at me with wide, bloodshot eyes. 'I thought maybe if we got straight in there, we could...'

My instinct was to tell her it wasn't her fault. But of course it was. I wasn't about to start comforting her.

'I *killed* them. It was all me. I always... want more from things. Push people. Bite off more than I can chew or however you want to put it. It's always paid off; it's been my strategy since day one, and it got me in my position. I always knew how bad they were, the people in our force. I was gonna change it from the inside and that meant taking risks. But I've taken one too many. Haven't I?'

I had to look away for a minute. Suddenly the lieutenant seemed like a confused, lost kid realizing they have no place in the world. I suddenly felt a sort of weight of expectation from her, like I had to come up with the perfect response to keep her from falling apart. I couldn't.

'Jack, what do we do?'

I sighed shakily. My mind just couldn't formulate any coherent thoughts, let alone figure out a sentence to put together. But I tried. 'I've lost count of the mistakes I've made in my life, and in this case, if I can even still call it that. What is this? Just chaos and bloodshed and horror. And we still don't know much at all.' I felt dizzy, nauseous. I focused on Ilsa's eyes. 'And my mistakes, and yes, *our* mistakes, have added to the bloodshed, to the chaos. How else would it have ever worked out, though? You didn't kill those officers—'

'But I didn't save them, either,' said Corral, a harshness in her voice. 'I don't feel like me. There's... There's a part of me that just wants to run. But that isn't me, Jack. I've never faced something like this before.'

Something was telling me that if we made it out alive, we would be facing more of this. And worse. But I didn't tell her that. If we weren't going to die, and if this was just the beginning, I thought it'd be best for her to discover that herself.

Corral sighed heavily. 'Look, you're the guy who took down a fucking giant before you even turned eighteen. Give me some . . . advice.'

I looked away.

I can't explain it but every time someone brings up my childhood, what happened in Arkansas all those years ago, I get a weird feeling, like a sense of embarrassment or shame. Something that's close to imposter syndrome, I guess. People don't mention it often anymore, but when they do, I go home at the end of the day and find myself looking in a mirror, the disheveled, magick bean-addicted, lousy cop staring back at me, laughing, telling me I have nothing else to live for.

I scratched the back of my head. 'Look, that was a long time ago, and the situation we're in now isn't related. If you want the truth, I can hardly remember what happened that day, or how I did it. I just know it's like I wasn't in control. A certain strength came to me and then the giant was dead, and I was alive.'

Corral looked back at me, dissatisfied. 'I admire you, and I want to believe in you.' She looked to her left slowly. 'I still don't trust the outlaw.'

Then, almost instinctively, I found myself saying, 'You'll have to learn to.' And that was true. We had no chance in hell of taking down Cole and learning the truth if those two were constantly at odds, pulling guns on each other every other hour. I realized I did trust Goldilocks. I didn't trust her to always make the right decision or to always be relied on, but I knew that she wanted to save these women and girls in the wood, and that she absolutely wanted Papa Bear decapitated, preferably by her own hands. When the time came, I would not intervene.

Besides, we were all outlaws now, anyway.

When Hatter had finished his work, what was fifteen minutes ago a violent bloody wound had become almost fully healed, at least on the outside.

Goldilocks, perched on the operating table, clamped her teeth together as she slowly raised her arm upward. I winced watching. 'It's . . . better,' she said, eyes closed.

Hatter stepped forward proudly, hands positioned behind his straight back. 'I would recommend resting it for a few days, midnight mandrake juice tends to develop a short temper when disturbed too much as it heals within the human body.'

That didn't sound too good, but it's not exactly like Goldilocks was going to listen.

She shook her head, rolling down her sleeve. 'Can't afford not to move. Just gimme somethin for the pain, y'know, for when I cross that bridge.'

There was a brief silence. Hatter looked into nothingness for a while before saying, 'Certainly. And as payment—'

'Oh no, not again,' groaned Goldilocks.

'As payment, you do not step foot in this study again. Any of you. And you most certainly do not attempt to arrest me or I will just kill you all.' He sniffed, scratched aggressively at one of his angular cheekbones, then smiled.

I could sense that Goldilocks's index finger was now itching to pull back on the revolver trigger. I looked across at her, saw a slight smile at the corner of her pursed lips.

'Oh, you wouldn't,' said Hatter, clearly sensing it, too, disappointment in his face. 'You wouldn't murder yet another member of your old family, Robicheaux. If you were to, I could make your life profoundly more difficult and painful long after you blasted those bullets into my brains.' He looked down the barrel of the revolver and licked his lips. 'I must admit, it would be an embarrassing way to go; there is no way of getting around that. Guns . . . Awful things. When an execution ought to occur, everyone would be much better off going about it the old way – a few drips of deadly matter and a word or two from some long-dead and accursed vernacular.'

'Yeah, well, not everyone has the time for that, Doctor,' I said.

'As for the Jack,' he said without looking at me. 'Perhaps one of these days he might realize that *time* is indeed in short supply. Instead of asking questions of me and my habits, no matter how peculiar he might find them, he would be better off going after the *true* villains.' He turned to me now, a grim look on his face. 'We're going to have to start tolerating each other very soon, my boy. I've got a feeling our paths will remain crossed on multiple planes of fleeting existence until we are ashes upon the ground.'

I grimaced, dreading the thought and running out of patience. 'Goldilocks, come on, we're done.' I said.

Slowly, Goldilocks got off the table, eyes trained on Hatter. 'Give me some sort of potion for when the pain kicks in, and we'll be on our way,' she said in a matter-of-fact tone. She lowered the gun slightly.

'Better,' said Hatter, and he reached into a metal tray holding an assortment of who-knows-what. He passed Goldilocks a small packet.

'What is it?' she asked as she took it from him.

'Ibuprofen,' said Hatter, and he burst into an absolute cacophony of deranged laughter – if you could call it laughter – wrapping his wiry arms around his stomach. It sounded like an army of rabid wolves with asthma stuffed into a small cage. That racket went on until we were back upstairs and out into the street.

It was getting dark in New York again now. We'd taken another setback and were low on numbers and morale. Goldilocks had been making the case for striking while we were angry and fervent, but we had no real strategy, and she seemed to forget we're not exactly all feral brigands with her particular skill set and apparent invincibility.

The coming night suited us just fine – I didn't want to think about how many cops were involved in what was now probably a state-wide search.

We needed to get somewhere where we knew we could be safe, to regroup and get it together. I thought about the bar from the night before, but at this point we couldn't risk getting over there without being spotted. It was too far away and our faces were surely plastered all over every news station by now. The powers that be desperately needed us eliminated. We were right behind them, and they were panicking. The thought of that gave me a little hope. But we weren't about to take on these monsters with just hope.

What I really wanted was to know how the chief felt right now. I wanted to see him squirming, hyperventilating behind his desk, dabbing at his sweating head with a drenched handkerchief, knowing we still weren't dead, knowing, of course, that the bear had nearly just ended his miserable existence. Maybe he was holed up somewhere deep underground now, a private jet on its way to whisk him away for early retirement. Cole was arrogant, but I wondered if he was so arrogant as to try to escape the bear and all the dealings he was obviously caught up in.

Something told me he couldn't leave yet, but we had to get to him before someone else did, or before he got to us.

Tonight we didn't stop for disguises, we just slithered through quiet parts of town, looking for some sort of shelter. Every five minutes we saw a cop car, and the occasional squad of King's Men, strolling down the streets. The more the night went on, the fewer civilians there were, and soon it began to look like martial law was in place.

Goldilocks pointed to an elevated parking lot to our left. 'There. We can hide there for a while, make our next move. Gives us a vantage point, we'll see 'em before they see us.'

And it's a damn good job one of us was still alert and had some life left, and not a walking bag of misery, because otherwise we would have been apprehended right there, and it would all be over.

I flinched as Goldilocks swung her good arm in the direction of something I didn't even get the chance to see. As she reached for something in her coat, I realized it was a cop, right in front of us.

He staggered back as Goldilocks brought out a shimmering knife. The cop was going for his gun but she was too fast, kicking his hand away from the holster, sliding up behind him, and bringing the knife to his throat.

'No, wait!' I called, reaching out desperately.

Too late. Goldilocks had already slashed the cop's neck from ear to ear.

The cop clutched at the fatal wound, wheezing and choking, blood spewing from his mouth and exposed throat. And I saw how young he was. Early twenties, maybe.

I looked away, hearing his final gurgles and the thump of his body hitting the concrete.

My eyes briefly met Corral's, whose head was in her shaking hands. She groaned and muttered, fingers trembling. Too distraught to even take Goldilocks on anymore.

I glanced down at the corpse, refusing to make eye contact with Goldilocks right now, my throat closed up and dry.

'We don't know how that woulda played out if I hadn't done that, alright?' Goldilocks started, her voice thick with tension. 'And we can't afford to dwell on it, either.'

I closed my eyes.

'Hell, I told you. We're gonna *have* to make these choices from here on out or we just ain't makin it out alive—'

'He's a fucking kid,' hissed Lieutenant Corral.

I looked up and saw Goldilocks chewing her lip, her eyes alive with both focus and unease. She stepped over the kid's corpse like he wasn't there, like she hadn't just murdered him, and got up in the face of Corral, whose head dropped slightly. She stood a few inches taller than the lieutenant, her arms planted stiffly by her sides.

I shifted closer to the two, my eyes darting around the dim streets and back.

'He was a cop – a cop who was lookin for us, to apprehend us, to kill us if he had to,' she said quietly. 'He was a cop workin for Chief fuckin Cole, a man who is *instrumental* in the abduction and murder of countless women and children.' She jabbed her fingers toward the ground with force. '*We* are trying to stop that man – all of 'em!' she hissed. 'So yeah, we may have to get a little fucked-up ourselves. Have some perspective, Lieutenant.'

And as Goldilocks turned away, I saw that, under the light of the glaring moon above, her eyebrows were slightly peaked, her parted lips were quivering, and her skin was paler than I'd ever seen it.

She stopped, wiped her blood-covered hand across her pants, and dragged the corpse across the concrete by the ankles, dumping it in a narrow alleyway for some helpless creature of the night to find. Just another body now.

Nobody said a word as we continued slithering along the streets, pausing and signaling occasionally at the sight of distant cops and King's Men on their patrols.

I thought about catching up to Goldilocks and offering words of alleviation, but I had nothing to say.

My throat was still closed up. Cold sweat leaked out of every pore. I imagined getting confronted by the King's Men or Cole himself there and then, how defenseless, how incapable of any kind of getaway I would be, how I would be leaving it up to Goldilocks and a semi-functioning Lieutenant Corral to save our asses.

I pictured myself projectile vomiting in the chief's face and making a run for it.

Then I came back to reality and sneered at my stupid thoughts, thoughts that were weighing down my failing brain and keeping me from staying vigilant out here in the middle of the city.

If I couldn't even stay lucid enough for this moment right now, then what they'd all said about me was true – I was a magick bean junkie, way out of my depth in this world, stumbling toward a predestined terminus that seemed to beckon more and more with every passing day. Flickering moments of hope, an occasional afternoon of happiness, glimpses of companionship and closeness – at the end of things, all this was to be shrouded in an unstoppable mist of dark.

'Stop feelin so sorry for yourself,' murmured Goldilocks with a sharp nudge that nearly toppled me into the road. 'Head up.'

'Head up,' I echoed feebly. No moping.

We managed to make our way onto the fourth floor of the parking lot undetected. Corral walked over to one of the openings and peered across the area, fingers gripping the cement wall.

Then I suddenly found myself clutching Goldilocks by the arm, a deep, burning sensation shooting through my chest then stomach.

She made a sharp shrieking sound and jerked back. '*Jack!*' she whisper-yelled.

Wrong arm. 'Shit, shit,' I said between breaths, 'you good? Agh!' I doubled over, arms crossed over my mid-section.

'What's happenin? Talk to me,' said Goldilocks while holding her shoulder, trying to repress the pain I'd stupidly just reintroduced to her.

I felt my eyes bulging. I blew out deep breaths and groaned. 'I don't— This hurts. *Shit*. This hasn't happened before,' I grunted. I looked around nervously, past the blurred faces of Goldilocks and Corral, as if I would find the remedy on the fourth floor of this parking structure.

Goldilocks scrambled at my clothes and my body got heavier. 'You injured, huh? You bleedin?' I heard her say. 'I don't see anything!'

Words and sounds got caught halfway up my throat. Streaks of purple, green, red, everything, they danced around in front of me, taking over my vision like a filter. Everything shook violently. I closed my eyes but couldn't escape. 'I need a . . .' Someone was whispering, someone was right up in my ear, speaking to me.

I wanted to see who it was, I wanted to open my eyes, turn my head, but none of that was happening.

I burned up, no longer feeling the ground beneath me.

Someone screamed as huge bloody fangs ripped at my arms, then my face. It was me who was screaming. A cold hand covered my mouth and the screams sank away.

'*Losing control,*' a voice said as flames danced across my eyes and burned me even more. Raw pain covered and filled me.

I was crawling now, dragging myself across harsh, cold concrete, alone. Then I began to rise, my legs struggling beneath me. Fresh air breezed across my face, through the hair that stuck to my forehead. Red and blue lights flickered in the distance, beneath lines of golden ones. They danced in the pitch dark.

I looked down, saw concrete and trees flying toward me.

A hand pressed against my contorting stomach, that same hand. I spun.

Goldilocks was there, eyes wide, her face twisted in shock or fear. I looked past her. Corral was there in the distance, hands in her pockets, no expression.

There were sirens.

'Shit,' I said, panting. 'I'm sorry . . . I'm sorry, I'm sorry, I—'

Goldilocks gripped hard on my shoulders. She seemed to be fighting the urge to shake me or launch me from this ledge, thirty feet aboveground.

She was whispering, eyes dancing across my face. 'What was . . . What did you . . .'

Corral stepped up to Goldilocks, hand held out. Goldilocks's eyes didn't leave me. 'We have to *go*,' called the lieutenant. 'They're here. They're here *now*.' I realized she finally wanted her gun back.

Goldilocks looked to Corral, then over her shoulder. After hesitating, she pulled out one of the handguns and shoved it into Corral's grip, eyes fixed on her.

And there was somebody here.

I looked beyond Goldilocks, beyond Corral. Someone stood behind her, deep in the shadows.

I tried to speak, to warn the lieutenant, but I couldn't.

Something washed over me – an invisible, thick mist that buried itself in my head.

Not again. Not now. I can't go back there.

But there was no pain this time, no burning, no screaming. Everything was quiet – I'd say tranquil, if I wasn't nearly shitting myself in fear. This was essentially a state of petrification, and if I needed to do something, to save myself or the others, I wouldn't be able to do it. It was my fear realized.

The figure either glided to me or I to it – there was no way of knowing for sure. Everything fell away. I realized both Goldilocks and Corral were gone.

I shouted with my mouth sealed shut, the sound of my own voice bellowing inside my head. As the figure drew nearer, a sense of familiarity and recognition shot through me, the weight of terror lifting off my shoulders.

'Oh, shit,' I murmured. 'This isn't usually . . . how this works.'

The witch gazed upon me with an invisible face. She stepped toward me in movements that didn't make any sense. *None* of this made sense.

Witches – the ones *I've* dealt with, at least – never tend to reveal themselves in the presence of more than one person. For this one to be doing so, there had to be a serious reason. Was I dying?

'What do you want?' I whispered. 'Is this it?'

The witch threw herself at me with jagged, impossible movements, and I screamed again – screamed as her black hole of a mouth practically enveloped my head. Everything was dark and I felt like I was barfing, but I wasn't. I didn't know what I was doing or where I was, couldn't figure out what the hell was happening at all.

Bright lights then: neon green, purple, red, blue, everything, swirling and dancing. A giddy sort of feeling passed through me. I looked down and my body wasn't there.

This is death, isn't it, my brain said. This wasn't how I imagined it to feel, but at least there was no pain.

No, this felt too wrong, too pleasant to be the end. I'd had thoughts before about death maybe being a relief, sure, but I never thought I'd be *giddy*. This wasn't death; this was good old-fashioned witchcraft. And it was going to save me. Again.

Something launched my body to the side and suddenly I was heaving rainbow vomit, sparkling, bright, shiny rainbow vomit.

I heard the voices of Goldilocks and Corral; they were yelling expletives and my name, maybe some insults, too, and I realized I was back.

The vomit – if that's what it was – bubbled and slithered on the concrete. I started to chuckle; I couldn't help it. I was really laughing, and it felt good, like ten magick beans were coursing through my veins.

I looked to where the witch had been standing, concealed in deep shadow. I realized she was still there, but fading. And then, as she evaporated back into nothing, back to whatever bittersweet hell she appeared to come from, words started to pass through my mind.

Goldilocks guided me to my feet, a mix of disgust and concern on her face, and my giggling faded as the words grew stronger. They were formed by an ancient tongue that seemed to translate in my head automatically. The sounds of their words were harsh and unforgiving, demanding to be listened to.

'*No more chances hereinafter. The harvester has neglected you one too many times. Your work is almost ended. Soon, the other will lead the way. The one that Death cannot snare. Chaos basks close to you, awaiting its nearing eruption. No more chances hereinafter.*'

As I blinked and regained my balance, the message faded away, replaced by Goldilocks's familiar voice.

'Jack, they're comin. Are you . . . Are you alright?' She was shaking.

I took her cold hands in mine. She looked down at them, her eyes glimmering with a film of tears.

A whisper shivered through my mind. '*We will sustain you no longer.*'

'It's going to be fine,' I said. And somehow, I meant it.

16

MISTER THUMB

'So you guys did see that, huh?' I said, loading my handgun.

Goldilocks nodded, terror still all over her face. It was as if we'd suddenly switched personalities.

Corral was backed up against the far wall, listening for something. I realized her gun was in her hand. If Goldilocks had returned it to her while I was out, I guess she really was scared right now.

'I don't know what the fuck you've gotten yourself into, Slade,' Corral hissed, 'but the explaining is going to have to come after we've dealt with *this*.'

I nodded. I was already watching, through the walls, beneath the ground. Someone was coming, and they were surrounded by a squad of King's Men.

'Whatever just went on with you, I wish you woulda gone about it without screaming at the top of your lungs,' Corral went on.

Goldilocks shot her a look of fury.

'Because now we are fucked.'

But I felt far from fucked. My whole body was warm and energized again, buzzing with power. Cryptic and deeply threatening message from the higher powers aside, it seemed they'd gifted me – for however long – an extremely potent and valuable dosage of magick bean, without the bean.

'Alright,' I said, ignoring Corral's fatalism as Goldilocks cocked her rifle, 'you two get behind me. And make sure you're close to cover.'

After a couple of seconds' hesitation, Corral clicked her tongue, scowled, and complied, joining Goldilocks beside a parked van.

I sensed our pursuers ascend another ramp. I felt that their guns were raised, but there was no way of knowing if they intended to shoot on sight. 'Nobody shoot,' I said, 'not unless—'

Goldilocks squirmed. 'Jack, I can take 'em out before they—'

'No. I got this.' And again, somehow I did believe I had this. As the magick coursed through my veins, I wondered if this was arrogance, overconfidence based on nothing, or if it was some kind of message from the witches that told me, for now, we were immortal.

I glanced around the parking lot, up, down and out into the streets, too. 'Oh,' I grunted.

King's Men were everywhere, lined up and down the roads, groups of them huddled on every street corner. They weren't moving. But the ones that were, the ones inside this building, were about to appear in front of us.

Slowly, I took a few steps forward, hands raised above my head.

Five King's Men stepped out onto our level and stopped. Then everything was quiet.

I squinted. The life form the King's Men had been surrounding all the way up here had become . . . shapeless, unreadable. I only knew it was even there through the lens of magick.

'Show yourself. Yeah, you,' I said, as if I'd actually seen the thing's response.

I peered over my shoulder at Goldilocks and Corral. They glowered, bemused. Tuning into the magick even more deeply, I started to form a more solid picture of what this thing was.

It was a man. A man who had done something to himself, something forbidden and magickal, tapping into sorcery that wasn't meant for him. I knew what that felt like, and as the mental image of the man grew stronger, I found myself hoping he would suffer similar consequences to me.

The image formed completely and the man himself, standing no more than two inches above the ground, shot up and expanded into a human shape, shifting into someone I recognized immediately, someone Corral no doubt recognized, too.

'No, *no*! Wait, wait,' Detective Bhatt pleaded. He hunched over, hands above his head, shuffling his feet along the ground, trying to back off.

'Now you stop right there,' I said, aiming my gun at his head. Through the walls I saw three more King's Men approaching. The sound of guns being primed clicked across the room. 'Shit.' I spun to face Goldilocks and Corral. 'You two, get down!'

I threw myself behind the nearest car. They did the same.

The sound of the King's Men's bullets thundering through the parking lot rocked my head, my senses far too elevated. It felt like someone smacking my head with a mallet over and over.

I grimaced, then felt a smile creep along my face. Adrenaline bubbled through me, fusing with the magick inside.

It wasn't like I would need all that good an aim; the magick would take care of that. I felt it.

I took a big breath in and stared right through the car I was sitting against. I saw everything, and the power was just pleading to burst through me and get the job done. So I raised my gun and fired at will.

I took down two of the King's Men myself, two shots each, they thumped against the wall with impossible force and collapsed in a pile of concrete.

A yelp came from Bhatt as he tried to scramble down the ramp to the floor below.

'Get behind me,' I called to Goldilocks and Corral, and ran to the top of the ramp. There were even more King's Men on the way, a lot of them, running in through the entrance of the ground floor.

We needed to hurry. This power inside me was one thing, but my partners were mortal right now, whatever Goldilocks might have argued.

I got Bhatt in my sights again.

Evidently, so had Goldilocks. 'Shall I take the shot?' she shouted behind me.

'No!' Bhatt squealed.

'Freeze, then!' I said.

He practically hurled the other King's Man in our direction. The soldier panicked, aiming neither here nor there. I took him down swiftly.

This time Goldilocks didn't wait for instructions. With a wince, she raised her rifle, peered down the sights, and took the shot.

The bullet ricocheted into the ground about an inch from his foot. She'd missed.

Bhatt screamed and fell anyway, writhing on the floor like a fish on land.

I ran toward him before he tried one of his shape-shifting tricks to get away.

'Don't you move, Bhatt,' said Corral, scrambling up to his flailing body. 'We got you, you son of a bitch.'

'You miss on purpose?' I asked Goldilocks while approaching Bhatt.

She smirked in reply.

Bhatt put his hands on his head and let out a deafening roar of frustration, fury, and insanity. My ears felt like they were bleeding now, and I ended up staggering back, cupping my ears and grimacing, but Goldilocks marched forward and rammed the butt of her rifle into his stomach to shut him up a little.

His eyes bulged as he folded over on the ground, the screams turning into gurgles and mutters.

Up close I saw how sickly he looked now, his dark complexion spotted with grayish blotches, forehead drenched with sweat. His eyes drooped, the sclera crimson with blood. Drool and foam rested on his top lip.

I recognized these symptoms. It was like looking in a mirror after a night of bean dependency.

He uttered a sharp, hacking cough, strings of blood coming up and dangling from his stubble. 'Don't . . . No, no, don't kill me,' he barely managed.

Corral approached him, and he whimpered as she pressed the barrel of her gun to his forehead.

I looked at her from the corner of my eye, sensing the King's Men getting nearer. 'Ilsa, we don't have time for this; we gotta get out.'

'No wound,' she murmured, tracing the barrel down to his neck. 'What is this?' she snarled.

He slowly glanced up, peering past the sodden black hair dangling across his face, the blood in his eyes glimmering in the harsh lights. He just grinned.

I grabbed him, twisting his body so he was facing away from the lieutenant, and put my gun to his head. He shouted something incoherently.

The King's Men had made it up to our level, all stopping at the bottom of the ramp, aiming their weapons at the four of us.

Bhatt flapped an arm around. 'No, no, no, stop!' he yelled. 'Don't you fire, don't you dare! You take your orders from me.'

The King's Men stayed perfectly still, lifeless but ever dangerous.

'Don't let them kill me,' he said to me hollowly. Then to the King's Men before us, 'St-stand— Stand down. Stand down now.'

They didn't move. I could almost feel Goldilocks's finger itching to pull the trigger, to take the chance, despite the odds being severely against us, out in the open.

Bhatt attempted to force some authority into his voice. 'Lower your weapons now, King's Men.' He glanced at me, then back to the squadron. 'I am in command. This is an order . . . you bastards.'

Then one of the King's Men began to make his way forward tentatively, weapon aimed right at my face. I reaffirmed my position, digging the barrel of my handgun into Bhatt's neck. He squealed once more.

'No, halt!' he yelled, his outreached arms trembling. 'Or I will have all of you eliminated.'

I raised my eyebrows.

The King's Man tilted his head slightly, now looking at Bhatt.

He raised his left arm and signaled something to the others with a quick motion.

All the King's Men gave way, lowering their weapons and apparently letting us walk past them.

Goldilocks scowled, her eyes darting to each of the soldiers in a cycle, her weapon still raised.

I looked to Corral. Her lips were scabbed, face drained of color. Her feet shifted on the ground but she didn't move forward. She seemed to be weighing our options.

I felt it in the air, the sudden lack of hostility from the King's Men. I tapped into it, closing my eyes, letting the power lead me. They weren't going to shoot us; they weren't going to apprehend us. Of course Bhatt was a coward, but missing out on the chance to get all three of us because he was so scared for his own life? I had to fight a grin.

I led the way forward.

'Jack,' said Goldilocks.

'We're gonna be just fine,' I said.

She hesitated, puffed her cheeks and followed, not taking her eyes or aim off the King's Men. Corral did the same, but her handgun dangled by her side.

The King's Men suddenly seemed completely devoid of life, standing soullessly like statues. They didn't move, didn't breathe. The only movement was the flicker of red and blue lights on their helmets and armor, blinking at different intervals.

I breathed in and tried to get a picture of the suffocating world outside these walls. It seemed like nearly every King's Man out on the streets had its attention turned to this parking complex. I breathed out and focused on taking one step at a time, my feet light but strong beneath me.

My senses had been scanning for one man above all the others, reaching out into the dark streets to find that heap of giant's shit. But there was still no sign of Cole here. Every time I thought about him and where he might be, the magick inside took on a more violent, wild shape, pressing against my flesh and rippling with a deathly desire. I had to be careful.

Beneath the distant murmur of the city and careful, rhythmic footsteps, I heard Detective Bhatt's quivering breaths. At first I thought the sound was slipping into delirious laughter, but it turned out to be more like a series of whimpers, then rageful muttering.

I tightened my grip on the back of his neck. 'You try anything, I'll feel it coming long before you get to even imagine standing over my corpse.' I secretly wondered why he wasn't going for his shrinking trick again. When he'd returned to normal size before, he appeared exhausted, drained.

That could mean a few things: It could mean he's a novice at this sort of magick, his body and soul easily overwhelmed by it; he's overdone it recently; or it's not exactly in his control.

Whatever it was, I realized I needed to get answers from him pretty quickly in case he returned to the size of an ant, flicked into a storm drain and escaped into the Hudson before I could royally squish him with the underside of my boot.

In near silence, we moved down to the ground floor of the parking lot. Beyond the walls, I watched for our pursuers without looking; everything revealed itself, clearer than ever, with next to no effort on my part.

I thought I could get used to this dosage, but I knew that beneath this sensation of complete power and control, raw, deciding fear still lingered, ready to pounce when the magick had worn off.

I tried not to think about that, about what was in store for me once the sorcery left my body.

The words of the shapeless witch reverberated through my head. Whether it was a memory of that oppressive but fleeting moment, or if she was still with me right now, I didn't know for sure.

I clasped my hand over Bhatt's mouth. He mumbled into it in a pathetic high pitch. Five King's Men marched down the street. I motioned to Corral and Goldilocks to stay perfectly still. They did.

A path to safety, or almost safety, reached out to me. Dead ahead, a narrow street of townhouses, no signs of life except for the odd cat or crow.

The King's Men split up, some heading into the parking lot through the entrance far to our left, the others roaming the streets. I heard something then. The King's Men from upstairs, they were in communication with someone. Other squads perhaps, and the chief himself, letting them know we had Bhatt.

'We have to move,' I whispered. 'That way.' I motioned toward the street ahead. We shifted onward.

Detective Bhatt rambled loudly. A splatter of blood met the pavement as the butt of my handgun connected with his jaw. I shoved him onto a public bench. Just as he was about to yell about that, I rammed the barrel of the gun into his gaping mouth.

I gripped the gun, feeling the friction as it scraped against his teeth and lodged in the back of his throat.

Goldilocks and Corral watched in silence.

Bhatt looked even more sickly now, like he was quickly fading from physical existence. His eyes widened, revealing the full extent of the damage to his eyeballs, next to no white even visible now, his pupils dilated unnaturally.

Only I saw these details, well away from the light of the streetlamps and townhouse windows, using the night as our protection from the King's Men and whoever else was out there.

While I stared back into his unblinking, crazy eyes, I had to push down the lurking, violent urges flickering inside me, close to the surface. An impulse to kill. I wondered how much of it was from the magick, and how much was from my raw loathing of this scum.

For now, I buried the rage, and pulled the gun from his throat, pressing it against his forehead instead.

Corral stepped up and tugged at his coat, confiscating his weapon. 'You won't be needing that,' she said in a low tone.

Bhatt murmured something and spat on the floor. Then he peered down the street vacantly and puffed out his cheeks. 'Well,' he said, quieter now, 'if you've got me – I mean, if you've *really* got me, and my useless friends don't show up – I suppose I can only blame myself.' He gesticulated with his hands while he spoke as if he was giving a presentation. 'This was always going to be my downfall, wasn't it? My passion for *life*.'

'Now who said anything about living?' I asked, pressing the gun to his head as a gentle reminder of his situation.

He snorted. 'No, you're not going to kill me, Jackson Slade.'

On another day, I would've secretly agreed. But today I was loaded with magick so potent I barely knew what my next move was going to be.

'It's funny how far you've fallen,' he went on, smiling. 'You're the boy who once slayed a beast so tall and ginormous, its head rose above the clouds, and nobody except you knew what the thing looked like until it fell! But tonight you weren't even able to step on a man no taller than the famed pill you adore so much. You can't even kill *me*, the man who killed your friends on behalf of your boss! I mean, it's just . . . just . . .' He trailed off, mock-exasperation on his face. Then he began to laugh, and gagged. 'Excuse me.' He gagged again. 'Your pardon.'

'What the fuck are you doing?' I said.

'Well, you see I . . . I'm not feeling too dandy.'

He didn't look dandy, either. I saw the skin on his face sagging slightly.

Goldilocks stepped forward now, standing as close to Bhatt as possible. 'You tryin something, huh?' she spat. 'Nobody's comin for you. You ain't worth the trouble to 'em anymore. You're stuck with us now, and we're the last people you're ever gonna spend time with. You're done.'

Whether that was true or not, Bhatt was in a state, in the palm of our collective hand.

He scrambled farther back on the bench, grasping at his face, panting sharply, erratically.

'Are you in pain?' I asked.

'Y-yes,' breathed Bhatt.

'Want me to make it stop?' I cocked the gun.

'*No*! No . . . You wouldn't. I can take it.'

I tuned in to my surroundings, making sure we weren't being closed in on. It seemed clear enough, but we needed to move, and Bhatt was making sure that didn't happen yet.

I grabbed him by the lapels of his coat. 'We keep walking. Any one of us is *more* than capable of killing you.'

Bhatt's breathing slowed. He didn't take his eyes off me. I saw realization dawning in them. He knew now I wasn't lying.

I checked the streets one more time, then let go of him.

'Where are we walking *to*?' he whispered.

'A ride,' I said.

'To where?'

I smiled. 'Wherever our boss is.'

Bhatt's already sagging face dropped.

After I'd scouted out a cruiser manned by only one officer, Goldilocks went in for the kill.

Corral had recommended she just incapacitate the cop, but Goldilocks cupped his mouth and sliced his throat instead.

The lieutenant's jaw clenched, but we weren't debating morals anymore. This was it.

I took the wheel, with Goldilocks and Corral sitting either side of Detective Bhatt. I started the engine and reached out with magick, searching for a King's Man-free zone nearby.

I found one a few blocks away and headed toward it. I concealed the vehicle in an alley and stopped the engine, turning my attention back to Bhatt.

As the hum of the engine faded, Bhatt stared back at me, Goldilocks and Corral glaring at him from either side.

'What?' He sounded like a defensive, guilty kid.

Goldilocks went first. She sneered at him with venom. 'What compels you to kidnap defenseless women and children and take 'em out to the woods? What's in it for you, other than your satisfaction, you twisted fuck?'

Bhatt sighed. 'No, no, no. *That* doesn't satisfy me at all; that's one of the many downers in this job—'

'This *job*?'

'What compels me is ambition, if you really have to know.' He swallowed. 'And fear.'

'What does that mean?' I asked.

Bhatt pointed at his chest with both thumbs, jabbing at himself. '*Means I'm not like them*! I'm not... It wasn't supposed to go like this. It's just... One thing led to another, and I had very little choice in where things went in the end. I couldn't turn back, I'm afraid.' His lip quivered slightly. 'And I *am* afraid.'

There was a yelp as Goldilocks smacked him in the face with her palm, then again. He leaned back in fear, almost climbing into Corral's lap.

The lieutenant shoved him away. 'So are we supposed to feel sorry for you? You're the fucking victim?' she said.

Bhatt's attention was on Corral then. He looked her up and down with near wonder. 'You, Lieutenant. I'll be honest, I'm surprised at you for not figuring me out.' He let out a whimper of a chuckle. 'You were supposed to know me so well.'

'Bhatt,' I said, watching the fury spread over Corral's face, 'enough.'

'You were supposed to be their help, their savior,' he went on.

'These innocent children, ripped away from their mothers and fathers in the middle of the streets – in broad daylight, no less! No one batted an eye. You *barely* did. And you're supposed to be, what, a hero? You even let *me* down, Ilsa.' Bhatt seemed to be tearing up, moved by his own arrogant words. 'I will not lie – there were times where I prayed to all the gods that someone like you would come along and catch us, catch *them*, and it would be over. But you never did—'

'I've heard enough—' Corral pulled out her handgun.

Bhatt closed his eyes.

'Stop!' I yelled. I reached out and snatched the gun from Ilsa's hand with ease.

If not for the magick in my veins, Bhatt would be dead.

Corral's teeth gnashed together. She grabbed her hair with both hands and tucked her chin into her chest, growling. 'I can't hear this!' she shouted.

I glared at Bhatt, whose eyes were wide with shock, as if he wasn't toying with his own mortality with his words.

'Okay, okay,' he said, hands raised. 'Listen, I can— I can make it up to you, all of you. I can *undo* the horrors I've been complicit in. You want to know where Cole is – that's why we're here, right? I can take you there. I can lead you there. I can!'

Goldilocks shot me a look.

Corral glared at Bhatt, then me, eyes red and glistening.

'If you don't kill me, I'll take you to Chief Cole.'

'I *will* kill you after, though,' said Goldilocks in a low tone.

Bhatt shrugged. 'I'm afraid there's a really long line. I don't trust you have the patience—'

'It's not just about Cole, is it?' I called out over the bickering.

Bhatt blinked.

'Snowdrop Wood,' I said.

'Yes,' said Bhatt.

'What the fuck is happening in there? I've seen things, heard things . . . I don't know what. Monsters, flames, screams. What's happening to the victims?'

The car was silent now. Bhatt fidgeted in his seat, looking to and from his shaking hands in his lap.

'Answer me,' I said, my voice getting louder.

'I don't know the politics of it all,' he said simply, quietly.

'There's a third party, ain't there?' said Goldilocks. 'It's not just Arminus and Cole. They're workin with someone else.'

I glanced at her, then Bhatt. His lips quivered again, more and more sweat glistening on his forehead. His breathing was thick and sharp, like he was on the verge of a panic attack.

'I expect you're right,' he finally said, 'but I'm not the one to ask. Really. I can give you Cole, and you can ask *him*. Not that I think you'll live long enough, but that's none of my business.'

'He's leading us into a trap,' said Corral.

I didn't take my eyes off Bhatt. I channeled the magick inside to essentially peer into his mind. I concentrated harder, trying to look past all the noise.

'He can't be trusted. We gotta find another way. This man feeds on chaos,' Corral added.

Bhatt seemed to smirk a little at that.

'He's leading us to our deaths, Jack,' she finished.

He stuck out his bottom lip and shrugged.

'No,' I said, turning to the wheel and starting the engine. 'No, he's not.'

We wound through the blocks of the city and joined the interstate. In the King's Men's cruiser, we were virtually hidden in plain sight.

Choppers flew by as the city faded behind us, disappearing into the low mist hanging from the black sky.

According to Bhatt, Cole's hideout was out of town, some random warehouse you wouldn't glance twice at. Along the way, I tried to get more out of him, more about his sorcery or curse or whatever it was. After betraying Cole, he'd decided to shut his mouth for a while.

He sat there like a lump of shit for almost the whole journey. I enjoyed the brief quiet.

The quiet ended once Goldilocks pulled a gun on him.

Bhatt gasped, jerking back in his seat.

'What are you doing, Robicheaux?' asked Corral.

Goldilocks cocked the gun. 'See, there's one more thing.'

I could sense the pressure of Goldilocks's finger on the trigger through enhanced senses. 'Don't,' I said. 'Don't fuck it up.'

'Now that they know they've lost you,' Goldilocks said, paying no attention to me or the lieutenant, 'they must figure there's every chance you've squealed, huh?'

'What? No I . . . Please, I'm very sick—'

'*I'll* show you sick,' she hissed. 'Arminus gonna run?'

I watched through the mirror. 'Jess—'

Bhatt's teeth chattered. 'I don't know—'

'Bullshit. They know we're closin in, all of 'em. They ain't just gonna sit there and do nothin; they'll all be on the move.'

'You don't know that,' I said. 'We have to go to Cole. *I* have to get Cole.' I felt rage bubbling in my stomach now, at the very thought of Cole, at the mental image of him getting away.

'You can get Cole,' spat Goldilocks, 'but you know what I have to do, too.'

Skyscrapers flew past us in a blur as we bolted along the interstate. My heart raced, thumped in my ears. The magick was either getting even stronger, or it was starting to mess me up.

'I'm gonna need you to make a turn,' Goldilocks said grimly.

Corral sighed. 'Robicheaux—'

'Jack.'

I shook my head slowly. Inside my head, I faced dozens of different outcomes, none of them good. They rushed at me, all at once, images and sounds. Death and blood and failure – that was all I saw.

My confidence was slipping. It was getting overrun by grim reality.

'Jack,' said Goldilocks again.

'Don't you point that gun at me,' I said.

A hint of a smirk crept along Goldilocks's lips. 'I know I ain't gonna need to.'

I took the exit.

Goldilocks directed me toward the storage container that held her bike. I quit weighing up paths and outcomes. I gave in to the fact that no matter what we did, this was probably almost over. And if nothing else, we would go down fighting on all fronts.

The storage was untouched, not a cop in sight around here. I undid my safety belt and went to open the door.

I stopped as Bhatt cleared his throat. He gave a little shrug, slumped in his seat, looking even more like a corpse than before.

'Bhatt?' I said.

His head lolled to the side. He looked at Goldilocks, blinking slowly. 'Make it fast,' he breathed. 'I don't know where he's headed, but he leaves tonight.'

Goldilocks's eyes were alive with conviction. She nodded. 'He's still here?'

Bhatt nodded. 'You won't . . . You won't,' he said, 'but *if* you manage to slay the bear . . . Tell him, from me—'

Goldilocks scowled. 'Naw, fuck you, Detective.' She slipped out of the car and slammed the door shut.

Bhatt grimaced and slunk down.

I joined Goldilocks outside the car. As I watched her then, a sickening, swirling sensation took hold of my stomach. And that was nothing to do with magick – it was plain old nerves. I swallowed hard, suddenly alive to the possibility I wouldn't see her again, one way or the other.

I held my hands out at my sides. 'Is this . . .'

Goldilocks stood there stiffly, looking down at the ground. 'This might be the only way we get 'em both,' she said. 'If we got Cole and actually made it out alive, the bear would disappear in an instant. I'm ... I'm sorry if this doesn't work.'

I shook my head, reached out with my senses. There was a foundation of violence, aggression, chaos ... grief. But right now, emanating from her and swallowing me up – terror.

Not for her, for me.

'Listen,' I said. 'Hamelin's evidence. He told me ... He told me it was hidden in some desk drawer, in the room he was living in, next to the bear's office, I think.' I felt a flicker of a smile on my lips. 'We could really do with acquiring that.'

Goldilocks's face was unchanged, her tongue wetting her bottom lip in thought, or anxiety.

'Now go,' I said.

She glanced up, then hurtled toward me, pulling me toward her, gripping me in a tight embrace. I held her in kind and patted her on the back, my nose filled with the smell of gun smoke and cold sweat.

'Go on, do it,' I said.

She pushed me away, nodding. She unlocked the shutter, then threw it open, revealing the bike.

She mounted it and looked my way. 'There ain't no rules anymore, Jack. They're gonna come for us no matter what we do. So just do whatever it takes. I promise you I'll do the same.'

I smiled. 'I don't doubt you.'

She took her helmet in her arms and seemed to hesitate. Then, 'Let's get these bastards.' She fixed the helmet on her head and slammed down the visor.

As the engine of the motorbike roared, I turned my attention away from the sinking feeling in my stomach and ducked back into the cruiser.

Corral watched as Goldilocks circled round and veered into the street, zipping into the night.

I heard the jingle of Bhatt's cuffs as he fidgeted in his seat. He tipped his head back and sighed melodramatically.

'Something you wanna get off your chest, Bhatt?' asked the lieutenant harshly as I started the engine.

'Just that... if I were in your shoes, I wouldn't be so leisurely, my friends.' He watched me in the mirror with sunken eyes. 'The clock is ticking. For all of us.' He managed an irritating, self-satisfied smile and closed his eyes.

I clicked my teeth and drove, feeling less than threatened by the ailing, cowardly captive cuffed in the back seat.

17

BLAIDD

As we got ever closer to our destination, I'd essentially fled from my body. With my physical being behind the wheel, the rest of me flew and spun through the suburbs, taking in every little detail, every movement and sound. With it being so late, there weren't many, but I couldn't afford to take chances.

So far, it seemed Bhatt wasn't leading us right into a trap. He really was selling out the people in charge of this whole thing just to keep his life for a few more days. I almost found that admirable.

Even as my senses swarmed around the blocks of run-down houses, junkyards, and warehouses, I managed to keep tabs on Bhatt. And so far, he was far from getting any stronger, and definitely wasn't going anywhere.

I briefly pictured a life with so much magick in me day after day, the things I could do, the things I could escape.

And *no more chances* whispered in my mind.

The closer we got, the stronger that unshakable sense of doubt that had been with me since the very beginning became. Even with all this magick in my veins, I was still fighting a constant battle with nauseating paranoia and anxiety.

I'd come to the conclusion that those feelings weren't going to leave me; they were going to stay with me until the end. However close that was.

Faceless, nameless people stood huddled in my mind. Slowly, they drifted apart. Dead ones littered the shapeless ground. A wave of flames engulfed them, burning them all to ash.

I stuffed the image back into my subconscious. Victims were still out there, begging for light. The flames hadn't taken everyone, not yet.

'Here,' breathed Bhatt.

I stopped the car a few yards from the warehouse. It sat there across the street, gray and unassuming, just like the hundreds of others that filled this area.

'You sure?' I said.

Bhatt was right – you wouldn't look twice at this place. And without him, there was no way we would have ended up where we were, here at the front door of Chief Cole's last refuge.

'Why there?' I asked. 'What's in there for him? He plan to just stay holed up until we're all dead?'

Corral's eyes flicked between me and Bhatt. Her tension filled the car. If the magick wasn't so powerful, it would've been disruptive.

'I suppose that would be the logical strategy for a man like him,' said Bhatt. 'But I've done what I said I'd do. My time is up.' He held up his hands, jingled the cuffs. 'Time to set me free.'

'No,' said Corral. 'That is not happening. You know it's not.'

'You're getting us inside, directly to the chief,' I said. 'Only then can you fuck off.'

Rows of ragged, badly painted houses lined both sides of the street. Their panes had splintered, screen doors warped, refusing to close. Everything was completely still for a while, except for a small-framed figure in the distance, shuffling down the sidewalk, hands stuffed into their raincoat pockets.

The thick clouds above moved quickly, like time was fast-forwarding. The street and buildings went from bright to dim as the moon floated in and out of view. For a while, I didn't move, the engine rumbling beneath me, causing a couple neighbors to stir, lights coming on, peeking through their blinds.

As I focused all my attention on that warehouse now, I started to make out figures inside. Not their physical shape, not their emotions or even sounds they make, just the presence of life.

But I should've been able to, with ease. Something was distorting my senses. They flickered, getting weaker the harder I tried to focus. It was like I was losing signal.

I turned to Bhatt. His skin looked dried up, his breathing thick and heavy. 'What's wrong with you?' I said. 'Are you doing this?'

He rolled his head to look me in the eyes. 'What?' he said, barely audible.

I peered back to the warehouse. If it wasn't Bhatt, then Cole had more than his usual detail of King's Men inside with him. Someone with magick capabilities was in there, maybe trying to shield him from me.

I grunted, quickly losing patience. Corral watched me with caution, her eyes glistening in the wavering moonlight, mouth slightly open.

And I sensed that she felt it, too, this uncanny sensation winding round us, round the whole street. She wouldn't need magick to feel this – it was powerful, enveloping, a dark essence emanating from inside the warehouse.

Bhatt's chattering teeth broke the cold silence. 'We should go,' he whispered.

'Where have you brought us?' I whispered back.

Corral tensed up even more.

Bhatt lolled his head from side to side, mouth tightly sealed.

'Answer me,' I said, slightly louder.

'I don't want this!' he blurted, and I shifted in my seat.

The magick was shaking, vibrating, distorting, my senses shifting into blurry pixels. Suddenly it was as if I was going blind.

'I don't want it,' he said again, loudly.

'Shut up,' said Corral shakily.

'What the fuck,' I whispered, turning to the warehouse.

It was somewhere in my mind, I think at first. But then it sounded so close, so loud, and it was like Corral and Bhatt could hear it, too. Cries and shrieks, wails of the lost children calling out until they were completely drowned out by the sound of roaring flames.

Not only did I hear it, I started to *feel* it, truly feel it reverberating throughout my soul. The pain, the loss, the sorrow, the absolute end of hope. These memories or experiences transferring from them to me. And it made me want to die.

I felt centuries of evil and terror flash through me in that instant. Visions of demonic faces, piercing, blood-drenched teeth and claws flickered before me. It all seemed to manifest into an unspeakable, palpable energy that entered me, lingering for the briefest of awful moments before passing through me.

I burned up from the inside out. Something was inside that building, something I wasn't ready to face.

Nobody should face this.

The blistering pain in my shoulder burned like all hell. Even gripping the handlebar of my bike caused a scorching sensation to instantly take over. But I had to fight through this pain or I would die, and dying before the bear did was not an option.

While I raced down the black country road, I tried to distract myself with plans. Wondered if Bloodstone's surveillance would be any different tonight now that the bear knew it was time to start panicking, and packing, according to the tiny asshat.

Best not to even think on it at this point. Relying on plans rather than my gut tended to cost me. If ever there was a night for going with my instinct, seemed this was it.

Whatever was about to happen, I was gonna have to make it perfect. Useless shooting arm or not.

From out here I could still make out the swarm of choppers on the horizon, way back at the city. I thought about Jack and what the hell he was gonna do without me.

I saw a hint of an orange glow on the horizon in front of me. I slowed down and lifted my visor, just to make sure they weren't headlights. They weren't. They were the lanterns that illuminated the main pathway to the doors of Bloodstone.

As I got closer, I realized they weren't the only lights visible, not tonight. At least three spotlights glared upon the lawn of the manor.

Now, they weren't there last time I checked, which was yesterday. A testament to how spooked the bear had become.

I smiled a little, then frowned when I realized how much harder they were gonna make my job tonight.

Whatever. An extra hurdle, no big deal – it would be dealt with.

I switched off the headlight and stopped the bike. I'd have to walk the rest of the way – couldn't risk any goons hearing the engine.

On my left was a clump of trees and bushes. They reminded me of Bluebeard, the freak. If he'd made it back to the manor, he was to be dead meat tonight, too. I concealed my bike in the bushes and kept to the side of the road as I moved forward.

The ground was still soaked from the rain. It made me think back to Snowdrop Wood and suddenly the pain in my shoulder made itself known again. I hissed and grabbed at it. Taking a bullet from a King's Man – how the hell did I let that happen?

I cursed Hatter for doing half a job and made for Bloodstone's perimeter, sticking to the tall brick wall.

I twisted and dropped into the weeds as two vehicles crawled along the road. Two NYPD cruisers. They slowed while passing the manor, then picked up speed and flashed their lights, heading for the city.

The question of Jack's fate crept into my brain again, but I had to let that go. I was here, he was out there – we'd made our choices, and now it was time to face the repercussions.

This wasn't about Jack; it was about revenge.

I felt my way along the slimy, mossy wall. In my final days as a member of Arminus's gang, I'd made preparations for a time like this, a time when I might need to make a little visit in the dead of night.

My hand bumped over the dislodged brick, one of the bricks I'd driven partially out of the wall when I'd made my escape.

A murmuring close by, on the other side of this wall. Two guys' voices, gruff and deep. Didn't recognize them.

I stayed completely still for a minute, controlling my breath and keeping my feet light on the ground.

Their loud voices, their mocking laughter, started to fade away as they patrolled farther down the wall, close to the front of the manor.

Using my good arm, I smacked one of the bricks with the palm of my hand, tensing my forearm and wrist. It budged.

I got down on my ass, feeling the cold, soggy dirt beneath me squelch. It sent a gross, shivering sensation up my back. I leaned on my undamaged side and kicked at the bricks, pausing every couple seconds, listening for voices or movement.

When the bricks gave in, I threw them to one side, but keeping one in my grip to use as either a weapon or distraction. The bricks grazed my head and dug at my back as I squeezed through the hole, kicking against the mushy ground.

I peered through the other side. The searchlight was only a few meters away, making a sweep from here to the front of the building.

I forced myself through and dashed over to the side of the manor, pressing myself against the wall, concealed in shadows, well out of the light's range.

The two guards casually stalked along – one with a heavy assault rifle, the other with a shotgun swinging lazily from his hand. Their guns wouldn't be of much use to them anymore.

I danced along the perimeter of Bloodstone Manor on the balls of my feet. I made no sound. The grass was well-kept here – no more squelching.

Seven windows lined the wall on the ground floor. I ducked, flowing past them all and quickly reaching the rear of the building. Needed to check for more goons. If I got surrounded here, it would all be over.

I placed the brick beside me, pulled out my pistol, and screwed on the suppressor.

More voices, distant footsteps, boots hitting concrete. I peered around the corner and, at a glance, counted about six patrolling assholes. Two of them had stationed themselves beside the illuminated swimming pool, one guy on the patio. Three guys strolled on the higher level by the trees at the back.

The detail was only a little heavier than it was when I scouted this place. These guys were nothing. I was gonna be fine.

Excitement swelled through my chest because when I took another glance, I noticed the propellers of a huge chopper protruding from the mass of pines fading into the black sky.

The bear's chopper. Arminus was still here.

Grabbing the brick again, I bit down on my lip and backed off from the corner of the building. I drifted all the way down and stopped at the other corner where those two guys stood.

They'd separated a little – shotgun guy stood right by the main gates. The other guard was out of my sight.

I was intent on walking through the front doors. After these guys were done, it was gonna be plain sailing.

The goon stepped closer to the gates, peering beyond them. I hoped it was me he was expecting, not backup.

I needed to make this quick.

I peered around the corner – two searchlights gliding across the lawn and three men with guns in total. Easy.

While the guard looked out the gate, I switched to the corner of the outer wall in silence, trampling on a bed of roses, almost slipping.

Dressed from head to toe in black, well inside the shadow, I was invisible for now.

The guard then made a big mistake. He didn't realize it until I'd sliced his throat open. He'd sauntered back down the side of the manor, casually peering into windows. Maybe he was checking for intruders. More likely he was trying to get a peep at some action.

Either way, he didn't find what he was looking for.

I swapped my pistol for my knife, which glistened in the moonlight. I noticed dried blood on it, blood from the kid cop. I cleaned it off and lurched forward.

His dying body squirmed against me and I felt the warmth of his blood as it spurted against my hand, the pressure of his weight agonizing against my shoulder.

I hissed in pain and cracked his skull with the brick in my other hand. It was a good release, but the pain was going nowhere. I would have to take it inside the manor with me.

The guard went limp, motionless on the floor. A heap of meat in a puddle of blood.

My movements were swift with adrenaline. But the burning pain still made this harder than it needed to be. I could've killed Hatter then.

I paused, listening. No one had heard the muffled whimper of the guard. I proceeded.

The other two guards out here stood either side of the doors to the manor.

They stared ahead blankly, mindlessly. I thought about two rapid bullets to each head, but I couldn't trust my arm.

The brick in my hand dripped with blood.

I made my decision in a split second.

I clattered the brick against the main gates after the spotlights cleared to the sides.

Both guards jumped, raised their guns, aiming everywhere and nowhere at once. Before they could do anything else, I sunk my blade into the nearest guard's throat. His rifle fell to the ground.

With my knife still lodged in his throat, the other guard turned to me and aimed.

My shot had to count.

I swung my bad arm in his direction and pulled the trigger.

The bullet went straight through his pathetic, terrified face.

His body fell back, tumbling off the small, concrete steps. He nestled in the bushes, all mangled and dead.

My teeth gnashed together. I let out a guttural growl and keeled over, gripping my shoulder as the pain swelled harder.

Finally, the guard with my knife in his throat stumbled down. He fell on his knees and looked up at me with bloodshot eyes. Blood spurted and poured from the wound in his neck.

I recognized the guy.

I hesitated.

I *would* recognize some of these people. Dwelling on it would be a fatal mistake.

I wrenched my knife from his neck and stuck it through his face instead. He gurgled and died. Just another heap of dead man on Papa Bear's front lawn.

With the arm that worked, I grabbed the corpse by the ankle and heaved it into the shadows. I pressed it up to the side of the manor with my boot so it was well out of view of the lights.

I snatched the set of keys from the other body's belt and flicked through them until I got to the big silver one.

My body was electric with energy. I was looking through lenses of red. Nothing was gonna stop me. This was it.

I shoved the key into the lock. It clicked. I opened the door and barely looked at the goon to my right before I killed him.

'Hey,' he went, '*what—*'

I pinned him to the wall with my blade. He kicked and scrambled there as his blazer turned crimson with blood. I tilted my head, wondering for a second if I'd just killed Arminus's right hand.

I breathed a sigh of relief when I realized it was just some other suit.

Bluebeard's demise was to be savored, relished. That man wasn't about to enjoy the mercy of a quick stab.

The official dropped dead as I took my knife back.

I took in the scents of old wood, burning candles, expensive liquor, and gunpowder. Home sweet home.

'Something's in there,' I said as we all stepped out into the damp cold air.

'Well, I would... hope so,' Bhatt said in between weak splutters. Specks of blood dashed against the frosted concrete as he spat.

'No,' I said, grimacing. 'Something more than just Cole, or King's Men. It's... Never mind.' I shook my head. There was very little need to talk to him about this.

Corral stepped beside me, looking up into my eyes with grave concern. She seemed to have aged ten years in the last twenty-four hours. 'I feel something.' She glanced toward the warehouse. 'You really can't see what it is?'

I shook my head.

Corral placed her hands on her hips and stood a few inches from Bhatt. 'What is this, hm? Your life is on the line here. Don't forget that.'

'Believe *me*, Lieutenant, I haven't forgotten.' There was a little more color in his voice now.

I watched him closely, both with my eyes and my power.

Corral stared at him sharply, waiting for an answer.

'I. Don't. *Know*,' he finally said. 'I've been kept in the fucking dark this entire operation, okay? If the chief has some sort of undetectable superpower with him in there, I know nothing about it. All I know is that *this* is his hideout.'

He paused, shifting his eyes across the street. Everything was so still. I wondered if the chief heard us breaking the silence.

Bhatt breathed in sharply, and I heard the effort it took for him to do so. 'Honestly, who knows what kind of allies a man such as he has made during all this,' he said. 'Or enemies.' He shrugged. 'Certainly not me.'

'What do you mean, enemies?' I asked.

'This . . . This dirty, dark, hellish *business*,' he spat, glaring past me toward the warehouse. 'The blackmail, the deals, leverage. The things they involve themselves in, oh, it's . . .

Corral stared daggers. 'Don't you *they* us, Bhatt. You *are* they.'

Bhatt ignored her. 'See, he's clearly made an enemy of the big bear, or they at least have a . . . rocky relationship – we all saw that with our own eyes just the other day.' He stuck out his bottom lip in that punchable way he does. 'A deal gone wrong, perhaps. Not holding his end of some bargain?'

Bhatt turned his attention to me then, eyes scanning me slowly, intently. He looked me up and down, smiling. 'You're almost definitely not prepared for whatever's inside that building. You know it. You feel it. You haven't been prepared for *any* of this, all this time. But you've gone ahead and done it all, anyway, regardless of the consequences. I like your style, Slade!' he announced, beaming now.

'Who are you?' I asked flatly.

He snorted and looked through me, his focus back on the warehouse again. 'Whoever I am, whatever happens in there, make the most of it all, won't you? I think some doors are about to close,' he said. 'But others will, of course, as they always do in these situations, *open*!'

'Want me to shut him up?' asked Corral. I saw she was aching to.

Bhatt turned. 'Oh, Ilsa, Ilsa, you tried that already, don't you remember?' He pressed the cuffs to his neck and stuck out his tongue, making a stupid, guttural bawl.

It became an authentic one as Corral planted her fist into his stomach.

I turned away and started to cross the street. Corral followed, her grip firmly around Bhatt's shoulder now as he staggered by her side.

I started to inspect the outside of the warehouse, searching for openings, or areas we might want to avoid. But my senses were nearly completely clouded now, so much it hurt to think. It was like my brain had just dried up and shrunk.

Whatever was in there had just overwhelmed my magick.

Looked like the part where I start to pay for my magick privileges was arriving at the worst possible time. And if it was because of that darkness in there, then it was probably always going to go this way. This is exactly what it wanted, what Cole wanted.

I looked at Bhatt. Was this what *he* wanted?

And as I saw the look of horror crawling across his face now, I thought probably not. He didn't have it in him to subject himself to this.

Corral's hands tightened into white fists, jaw clenching, pulsing.

That *thing* in there, that void, it was spreading.

'Holy *shit*,' hissed Bhatt, and he started walking backward, shaking his head.

'No,' I said, grabbing him by the arm. 'No you don't.' I hurled him in front of us so he was right next to the door. He glanced at it, then at us. He looked like he was about to burst into tears. 'You can't,' he whispered.

That feeling. It felt like decay, poison. Pure misery. I couldn't think straight.

But one thing I did know – Bhatt was going to lead the way now.

'Get that door open,' I said.

'We— We should call backup,' said Corral. She sounded short of breath.

'Hey,' I said quietly, shaking my head. 'There *is* no backup.'

Corral peered at the ground, the houses across the street, at Bhatt, the night sky, and finally at me. 'Right . . . right,' she breathed.

I pulled my gun on Bhatt, who was still facing away from the door. 'Open it,' I said. 'Now.'

He tried the door handle, half-assed, then looked back at me.

'Can you use your magick?' I asked impatiently. I noticed the gun was shaking in my grasp. *I* was shaking.

Bhatt stammered. 'Magick? I— If I use my magick, I'm f—'

I stormed over and grabbed him by the hair, then slammed his face against the door. '*Now.*'

He panted, screwed up his face. He spat some more blood on the ground and looked down at his hands.

'Don't try anything.'

'Shut *up*, I need to concentrate,' he moaned. 'I'm weak enough as it is.' He closed his eyes. His fingers began to flicker and shake.

Then his index stiffened and pointed at the lock. A red streak flowed from him, swirling and weaving through the gap.

It vanished suddenly and Bhatt gasped like he'd been holding his breath. Beads of sweat trickled from his nose and hair.

There was a click as the door unlocked.

Corral gripped Bhatt by the arm again and pulled him back.

I opened the door. It squealed and groaned horribly. I winced, looked at Bhatt, then stepped in.

'What?' he spat, shaking. 'Not even a *thank you*?'

We walked into the building, walked head-on into the horrors that had started twisting our minds, distorting our senses until they were almost useless.

The first thing I noticed through my shaking vision was the vines of moss that climbed the tiled walls on either side. The hallway was airlessly narrow, damp, and reeked like piss.

In some other room, a liquid dripped onto the floor rhythmically. I wondered if it was blood. The only other sound I heard right now was Bhatt's labored breaths as we trudged through the hallway.

My whole body began to feel weightless. A biting, prickling stirring twinged in my chest.

The closer we got to the source of this darkness, this *hex*, the weaker I felt, as if my life force was invisibly leaking from me.

For a brief moment, I scrunched my eyes shut, desperately looking within myself for some power, some magick that shouldn't be mine. If it was still there, it was buried beneath that other power.

'There's still time to turn around,' whispered Detective Bhatt behind me, desperation thick in his croaking whisper.

I heard the sounds of boots scraping on the floor and clothes crumpling. Corral giving him a shove and glare, I assumed.

'What is that?' I whispered to myself.

A door to my left, a tiny square window at eye level. Peering past the grime, I could make out illustrations and markings, maybe writing, too, words made up of some forgotten language.

The room looked like an abandoned prison cell. A single rotten mattress sat diagonally across the floor. The markings were sprawled all over the walls. The centerpiece showed a tower of red flames surrounding a horde of bodies. Beneath the flames, two black eyes, smiling fangs.

Corral said nothing. Bhatt, for once, said nothing.

Instead, we all looked to the doors at the end of this hall. That's where it was, the evil. The doors seemed to be pulsing, beckoning. Our legs transported us toward them. This was it.

Chief Cole was on the floor. Groveling, sweat pouring out of him, darkening his white shirt at the armpits, between his rolls, all over his back. His tie hung loose over his chest, pants rolled up and ripped, face covered in black and green blemishes. He was begging to shadows at the end of the room.

He swiveled to face us as we entered the room. His mouth was gaping, his eyes bulging. He stumbled to his feet and began lurching toward us. I didn't move. My eyes were transfixed on the shadows behind him.

Suddenly, he froze, a dark blur enveloping him.

'Jack,' said Corral, voice shaking.

Chief Cole growled where he stood, arms squashed up to his sides, his face twisted in rage. 'So you would bring them *here*!' he roared, and I realized he wasn't talking to me.

Detective Bhatt took a few steps forward. He staggered one way, then the other, hands still shaking in their cuffs.

Corral was so overwhelmed, she'd just let him go.

Bhatt stood a couple meters away from me, looking the chief up and down, seemingly ignoring the presence in the back of the warehouse. Dim light, a toxic sort of green, streamed through small windows high up on the walls and illuminated the side of Bhatt's face. His skin wasn't sagging anymore.

I tried to stay alert and watch all three – him, Cole, and the shadow. Suddenly, I noticed motionless figures around the perimeter of the warehouse. King's Men.

'Well, your *grace*,' drawled Bhatt, 'from where I'm standing right now, it looks like you were just about finished either way!' Then he tilted his head, peering past the chief. 'Hello!' he called into the darkness.

The shadows didn't speak, but the swirling, probing darkness was *there*.

'Of all the officers in my ranks. Of *all* the officers . . .' Cole gnashed his teeth together in a grim smile. 'You're going to die, boy. You're going to die! And you,' he shot me the same look. 'What are you thinking, hm? Did you come here to arrest me? To take me into custody and put me behind bars? In what reality was *that* going to happen?' His voice was high, shrieking in delirium. He was never going to admit it, but he clearly understood it was over for him, whatever happened to the rest of us.

The dark force around his giant body drifted away. His limbs relaxed.

I kept my mouth shut. I couldn't speak, only observe, anticipating some unknown horror.

At the mere sight of us, the chief had gone from seemingly pleading for his life to returning to his usual, tyrannizing self.

I felt the shadow's magick ease off, as if it was sitting back, soaking in the entertainment.

And so did Cole because a look of slight confusion washed over his crumpled face, and he peered tentatively over his shoulder.

'You have . . .' he whispered, '*no* idea what you're dealing with here.' He chuckled then, and turned back to face us.

'Tell us,' I said, my heart pounding. 'Tell us what we're dealing with. What have *you* been dealing with?' I looked into the shadows and just saw dark.

But Cole had turned his attention back to Bhatt, who had a sliver of a smirk forming on his lips. 'I suppose I should thank you, Detective Bhatt,' he said between wheezes. 'Useless as you are, bringing this vermin to me might have actually been the most I could ever have asked of you. You failed, oh you failed spectacularly. However, with the five of us standing here tonight, I shall just finish the job myself. Get my hands a little dirty.'

And he pulled a handgun from his jacket, surprisingly quickly. This time there was no intervention from the dark.

I'd started to raise my own gun when I felt Cole's intentions a split second before he did it, but I was still slow. My movements felt lethargic, weighty.

Bhatt chuckled loudly as Corral drew her weapon and aimed it at the chief. She took a few steps forward.

'The *valiant* Lieutenant Ilsa Corral!' boomed Cole. 'I know all about you and your escapades now, my dear, and it's all *very* impressive. All this, well, it all *started* with you, really, didn't it? You and your ragtag band of rebels. Who'd have thought!?' Cole licked at his lips with a fat tongue. There was even more sweat forming on his head. 'Though, where are they all now? Not *dead* are they? It's a shame all your work has been for nothing, and that you got your loyal followers killed in the process.'

With the shadow's magick quieting, my own seemed to be flickering with signs of purpose. And I felt Bhatt's energy returning, growing. I gave him a sideways look just before he stepped even closer to Cole.

Surely he could shrink out of those cuffs whenever he felt like it now.

There was a click as Bhatt tilted his head and worked his shoulders. He exhaled loudly. 'You think I failed?' he asked, his voice now full of vigor, a hint of anger. 'I believe it was you who once said that I am a man who knows how to make the most of any given situation, right?'

Corral had her gun between Bhatt and the chief now. 'Bhatt,' she said. 'Stop talking. Stand down.'

Bhatt was only about a meter away from the chief, right in front of me and the lieutenant.

'You have been on the losing side for a *very* long time now,' Bhatt went on. 'Naturally, for me, that meant that I had to find opportunities . . . elsewhere.'

Cole scowled, his gun pointed lazily at Bhatt's chest.

'This venture of mine will thrive and succeed in amongst chaos, Mister Cole.'

'Venture?' spat Cole.

Bhatt's tone became solemn. 'I'm not lying when I say I don't know what's lurking back there in those shadows, when I say I don't know who has you on their leash. And I *promise* you I don't wish to find out by just walking up to it. But I would expect whatever it is to be an awfully fun entity to play around with after you're gone. I *feel* the energy, and it's . . . *ahhhh*,' he exhaled, head tipping back, eyes closing. He stepped back a few paces, slowly, like he was drifting.

Corral stepped back, too, her gun aimed at the back of his skull. She flashed me a grim look.

My gun stayed on Cole.

And Cole looked enraged.

'How *dare* . . . Is that a *threat*!?' the chief shrieked.

And I felt a ripple of terror blast from my stomach into my brain. I was too late. 'No, *wait*!' I heard myself yell.

'Oh, boy,' murmured Bhatt with a smile. And in a horrible flash, he was no longer there.

The cuffs clattered to the ground.

At the same time, Cole's handgun went off, a split-second before mine.

His bullet scorched through the empty space where Bhatt should have been. And ripped through Ilsa Corral's forehead.

Her small frame whipped backward. Her head cracked against the ground. A pool of blood instantly surrounded her body. Dead.

Chief Cole's body folded and collapsed to the ground, my bullet lodged in his brain.

'*No*,' I breathed through my teeth, looking down at Corral's lifeless body. I stumbled across the growing pool of crimson and knelt beside her. My legs lost their feeling. Everything turned white for a moment.

A clicking sound echoed around the warehouse. I looked up, my head suddenly weighing a ton. The King's Men had their guns pointed at me. They were pulling the triggers. Nothing was happening. Red magick swirled around their guns.

Then Detective Bhatt appeared again, standing above me. He peered down at Corral, his mouth hanging open. He looked at me, pointing at her dead body. His eyes were wide. 'Oh . . . dear. That's not exactly what I meant to—'

I shot up and charged into him, putting everything behind my weight. I screamed, tackling him to the ground. My fist met his face. It was all I wanted to do, forever. I punched, and punched, and punched.

With a wave of his hand, he flung me across the room, a red streak of power blasting out of him.

I crashed into the ground, too close to the shadow. I scrambled away from it and back toward Bhatt desperately because I wasn't done with splitting open his face.

What was flowing through me didn't feel like magick anymore; it was just rage and hate.

I spotted movement from Cole out the corner of my eye. He was still moving, still alive in a heap, groaning, guttural sounds distorted by the blood of giants pouring from his mouth.

But I didn't care right now. I wanted Bhatt.

His expression became aggressive, determined. He blasted more magick at me and I crashed to the floor again. I screamed and roared in frustration, pounding the concrete with bloody fists.

Bhatt clawed at his face and shook his head like a wet dog. '*Wow*!' he yelled. 'You caught me out a little there.'

I yelled something at him, don't know what, and reached out for my gun. It was nowhere near me. My eyes flicked to Corral's corpse again. I closed my eyes and made a weeping sound.

'Don't worry,' Bhatt said, his voice suddenly near.

I swiped out at air.

'Don't worry because we're gonna do this again sometime. You can count on that.' His coat flapped across my face as he turned and walked away.

I slammed the ground, managing to haul myself onto my knees.

Bhatt stopped and glanced around the room. 'I should level the playing field before I go. After *all* you've put up with, maybe you've at least earned that.'

Effortlessly, he weaved a horrible, groaning flow of magick that swirled around the warehouse and annihilated each King's Man. They became pieces on the ground, then burned.

'We were never in any real danger,' he said. 'I wouldn't let that happen – not yet.'

My eyes dropped to Corral's corpse again. I couldn't help it.

'Ah, yes, well . . . There is that.'

My fists clenched by my sides.

'But you can't say I was wrong! Doors have certainly opened tonight, Jack. Now it's up to you. What will you do now?' He made for a corner of the room, stopped, and turned back around. 'It's a fresh start. So let me reintroduce myself. The name's Tommy Thumb,' he said with a smile. He jerked his head at Cole, and at the shadow. 'Now, go on. Finish what you started. If – *when* – you make it out, I'll be waiting, somewhere down the line.' His smiled deepened, he waved, and shrunk into a dot on the other side of the room. Gone again.

I pushed myself to my feet and turned to Cole.

He spat out more blood and scrambled up. His face was crimson with blood, a black hole in the center of his head. Bits of his brain sat by his feet.

And as that dark power, that essence of pure evil behind him grew once again, it didn't overwhelm me. It didn't drown out my senses or my magick.

It joined them.

18

ONCE UPON A NIGHTMARE

Flames lined the hallway ahead of me. Fluttering, teasing flames, protruding from steel brackets fixed to the walls.

And just like that, it occurred to me I could burn this whole place down, right now, tonight. The victims weren't here anymore. The only people left in this building were accomplices of that grizzly shit.

But for now, I reloaded my gun and scurried down the silent hall. I wondered how long this silence would last, how long it would be until the tranquility was destroyed by gunfire, and Arminus's final, dying roars.

There was a low rumble of conversation coming from one of the open doors on my right. I came to a stop.

'The fuck do you mean, not responding?' one guy said.

'I don't know. He ain't saying anything back. Whaddaya want me to tell ya?' said another.

I silently darted past the open door of the lounge area, caught a glimpse of the fireplace, a table with booze on it, a few shadows.

So they were about to find out about the bodies already. Fine. I'd just have to make this even quicker.

Third floor. Papa's office. I needed to be there before he fled.

I got moving, heading for the stairwell at the end of the hallway. I spun, walking backward at pace as I came up to the double doors.

Two guards stepped out from the lounge and into the hallway. They checked out the main entrance then glanced my way. But not before I slipped through the doors.

Someone yelled. They'd found the bodies.

Now it was time to run.

I gripped the wooden handrail and flew up the spiral stairs. The farther into Bloodstone I got, the worse the burning in my shoulder seared.

With every minute, there were more reasons to get this done quickly.

I made it up to the second floor and stopped. Above me was a clamoring, a rush of running footsteps.

So, it was time for the place to burn.

I took out my rifle and smacked one of the torches with it. It dropped to the carpet and began to spread beautifully. I knocked out another one.

The flames were violent, growing quickly. They licked at the walls and the framed paintings that covered them. They charred oak until it was black.

I got back to the stairwell. The alarms sounded.

The goons were going to flee at the sight of flames and the ringing of alarms, no doubt about it. They weren't here out of loyalty; they were here for riches. No riches here, not for much longer. Just fire.

I heard them through the old walls, the thin ceiling. Muffled yells of panic, scattering footsteps.

People screamed and swore, probably climbing all over each other to make it out first.

There were voices I recognized. I had to bury ghostly memories that flared up then. *This was the only way*, I told myself. Fuck them.

I froze as I listened to the chaos around me, feeling the heat grow and press against the walls. Because within that chaos, the clamor of frantic treading and fighting, was the sound of slow, methodical footsteps.

Someone sure as hell wasn't bothered about the fire. They were happy to go at their own pace. I listened to the rhythm.

Stomp. Drag. Click.

And it got louder, closer.

This person wasn't leaving. They were approaching me.

'Shit,' I whispered as I raised my gun. And I scoffed because I knew who this was, who it had to be. Of course it had to be him, one last time. Yeah, *of course* he was here, to cost me valuable seconds, to assume the role of Papa Bear's last line of defense. Fucking bootlicker.

'It's you, isn't it?' said that rasping, slimy voice. 'Look how *far* you've come, you sweet little girl.'

I swiveled, lashing out and swiping another torch, which clattered to the ground. Flames spread and grew. Smoke flowed down my throat.

I was convinced that voice – Bluebeard's voice, his breath – was sighing down my neck. But he wasn't there.

I gasped, covering my nose and mouth desperately with my turtleneck. My eyes stung and watered, my nose fizzed, felt like it was about to start bleeding.

'Oh you can just stand there, if you like.' His voice was somehow everywhere and nowhere.

Stomp. Drag. Click. And the roaring of flames rising.

'The flames will just take us both. Oh, my beautiful, darling Goldilocks, wouldn't that be a moving ending to our lives?'

I wanted to go, to leave, to chase down the bear. But I couldn't – Bluebeard was here and I wanted him to die. Needed it.

I coughed and retched.

'*Where the fuck are you!?*' I screamed.

He chuckled. 'Always near, sweetheart.'

A steel cane crashed against my throat. I gripped at it, choking and spluttering. He pressed it harder against my neck, his other arm wrapped around my waist from behind. I threw out my leg and connected with his balls.

He yelped or laughed, and lessened his grip.

I spun and went to shoot, but he knocked the gun out of my hand with his cane, then jabbed me between the eyes with its end.

It was enough to send me to the floor – the melting, boiling floor. Flames reached for me as they climbed all over the walls.

I shot back up. Bluebeard was grinning at me. And I noticed then that he didn't even have a gun. His eyes dropped to my handgun, lying at his feet. He stepped on it, and swiped it back into the fire.

I remembered the knife, covered in blood.

Bluebeard chuckled as it appeared in my hand. His eyes widened in excitement as he saw me hesitate.

No. A knife was too quick, too merciful for this scum.

I gripped the handle hard and threw it. The knife spun through the air in a blur, nestling in Bluebeard's shoulder.

And Bluebeard's smile only grew, just like I knew it would.

I screamed, and this time threw myself at him. My hand clasped around the knife handle sticking out of his shoulder. My other hand gripped his throat, my nails sinking into his skin, and we crashed to the floor.

Searing pain shot down my shoulder and into my chest, my heart. But with my good arm, I struck and struck, punching and clawing at this piece of shit, this raping, murdering psychopath.

His screams grew into laughter, then back into screams. I reveled in his agony, forgetting the burning world around me for what felt like a lifetime. There was blood under my nails, over my hands, in my eyes.

I stared down at his torn flesh. And I enjoyed that sight.

His laughter grew, and I let out a scream of torture as a knife burst through my flesh, *my* shoulder. My adrenaline vanished, and

I tumbled to the side, gripping the reopened wound.

Tears invaded my eyes as I stared up at the ceiling. I was clouded by overwhelming heat, flames inches away from my head. I was in agony, an agony I'd never felt before. I saw his blurred figure, the shine of his black hair, the navy blue of his goatee, his gaunt figure swimming and rippling in the heat, the whiteness of his teeth as he grinned down at me.

Until now, I didn't know how it felt to lose.

I was gonna make sure I never felt it again.

I wrapped my legs around his damaged one, putting all the strength I had left into my calves. I lurched to the side and pulled him toward me. He fell, arms flailing wildly, and slammed against the wall. He screamed as flames roared in his face then took him in an embrace. They swallowed his head and caressed his skin. He wailed and shrieked. He couldn't even laugh anymore.

But I could, and I did – I laughed, watching the fire consume him. But I didn't smile for long because my eyes caught this shimmering, this glistening, and I heard scraping on the melting wood.

I saw that his belt buckle was undone.

My nails clawed at my cheek, physical pain falling away a little, replaced by nausea, dread, and an extreme fear. A whirlwind of thoughts took me over in seconds as I lay there frozen, weak.

As he'd stood over my dying body, in the middle of this burning mansion, he was going to rape me. Rape me, and burn to death in the process.

This is what we were dealing with, and he had to die now. But I couldn't move.

And I couldn't see because more tears had glazed my eyes. I was looking at nothing when I realized the screaming had stopped and turned into grunts and whimpers.

For a second, I thought he was dead, but then his boot struck the side of my head. I clambered over to the wall, the crackling and blazing fire suddenly deafening.

I felt helpless, weak, useless.

As I turned, I saw Bluebeard, hunched over and growling, stumbling away into the distance. He seemed to walk into the weaving fire.

Was I about to let him get away again?

'*Goldilocks!*' roared a voice behind me.

Blood covering my face, my dried mouth hanging open, eyes drenched in tears, slowly, I turned my head and looked down the hall.

Arminus strode through the fire. The hall seemed like it shook with every step he took. His face was blank, observing. His snout reflected the flames swallowing his home. His black eyes looked beyond me at his right-hand man, what I'd done to him.

The flames surrounded Arminus, but they didn't touch him. I saw a patch on his neck where fur wouldn't grow, one of the scars I'd given him.

Arminus was here. This was the moment I'd craved for so long. It was a moment I'd lost months of sleep over.

And it had been served up to me in a way I never imagined. In this reality, I stood before him with no weapon, all my strength gone, my *fight* gone. In this reality, I was going to die.

More importantly, I was going to fail.

'This was my home,' said Arminus. His black eyes were blank. 'Why did you do this?' His gaze was on the floor. His voice was barely audible over the roaring fire.

My eyes were fixed on his claws. They shimmered red and orange in the light of flames.

He stepped forward, slowly, methodically.

'*Boss!*' yelled Bluebeard somewhere in the distance.

Arminus was next to me now. His frame towered over me. I was staring into fur and a giant waistcoat. Nothing was in my head.

I just waited for the end.

But there was no sign of it coming. The claws stayed there, limp by his sides. His gaze stayed fixed on the floor.

I looked up at him, staring blankly at the profile of his face.

He didn't even look at me. Instead he walked on, *trudged* on, surrounded by all this madness.

I sidestepped as he went, my body nearly flat against the small part of this wall not covered in fire.

I audibly gasped, gripping my own neck, delirium washing over me.

He couldn't do it. Something was wrong – Arminus couldn't kill me. And I physically couldn't kill him.

'Why?' I called to his back. I couldn't stop myself. 'Why won't you do it? Why won't you kill me?' I stumbled where I stood, grasping my useless right arm.

My chest vibrated as he let out a low, guttural rumble.

'I'm still part of it all, that right?' I said. 'You can't do it . . . You can't do it because in some twisted, fucked-up way, you still love me. You love me like I'm your own *kid*! To you, I'm still in this . . . this rotten *family*.' Tears streamed. '*Well, I don't want it!*' I screamed, '*I don't fuckin want it!*'

The world shook as he roared. I fell back, enclosed between flames. A paw came lashing through the burning air.

The last thing I saw with the eye that Arminus took was the claw, the claw that shimmered with crimson flames as it sunk into my socket.

I screamed and screamed and fell into the dark.

'*How?*' I growled. 'How are you still alive?'

Strings of blood fell from Chief Cole's mouth. His eyes rolled in his head as he gurgled and wheezed.

I felt that dark energy inside me now. I wasn't just observing it, or being drained by it; some of it belonged to me. It swelled and burst through me as I swung a fist into Cole's bloodied head. It swung back. I heard his blood splatter across the concrete and longed to hear it again.

I struck, connecting with his jaw. He stumbled back, almost toppling over, but somehow remained on his feet.

I had no regard for my life now. Consequences didn't exist in this moment. Only my rage existed. Only the chief existed.

Control was gone. Awareness was gone. A side of me I didn't know existed had taken over, and it turned Chief Cole's face into mush.

My knuckles were busted open, my limbs shook violently, but strength was back on my side, and Cole was on the verge of death.

I wiped the blood from my eyes and realized I'd stumbled back, deep into the darkness at the back of the room – the cold, deep, endless shadow.

My body seemed to slow down as the darkness enveloped me. My teeth gnashed, not from adrenaline but from fear. I didn't, or couldn't, turn to face it. Instead, I fell to the ground, gasping and shaking.

My palms smacked against the concrete and I started crawling, dragging my fingers through cold blood.

Then the shadow spoke.

'Ahhh, dear lad. This fear that seizes you, let it go. It is only within your mind. Do away with such trivialities and seek what you came for. It is so close.'

The voice was visceral, penetrating. It was a voice that could command forces you didn't know existed. A rough, rich, pulsating voice. It sounded like it belonged to a force that'd watched centuries pass by.

I couldn't help but turn then. I looked right into the abyss. Two orbs swam there, a sort of rotten yellow. They looked weak and dry, but somehow also eternal, all-seeing.

'Let me look upon you,' ordered the voice. 'Yes. Yes, it is you. Jackson Slade. The one who shall lead me to her. Ahh, I have seen that you will uncover all. You'll cast the truth out into the open for everyone to witness.'

'I don't know what the fuck you're talking about,' I croaked. 'Stop with . . . Stop it all. I'm exhausted.'

'Such a pity. Exhausted or otherwise, I have seen that you are the vessel. Therefore your work is not done. Because first, before you give up, you *will* bring me to her. To that primal *power*.'

I stood there with my mouth hanging open. I heard more blood landing on concrete behind me.

'*Exhausted*,' spat the voice. 'You do not know the meaning of exhaustion!' Those eyes grew then, black cracks becoming visible on the edges. 'And you, Cole!' it roared. 'As I was saying, before we were joined by this bout of brief chaos, *you*, giant's blood, have outlived your practicality. The ministrations you have offered are no longer required. I have feasted, and will continue to feast without you. You are compromised, drastically weakened.' There was almost a sadness in that voice.

I finally tore my eyes away from the yellow orbs and watched Cole rise above the ground. His arms shot out horizontally, blood dripping from his lolling head to the floor.

He looked unrecognizable after the damage I'd done. Both pride and horror swelled in my chest.

'Your incompetence could have cost myself, the sisterhood, *everyone*, everything. If you were to fail so spectacularly at this juncture, what chance would you have had beyond it? You have, albeit barely, served your purpose. Thus, your termination is upon you.'

As he levitated closer to the shadow, Cole whispered something. He spat out another stream of blood and squirmed in the air. He lifted his distorted face. 'You . . . can't,' he murmured.

The yellow eyes glared and the voice chuckled, giddy. 'Oh, you and I both know that, yes, I certainly *can*.'

'Kill Slade! Take him!' pleaded Cole. 'You know he's the one you want. He's the one who's been getting in your way all this time. *He's* the threat to your work, my king! My king, I am begging you now, *begging!'*

'As you should.' A huge, mangled hand of claws grew out of the darkness. In the dim light, I could just about see the gray-black matted fur, covered with scars and bumps, spotted with something like dried blood.

'My king!' screamed Cole.

'I thought it was you who art the king?' said the beast in a mocking tone.

I looked between them both, helpless.

'I am the descendant— I am the blood of giants, the blood of the old king . . .' stammered the chief. 'Old King Cole's fury lies within me!' he whimpered.

'Ohhh, do shut up,' growled the shadow.

'Wait,' I found myself saying.

'Slade! Come on, my boy, do the right thing once more. All will be forgiven!' Cole flapped his arms around, floating in the air.

'I see what you desire, Jackson Slade. Are you to do as I said, and seek what you came for? The man was never to be incarcerated, was he? You always wanted *this*.'

And before I could even think, the shadow channeled its power right through me. Suddenly, I was the one hanging Cole in the air; it was me in complete control, staring across at the man I hated so much, making him squirm and scream.

I let go of the power inside.

There was an awful sound, a crunch, followed by a splat. Cole's screams became monstrous gurgles and howls, his body distorting and twisting and shrinking until it became a ball of flesh and bone.

My hand hovered before me, a black mist of energy streaming from my fingertips into the mound that was Cole.

He shrunk more and more. I saw his twisted, bloodied face among the mess of broken human. Then it all vanished—

—and came back again in the form of an explosion, an eruption of blood and bone. It broke out across the whole warehouse, covering my entire body. I gagged, threw up barf and black mist. I fell to my knees.

'How you have longed for that,' announced the shadow.

I wasn't sure I agreed.

'Continue, now. On with your journey. There is much to be discovered. In finding truths, you will satisfy your own needs as well as serve me. When I have the girl in my possession once more, it will be you who is sacrificed. I tell you that with certainty, young one, and perhaps slight regret. The path is oh so foggy. It is vague and lit only by gray clouds, but there are some paving stones along the way that I can see, clear as I see you before me now, heaving up your illness.'

I threw up the last of what I had in me, my vision fading, head spinning.

'I will leave you with this. The power you are about to stumble upon will be something that exists far beyond your comprehension. I don't believe there is a person in this city, perhaps even this entire realm, who can fully grasp the implications of the woman who lurks here, and what she holds within her. But I do. So when this darkness is visited upon you, it will tear apart everything you love, and everything you hate. It will leave only ruin and fire. There is precious little to be done about this, I fear.' The voice chuckled grimly. 'The power I speak of, well, it makes me seem a mere trickster!'

'But what the fuck are you?' I managed, holding my twisted stomach.

'Another time,' said the shadow. 'And there *will* be another time, of that you can be sure. For now, though, rest. And rest deep and well. The embers grow, the fire spreads, a girl with death in her heart arises once more.'

'Who?' I croaked.

The eyes narrowed, glancing around the room cautiously. The shadow's voice dropped into a near whisper. 'This precious girl, with eyes as red as roses, her skin the white of snow, and hair the black of ravens. Her heart does not beat, yet she is more alive than any of us. One day, you will take me to her, and maybe then you will understand.'

A gust of cold air swept through the building, blowing my hair across my bloodied face. The shadow, the abyss, shifted, and the creature stepped out of it.

'And if you do not understand,' it said, its eyes fixed upon the blood and guts that covered the floor, 'well, that really has very little effect on anything that comes after. For you have so little a part to play in this, Jackson Slade, slayer of giants. It is not about you. It is about me, and it is about *her*.'

Its fur was matted, scarred all over. Its wolf's face was distorted, grotesque, like it'd been pulled apart and rearranged time after time. It walked on bony hind legs, still towering above me, despite hunching over almost horizontally. A black, thick cloak was wrapped around its frail body.

The thing reached out a long, rotten claw, and scooped up a mound of flesh, holding it up to its huge teeth. Blood and guts dripped between its claws. It forced the bits of Cole into its jaw.

When the yellow eyes met mine again, I forced myself to look away. I backed away, praying I ended up close to the exit.

I realized it was prowling over to the corpse of Ilsa Corral. I gagged and turned and stumbled for the door.

'Yes,' growled the beast. 'Fare thee well, lad, and leave me to my ceremony. For the *blaidd roi* feasts again this night!'

My head scorched and blazed from the inside. My hands were sticky with my blood. All I heard was roaring. All I felt was fire, inside and out.

I screamed and cried. I crawled and kicked my boots into the ground.

I couldn't see a thing.

I pressed a hand to my left eye, tried to open it. I screamed again, and started to doubt anything was real.

When I tried to open my other eye, my head and body were bolted with an unbearable agony.

I had failed.

Arminus was going to make it, and he'd almost killed me doing it.

Almost.

I was still living. I still clung to life now.

And as long I was alive, there was the possibility of finishing the job.

Slowly, painfully, I just about opened my one eye. I could at least see a couple meters ahead of me.

I slammed my fists down on the wooden panels and heaved my body along the hot floor. I'd made it through the worst of the fire, surely. The flames were gonna grow, gonna catch me if I didn't move fast enough.

I saw, barely, but I could work with it if I made it through this pain. This pain that was everywhere, this torture that ate away at me.

It didn't matter. I would *make* it not matter. I was alive.

I just had to keep on living, keep on moving.

Hamelin's room, it was so close. I wasn't about to come out of here empty-handed – not a chance in hell.

The blood on my hands was mostly my own. I'd sooner just burn to death here than leave like this.

The double doors to Arminus's office swelled with heat at the end of the hall. I crawled and crawled. I just didn't have the strength to stand. I didn't trust myself, didn't trust my legs to stop me falling into fire.

My lungs weren't working, my legs couldn't hold me, my sight was nearly gone, but Hamelin's room, it was right here.

I gasped and yelled when I realized the door was right by me.

Smoke was streaming along the hall and underneath the door frame.

With a shaking, crimson hand, I grabbed the door handle and let my body fall against the door, swinging it wide open.

I coughed and spluttered and wheezed. Everything looked gray and formless. For a few seconds, I couldn't make out the bed from the desk.

I grabbed something, a cabinet I think, and forced myself onto my feet. My knees buckled. I kept going.

I ripped open a drawer, tore its contents out. Pens, scrap paper, a knife – I took that – and then, right at the bottom, a thin piece of wood, fitted loosely into the drawer.

My hands shook even more as I flicked the blade out and lodged it beneath the wood.

A folder. I tried to make out the words on it, my working eye barely opening. The folder was labeled 'Koppelberg.'

A weeping sound burst out of me. I stuffed the folder beneath my jacket and rushed out of the room.

Then a lightness flitted through me. It was a hope, a shred of stupid, gleaming hope. Why? What right did I have to feel hope?

I hugged the evidence to my chest, staring into the hall of flames. My lungs felt non-existent now. I had the urge to vomit but nothing was happening, nothing was working like it was supposed to.

I peered out the window to my side, nothing but blackness outside. The drop was too far. Not an option.

Then I looked again at the face that stared back at me. I let out a whimper, my limbs weakening, nearly dropping the folder to the floor.

Only one eye stared back. The other was a bloody pulp of caved-in flesh.

I tore myself away from my reflection, gritting my teeth together. Forget it. I was still *alive*.

I threw myself through the worst of the flames, the final stretch of hallway before the staircase, my only way back out. I crashed through the doors, flames licking at me from every direction, the burning just another layer of pain that I wasn't gonna let kill me.

I rolled across the floor and hurled myself against the wall, barely able to tell where I was. The stench of smoke filled my nose as I clattered down the stairs.

Down here, the fire wasn't so furious. Maybe the worst was over. Maybe I really wasn't gonna die in here.

Maybe my lungs would just fail me when I was out.

But I had the evidence.

The night's sky taunted me as I stumbled toward it. I heard crashing behind me as part of the building started to collapse. I didn't turn my head, I kept going, kept going with the very last of what I had left.

My vision was completely gone now. All I saw was white.

My hands touched something sharp and cold, then my spirit detached from me.

I'd found myself almost grateful Bhatt, this Tommy Thumb, had shrunk and fucked off down some sewer, leaving his cruiser behind.

In complete delirium, I'd burst out of the warehouse, running from the horror inside, and thrown myself into the car with one person on my mind. Goldilocks could still be out there – I absolutely believed she was.

Maybe I only believed that because I *had* to, because I wouldn't have been able to deal with losing her, not tonight.

The image of the wolf beast devouring Corral's body had played and replayed in my mind as I raced through the back roads, silently and numbly praying to every god to let Goldilocks be okay. The gods were the last beings I should've been asking – they had nothing for me, nothing for us.

And when I'd seen the blazing fire on the horizon, reaching for the moon, white and crimson flames against black sky, I'd felt it in my heart somehow, felt the truth. The truth was, she was holding onto life.

She was there on the ground, her ashen face turned black with fumes, patches of her jacket and pants melted away, revealing seared flesh. One eye was closed, the other wasn't there at all. Her hair was splayed out around her, streaked with black ash, but still the white-gold shined through.

And somehow, after all this horrific pain she would have gone through, her face was the picture of calm. I'd never seen her look more content than now, here so far away from consciousness.

I'd almost choked in panic and fear as I fell by her side, checking desperately for a pulse, listening for her breaths under the deafening chorus of rising flames.

And I was right. She was alive, if only just.

We were both alive.

Whatever was to happen next, right now, we were both survivors of this hellish night. I let out silent cries, tears streamed down my face as I held her head in my lap.

The crying only became more suffocating when I noticed the folder sticking out from her jacket. Hamelin's evidence. She'd got it.

And then the King's Men came. The choppers descended, the firefighters and cruisers pulled up. Weapons were raised. They all closed in on us.

I looked to the stars, placed Goldilocks's sleeping head softly onto the grass, and faced them all. Commands and threats echoed through the open space, a distorted voice ordering me to surrender.

I just found myself walking, stumbling down the path, the folder hanging by my side. I stopped, staring at the army in front of me blankly.

A silhouette of a man stuck out to me. He emerged from a black car, holding out his arms and shouting things at the King's Men.

His coat flapped wildly under the choppers, hat flying away.

I chewed on my tongue, thinking about what we'd done, what had been set in motion, no matter what happened to us.

Right now, there was nothing I could do. There was no one else left to save us. Whatever was about to happen, had to happen. There was nowhere else to go.

I looked back at Goldilocks's body on the ground, Bloodstone in flames behind her.

I smiled, and let fate take over.

Something shot into my neck, and oblivion took me.

It felt like just seconds later the synthetic odor of hospital was flowing up my nose.

My eyes burned as I gazed into a white void. I closed them, my breaths shaky and hollow, heartbeat thudding.

I tried again, gripping the sheets below me and attempting to force myself upright. The void was just a ceiling.

My hand appeared in front of me, all pale and wired up. I hissed through gritted teeth, all that adrenaline long gone, now just aching, discomfort.

I looked to the monitor by my bed, and found myself reaching for it. I tapped the screen, as if this machinery would give me the answers to the storm of questions bombarding my head.

'Looking for the off switch by any chance, Detective?'

I gasped at the sound of the smooth, sophisticated, and mildly threatening voice coming from the corner of the room, and shrank back into the bed. The voice belonged to a man with a lean frame, sinking into an armchair in a relaxed posture like he was in the comfort of his own home. I squinted, just making out an expensive-looking suit, dark skin, then his graying slicked-back hair, and the extent of his fairly short stature when he rose to his feet.

The man must have seen the look of recognition fall over my face because he smiled and said, 'No. Don't worry. *I'm* not going to be switching it off for you. No sense in that.' He stepped closer, fully visible now under the harsh light of the hospital room, holding a fancy fedora to his stomach.

'Governor Charming,' I stated.

He peered over his dainty glasses with a slight frown, then picked up a jug of water, pouring a glass. I expected him to lift the glass to his mouth, but instead he held it out to me, tapping it lightly with his ringed finger.

I took it with a shaking hand, the governor not letting go until it was clear enough I wasn't about to spill it all over the wires holding me to this bed. Heavy rain rattled against the window like some force trying to break in.

Charming's eyes flicked to the heart monitor while I downed the glass. 'You and the girl seemed to put yourself through all of the known hells to do what you did,' he said, his assertive voice not giving anything away. 'Why?'

My mind went almost blank then, nothing there besides the faint memory of Goldilocks lying on the grass, burned up, nearly dead. It seemed so long ago.

Governor Charming shook his head slightly, his dark eyes glancing down. 'It's fine. I shouldn't pry. Not yet. You've been in a coma for over three weeks, Jackson. The doctors are still trying to figure out what precisely caused your injuries, your affliction. They suspect something along the lines of a magickal nature. Though at this stage it seems the magick employed was anything *but* natural.'

I said nothing, hoping he would, for now at least, stick to his vow of not prying.

'Where is she?' I asked.

Charming opened his mouth, closed it, then took off his glasses. He peered down at them for a few seconds and placed them back on his face. He sighed. 'Missing.'

I realized I'd been holding my breath, and let out a sharp sigh that burned my chest. I think that was just about the best answer I could've asked for.

'Her wounds are significant. Her right eye, gone.' He gazed around the hospital room. 'She essentially vanished from this hospital as soon as she was well enough to move, it seems.'

I smiled, and glanced toward the rain-covered window, water rippling down the glass.

'She's out there somewhere, Slade. Wounded, in a monumental amount of danger.'

I waited for Charming to ask me where she might've gone, but it never happened. 'She'll be fine,' I said, mostly to myself.' My smile faded and I turned to face the governor again, the memory of the evidence concealed beneath her burned jacket returning to me. 'The evidence,' I said. 'Where is it?'

He walked over to his seat at the back of the room, picked up a briefcase, and returned to the side of the bed with a grim look on his face.

'You don't understand. You don't understand how valuable that is,' I said, rising in my bed.

'Oh, I do. But see, this evidence is a mess, barely readable. What I *can* make out is damning stuff, to say the very least, but there is work to be done here.' He paused and glanced at the floor before making eye contact again. 'One thing we did find was the location known as Koppelberg Hill. And there, we found some of the victims. Only a few were alive.' He swallowed. 'When they are ready, we'll hear what they have to say.'

'*Ready*?' I said, my voice getting louder as I pressed my palms hard into the mattress, attempting to sit up farther. 'We can't imagine what they've been through. What they've seen. You look after those kids, Charming. They'll talk in their own time.' I pointed a shaky finger toward his face.

Charming's eyes glanced over at the monitor. 'Rest,' he whispered. 'Breathe.'

'No, *listen*. I know what you are. You're a slimy bastard. You lie for fun. You lie more for votes. If you're here to make my life harder than it's already become, just unplug this fucking machine now. I guess you're implicated in this stuff, anyway, right? You'd have to be. You're all the same. All this happened under your nose—'

'You're a good man, Jack. I can tell,' said Charming impatiently. 'But listen to yourself. You're naive, so young at heart. Obviously you have limited knowledge of how things really work around here. I'm not sure how much power you think I actually have—'

'You're the *governor* of New York! Head of the famous and feared Charming dynasty—'

'Governor,' spat Charming, 'is nothing more than a title today. If there was anything I could have done to put an end to this horror before now, have no doubt in your mind I would have—'

'I know more than enough about your family to recognize how little integrity you guys have. You've been promising solutions for decades, but what you've always delivered at the end has been a system of ingrained corruption from top to bottom.'

Charming smiled grimly. 'Or perhaps I'm just trapped in that system, same as you. You've done things you're not proud of because of it. I *know* your record, but I'm willing to look past it. Perhaps you should give me a chance in return. I am not my family.' He sighed.

I felt my wrists buckling with tension.

'Understand this,' he continued. 'If the people you've been going after even got the slightest suspicion about me, a hint of a scent of betrayal, it would be the end of me and all I hold dear. You might perceive that as cowardly, but I have to play this role for the good of the many. We might never see what comes of our work; I'm almost certain I won't. But nevertheless, we must do our duty. We are the only ones who can keep the monsters from breaching the wall.'

'I think it's a little late for that. How many are dead? How many have been . . . have been sacrificed?' I suddenly felt faint, nauseous. Depressed. 'We're losing people every day.'

Governor Charming adjusted his glasses, his eyes glancing around the room as he thought. 'Chief Cole is dead. Arminus appears to have fled the state. And that is thanks to you and those who have given so much for the good of the world. Without the work of the lieutenant, and Officer Piper, and—'

'Ilsa Corral,' I spat. 'Rich Hamelin. Detective Vesryn.' And . . . the others. They died before I could even learn their names. My fists clenched.

'Without their work, and the work built upon it, things would be so much worse. This is only just beginning, Jack.'

I shook my head, so many broken thoughts flitting around in my mind. 'Those people . . . Goldilocks. She's someone who's doing good, not you.'

'The outlaw is too far gone,' said Charming, putting authority into his voice now. 'She's done too much, too much that outweighs the good.'

'You'd still arrest her?'

'I must continue this front if anything's going to get done on my end. The incarceration of Jessica Robicheaux would be an unfortunate but necessary play.'

'Fuck you,' I growled. 'If you're going to arrest her, then just take me, too.' I laughed, an ugly, vicious snicker. 'You'd have to get hold of her first. She'd kill you. She'd kill anyone you sent.'

'I'm not sure about that—'

'You should be,' I said, shooting him a look. 'This fight isn't going on without her. I couldn't do it without her, wouldn't even try. Neither of us needs your permission, anyway. You come for her, everything will go down in flames. We all lose.' I took a few breaths, my hand resting against my throbbing throat. 'You don't know what I've seen. What I know. You have no fucking clue what's really out there. If you did, there's not a chance you'd be talking like this.'

Governor Charming stood completely still, his face hard and unreadable.

'All the death . . . And all the death yet to come. That thing that tore Cole apart. It's . . . It's fucked. It's all fucked. And I don't think it's even started yet. Something's coming. And you should be prepared to lose a lot of people. I'm scared. So be straight with me. If you're not, well, then you're an enemy. There's no other way. Quit the games. This isn't some shameless political campaign. You're used to playing with people's lives, I guess, but this is a whole other fucking monster.'

Governor Charming swallowed then, his head tilting down. I caught a slight twitch at the corner of his mouth. 'I will do what I can,' he said, then tapped the evidence briefcase and placed the fedora on his head. 'I'll need more information from you, soon as possible. Every last detail. Nothing held back. The evidence will be safe with me.'

I inhaled sharply, cold sweat gathering on my forehead.

Charming stepped toward the door and turned. 'I'm sorry for what you went through, Detective Slade. Sincerely. None of this should ever have happened.'

Rain crashed against the window. I stared at the foot of the bed, feeling weightless, entirely exhausted. 'But it's happened,' I said. 'And is still happening.'

'Rest, Jackson. You're safe for now. After all, I'm the reason those King's Men didn't kill you back at the manor. They are stationed outside your door. They'll see to it that no one else disturbs you. When you're ready, you can tell me everything there is to know. And we'll talk about the outlaw.'

He opened the door.

'Who are you, Governor?' I said, barely audible.

He may not have even heard me because then he was just gone.

The door closed, and I lay there alone with my agony.

All I'd had in that hospital room was time. Too much time. The decay and subsequent recovery of my body was painful. Day after day of nothing but reflection was worse.

When the longest month of my life was over, I tried to tell Governor Charming everything I could. It was an impossible task. What good were words?

The fallout was grim and blood-boiling. In the end, the media had reported that a lone police officer called Piper was – through the aid of a now-deceased local nightclub manager named Hansel Freeman – responsible for the abductions. That he had drowned children in the river at Koppelberg Hill. The NYPD's statement declared this Officer Piper had been one bad apple.

My half-empty beer bottle had put a hole through the TV.

Down the line, Governor Charming deemed my old apartment downtown safe, informed me I could carry on living there with no worry about coming home one night to unwanted company. I deemed his conjecture a whole lot of bullshit.

I only returned home once, to gather the few belongings I owned, before I abandoned the place. Half-expecting someone there to put my lights out, I instead found a fat sack of banknotes.

More importantly, attached to it was a note:

I can't carry all this. Here's your share. As I'm sure you figured, I'm fine. I know you will be, too. Don't look for me; I'll find you. This time I won't shoot you in the heart. We got work to do, and monsters to put down.

~ G

Afterword

Thank you for reading till the end. But this is only the end of the beginning, and hopefully the beginning of something really cool. I'd be grateful – eternally, perhaps – if you take a further couple of minutes out of your day to leave a review on Amazon or Goodreads, or both.

Hopefully see you at the sequel, and all the ones that follow.

Printed in Great Britain
by Amazon